PLANET FRED

A space-slime continuum adventure

Jim Stein

Also by Jim Stein:

Legends Walk Series

Strange Tidings
Strange Omens
Strange Medicine

This book is a work of fiction. Names, characters, places, and events are purely fictitious and stem from the author's imagination. Any resemblance or similarity to actual people, places, and events is purely coincidental.

Digital ISBN: 978-1-7335629-4-2
Print ISBN: 978-1-7335629-5-9

First printing, 2020

Jagged Sky Books
P.O. Box #254
Bradford, Pa 16701

Cover art by Katie Stein
Cover design by Kris Norris
Edited by Caroline Miller

Dedicated to Charles "Bud" Stein, the best father, mentor, and friend my sister and I could ever have hoped for.

A special thank you to the caregivers, friends, and volunteers who helped Dad and our family.

Please consider supporting your local hospice and the organizations dedicated to combatting conditions & diseases that too often steal away our loved ones.

Acknowledgements

Thank you to all the people who helped *Planet Fred* reach escape velocity and the gravitational pull of my inner-critic:

Claudia, Joncine, and John for their attentive beta-reading,

Caroline for excellent and speedy editing services,

Katie for the wonderful oil paintings of front and back covers, (please note that Reemer the sea-slug is not to scale)

the talented Kris Norris for incorporating the paintings into professional print and ebook cover designs,

my advanced reader street team for giving *Planet Fred* an early read and letting others know the good, the bad, and the ugly,

and to you the reader, without whom there's really no point in storytelling.

Visit https://JimSteinBooks.com/subscribe to get a free ebook, join my reader community, and sign up for my infrequent newsletter.

Prologue

HARRY WAS the first casualty, going down under a spray of paralysis needles riding a puff of gas from the tree he examined. Nancy, the mission botanist, sat on her heels prodding a legless mass of mobile lichen in an attempt to discern how the alien plant moved. Her lanky assistant shielded her from the darts, went rigid, and fell toward the tree. Snakelike roots erupted from the ground to snare his torso.

Nancy clawed at the tendrils, but in moments a brown cocoon enveloped her friend, leaving only darting blue eyes bright with fear. Nancy redoubled her efforts, but roots twisted around her ankles. She tore free and ran for help.

Adrenaline fueled her dash back to the landing site, back toward the screams. Giant flat-leafed things covered the ship's hull. The Endeavor's crew fought in pockets across the clearing.

Greg, the ship's cook, defended the dining pavilion, swinging his meat cleaver and hurling insults at the giant salad components that cornered him. When the gutsy Philippine sank his blade squarely into what looked like a walking radish, white streamers shot out to harpoon the cook's arm. Blood oozed from the tiny perforations, and the bulbous red creature pulled the cords tight, reeling the man toward a gaping maw that opened just below the cleaver.

Nancy dashed forward and wrapped her arms around the cook's legs, pulling with all her might, and came away with a shoe in each hand. Greg stopped struggling, his legs hung limp, and the radish consumed the small man.

The clearing grew quiet except for the rustling of alien plants huddled over prone crewmembers. Nancy ran for the nearest crumpled form but three oversized walking sticks with thorny arms moved to intercept her. So Nancy Dickenson did something only a trained botanist might think of; she sprinted away in blind panic.

1. Run for Your Life

F RED, A stupid planet with a stupid name. Nancy cursed as jungle vines and brambles tore at her. Blood seeped down to mix with the red already staining her hands and dripped to the loamy soil. Feeding the voracious jungle wasn't a good idea, but it couldn't be helped. She ran on, desperate to get away from their landing site, away from ground zero. Even as her heart raced, part of her wanted to turn back, to help the others. But she'd already failed them.

Her legs burned as she ran and screamed out her frustration in blistering curses. Planet Fred was supposed to be paradise, especially for a thirty-three-year-old botanist eager to discover new species. The surface temperature never exceeded one hundred and twenty degrees Fahrenheit, nor dipped below forty-three. Its oceans teamed with nutrient dense invertebrates and fish. And the sole intelligent species was a race of aquatic slugs so vain that the navy planned to trade mirrors to purchase huge mineral reserves.

But Nancy's assignment to the poorly named world was a dream turned nightmare. While there were indeed thousands of undiscovered plants to study, too many had insatiable appetites. Poor Harry had been her closest friend aboard ship, the mission's soil specialist, and so excited to explore the world his father discovered.

As a ranking officer in the Interstellar Astronomical Bureau and senior planetologist on the first expedition to this world, Commander Gregory Coppola lobbied hard for Fred's unique designation. Harry always got a wistful twinkle in his eyes when Nancy asked why his father had pushed for the strange name. But he'd never shared the inside joke. And now he never would.

The memory of Harry's eyes bright with fear spurred Nancy on. She darted around a woody clump that reached out with flexible trunks covered in thorns. This planet didn't even have mammals; why were alien plants so hungry for human flesh? It was no wonder that the sea slug nation rose to the top of the evolutionary ladder—any land-based competition became plant food.

Nancy plunged through a thicket of whipping vines onto flat sand, a narrow beach that valiantly held the jungle at arm's length. She should have pulled off her boots and sealed her field kit. But the images and screams drove her into the placid water with clawing overhand strokes—as if she could tunnel her way off this godforsaken planet. Fire raced along her arms as saltwater soaked into hundreds of cuts, then along her shoulders and legs as she struggled to make progress.

The current pulled left as she made for a tan smear sitting low on the water. Miraculously, Nancy managed to stroke straight for the little island despite the stiff current. She pulled herself onto the sandy spit through a haze of grief and pain, eyes darting left and right, searching—sugar-white sands, rock crests, not a speck of green. No plants. With a ragged sigh, she collapsed on the wet sand and the world faded.

Hours later Nancy Dickenson, champion of all things green, sat on her little bit of offshore archipelago, focusing years of study and training to plot revenge on the things she loved most. She scrubbed her arms, trying to clean off the more tenacious stains and blood. Red blotches rose on the back of her hands and pale forearms from the constant attention, but at least the melanin enhancers were keeping up. A quick look in the hand mirror from her pouch confirmed she wasn't burning under the brutal, alien sun, but the med darkened the freckles around a pert nose and gave her short black hair a healthy showroom shine. The sheen highlighted a few annoying gray strands that had come out of nowhere over the past year. Nancy rubbed at a red stain on her right temple, attempting to wipe away the bit of dried blood that should have washed off on the swim.

A squelch halfway between the twisting of a balloon and mashed potatoes oozing from a clenched fist brought Nancy out of her brooding.

"Your move, sister," the translator on her left wrist intoned in a pleasant—though somewhat mechanical—male voice.

Subcutaneous muscles rippled as her four-foot-long opponent slid away from the slimy X it made on the tic-tac-toe board in the sand. She had no idea how the translation device knew the slug's gender. Harry said the males were more pea-green than the pus-yellow females. But he was dead now, and Nancy couldn't tell the difference. A glob of sickly mucus splatted against her already filthy shirt.

"Ugh, that's disgusting, Reemer."

The wrist translator turned her sentiment into flatulent sounds punctuated with a rolling splat for the slug's name. Nancy scraped the offensive projectile off her shirt, leaving a glistening patch. The glob hanging from her bangs refracted the setting sun like nauseating jewelry. A hissing squeal vibrated from the slug.

"My apologies. Unavoidable ejection," the translator dutifully droned, but the device laid snickering laughter over his polite words.

Nancy glared at her companion, marked an O in the center of the board, and drew a line from corner to corner.

"That's the name of the game, tic-tac-toe. You lose—again."

Her device tried valiantly to keep up with the slobbering, sputtering obscenities that streamed from the little alien. The glistening slime covering Reemer turned milky white as pustules on his thick hide ruptured in agitation.

"You cheated!" he accused. "You must have cheated again."

Nancy sighed and summoned patience. "No, I told you there can be three symbols on the diagonal. Like this."

She ran her finger along first one diagonal, then the other. Curiously, the little creatures saw the world in right angles. Her hours with Reemer confirmed that he even traveled using only perpendicular movements, often heading off at a ninety-degree angle and zigzagging to his destination instead of traveling in a straight line. Reemer sat on his tail end, eyestalks following the motion of her hand, but it was no use. Some connection just didn't fire in whatever the species used for a brain.

Nancy erased the board with a slap, then swatted at a sharp sting on her arm. The tiny seedling chomping on her disintegrated with a satisfying high-pitched squeal. Their little island was devoid of dangerous plant life, discounting the moss coating several boulders. Laying down on those would probably result in losing a layer of skin. But the wind occasionally brought in drifting seedlings every bit as voracious as their mainland parents. What a world.

Her swim through the crystal-clear waters to the little offshore island couldn't have been far, but she'd collapsed in exhaustion from the effort and adrenaline crash, then woke to the glimmering eye stalks of some new horror and almost had a heart attack. Reemer had been good-natured about her nearly skewering him before she realized he wasn't a voracious plant.

The research site was far behind thanks to the island itself, which drifted with the warm coastal current instead of staying put like a sensible land mass. Now, miles of hostile territory stood between her and the ship. If other survivors sent out a distress signal, the navy might already be on its way. She couldn't afford to drift away from potential rescue.

"Sorry," Nancy said, referring to the abrupt ending of the game. "Reemer, you must know the jungle. How hard would it be to get back to my base camp?"

"Easy! Islands circle back around," squelched the alien, his tiny mouth forming a childlike O as he stared at the erased board.

"Perfect. How long?" Nancy felt the ghost of a smile tug her lips.

Reemer studied the passing shoreline for a moment. "Nine months." The translator again pumped echoing laughter behind his words.

"We'll starve!" And miss any chance of rescue.

Nancy scowled as the slug hissed like a flatulent balloon. He thought this was funny.

"Not starve. Fun trip. I'll catch fish."

"I'm sick of—"

But her companion shot across the narrow beach, straight into the water. Pale green mucus glistened on the sand where he'd been. Their navy briefing had mentioned the intelligent slugs. The Squinch moved fast for an invertebrate race, much faster than terrestrial slugs.

Ten minutes later, the water rippled as a green shimmer with a billowing black end made its way ashore. Water sheeted off Reemer, and the dark segment on his tail resolved into a large flatfish. Its wing-like fins flapped weakly, revealing a white underbelly like the skates back home. The fish was stuck fast to a ropey appendage protruding from the alien's hind end. A vein along the obscene looking thing pulsed once, and the fish grew still. Barbs along the end of Reemer's hunting whip retracted, and the arrowhead slid from the fish's flesh as the appendage snaked back beneath him, and Reemer gave a little shiver of delight.

"Food," he announced.

The fish was bigger than the slug, with fat, meaty wings. Nancy retrieved what looked like a silver pistol grip without a barrel from her field bag. She used the sample cutter to carve off strips, but the little laser wasn't suited to cooking. At her request, Reemer ducked back into the sea and returned with a leafy plant. She wrapped the seaweed around the fish and did her best to visualize sushi.

The alien's dining style was…different. Reemer moved over to the carcass and promptly threw up. The noxious mass of goo teamed with wriggling white specks. Nancy's dining fantasy vanished. The sushi roll clawed at her innards, but she couldn't look away. Reemer blew out an opaque bubble and slapped it into the putrid mess. It spread over the fish carcass, pushing through the puke. Unless she was badly mistaken, the Squinch just coughed up his stomach to digest the fish.

An eternity later, Reemer slurped his organ back inside and proceeded to suck up his meal with one eyestalk tilted back to watch her. Nancy clamped a hand over an involuntary gag and stumbled to the water.

2. Here for the Party

C APTAIN VEECH Gekko parked his ship in a geostationary orbit over Greenorb's southern continent while his crew prepared the shuttle. He preferred making planetfall with the smaller craft, rather than trying to land the half-mile long behemoth that covered the interstellar distances so well without complaint. Well, without much complaint—or more accurately— with criticisms that could be easily tuned out. As with so many of the advanced races, the human crew relied on the ship's artificial intelligence—or AI—for navigation and life support functions. Normally that wouldn't have been a problem, but QUEN—short for QUantum Elementary Navigation system—had developed a distinct personality. And she excelled at tormenting the crew, particularly the men.

The personality emerged shortly after Veech won QUEN in a dockside card game. Gambling was technically prohibited, but for a small kickback, the port authorities ignored low-stakes games. Something went haywire during the computer system's abrupt transplant from a cushy space liner to the dilapidated exploration class starship.

QUEN insisted she did her job superbly: recycling fresh air to the recreation decks, keeping the passengers well fed, and plotting smooth routes between holiday ports. His crew held a distinctly different opinion. Every watch team got treated to spot emergencies such as shutting down atmospheric venting to the nonexistent recreation deck. The gourmet meals that randomly appeared were greeted with enthusiasm, until food stores ran dangerously low and he was forced to implement rationing. Worst of all, the damn ship kept re-routing toward vacation spots, which required manual reprogramming of the nav computer. Not that he wouldn't welcome some fun and sun, but the mission came first despite QUEN's pointed suggestions.

"All hands, man the lander," Veech called over the ship's intercom. He turned to address the mass of displays and controls that covered the front bulkhead of his bridge. "QUEN, we're heading down. Just stay in orbit and don't do anything."

"Certainly, Veechy dear. I've got some wonderful charts to look through for that romantic getaway you've been hinting at." A bright green light on the console winked suggestively.

He gaped, then shook himself. "No vacations. We're here on business. Just keep the ship functioning, okay?"

"You're so cute when you get embarrassed, lover." The infuriating green light winked again. "I won't let the crew in on our little secret. Run along and let me take care of everything. Kisses."

The instrument bank went dark except for the mellow twinkling of a handful of scattered readouts. The AI had withdrawn to plan its delusional tryst, and Veech cursed under his breath. Why did he get all the nut cases? Not just the goofy computer, but his current crew left a lot to be desired. None of them had decent credentials. Most didn't even admit to a permanent address. He grudgingly amended that thought. A couple were okay. Craig Finkle, the ship's Jack—as in jack of all trades—seemed decent enough, as did Jake Farnsly, his tech specialist. Veech sailed with Finkle before, but Farnsly was a greenhorn to deep space. But the kid was sharp with the gear and a passable pilot.

It seemed appropriate to bring a greenhorn to hunt on planet Greenorb. Most folks didn't use the official name because Fred was clearly meant as some sort of witty pun for those of superior intellect and inferior social skills running in scientific circles. Nevertheless, the illicit hunt that took place on the remote planet every five years drew ships from across the galaxy. The whispered rewards had always been taunting, though too good to be true. But QUEN's meddling and several poorly executed jobs left Veech desperate.

Now, he felt like an outsider on his own ship, a bus driver for hire. Most of the crew had hunted here before with Urneck Grint. Grint paid up front on a standard contract including watch rotations and duties in space for the crew, but Veech remained in the dark on details of the planet-side mission. Similar expeditions always turned a profit, so they clearly sought something of supreme value. He just didn't know what, and that frustrated the self-made spacer.

Captain Gekko strode through rusty corridors toward launch bay number two. What a joke. The ship only had one bay. A prior owner attempted to impress potential customers by exaggerating the ship's capabilities. The sole mess deck boasted a placard designating the space four of five, locating one of the thirty two supposed bathrooms should be a breeze, and the auxiliary bridge was in fact the only one he had ever run across in the fifteen years he'd owned Fatal Beauty. Still, the eccentric numbering added a certain charm to his baby, and Veech had never been much inclined to relabel it all.

Eight crew members, six men and two women, met him in the shuttle launch bay and made ready to descend to the surface of Greenorb, aka planet Fred. Veech took a seat behind the pilot and tried not to stare at the scruffy lot while they prepared for launch. The men reeked of danger, but at least the women weren't too hard on his old eyes.

"Don't forget your sunscreen," chimed a feminine voice from the ubiquitous speaker system around the loading docks.

"Give it a rest will ya, QUEN? We're working." Jake dumped another armload of water skis, beach balls, and fishing gear out of the shuttle's hatch.

As the equipment clattered to the plasti-metal floor, Jake wondered for the hundredth time what he'd gotten himself into. He'd only been in the civilian space force for three years, and work was hard to come by with that little experience. Signing on with Captain Gekko should have been a dream come true. The old spacer lived up to his reputation and the wages were more than fair. But Jake hadn't bargained for the surly crew and haywire AI.

"Darling, you're so tense. I'll order you up a nice massage planet side."

A pink foaming drink, complete with miniature umbrella, materialized in the young technician's hand just as he reached to secure the hatch. Sweet liquid splashed down his arm and soaked his khaki shirt to the waist. Thankfully, the replicator was a shipboard system, so her games would end after shuttle launch.

"Don't miss the luau—"

The slamming hatch cut off QUEN's recommendations. Jake muttered under his breath as he wiped his shirt and walked to the rear of the command module to strap in. The small craft would link up with the much larger shuttle body shortly after launch.

"Should've gone before we left." Pete, a gnarled old fellow with a deep scar across his left cheek, giggled at his own joke and looked around to see if the others would join in—they didn't.

The rest of the crew was a somber lot. Jake had seen that much before signing up, but they needed a strong tech-head. Even before crew bonuses for a successful mission, the pay enticed him to ignore his better judgment. For the chance to retire young, he could put up with a few shady, tight-jawed characters.

Still, Cheeky Pete tried his patience. The old man could supposedly track across terrain from bare rock to swamp lands, but he never shut up and didn't mind talking just to himself. The old coot had done a minor job with the team lead but was essentially an outsider—just like Jake. If the guy wasn't careful, one of the others was likely to beat him senseless.

For the most part, the core crew ignored Jake, Pete, and Craig, a big man with wavy blond hair and next to no experience. The other three men were cut from the same cloth, wide cloth, with bulging muscles and features of stone. He wondered how they maintained their hardened physiques in spite of never stepping into the ship's gym. They might crank the gravity up in their quarters, but that was a hard way to stay in shape and tough on internal organs.

For planetfall, Captain Gekko sat behind the pilots, a pair of granite twins named Ray and Jay. Ray-Jay guided the pilot module smoothly out of the bay and settled them like a blister onto the much larger shuttle body moored off the starboard side. Their captain studied a hologram of the planet below. Patches of color and numbers decorated the sphere, showing everything from temperature gradients to topology. Gekko had selected their landing site based on information from Ray-Jay, hours of studying the planet's model, and consultations with Urneck—who would be in charge planet side. He'd let slip they were after some sort of rare plant. No one offered additional insights, so Jake tended to keep his head down and focus on his job of maintaining the trackers and communication equipment.

Urneck sat across from Jake and polished a blaster that already held a painful shine. The weapons officer caught him watching, grinned, and raised the gun to point at Jake's chest. Jake should have been used to these antics, but sweat popped out on his forehead.

"Fight with your girlfriend, J?" Urneck finally lowered the weapon and gave his customary wink from beneath bushy brown brows that matched his close-cropped hair.

Jake counted stars through the observation port and willed his pulse to slow. Urneck's fascination with destructive devices kept Jake on edge. The man was tech-savvy and could probably do Jake's job if not for the constant inventories and checks on the ammunition, charge modules, and guns. But that wink seemed like a clear surrogate for pulling the trigger. His ready grin and shining eyes made it easy to imagine the fellow laughing over your partially vaporized corpse as he continued to polish the gun that just blew a hole through you. Rather than engage in polite banter with a friendly maniac or trade cackling insults with Pete, Jake watched the ship's quiet descent to the green and turquoise surface.

3. Landfall

N ANCY FOUGHT her stomach's urgent need to set the pseudo-sushi free to again swim the tepid oceans. One of Reemer's eyestalks tracked across the sky as if following a bird. But before she could look, the slug returned to his meal with noisy gusto. He swayed and shivered as Nancy lost her battle. Amidst prayers for death and sputtered curses, the violent heaves finally trailed off into weak little coughs.

"Are you done?" she gasped, refusing to look up.

"Just finished," came the translated reply.

Nancy heaved a sigh and turned to chastise the alien. A baseball-sized glob of molten fish dangled from the slug's mouth. His eyestalks swiveled in opposite directions as he slurped down the wriggling mess with another shiver of delight.

"Ugh," was all she managed before again doubling over.

Her sides ached as she scrubbed sand across her mouth. A sip of sweet, brackish water helped wash away the taste of bile. The translator sputtered static in a vain attempt to interpret the quiet sounds drifting from the Squinch—probably more laughter. Miserable slug. She glared up at Reemer, but the Squinch's eyestalks scanned the sky. Nancy caught a flash of something just as it disappeared over the trees.

"What was that?" she demanded.

"A flatfish. Didn't you like it?"

"Not that… That." Nancy's finger stabbed skyward. "What did you see?"

"Nice clouds…hot sun…blue, almost purple, sky!" the translator sputtered.

Escargot was not a delicacy she craved, but the look she shot Reemer was laced with garlic and butter. She scooped up a handful of dry sand and stomped forward. Reemer looked on with what may have been a smug expression. Nancy threw the sand on him.

The alien wailed and writhed as tiny bumps popped up all over his leathery-looking hide. Nancy tuned out the translated obscenities. Reemer made for the water, but she blocked his path, her foot poised to kick more sand.

"Get it off!" Reemer screamed as milky fluid oozed from the bumps along his back.

Earth slugs shriveled and died when dowsed with salt. The effect on Reemer was similar. But sand wasn't salt, and the over-dramatic alien certainly suffered no more than mild discomfort. Still, he played it up for all he was worth. Nancy stood her ground. Squinch biology had to be equipped to deal with blowing sand. Even so, an impressive torrent of fluid ran off Reemer as the translator sputtered out one last obscenity.

"Please," the device whined into the sudden silence.

"What was it?" Nancy demanded.

The glistening antennae drooped. "One of your flying machines."

"From my camp?"

"Looked different, fatter, but it flew." Reemer edged around her and slid into the water with a sigh.

Nancy let him go. A ship! The chances of another mission visiting this exact section of Fred were pretty slim, especially considering the Squinch delegates who normally dealt in mineral transactions were farther north. If the crew managed to beat back the attack, they would be out searching for survivors. But they obviously hadn't spotted her little slice of paradise.

Reemer emerged from the ocean firing off directives. "Don't ever do that again, you overgrown… Hey, where're you going?"

Nancy collected her now dry belongings and repacked her tool pouch. She zipped the waterproof lining this time and slung the strap over one shoulder to free her hands for the swim. The mainland drifted beyond easy reach, but a peninsula jutted out into the ocean ahead. If the currents held, they'd pass within a hundred yards. Her right foot grew oddly warm. She glared down at Reemer and the puddle extending out from under the disgusting alien.

"What?" he asked.

"It's been fun, but I'm going to find that shuttle."

Nancy waded into the water as the peninsula drew near. Twenty feet out, the false bottom disappeared, forcing her into a swim through deep water only slightly cooler than the shallows. Halfway to the spit of land, she realized she'd misjudged the swift current. Swimming was not part of her regular workout. She swept past the spit of land, her hundred-yard swim turning into a half-mile.

Nancy's heart pounded in her ears as she struggled to maintain a steady overhand stroke. Shortness of breath forced her to alternate gliding along on her side, then her back. But for every restful stroke she took, the mainland dropped farther away, forcing her to work that much harder to retake the progress she'd made. Fred's aquatic life was not well documented, and images arose of sharp-toothed predators and leviathans rising from the depths to swallow her whole.

Through a haze of fatigue, Nancy felt something firm but yielding strike her foot. It was large, very large. She kicked off, striking out with renewed vigor toward the approaching shoreline. But with each kick, the monster rose beneath her, slapping the backs of her feet, her elbows, her hands. Its hide was packed sand; the thing was enormous; and…it was Fred. Nancy laughed and staggered upright in the shallows.

The broad sandy beach was barren of malevolent plant life, though a single lump jutted from the sand off to her right. It was short and squat, about three feet of greenish bulk. Nancy wiped water from her eyes and splashed ashore, angling away from the mass. She could outrun a wad of carnivorous moss or seaweed, but would have to rest soon. The thing moved with fluid motion toward her, then raised on one end and issued a warning hiss that ended in a chorus of sounds worthy of a warthog stricken with food poisoning.

"You swim slow," came a muffled voice from Nancy's side. She unzipped her pouch and slipped the translator back on her wrist.

"Reemer, how the hell did you get here?"

"Followed, then went ahead."

"But why?" Nancy plopped down, savoring the feel of powdery sand as it leeched water from her clothes.

"Adventure. You and me."

Nancy eyed her uninvited companion. A thrill-seeking slug wasn't exactly a valuable asset. Reemer had outpaced her coming ashore, but she doubted the little guy could keep up on land. As she pondered how this arrangement might work, a murky liquid with oily blue swirls seeped out of the Squinch's rear end. Noxious fumes sent tears coursing down her cheeks. She gagged and retched, faint to the point of passing out when an afternoon breeze blessedly carried the stench away.

Reemer's mouth formed its little O as he leaned forward expectantly. She was too tired to argue. Having company in this hostile jungle—even the company of a disgusting excuse for a species—was better than going it alone. With a weary sigh she nodded, stretched out, and closed her eyes for a quick nap.

4. The Shuttle

"COME ON, REEMER!" Nancy plowed down the dirt trail, while her companion zigzagged in her wake.

There ought to be another term for Reemer's movement. Zigzag implied diagonals, which was exactly what the little fellow avoided, preferring ninety degree turns. Since the trail didn't run straight, the slug's wiring forced him to alternate between a straight line forward and bouncing from side to side like a ping-pong ball. She watched the slug turn left at the path's edge and then right to keep from going off the other side.

"Right behind you, fearless leader."

Nancy eyed the glistening trail crisscrossing the bare earth. No one would deliberately put that much effort into moving such a short distance. She sighed and studied their surroundings. The trail itself was an enigma. Fred wasn't supposed to have land animals, but they had walked for hours on similar paths. The forest remained quiet except for those nasty floating stingers. She'd collected dozens of itchy welts, but the rising wind now blew the seedlings away.

Branches along their back trail swayed and creaked. Nancy whipped around, but it was just the wind. Clouds piled overhead in a crimson canopy, turning their loamy path into a bloody stream under the ruddy light. Anxiety hastened her steps as she forged on feeling very exposed. If flood waters had cut this particular path, they were in exactly the wrong place.

"Big storm coming." The translator managed to distinguish the alien's gusty speech from the howling wind.

"No kidding!" Nancy shouted over a violent gust that smelled of rain. "Head for that cliff. Some shelter is better than none."

A dark rocky outcropping crouched beyond the whipping branches of a squat tree with elephant-ear leaves off to their left. She left the trail, heading for the meager cover. The lone tree sat among sparse underbrush. It looked as battered by the winds as they, but to be safe, she gave it a wide berth. The slug turned off the trail and put on a burst of speed. As usual, his direction didn't match her own.

"Drop leaf!" Reemer called as he vectored wide to her right, antenna scissoring in the wind.

"To the rocks, Reemer!"

A palm-sized leaf shot past her, then another. Wind tore handfuls of leaves off the tree, sending them tumbling past. Nancy struggled to see through the gathering gloom, flying debris, and her own whipping hair. She clawed the strands out of her eyes only to have them replaced by more, across her face, arms, and neck. The feather-light touch built as the wind pressed in, fighting her progress.

Nancy found her feet slipping in the rich soil as she struggled forward. She squinted into the wind, but there was no sign of Reemer, only swaying underbrush and the now leafless tree. Turning downwind gave her streaming eyes a break, but instead of the little alien, a flock of green birds hung in midair, flapping against the wind to hold their position.

The first fat raindrops splatted down. Nancy turned back toward the rocks, but couldn't make progress against the howling wind. The birds fared better, pressing close and converging behind her—no, not birds at all. Those were leaves. Rather than the elephant ears blowing away, they clustered just beyond her. Nancy raised a hand to wipe at the hair plastered to her cheek, and several of the leaves danced in response. She shoved her right foot forward, and another group of leaves skittered along at ground level, matching the motion. The wind wasn't holding her in place. She'd waded into hundreds of thin strings, fishing lines tethering each leaf to its branch.

Some leaves spun wildly while others simply rocked on their invisible cord, string-bound UFOs from an old B-rated movie headed her way. Nancy back-peddled to let them pass, but as the pressure of the threads across her front eased, similar force build across her back. She managed a half-dozen steps before losing traction.

With slack in their lines, a handful of leaves accelerated. One of the spinners shot past her stomach and yanked the front of her shirt taut. The spinning leaf trailed nasty barbed hooks that caught fast in the material. She tried to pull free, but the leaf's tether was tough and stretchy. As she worked at the hook, one of the stable leaves sliced across her forearm on its way back to the tree. Blood seeped from the razor thin line it left, and pain seared across her arm a moment later. The adaptation was ingenious: specialized leaves to hold prey while others sliced it to bits.

Nancy didn't savor death by a thousand cuts. With a frantic twist, she broke free, but two more hooked leaves bit into her arm and thigh. There was no pain, the barbs clearly laced with a natural anesthetic. Fresh fire across her thigh and neck attested to the fact that the razor leaves were not similarly treated. The wall of leaves drew close, and struggling only meshed her more tightly in the strands. Nancy fumbled at her pouch for the sample cutter. The threads weren't impervious to the little laser, but they were tough. Each thin line took several seconds before parting with a flash under the invisible beam.

The wind howled on as the laser worked through line after line. Nancy grabbed at the last hook, intent on regaining enough mobility to back away from the approaching death. Before she could bring the cutter to bear, the leaf popped off its tether to hang against her stomach like a giant earring.

A slash of fire across her cheek snapped her back into action. She struggled back three steps, scraped a handful of cords off her chest, and thumbed the little laser to life. A razor leaf stabbed her foot, then spun downwind, tumbling into the wall of leaves that was now only steps away. But the mass moved erratically, their orderly progress disintegrating into chaos. The nearest leaves swerved wildly, some slapping the ground, others breaking from their tethers to career downwind. The tension in her bundle of lines lessened as leaves broke free.

"Is it working?" Reemer called out from the right.

The Squinch circled the attacking tree. More leaves fell away. Perhaps a third of them had dropped off like…well leaves. Hot welts rose on her bare skin when the empty lines retracted at searing speed.

"Whatever you're doing, do it faster!"

The slug ducked his head, and his skin darkened through deep olive to purple. The translator couldn't form proper words out of the sounds that swept passed on hurricane force winds. "Uhhhm… Eahhhhck… Heetttahhhhhhh"

The leading edge of the remaining green mass shimmered and vibrated. With an audible snap, the entire flock tumbled away on the storm. Nancy gasped as a hundred kite stings burned parallel lines across her from head to toe.

Her knees buckled as the pressure vanished, and she staggered toward Reemer. The driving wind helped her stay upright and the lee of the tree afforded some protection, but they still needed cover. Blood from dozens of razor and hook wounds seeped through her clothes and sweat stung her eyes. Reemer looked similarly exhausted. His skin had lightened to the pale khaki of a garden slug. Dirt and humus stuck fast to his protective slime. The alien looked small and deflated.

"You okay?" Nancy asked.

"Give me a minute," Reemer gasped, struggling to rise. "It worked?"

"I don't know what you did, but you saved me."

Nancy hesitantly bent to stroke the top of the little alien's head. Slime and debris clogged her fingers as she scratched between his antennae. Reemer nuzzled his warm gooey head into her palm, demanding more attention in spite of his exhaustion. With a nod of determination, she pursed her lips and lowered them to a relatively clean spot near his right antenna. Just before contact, her nose wrinkled at a truly foul odor.

Squinch did not generally smell bad; their scent was reminiscent of overripe apples but not unpleasant. The botanist clenched her jaw to keep her stomach at bay and looked for the source. Clods of matter ringed the ground beneath the tree. The air above each shimmered as if trying to escape the vile stench. Some were single mounds, others formed lines of putrid white-gray material that defied classification as simply liquid or solid. Even the sporadic fat raindrops seemed to miss those on purpose. Vague shimmers of mucus trailed off from the end of each mound. The nearest disappeared beneath the alien.

"How did you stop it?" She backed away as Reemer swiveled around to replace the top of his head with a mouth as close to puckered as he could manage.

"I gave the tree food so it didn't need you!"

She looked from slug to mounds as realization dawned.

"You crapped me free."

"I saved you."

"With crap."

"With excess biological by-products." The translator added quiet snickering.

Nancy took a ragged breath, pressed her lips tight, and strode off toward the rocks.

"No kisses?"

"Crap."

5. What's for Dinner

T HE STORM threatened throughout the night, just on the edge of breaking. Nancy and Reemer wedged themselves between half-buried boulders. The arrangement was uncomfortable, but she managed to drift in and out of fitful sleep. She jolted awake before dawn as lightning blazed across the sky in searing horizontal cracks. The rain arrived soon after in dense curtains that sent rivers to converge at the base of the rocks. They huddled, miserable and wet, for the better part of an hour. Just as standing water closed over her feet, the rain cut off and the storm disappeared so fast that Nancy wondered if she was still in Kansas.

Sunshine angled across the sodden landscape, coaxing steam from the ground. Reemer splashed about in the puddles while Nancy wrung water from her shoes and scanned the woods. They needed to head north, but there was no way to tell how far the shuttle had gone before landing. After teasing a cup of water from each shoe, they trudged on. Before long, hunger rumbled in Nancy's belly.

"I dislike your appendages," intoned the translator.

Nancy eyed her companion. "What's that supposed to mean?"

Reemer tilted his head in a kind of half shrug. "I didn't say anything."

They continued in silence, and Nancy found herself fondly remembering the flatfish they had shared just yesterday. The knot of emptiness protested that it had surely been at least a week.

"Your antenna is limp with rejection."

Nancy stopped dead in her tracks. If Reemer had been capable of following her without using his absurd ninety-degree turns, he would have slapped into the back of her legs. As it was, he scuttled past to the edge of the path before looking back, eyestalks raised in question.

"All right, sluggo. What gives?"

"Gives what?"

Nancy shook the wrist translator at him. "You said my antenna was limp."

"You're the one muttering. I didn't know humans spoke without their mouth. You must have secondary communication organs like the Squinch."

Muscles rippled and lifted the amorphous skirt that undulated when Reemer traveled. Five puffy slots beneath looked like deep belly-buttons coated with a mixture of petroleum and grape jelly, until they pinched shut into the unnerving semblance of tiny mouths.

"See," Reemer declared excitedly. To Nancy's chagrin, slime and air blurped from the orifices with a calliope of sounds one might expect from an accordion made of rotten meat. "See, see, see?" her translator sang, harmonizing the word into complex chords reminiscent of classical music, Chopin perhaps.

As the slug burped out beautiful music, the answer to her original question came clear and laughter spilled forth. The tension coiled in her chest eased as she tried to get herself under control.

Reemer let his chorus trail off, mouth agape. Nancy gasped for air and wiped her eyes.

"My stomach growled…the translator thought—" Giggles erupted, making it impossible to continue.

Reemer joined in the laughter this time. Mercifully, his skirt dropped, leaving a thin green fold along the length of his body. Nancy suspected those little mouths—yes, it was better to think of them as mouths—were hard at work because the translator tinkled with music as they guffawed. Vertical creases crossed the horizontal one as Reemer scrunched and wriggled. He got the joke readily enough, but then why not? The fellow must have a sense of humor given his disgusting antics at her expense. Nancy got herself back under control, but Reemer continued to writhe and gasp for air. His music became stringent and creases crisscrossed his entire body.

"Get it off," he pleaded, the background music now harsh and discordant.

The lines weren't creases or folds at all. Green tendrils wove around Reemer. He slid sideways as the living net hauled him off the trail. Nancy had her cutter out in an instant, but he was wrapped so tight that she'd have to slice his skin to get at each cord. She looked for a leading edge, but the net grew from the ground beneath Reemer and moved with him, leaving nothing for her to attack.

"Net vine, it'll pull me under!"

"What's the plant look like?" Nancy slapped aside underbrush, following the bound alien. "I need something to work with."

"Purple…vine. Fish leaf…murpfff…soup…pickle," the Squinch sputtered.

Fleshy bits of Reemer's hide puffed up between the constricting weave as his skirt sank into soft soil. Nancy didn't see any purple fish or pickles, but a flash of blue caught her eye. A thin curly vine lurked among the leaves of the underbrush, and a dirty-blue runner shot along the ground to another group of bushes.

"Wait here." Nancy gave the universal palm-out hand signal that worked so well on terrestrial canine and alien slugs bound by carnivorous plants and headed off to follow the vine.

"Murndork…grimp?"

The blue vine thickened, coursing around rocks and dead trees. Thirty yards away, the vine branched up the back side of a dead tree. Now as thick as her wrist, hair-like tendrils anchored the woody stem to the rotting bark. The vine climbed high and spread out overhead. A canopy of purple laced through the bare branches of the dead trees that bore the nasty plant. Nancy shot an anxious glance back. Reemer barely moved.

Other blue tendrils snaked down tree trunks to spread like veins across the landscape, but the purple ones all branched up from a cone atop a woody root in the middle of the dead grove. She dashed over with the cutter in hand. Within moments, wisps of smoke rose from the foot-thick root, and the vines overhead jerked and danced in agitation. No use—cutting through would take hours with the small tool.

"Runfthhhh!" Reemer cried.

Nancy ran back to slug. The top of his back and his head were still above the surface, but the vines had him in a punishing grip thanks to her cutting. The flesh sticking between the cords looked about to burst.

"Let me think."

The weave loosened enough for Reemer take a ragged breath, then tightened again. Like the Venus flytrap, the plant probably used fluid pressure rather than muscles. Such mechanisms could spring traps, but weren't well suited for prolonged movement, though this plant seemed to have more than enough stamina to finish burying her companion. She examined the thick silvery leaves hanging from the lower vines. They were teardrop shaped with a flared end and did resemble fish on a line. She plucked the nearest and found it surprisingly heavy, more like a fruit.

She winced at a gasp from Reemer. The plant didn't appreciate its leaves being picked any more than it liked the notion of being hacked off at the root. She could think better if the thing would just settle down…or…sleep! Plants didn't slumber, but they did hibernate! Nancy ran back to the main stem.

"Noooooooooooo!" Reemer cried, the weave having shifted off one of his mouths.

Nancy ignored him, adjusted a setting on the little device, and pushed the business end down against the root. Instead of smoke, wisps of fog drifted from where the wide blue beam met wood. Frost formed on the bark as Nancy worked around the root. The leaves jangled for a frightening moment, then went still. Although the little unit grew hot, she kept at it until ice fully coated the stem.

Nancy hurried back to her companion, ripped away the loose netting, and dug Reemer out. He curled into a ball, so she scooped him up and staggered back to the trail, cooing reassurances between ragged breaths. The slug was heavier than she would have guessed. When Reemer finally poked his head out to look around, Nancy nodded and left to finish the job.

She returned wearing a humorless grin. "Let's go."

Rather than waste words, the alien moved out as fast as his canted travel allowed. The trick to not getting surprised again was to watch for telltale signs: leaves where none should be, lone trees or ones surrounded by deadwood, that sort of thing. They settled into a routine of walk, dodge, and fight, incapacitating aggressive denizens as necessary. Nancy's hibernation trick worked with vines and bushes, but her small tool lacked the power to be effective on the nastier trees.

By afternoon, the pair moved beyond the dense pocket of predatory plants. Though still watchful, the respite from constant danger left time to think. Nancy nibbled a silver-purple fruit and ducked a low hanging branch that tried to look innocent and uninterested in the pair. The net vine leaves tested as edible and tasted of eggplant and banana.

Freezing that first net vine into hibernation hadn't been enough. Nancy felt her cheeks warm, thinking of how she had returned to garrote the main stem. The ring she'd cut around its root would kill the vine in short order. Once dormant, freeing Reemer had been simple. The little alien was shaken, but fine. So why had she felt the need to mortally wound the helpless plant? Grad student Nancy, who transplanted weeds under the exasperated whispers of her professors, would have been appalled. She'd grown up going out of her way to help all living creatures. Now, on this beautiful alien world, she found herself deliberately destroying indigenous life.

These plants hadn't attacked Endeavor, but Harry's frightened eyes muddied her thoughts and painted them all the same. The vine she condemned would have reduced Reemer to nutrient sludge. The jungle felt sinister—malevolent—and had to be stopped. Compassion fled as Nancy clenched her jaw and slashed at a cabbage-looking thing creeping toward the path. She had sharpened her walking stick into a flat-edged spade. A handful of leaves dropped off the cabbage and the creature tried to scuttle away. Her spear lanced out again, biting deep into the dirt as it impaled the thing. It died amid shuddering leaves. For Harry.

By midday, the blue-white sun sat fat on the horizon, cooler than Earth's star, but sufficient to produce a sauna that drenched Nancy's clothes and plastered black curls against her neck. The Squinch ambled along unperturbed, occasionally commenting on the flora. His spirits seemed high, but Nancy noticed he stopped well short of the path's edge now, and his antennae were in constant motion.

They rested in a grassy clearing atop a knoll modeled after a friar's haircut. Grass formed the pale pate, while hairy black vines hung from the surrounding trees. Nancy bit into another purple fruit and studied the circle of trees. Silver flashed for an instant on the slope ahead. Her heart raced, but they'd have to move quickly to get there before dark.

The botanist gathered her few belongings and prodded the Squinch. He woke in a seething, bubbling mass of complaints. Nancy abandoned the path and headed toward the distant glint of what she hoped was the shuttle. Reemer kept up a running commentary on any plant he thought moved too much as she hacked a path forward. Less than an hour later, they stumbled into another clearing.

The ship that flattened the grass was segmented along its length like a giant beetle. Instead of a few sturdy landing struts, dozens of spindly legs extended from a craft that could span two football fields. The hull shown blue like overheated metal in the fading light. An array of nozzles poked from the craft's tail end, deep space thrusters. Its shape, color, and design were bizarre and nothing the navy would use.

They stepped close, and she looked to Reemer for an opinion as something cold and unyielding clamped around her neck. Nancy grabbed at a red-blue claw covered in coarse little bumps. It didn't budge. Teeth lined each half of the claw, making it difficult to swallow. Her assailant, a giant lobster, scuttled out from the forest of legs supporting the strange craft. It regarded her with swiveling eyestalks and constantly moving mouth parts.

"Do something, Reemer."

The slug leapt into action, shooting back from the brutish crustacean. It was a sign of his single-minded purpose that Reemer executed the maneuver in absolute silence, forgoing wasted words. The move would have been more impressive if Nancy had been able to witness the undoubtedly heroic and ingenious plan upon which the Squinch launched to free her and incapacitate her assailant.

Unfortunately, Reemer failed to notice several other shelled aliens until he backed into one and ran a slimy three feet up the thing's carapace before being hauled into the air. At least her own captor hadn't tried to lift her by the neck. The aliens stood with eyestalks swirling and mandibles working soundlessly.

"We mean no harm," Nancy choked out. "I need help. The plants have gone mad."

Burping, gaseous sounds spewed from her stupid translator. She cringed at the Squinch translation, but her captors grew excited. They hissed, clicked, and pointed at her wrist. Their exchange recalibrated her device, which dutifully issued a chorus of mechanical laughter and guffaws. The lobsters thrust her and Reemer into a small compartment that descended from the ship like a shaftless elevator. Nancy rubbed her neck as the claw withdrew, the door closed, and an offensive odor wafted from the Squinch.

The walls were solid, but the ceiling glowed and bathed their prison in a dim twilight. Thankfully, the floor was a spongy composite that made sitting and waiting bearable. Botanist and Squinch exchanged thoughts on their predicament. Neither had ever seen the likes of these creatures. Humans were the only ones with a permanent interest in the Squinch's world, but Reemer knew other races visited around the time of the jungle's awakening. Even with their protective slime coating, the Squinch didn't venture ashore much during those periods, so information on the other races was minimal.

A long hour later, the door opened, and claws hauled them into pale moonlight. A small yellow-shelled alien slapped a two-inch metal plate to the side of Nancy's ankle and a similar plate to Reemer's back. The skin under the plate stung and prickled horribly, but the sensation quickly faded. Satisfied, the alien restraining them backed away. The creatures' shells were mainly red but had overtones of blues, yellows, and greens. Plus they varied in size, so Nancy found it easy to distinguish individuals.

As Little Yellow shambled off, Nancy looked down at the silver tether and smirked. As invertebrates, these overgrown lobsters probably didn't realize a human could afford to lose a bit of skin. The same might not be true for Reemer, but once she was free the slug could just drag the leash behind him. Nancy tugged hard and frowned. Rather than stretching her skin, the plate jerked deep in her ankle as if fused to bone.

"What do you want?" She glared at the retreating alien.

The translator got the language right, thanks to background clicking among the others who scurried about in obvious preparation. The creature she addressed turned baleful, antenna-mounted eyes on Nancy's translator, then her face.

"We Lobstra dislike spies. The captain may yet order your legs pulled off."

Nancy shuddered, pushed down her panic, and latched onto the creature's other words. The translator may simply have put things into a reference she could understand, but what were the chances that this race would call themselves Lobstra? A giggle slipped out. Maybe she could fend them off with clarified butter or bring them to their knees with the smell of a New England bisque.

Her giddy ponderings drove away thoughts of bloody stumps and let her take stock of the activity. Lobstra loaded supplies and equipment onto hoversleds ranging from sleek narrow cargo skids to massive patrol craft with enclosed deck houses. When a skid was full, an alien clicked out commands and the sled would rise and bob complacently awaiting its next command.

A few of these smaller sleds appeared sulky, slowly deigning to hover only after much coaxing. This was surely a simple matter of the transports being overloaded. Although, one sled followed and bumped its controller until the exasperated Lobstra drew a weapon. Faced with the dish-shaped muzzle of the energy pistol and a stream of clicking threats, the transport swung back into line, but as the Lobstra turned away, the sled tilted and a fragile-looking container tumbled from its rear deck.

Soon enough, the sleds and Lobstra formed a loose line, and the ship's hatches closed. A big, dark red Lobstra clicked muffled words into the device around his neck. The massive ship shimmered, went vaguely transparent, and then snapped back into focus, an occasional spark of energy the only telltale sign of the force-field along its hull.

Why scores of giant lobsters, a slug, and one human set off into the night remained a mystery. The few big vehicles—the forty-footers that could easily have carried everyone—trundled along at the back of the formation, piloted by small crews while the rest of the aliens set out on foot.

The clearing opened onto a plain, and they made good time before smashing back into dense jungle that teamed with even more predatory vegetation by night. The Lobstra met the inhabitants' aggression with massive firepower. It was a testament to the recent rain that the landscape didn't go up in flames. The flash of pulse rifles and stench of scorched vegetation marked the group's progress.

In addition to illumination by weaponry, Lobstra shoulder-mounted light wafers bleached out the daytime colors. Deep black pockets between the trees provided a flat contrast to the dazzling beams that crisscrossed their path. The light show made it difficult to watch her footing, especially since Nancy also scanned for anything nasty that might have slipped through the aliens ahead.

Reemer managed their tethered arrangement well enough. After trials, errors, and several embarrassing suggestions from her companion about how to better use her legs—some of those still made Nancy blush—she'd simply left Reemer to follow behind. They were nestled in the back third of the procession, with Lobstra fanned out behind and ahead. Reemer zigzagged along, and Nancy tried her best to not imagine the slug as a fishing lure.

Scrabbling sounded in bushes to the party's left. The big leader's light caught the edge of something disappearing in a rush of leaves. The group turned and pursued the retreating noise. As they moved through the underbrush, the rustling multiplied, and the group spread out. They poked the vegetation with weapons and claws, startling two needler saplings into attacking. Thick shells deflected the paralyzing darts that had taken Harry just days ago. Claws made short work of the little trees, and as she passed, Nancy took perverse satisfaction in adding to the wounds with her cutter.

Still, the fleeing creatures stayed ahead of the Lobstra, and Nancy soon found herself well behind her captors. She considered running, but the tether was problematic and walking the jungle at night seemed foolish. They headed south, away from the mountains and the Endeavor. She needed a plan.

Reemer shot past with a squeal. The ground behind him churned as something tunneled along in pursuit below the surface. It was nearly on top of him—or rather, under him—when the tether reached its limit. He jerked to a stop, his front end stretched like a rubber band, and he rebounded back along the leash to land with a sick plop. The thing in the ground burrowed past. A dozen paces beyond, the ground erupted, and a mass of snakelike heads poked into the air. Nasty barbed hooks festooned the final third of each appendage, which ended in a mouth lined with ridges.

The vines rose on a single root that sliced through the dirt as it doubled back toward Reemer. Something larger buckled and bulged beneath the ground. Reemer made it back to her side. She scooped the slug up under her arm and jumped aside just as the plant struck, a living flail that missed by inches. The heads shook and wriggled to clean off dead leaves and debris snagged by their hooks.

The search lights continued to swing back and forth through the woods ahead, the Lobstra unaware or uninterested in their predicament. The creature oriented on them again, perhaps tracking body heat because neither of them had moved a muscle. Nancy set Reemer down, picked up a rock, and threw it into the plant's path. The vines slapped down in unison, so it also sensed movement. The translucent patches behind the hooks likely provided rudimentary vision. Thin fettuccini tendrils shot from each head, skewering and shattering the rock. This plant definitely ranks as an overachiever in the hungry department.

The trusty cutter was again in her hands, but Nancy doubted she could get close enough to use it. By the smell of her companion, Reemer already tried his fertilizer trick—or perhaps that had been unintentional. She squeezed close to the slug, setting off a wave of nausea that had nothing to do with her impending death.

The mop of vines glided forward, scattering the broken rock and rearing up to strike. No one was close enough to help. She brandished her cutter, determined to make a fight of it, to die trying. A stray beam of light swept the ground. The plant paused, swung around, and zipped off in the opposite direction. The living flail raced toward the source of light, a lone Lobstra emerging from the trees. Not even the thick shells of her captors would protect them from this plant.

Nancy's moral battle was brief. Though a prisoner, neither she nor Reemer had been abused. At worst they'd been ignored. The questing vines pulled underground. A barely perceptible heave in the dirt closed on the unsuspecting Lobstra. Clicking screams filled her imagination and put Nancy's feet in motion. Reemer was taken by surprise and dragged along behind, stuttering curses that he finally had to abandon in order to right himself and scurry along on the tether.

The Lobstra was maybe fifty feet ahead, the plant only twenty. It moved cautiously now, perhaps due to the size of this prey. The hulking alien leader faced the other way, oblivious to the danger as he poked his blaster into a thicket. Her foot caught on a raised patch of dirt. A ridge flowed off toward the buried plant, an amazingly long main root that Nancy followed.

"Look out!" She yelled as sinuous vines burst forth at the Lobstra's feet.

Clicks bubbled from her translator. The Lobstra leader whirled, noted his peril, and leapt back with astounding grace. It was a seamless movement that no human could hope to emulate. Unfortunately, as the bunched legs sprang back, the plant slapped forward, catching a spindly white appendage. The Lobstra was brought up short mid-jump as root tendrils trapped and speared through the leg. He howled, in a clicking sort of way, and snapped at the vines with his powerful claw, but one speared the pincer, anchoring it at the alien's side.

The Lobstra fought with quiet determination, methodically bringing the blaster in his free claw to bear. Each shot severed or forced a vine back, only to have it replaced by another erupting from the earth. The leg he'd been pulled down by was a mess of shattered shell and white fluffy meat and the pinned battle claw cracked down the middle. His oblivious companions beat the bushes ahead in search of their elusive quarry.

Nancy waved the cutter in frustration. Getting close enough to lase individual vines would get her snared before doing any good. This had to be another case of cutting evil off at the root. She kicked and scraped at the ridged dirt, revealing the warty root that lead to those deadly heads.

Another vine lashed the alien and a bulbous knot on the main root deflated. A second later, it swelled as another knot sank in time with the next attack. Five of the supple pockets ringed the stem, bladders providing liquid pressure for movement. Nancy traded the laser for her knife and stabbed a rising lump. Rather than biting into hardwood, the blade sank to the hilt. Oily sap sprayed across her hand. As the knot cycled to refill, more sap drained out through the gash.

Nancy burst two more knots before sparing a glance at the Lobstra. Half the killer vines lay twitching at his feet. The Lobstra tried to level his weapon, but it shook spasmodically. She sliced down again and again. Oil spewed and within seconds the deadly plant lay helpless. The situation finally registered on the monstrous plant intelligence driving the creature. The root slid back through the earth, dragging off the lifeless mop.

Lights moved out of the woods now. Nancy hurried to the injured Lobstra and went to work cutting away the severed heads that skewered his shell. His eyestalks followed her flashing knife, but he made no move to stop her. Angry clicking foreshadowed the arrival of the others. Her translator couldn't keep up, but leveled weapons and threatening claws made their intent clear. Nancy looked from dripping knife to the shattered limbs.

Thankfully, the ground was still littered with crushed vines. No one could look at that mess and think a tiny human had overpowered the massive armored alien leader. Surely comprehension just now dawned in the eyes of the new arrivals, the foremost of whom reached forward with a hiss of escaping air, paramount to a human's sigh of relief. But rather than patting her shoulder in thanks, the reaching claw clamped around her upper arm, wrenching it outward until she dropped the knife. The other claw moved to her neck.

"No, I—"

A mass of studded burgundy shot past, cutting off her words and slamming the menacing claw away. On his backswing, the leader clamped down hard on the claw that crushed Nancy's arm, grasping it just above the spiny elbow armor. The pressure eased immediately, and blood flowed back to her tingling fingers.

"Use your wits, Joda." The leader's clicks were strong and harsh, even if he stood awkwardly to favor his wounded legs. "The girl saved me. None of you fools lifted a claw. Would you rather see these burst me open like a rapid ascent from the depths?" He pushed her attacker away and kicked at the plant's remains.

"We didn't know." Joda's claw twitched feebly as it regained some measure of mobility. "That Budra was giving us a hell of a time. We nearly had it, but it vanished. Then the alien was cutting at you."

"A lure," Nancy murmured.

"Explain, human," the leader demanded.

Nancy started, not realizing she'd spoken out loud. Waving eyestalks regarded her, and a growl from the translator spurred her to elaborate. "It had to be a decoy. The plant drew you off so it could get one or two alone. That's why your people never caught anything. Their quarry stayed just ahead, keeping everyone busy. Then when its meal was foiled…"

"The beasty took its hunters and lures away," the leader concluded.

"Exactly! Too tough of a meal."

The Lobstra regarded her before reaching forward. She couldn't help cringing, but he ushered her toward a ring of boulders that rose from the grassy plain.

"We make camp," he called to the group, then addressed her directly. "You and I must talk."

"Stupid brutes can't travel at a decent pace. Umphh." Reemer huffed along behind them.

The slug must really be out of sorts because the Lobstra's injuries had them slowly ambling. By the time they made the rocks, Nancy's shoulders ached from supporting the sagging Lobstra. He sank to a wide flat stone with a sigh. Reemer sputtered up and collapsed.

She supposed the Lobstra was going to make it. No one bothered with any sort of medical attention. The other aliens busily set up camp, unloading the necessary items from their pet hover-sleds. Their leader shifted restlessly, then groomed himself with the tiny legs that normally hung limp below his throat.

Nancy tried not to cringe when she realized he was daintily stuffing bits of debris into his mouth. If she didn't know any better, she would say he was stalling. He finally looked up and spoke, though he kept pushing tidbits between his mandibles.

"Human…"

"My name is Nancy Dickenson. Or Doctor Dickenson if you like."

Something akin to a smile might have crossed the alien features, the mandibles swung outward and the hair-like spines that lined them curved up. "Yes, of course. I am Captain Luftew or just Captain. I suppose I should thank you."

Anger boiled, burning her face. "Don't strain yourself, Captain. I only did what any self-respecting person would. If you prefer, next time I'll let you be split into little itsy-bitsy pieces and eaten alive. Then you won't have any worries, like prisoners wondering where the hell you're going and what the hell you want from them!" Sweat beaded on her forehead in spite of the mild night air.

"You will recall I returned the favor and stopped Joda from clipping off your head."

Damn, he had. Of course, a captain was responsible for his crew's actions. A small consolation, but he would have had to live with her death on his conscience. At least that was how a human crew functioned. Filtering everything through the translator made reading the situation difficult. She'd give him the benefit of doubt for the time being.

"I do appreciate that, Captain. You were saying?"

"You must understand our lack of enthusiasm at having you and your companion along. We seek the ultimate prize. The nectar will be ours this cycle."

"Why drag us along? We don't care about any prizes."

The captain lifted shoulders and forelegs in what passed for a shrug. "We cannot have you giving our location and numbers to competing expeditions. The alternative to holding you is…less than pleasant." The captain studied his good claw, which again looked menacing. He hastily dropped it and leaned forward. "We need not talk about what will not be. I assumed the Squinch led, but you are stronger and adept at dealing with the jungle. I would have your skills in our hunt."

A job offer! For a plant assassin? Nancy considered as she looked down at Reemer, who now snoozed against the base of the boulder. Helping the Lobstra would elevate them from prisoners to consultants, and give Nancy a chance to strike back at this horrid planet—to balance the scales for her dead shipmates. This could be a win-win, especially if an opportunity arose to steer the group toward Endeavor. The captain was eager for an edge in their bizarre hunt, but she needed more than satisfaction in return for her efforts.

"This prize must be valuable. I need to know more to decide."

"Cycle end and you know so little?" A chuckle bubbled from him. "Ah well, it is common knowledge that this planet, this jungle, comes to life every fifth year. Aside from gorging on flesh, it protects the quinquennial nectar. The demon queen that produces it is never in the same place and will be guarded by the most vicious denizens. If fortune smiles on us, we will find it first, milk the nectar, and become wealthy on a scale with royalty."

"If I help, I would share in that wealth."

The captain went back to his grooming. "No need for that. We can ensure you return to your own kind, if that is your desire."

So he'd deduced her current situation—at least in part. Better that than dealing with an imbecile. Still, the deal left her only a vague promise. Luftew seemed implacable, with an air of confidence and command that demanded admiration. So many commanders lorded their positions or played the bully, but he reminded her of Captain Gunthall, commander of the expedition. Although hopelessly outnumbered by geeky scientists, the man had managed to control the brilliant diverse personalities with aplomb and consistent good nature. This Lobstra, though significantly harder-skinned, seemed to be of a similar temperament. But even a lowly botanist needed credits for the basics of life.

"Now, where on Earth would you drop me off? I'll have expenses to make it all the way home." Nancy patted the captain's good claw and ticked items off on her fingers. "Ship's passage, new research equipment, and fresh food all have a price. I'd think ten percent would cover things."

Spiny hairs curved up to the captain's eyestalks in surprise. He let out another bubbling laugh, and they both settled back to enjoy some serious haggling.

6. Humans

V EECH'S CREW crouched in a semi-circle around the
diagram he'd sketched in the dirt, eager to start their assault.
But a sneer twisted Urneck Grint's mouth. The weapons tech tried
his patience. The jerk wanted digital maps and imagery piped over
wireless comms to the heads-up display in his helmet. Never mind
that the damned snakes were just over the rise. You could see them
by simply standing up. Sometimes, old-fashioned planning was the
best. Leave technology for where it was absolutely needed.

"Everyone got it? We hit the snakes hard and fast. Don't linger.
Esha are damned nasty." Captain Gekko dusted off his hands.

The team checked their weapons, and the green kid, Jake,
looked to his tracking equipment. That was the only essential gear
this little raid needed. Once planted, a pin-sized transmitter would
let them track the rival group. Even though the snakes had no ears,
Veech flinched at the sound of his people getting ready. This
certainly wasn't a crack special ops group like the Spacers, those
silent, dedicated individuals he'd never see again. But it would have
to do.

"Thank you so much, Captain." Impossibly, Urneck's sneer intensified before he turned to the others. "If things heat up, set your beams to plasma mode. That'll split their hides, but hit them in the face or neck. Nothing else slows them down. Your gear set, Greenhorn?"

Jake Farnsley looked up from his checks. "Ready, relay's working fine."

"Let's get moving then." Urneck paused as Veech pointedly cleared his throat. "That is of course if the captain is ready. Yes? Okay, boys and girls, let's move."

The big weapons tech took the twins and others off to the snakes' flank, leaving Veech to lead the remaining men in through the front door—as it were. The general idea was to harass the aliens, splitting their attention long enough for Jake to slip in and plant the tracker. But would Urneck keep to the plan, firing for distraction and not to kill? The last thing they needed was a blood feud. He wished all the jobs were as simple as yesterday. The insect-like Gants didn't even bother to set out guards, so Jake and Craig Finkle had simply deactivated a section of shielding, slipped in, and planted the bug. Smooth.

Snakes, on the other hand, were a paranoid lot. They posted guards, and the entire camp would descend in a frenzy on intrusive scents or vibrations. The evolutionary trait helped the deaf race survive, but it guaranteed failure of any covert infiltration.

Veech signaled his team to halt just shy of the first guard post. He gave Jake a thumbs up and reassuring wink. Mustering the gesture was difficult. He clearly didn't have the control and authority an expedition's captain should, much less the respect of this crew. Then there was Urneck. Images of Long John Silver's bloody mutiny flashed through his mind as he peered to the south, willing Urneck to follow the plan. Farnsley might be young, but at least the kid held to the chain of command. Finkle seemed okay too, but the others supported the weapons tech.

A percussive blast thumped in his chest. A half-dozen brilliant green-yellow stars blossomed overhead, simulating midday and sending snakes in all directions. Urneck's team would be moving in to set off decoys. Vibration and noise from the devices combined with the detonations and flares should overwhelm the snakes' delicate senses. As the camp dissolved into slithering chaos, his men lobbed incendiary devices into the trees along the camp. The heat signatures would put any staunch snakes over the edge. It also signaled Jake Farnsley to move in.

* * *

The whoosh of ignition in the trees got Jake's attention. Yellow and blue flames licked up quickly, consuming who knew what nasties. As the first treetop flared bright, he crept forward with the transceiver clutched in one hand and a dispersion pistol in the other. He preferred to avoid guns, but the non-lethal weapon was a decent compromise. It shot a scattering of mass-increasing gel pellets that clung to the target, pulling additional mass from their surroundings. The gel only retained cohesion and the debilitating mass for two to three minutes, arguably enough time to elude an assailant.

The camp was a nightmare. Snakes beat against the ground with tiny arms extending from their elongated bodies at neck and waist. Others lay with their head on the ground and tongue flicking out every few seconds. The flares must have blinded them because every reptilian eye was hazed over. The snakes ignored him as he picked his way toward the objective.

As he stepped around a prone snake, the creature blinked. The cloudy film was a set of eyelids shutting down external inputs to help the aliens deal with the commotion. Jake hurried past a row of metallic tubes that served as tents and clattered up the ramp onto a massive transport. Wind drove choking smoke into his face as he knelt and activated his tracker. A needle-thin tube extended from the head of the device, snaked into the cooling vent under the control panel, and planted the tracker nodule.

The electronically neutral device utilized passive trace elements and was virtually undetectable unless you knew what to look for. Active tracking by satellite used x-band rebound technology to pinpoint each tracker's location. QUEN set that bird in orbit just before the crew launched. Tracking wasn't done from the main ship as a precaution against retaliation. No big deal if angry aliens destroyed the relatively inexpensive satellite, but if QUEN and Fatal Beauty were taken, the humans would be stranded.

Job complete, Jake slipped back through the rows of tube-tents. Craig Finkle crouched by the disabled guard and returned his thumbs up with a smile as he fired off a green flare to signal withdrawal. The crew continued their merry dispensing of confusion for another minute before the commotion died down.

Jake's left foot caught on something as he passed the last tent. He peered down to see why his foot had gone on strike and looked into milky snake eyes. The creature was rigid with neural overload, but had struck out instinctively at his foot. Pain shot up his calf. Jake tried to pry the reptilian mouth open, but couldn't get enough leverage. He waved frantically for Craig, then dropped onto his backside. Cotton muffled the world and the leg went blessedly numb, so nothing to worry about. He sank to the ground, wishing for a fluffy pillow.

A moment later, Craig loomed over his comfy spot. It was inconsiderate of the beefy man to swing drunkenly like that, though it only mattered in a distant, abstract sort of way. Jake rolled his head to look down as something jerked his leg. The snake still had his ankle in a vice-grip, and Craig kicked the alien's head. Funny.

"Two points." Jake grinned at the joke. "Again!"

Soft thrashing inside the tent meant the beastie was coming out of its stupor. Maybe it had pillows to share.

Captain Gekko took Craig's place and knelt to examine the snake. Jake giggled at the sudden arrival of his boss. Gekko dug curiously tanned thumbs behind the jaw. How on Earth did the man maintain a total body suntan in space? The comatose reptile didn't seem to mind as the thumbs forced its mouth open just enough for Craig to drag Jake's ankle and petulant foot away from the creature. Four rotating fangs slipped from tiny punctures in his skin, leaving wet yellow lines across the top of his boot. Interesting that it had a pair of fangs on each side of the mouth. Perhaps they shed dull fangs like a shark lost old teeth.

Jake floated across the ground, unable to feel the arms hooked under him. He couldn't feel much of anything, and the buzz of charging capacitors filled his ears. The captain looked worried as he keyed something into the ship's comm link. That was surprising. Standing orders limited off-world transmissions to extreme emergencies to prevent aliens from intercepting communications. Even if they couldn't break the transmission's encryption, some of these races were tech savvy enough to pinpoint its origin and calculate the ship's orbit.

The captain muttered at Urneck Grint who immediately vanished. Jake wished people would stop popping in and out. The big man returned with a medipak, unzipped the protective bag, and withdrew a nasty looking syringe. The two-inch needle glinted, and a drop of green liquid fell from its tip. Some poor bastard must have caught one of the tropical viruses they'd been warned about. Jake wondered who.

7. A Turning Point

N ANCY WAITED with the Lobstra on watch. The column would advance when hulking Joda and his security team finished smashing another corridor through the dense vines ahead. The acrid scent of crushed greenery was sharp in the air, making her eyes water. Another impact rifle pulse shook the ground and flattened twenty feet of vegetation. The aliens preferred to bludgeon their way through impassable undergrowth.

This time, they'd hit a field of what looked like raspberry plants. True to the menacing nature of the stupid planet, these vines weren't happy to simply block their path. The spiny tentacles lashed at the approaching group, severing legs from two Lobstra. Luckily, the creatures had more of the spindly appendages than they needed, and the pair seemed none the worse for wear.

Nancy chewed her lip. Over the past two days, Captain Luftew had picked her brain for vulnerabilities of plants they expected to encounter. Those sessions confirmed her own observations, but also gave new insights to Fred's flora. She was certain that the mobile—and therefore more dangerous—inhabitants used one of three methods for locomotion: hydrostatic pressure, like the creature that injured the Lobstra captain; compressed gasses, like the needlers; or true tissue contraction. Plant cell physiology limited those using contraction to slower movement like the crawling cabbage.

A surveillance drone showed killer raspberries stretching for miles. The slow progress left ample time for more discussion, so at the next stop Nancy headed back to Captain Luftew. A hammer fisted blow from the impact rifle caused her to stumble and almost step on Reemer. Although the captain had removed their tether, the slug stuck close and remained in a foul humor. That wasn't by any means out of character, except that his comments held more rancor than usual.

"Off to see your boyfriend?" Reemer asked as they approached the command group.

"You're making even less sense than usual."

Reemer "accidentally" ran over Nancy's foot when she stopped to admonish him, leaving a translucent green trail across the toe of her right boot.

"The rockhead can't speak your language. Too much shell, not enough brains."

"What's gotten into you? Even we can't talk without this." She held up her hand and pointed at the translator, then spun around to cover the remaining few yards to the captain.

Reemer slunk along behind her, muttering obscenities. Nancy fingered the translator's gain adjustment, which usually spared her from background chatter and the bulk of the slug's crude comments. Reemer's expletive binge drove her to use the maximum setting, which still only filtered out maybe half of his foul language as they walked.

Captain Luftew was deep in clicking conversation with Little Yellow, or Meinish as she'd heard him called. None of the crustaceans had surnames. Her translator let out a happy little sigh and shifted away from the slug's blistering language to work on the Lobstra's discussion.

"Another two miles," Meinish concluded.

The captain merely nodded and turned his eyestalks on Nancy. Meinish regarded her briefly, gave a dismissive shrug, and shambled off.

"Sorry to interrupt." Nancy's resolve slipped in the presence of the confident captain. She sputtered, trying to frame her thoughts. "Two miles? Then what?"

The captain consulted a handheld—or rather claw-held—device strapped to his left foreclaw, making use of the healing appendage. "To get clear of these vines. Then Meinish sets a course to the west."

"He has a search pattern?" Nancy squinted at the little map display crisscrossed with lines and alien writing.

"Meinish has divided the landscape into grids. We search each for signs of the quarry before moving to the next selection."

Nancy shuffled, earning a squawk from Reemer as her foot glanced off his slimy skirt. "We've been in one grid for days. There must be a hundred sections there." She jabbed a finger at his display. "This will take forever."

"Be calm, Nancy." Luftew waved his smaller claws. "The grids are randomly selected. If Providence wills it, we'll find our quarry before the others."

Nancy argued for a more logical process of elimination, but found herself up against an indefatigable resolve to ignore logic. She'd thrown in with alien gamblers, a race that worshipped and trusted their success to gods of luck. Her prior impression of the captain as a steadfast, logical person crumbled, replaced by the image of a simpleton who stumbled along hoping things went well. How long would they blindly search for this elusive nectar? Surely the other searchers used a scientific method, while the meandering Lobstra pecked away at their random grids.

A clicking whistle signaled it was time to move on. Nancy cast about desperately as the aliens obediently trudged down the newly formed path. This was insane!

"Captain!" Nancy hadn't meant to shout, but it got Luftew's attention. "There's a better way. Plants follow patterns and cluster where the conditions are favorable. With a little examination, we can pinpoint the most likely locations."

"Trusting chance is our way." He turned again to go.

Nancy thought furiously. With a little more info on this plant, the continent's topology, and the local climate she could develop a reasonable model.

"And you've found this nectar how many times?"

"What search pattern would you propose?" The captain paused.

"First I've got to assess the available information."

"We keep moving." He shambled away, making her heart sink. "Talk to Joda for what you need. No promises."

Joda was the captain's Lobstra through and through. Although he appeared to be about as imaginative as a bag of rocks, the idea of improving the odds intrigued him. Unfortunately, little yellow Meinish held all the planetary data. Due to his small stature, Nancy had assumed he was young, but the head searcher turned out to be the oldest crewmember and had been on a half a dozen hunts.

Meinish proved to be an acerbic fellow, sharing information only grudgingly. But with Captain Luftew's orders as incentive, Nancy eventually collected what data the old curmudgeon recorded over the decades. There was no disguising the fact he resented her attempts to narrow down his search. Nancy worried he might rebel at any moment.

"Swamp, that's all swamp." Meinish jabbed the stylus at several lowland areas on the vidpad they studied. "Nasty vines down there, big as your shell. Eerie lights too."

"You've been there before?" Nancy asked.

"Three cycles back. Nothing but water and weeds, mean weeds." He consulted the computer embedded in his worktable. "We'll be down there in two days, three at most. Then, you can see for yourself."

"But you said this queen plant thing is like a cactus, an arid-loving succulent." Nancy sat back on her heels. "It'd rot in conditions like that. Why waste the time?"

The searcher waved a misshapen yellow claw under her nose. Small white cones resembling barnacles decorated the bumpy shell. "Human, the random selector ordains that grid. No better or worse than anywhere you'd have us look. Fifty-fifty chance the monster'll be there. Wait, I take that back. There's a better chance of her being there, cause luck's on our side. You can plan all you want, but it's for naught if you look in the wrong place. I'm not gonna let the captain be constrained like that."

Nancy counted to ten, looked at Meinish's arched back, and added another five for good measure. "At least tell me about the minions that surround the queen. You've seen two types?"

Air and bubbles gurgled from his mouth parts, deflating some critical internal organ that had kept his crusty old shell arched in its defensive posture. He seemed happy to drop the topic of search areas. Years of failed missions where he had moved from apprentice, to assistant, to master searcher left Meinish pretty touchy.

"Well, that's an odd thing. One is sorta like the queen, all green with spines and needles. They walk around too, just like real people, only all they want to do is poison ya, then suck your innards out. Ain't got feet, just stubby little legs, three of 'em that sort of roll along the dirt."

"You've gotten close then?"

"Course I have. First cycle, as a young'un. Chance was with us. Queen was in the first damned grid we hit. Cowered behind those little green bastards. We would have mowed through them like nothing if it weren't for the other ones."

"The second kind?"

Meinish bobbed his upper torso in an approximation of a human nod. "Never got at them, nor the queen for that matter. Not too certain what the others are. Blasters and impact rifles didn't seem to faze them. They just kept coming. Chased us so far back that the greens got away."

"What did those ones look like?"

"Hard to say." The claw holding the stylus scratched the base of an eyestalk. "All types of nightmares. Big black devils with fiery eyes as I recall. Others saw metallic monsters that shot out flame to broil you alive. One fellow fainted when he saw a vee-shaped shadow tree crack and splinter the shell of his shipmates before flaming them." He scratches some more. "Course that was sort of odd, since we didn't lose anyone that trip. Remember I was young, but I don't recall anyone having to be patched up that badly."

Nancy considered this for a moment. "So basically a wide variety of dark creatures, all with some sort of fiery weapon?"

"Well, there were flowers everywhere, big white ones with fluffy middles. Didn't smell at first, but in the commotion of the devils attacking, I remember the air was thick with their perfume. Fighting must have shaken it loose. But they wasn't in the fight, just all around the outside. Sort of like a boundary."

"Really, flowers?"

"On tall stalks with curled yellow leaves shaped like pincers. I couldn't read what was printed on them. Now listen, missy, I need to get back to my charts. Get the official records off Drissa, she's the specialist. The captain's gonna call for the next grid soon, and I want to give him the most random selection possible."

Meinish turned to a side table and scrawled notes on a stained and ragged chart he had pinned flat. Although much of his so-called planning was done on the computer, the crustacean practically fawned over the ancient map.

Metal monsters and flower claws didn't make much sense. His description made it sound like the crew had been hallucinating. But then again, Fred was a strange world. She needed more solid information to help lay out a plan. Stumbling around at random was not going to get them anywhere. If she could narrow down their quarry's habitat and the searcher would see reason, she might yet steer this expedition in the right direction, maybe even toward Endeavor.

Nancy had wasted the better part of a week tromping through the jungle. If her expedition had survived, they could already be in orbit rather than risk more casualties. With crewmembers unaccounted for, protocol would be to leave an emergency transmitter behind. She could call for help if she got to that theoretical radio.

Her first order of business was to apply some rigorous logic to determine where this nectar plant and its legion of protectors might hide. Meinish wouldn't be easily swayed from his confounding trust in chance. She left him happily hunched over his precious chart, plotting out actions unfettered by logic. Movement in her peripheral vision made her look back. Reemer dangled from a tree limb just above Meinish's table.

The tree must have scooped up the Squinch for a snack. Her spike of panic turned to confusion. No, the tree was a well-mannered species akin to the white birch. To be fair, most of the jungle acted in an appropriately benign manner. It was just difficult to see the forest for the trees when some of them were out for blood.

What is he up to? She vowed to pay more attention to the slug. Reemer had grown increasingly irascible, and his hide had lost its healthy green glow. He could be coming down with something, but that didn't explain why he dangled from a branch high above the table with his skirt spread wide.

"Banzai!" her translator cried as Reemer launched from his perch like a flying squirrel.

He hit Meinish's chart dead center with a resounding thwack that blasted slime across table, computers, and the surprised Lobstra. It was like a belly flop into jelly, but replace the condiment with a noxious mixture of bodily fluids. The idiot! Nancy would get equal blame for the stunt. She hurried back, hoping Meinish's map wasn't ruined. The Lobstra rose high on his hind legs, claws shaking, and turned on Reemer.

But when the storm broke it was something entirely unexpected. Meinish slapped his massive claws down to either side of Reemer and unleashed a stream of sputtering clicks right into his face. Incredibly, laughter erupted from the translator, a true belly laugh. Both aliens wriggled and laughed, slapping and poking at each other like drunken fraternity brothers. Nancy stalked across the last few feet to ground zero. Reemer must have read her stormy eyes because he got himself under control rather quickly.

"Too tempting," he fluttered in apology.

"And you?" Nancy turned her glare on the Lobstra who idly pushed globs of goo together to form a small mountain over a similarly shaped range on the map. "Your map is ruined. What about your responsibility to be random for Captain Luftew?"

The translator wasn't great with inflections, but its tone matched the youthful glint in the searcher's eyestalks. "Made of synthpaper. Can't even burn the stuff. What could be more unexpected than a giant slug dropping from the sky and spattering me with luck knows what? He's a marvel of arbitrary behavior."

Reemer laughed in delight and launched a jet of liquid onto the searcher's lower carapace. Nancy was in the splash zone and collected new yellow stains on her much abused jumpsuit.

"You see?" the Lobstra quipped. "Wonderfully unpredictable. I had my doubts when destiny brought you to us, but things are looking up."

With that he turned back to his chart and Reemer. Meinish clicked, Reemer flubbered, and Nancy didn't have the slightest idea if the two could understand each other. Meinish swept the excretions from his map with those tiny scrubbing arms, but his battle claw slipped, sending him face down into the mess.

"Wonderful!" was all that came through the translator.

"Amazing," Nancy muttered and headed off in search of Drissa and a secluded nook. There was more information to collect and ideas to work out.

Drissa, a refreshingly sane Lobstra and the chief medic, happily provided what she had on the local flora. Like Nancy, she chafed at their questionable progress. But then, what scientific mind wouldn't? Her records were sparse on detail, but proved less confusing than Meinish's stories of metal and tattooed plants.

As Meinish predicted, two days later they crossed into swampland. Nancy finished her assessment during their lunch stop on the third day. She rubbed at a red patch on her arm, where a wayward seedling chomped out a tiny ball of flesh. The wetlands produced more of the little devils, an interesting parallel to Earth's mosquito. Perhaps the parent plants were aquatic.

She found the captain in conversation with his searcher and Joda. Reemer wallowed about, staying close to his new friend, but not intruding on the discussion. His skin was a mottled map of dry patches, making him look like a mobile atlas. She headed toward him, letting the Lobstra finish their discussion.

"Are you okay?"

"Fine, I'm waiting on the searcher. He's taking me to a mineral spring." Reemer puffed up to his full height.

He put great emphasis on Meinish's title. If Nancy didn't know better, she'd swear he was mad at her. If only there were some way to tell.

"Are you mad at me?" The question seemed a logical way to find out.

"Why, because we're traipsing through the jungle, far from the sea, and dodging death at every corner? No, it's great."

"But you insisted on coming."

"Yeah, so sue me." With a whoosh of air, Reemer deflated.

The Lobstra finished their conversation. Reemer turned abruptly and called out to Meinish. In a moment he was by the yellow Lobstra's side, pointedly ignoring Nancy and pitching a ball of slime at Joda. After surreptitiously checking to see if Nancy watched, the slug chortled overly loud. Whatever.

"Captain, could I have a word?" She turned to the leader.

The Lobstra nodded and leaned back on his tail in what the botanist had come to recognize as a posture of relaxation.

"I have those alternate search areas. From what we know of the quarry, I assure you it won't be in any wetlands."

The captain leaned forward. Nancy mistook the gesture for interest until he spoke. "Ridiculous. I appreciate your help so far, but our success is in Her claws now, not yours. I won't spurn Lady Luck."

"But you're wasting time. Your own records show this is a succulent-class lifeform. Moisture makes it rot. You want to look at higher elevations, where it's arid. I'll show you."

Jim Stein

Nancy presented three locations where the queen, which the Lobstra referred to as the Szooda, was most likely to be found. With every word the captain's shell seemed to thicken.

"You're saying the Szooda could be in one of these areas you've plotted?"

"It's very likely." Perhaps he was coming around.

He called Meinish back over and asked, "Does your algorithm include these three areas the good doctor circled?"

Meinish studied the simple map on which Nancy had painstakingly annotated her search criteria, assumptions, and conclusions. "No, sir. We use square grids."

The captain brightened. "Can we run the next random selection with circular locations?'

"Sure can. More overlaps, so the numbers will go up maybe twenty percent. Our Lady will like having more possible outcomes."

"Excellent! Doctor, Providence will make use of your inputs after all."

"Look, you've got it all wrong." Nancy nearly sobbed in frustration and swept out her hands to encompass most of the map. "These areas have no Szooda. None. Pretend they aren't on the map." She pointed at several areas outlined in red. "It could be in these places. Could be." Then she jabbed a finger at the tight circles, cycling through the three zones. "Here is where the Szooda should be if it hasn't been chased to a less ideal location."

Amazingly, it took Reemer joining them for her to make progress. He burbled and squeaked his way into the discourse, leaving Nancy feeling ignored. In the end the searcher agreed to modify his algorithm. He'd use only her highly probable and less likely—but possible—locations. The selection would still be infuriatingly arbitrary, but did improve their chances dramatically. If they were lucky.

8. Unsavory Cookout

F ATE AND the other assorted euphemisms Lobstra used for their deity had not been kind to Nancy. Meinish's algorithm didn't select one of her hot spots or even an area near the scientific team's landing site. Moving away from the wetlands was a small consolation. She hadn't looked forward to wading through stinking water, and swamp-borne flora adapted peculiar survival traits. She had no desire to see what such adaptations might yield, and that fact bothered her. Where's my passion?

Once the captain changed the search parameters, Meinish grew inexplicably friendly. More often than not Nancy found him riding the same hoversled or walking with her. Though, that could have been to get away from the Squinch's increasingly foul temper.

"What's gotten into Reemer?" Nancy asked, desperate to stop Meinish's discourse on random selection and chaos theory.

"Dunno, Lass. We were having a grand time a few days ago. Never knew when he'd spew slime or let off a stinker." Meinish laughed as he hobbled along. The feelers and legs down his left side didn't work as smoothly as the others, giving him an uneven stride. "But that boy's gotten downright surly. He took the change in plans hard, don't like where we're headed maybe."

Nancy found that difficult to believe. Reemer longed for the adventure and opportunities to pull juvenile pranks. He wouldn't care where they traveled. The Squinch excelled at being self-absorbed, but it would be easier on everyone if she could get him out of his funk.

"I might have something." Nancy fished a small round reflector from the depths of her pouch.

Her old crew had joked about the Squinch mirror fetish. Now was a good time to hunt up Reemer and see if the rumors were true. The sleds lined up for a rest stop where the jungle gave way to forest conifers that thankfully were not hurling projectiles. The gecko strips on the back of the mirror clung to her palm with microscopic hairs. Nancy ripped it loose and went in search of her companion.

She circled the camp twice before spotting the slug slipping into a dense stand of spindly trees, no doubt off to pout. She followed his glistening trail a good thirty yards. Daylight filtered from behind as the trees swallowed the sound of bustling Lobstra. Ahead lay gloom and shadows.

"Reemer? Stop moping and come out."

Wet rustling came from just ahead. The translator couldn't decide on a specific meaning and gave up with a disgusted hum.

"I've got a nice little mirror for you," she coaxed, her translator sputtering Squinch.

The rustling grew louder. One glistening antenna poked out from behind a boulder. The inquisitive appendage was bright green with rust colored spots and held an eye filled with angry red spider-veins.

"You look awful!" Nancy winced.

She stepped toward the boulder, but Reemer squealed high and loud, sounding for all the worlds like he was roasting on hot coals. The translator sputtered out nonsense, seemed to realize its mistake, and fell silent. Then the entire boulder heaved, and Nancy found herself confronted by a mass of flesh.

The slug's gray mottled body, which had looked so rock-like, was the size of an elephant. The head with its single antenna towered over her as the slug reared up. How had the Squinch changed and grown so large in just a few hours?

"Reemer?" Nancy held out the mirror, trying to ignore his angry hisses. A bulge appeared in his midsection and lengthened into a pseudo arm that snaked out to take her offering. The eyestalk shifted from left to right, studying his reflection.

"Nice isn't it?" Nancy asked as she flicked slime from her fingers.

Reemer tore his gaze from the reflection and glared at Nancy. On a scale from one to ten, he certainly didn't look happy. A second bulge appeared below his neck. The skin stretched and tore open to reveal a gaping mouth lined with sharp cartilage. The slug lunged for her.

The hideous new mouth closed over her hand and pain flared as it sawed at her wrist. A blur of green from her right and yellow from her left converged in wailing attack. The yellow resolved into Meinish, limbs flailing and claws slicing through the mottled hide to expose crescents of whitish meat beneath. Reemer, the real Reemer, attacked from the right. He smashed into the larger slug with an explosion of slime that dowsed her with mucus.

Meinish clearly hurt the creature, but it refused to let go. Nancy's knees buckled, but the grating mouth clamped over her hand kept her upright. Reemer was less effective. He nibbled at the larger slug's head, trying to get hold of its antenna, but her attacker simply stretched its neck higher than her little companion could reach. Another mouth-bulge formed beside Reemer.

"Reemer, look out!"

Reemer turned away, but rather than retreating, the ropy fishing tail shot from his posterior. The barbed tip sank deep into the flesh between the newly forming mouth and the one biting her hand. The mouth went slack, and she stumbled away, blood dripping freely from limp fingers.

The air hummed. A brilliant white disruptor beam caught the beast full in the face. Its eyestalk stretched back and disintegrated into goo that jetted away in the beam. The face went next, melting like wax. Reemer and Meinish scuttled back as the headless mass quivered and rolled onto its side.

Joda emerged from the trees, his weapon still trained on the monster. He spared her a glance, crossed to Meinish, and scolded the old Lobstra for his foolishness while managing to click with relief.

Time skipped forward. Nancy woke on her back to the smell of antiseptic and clouds moving overhead. Her wrist ached horribly, but rotated smoothly so nothing was broken. She lay atop blankets among cargo containers in the back of a moving hoversled. A yellow container shifted, revealing a familiar face.

"You all right, missy?" The old searcher sat with his back to her, mouth feelers whirling incessantly.

"Wrist hurts like hell, but I think it's okay. Did I faint?"

Windy bubbling answered instead of the Lobstra as Reemer crowded into her little alcove. "Dead away. Slurg venom could have killed you."

Nancy recoiled and immediately regretted it when her friend's antenna drooped. She forced herself to relax but couldn't move closer to apologize.

"Sorry, just nerves." She studied the smooth surface of the crate she huddled against. "What's a Slurg?"

"A big ugly slug with no style at all," Reemer said.

"Right nasty beasty," Meinish agreed. "Chomped your hand good. Would've been worse if Joda hadn't blasted its head off."

"I thought it was… I gave it a mirror. Then, you two tried to stop it."

"A poor mess we made of that, missy."

Nancy pushed to her feet and put her good hand on Meinish's head. "No, you were wonderful, battle claws flying—"

Nancy planted a grateful kiss right on the surprised old Lobstra's face. It was salty and feathery, like kissing a catfish with a moustache. She rounded on Reemer.

"And you, little hero"–she drew in a deep breath and reached for the slug—"kicked monster ass!"

Of course Reemer was wet and slimy, but surprisingly sweet like she'd smacked her lips into molasses. His sagging antenna straightened, and his skin wriggled in pleasure, shifting through green and yellow hues before settling back to somewhere in between. It still didn't look like a particularly healthy color, but for a change he seemed happy.

They lapsed into companionable silence. Nancy took the opportunity to examine her wrist. A clear flexible compound coated her forearm and sealed shut a nasty crescent-shaped gash. She gingerly flexed her fingers and smiled when everything worked properly. At least the monstrosity that attacked her was dead. She said as much.

"Not dead, but he won't be bothering anyone for quite a while," Meinish replied.

"You're kidding. It had no head! Nothing could survive that."

"I've seen worse myself." Reemer shrugged with his sensory antennae. "Nothing special about the head, though losing an eyestalk is rough. She might blunder into some tree that'll finish the job unless her crew finds her first. Slurg are surly, but they take care of their own."

Was he joking? Some terrestrial species like earthworms could survive and even thrive on being cut into pieces, but she assumed the Squinch—and now the Slurg—had a nervous system tying into higher brain functions. Perhaps with no protective skull an exposed appendage wasn't the best place to store one's mental faculties, but it was difficult to override preconceived notions on anatomy.

"How do you know it was female?"

Reemer's eyestalks swiveled, reflecting the setting sun. "Aside from those come-hither antenna? She might have been mean, but you can't deny she was drop dead gorgeous. Big gal, and that slime, her scent…mmmm"

"She nearly chomped you!" Nancy reminded him. "Are you drooling?"

The pink rabbit laughed its sad little laugh and turned mournful eyes on Nancy. She didn't know why the presumptuous little critter was unhappy with her. Traipsing all this way to find its nest certainly showed interest and caring. But instead of congratulating Nancy on her tenacity and tracking skills, one furry pink paw whipped a mallet around and struck the big drum strapped to its stomach. The rabbit spun and headed down the trail. Nancy followed, involuntarily marching to the drum. She tried skipping a step, but all that did was make the opposite foot fall with each beat. The tempo increased as they moved through the forest, the critter staying just ahead of her.

The edges of the trail were unnaturally crisp where brown dirt gave way to jungle groundcover. The manicured path led into a trap, but her feet moved on to the drum's cadence. She worked her way to the edge of the path and grabbed a handful of vines. Instead of slowing her down, sharp blades sliced and slipped from her grasp. The rabbit grew larger, his pink fur mottled with green overtones. The giant cylindrical battery that he wore like a backpack caught her eye. Silver letters gleamed on the black surface, but rather than a brand name it simply read, "No."

Heart racing, desperate, she drew the laser and keyed it to full power. The beam struck the battery, and a muted explosion sent fur flying as the creature disintegrated. Nancy's feet stopped so suddenly that she fell, flinging an arm up to keep from smashing her nose into the dirt, dirt that smelled hot and sweet. She rolled onto her back and marveled at the drifting fluff.

The sun picked that moment to set, painting the white and pink debris green. Nancy laughed as the storm of green swirled around her in a slow tornado. The fluff became big fat leaves. Not the cutting ones of the fisher tree, but three-dimensional wedges the size of two hands spread against each other. They swirled and flapped filling her head with regret. Regret for the tree they had lost. The regret of fall leaves doomed to drift forever, to gather in rotting piles. Regret and blame. They blamed her!

The maelstrom bobbed in unison as their collective accusation came clear. She blew up the bunny in self-defense. If it hadn't been towing her along, making her chase it—the leaves zipped about in a frenzy as the tornado raged faster and pressed close. Perhaps they were from a carnivorous tree after all. Energy rifles roared and the little swarm turned as one and fled.

* * *

Nancy blinked, willing her surroundings into focus. The smooth rocking of the hoversled had stopped and there was some sort of commotion, but her warm nest of blankets nudged her back toward sleep. A scream brought her fully awake as spatters of gunfire erupted. She crawled out from among her containers and found Reemer huddled under an overhang.

"What's going on?" she whispered.

"What makes you think I know? Just been napping and then the yelling started, and now the weapons. Sounds like the shellbacks are getting pummeled."

Nancy wrinkled her nose at the petulant attitude as well as the stench wafting off Reemer. Puddles of thick liquid covered most of the deck in the Squinch's hiding place. She moved to the edge of the sled and peered over the gunwale. Heat washed up as she tried to make sense of the scene.

The Lobstra were ringed in by towering stalks of green and silver. The plants had thick central stems like field corn, but rather than ears they bristled with oval flower heads, reminiscent of sun flowers. The center of each flower was mirror bright and ringed with broad silver leaves. The weapons fire came from the Lobstra themselves as they tried to cut the plants down.

A beefy blue crewmember leveled his rifle and fired. He hit a stalk and the plant toppled. Unfortunately, his beam also struck one of the flowers and the energy reflected off to the right and took a chunk out of a cargo sled. Flowers shifted to fill the gap as plants filled in from behind.

"If you've got any tricks up your sleeve, lassie, now would be a good time." Meinish scuttled low across the deck on his good side to join her.

Burns marred the old searcher's back, and his top left feeler was missing. Another stray energy bolt shot across the circle, struck a flower, and reflected back to sear one of the crew.

"Stop using lasers, you damned fools!" Meinish clacked his battle claw. "Blaster cores are almost drained, and we can't get close enough to clip them. Lomjack tried, they focused on him, and the poor bastard fried. Tain't nothin' we Lobstra fear more'n being cooked alive. Better to risk blasting ourselves into the next life."

Sweat and smoke stung her eyes as she studied the scene. Sunflower heads turned to drive back anything close, but most focused on the center of the encroaching circle. Smoke and steam rose from twenty feet of bare ground awash in painfully bright light. The Lobstra punched holes in the attacking line, but it wasn't enough. The circle continued to shrink, which meant less flowers needed to maintain the attack. Their maneuvering room dwindled with each passing minute as the plants herded sleds and crew toward the central kill zone.

Nancy hopped off the sled. Several mirrored heads swiveled to drive Joda's security people back from a failed charge. Either the flowers responded to movement or something in the root structure sensed approaching vibrations. If they could get a couple Lobstra through the ring, their claws would make short work of things. She hurried to the rear of the supply sled, tore open a crate, and hurled a foil-wrapped food packet at the advancing line. Several vegetative heads swiveled, tracking the projectile. It landed short of the ring and shone brightly in the focused rays. Seconds later, the mirrored flowers turned back to the center. The plants probably sensed movement through light contrast using photosensitive receptors.

"Can we can wet someone down? Keep them cool enough to get behind the plants."

"Tried that." The searcher wagged his head. "The water turned to steam so fast we lost little Truid. Poor bloke died screaming."

Three concentric rings made up the battlefield. The smoldering center shrank as the trap contracted. Grass blackened, just shy of bursting into flames. The Lobstra, their hoversleds, and equipment floated in the safe zone, keeping a thirty-foot buffer from the center and from the plants. Any closer to the center and they risked stumbling into the heat. Any nearer the outer ring and they were targeted directly. As the plants drew closer, the silver packet she's thrown disappeared behind the advance.

Nancy tore open another package and an orange cascade of what looked to be water-packed fisheyes spilled to the deck. Reemer surged past, knocked her aside, and slurped up the orange balls. The feather-light packaging was tough and flexible.

"Do you have survival blankets or anything else made of this stuff? We need enough to cover someone and reflect the heat." She pushed the empty pouch at Meinish.

"We got large ones." He spread his claws indicating a handbag sized pouch. "Could glue a bunch together."

A shriek sounded high and bright above the fighting, then cut off abruptly. Two Lobstra hauled an unconscious crewmember away from the blackened center and hefted it up onto a sled. Equipment and people were packed tight and the jostling had pushed the female Lobstra into the heat.

"Not enough time." Cloying smoke rose thickly from the center to sting eyes and throat. It would only take a light breeze to ignite the grass. Nancy grabbed a handful of the food packets and hurled them. Silver flowers swiveled wildly, tracking the projectiles. "Make them focus on something else."

Meinish caught on quick, tore the top off a new container, and used his small feeding claws to hurl a stream of projectiles. More flowers turned, trying to bake the assumed threats.

"Stop yer shootin' and make 'em turn!"

Energy blasts were replaced by flying debris, packages, and phlegm. The latter came from Reemer, who pulled out of his funk enough to hack up great gobs of mucus. The center of the trap cooled as the attack lost focus.

"This won't last long," Joda called from their left.

True. Packets fell in a heavy silver rain as the Lobstra tore into their supplies, but empty containers were being dumped from the sleds at an alarming rate. They would run out of ammo soon.

A low grinding rose amid the thwacking cadence. The sound grew louder, echoing from beyond the wall of death. Dozens of brown-green wedges rose above the silver flowers, new weapons—no, the heads of giant insects. The newcomers tore into the stalks with powerful mandibles. Flowers toppled to the ground, and the suffocating heat winked out. Dozens of elongated brown faces with bulbous green eyes swiveled in unison to study the trapped group.

"Weapons!" Captain Luftew bellowed.

9. Going Mental

H EADLESS STALKS fell to the ground, and in moments the heat trap was reduced to a carpet of wet stems. Confronted with a swarm of giant insects, the Lobstra pulled into a defensive ring with Nancy and Reemer at its center. The insects boasted exoskeletons, but were delicate and bright compared to the beefy Crustacea. An individual would be no match for any of Luftew's people, but there were just too many.

The bugs stood six feet tall with light green bodies, brown accents, and little variation to help distinguish individuals. Feathery-edged devices swung from utilitarian belts as they stepped through the dead stalks on four spindly legs. Their upper arms articulated with triple joints and ended in tapered combs like those of a praying mantis.

They encircled the Lobstra, but paid them little heed. The alien insects picked though the dead stalks looking for the silver flower heads. They'd rotate the flowers with those wicked-looking forearms while chewing off the reflective surface, then dropped the white corpse and move on to another. Individuals paused in their foraging to raise up on their four rear legs with combs tucked tight to their chests. Those immobile observers grew in numbers, attentive prairie dogs swaying and watching.

Joda leveled his weapon at the nearest insect. The newcomers pivoted in unison, combed hands flashed to belts, and every insect leveled a pair of sinister looking tubes. Deadly projectiles would fly from the quad-barreled weapons at any moment, turning the scene into a bloodbath. At least a hundred insects surrounded them. Where did they all come from?

Lobstra antennae and feelers bristled with tension as the standoff stretched on. The insects felt…different, patient yet resolute. They wanted to return to feasting, but would deal with— would destroy—the threat confronting them if necessary. Reading so much from the body language of alien creatures should be impossible, yet Nancy couldn't help empathizing. This new race saved them from being burned alive and for their trouble were now forced into a confrontation. It just wasn't right. The jungle is the real enemy.

"Stop it!" Nancy shouldered forward and rounded on Joda.

The big Lobstra skirted sideways to retrain his blaster on the nearest insect. A short-side step again blocked his line of fire.

"Get out of the way, human," the security chief growled—or at least that's how the translator rendered his rapid clicking.

"This is ridiculous. They saved us, so you want to kill them?"

"We just happened to be in the way." Joda tried again to get a bead on an insect.

"They're hungry for plants. Let them eat." Nancy swept an arm out toward the strangers, causing several to again take up swaying.

"Human…" The translator followed the word with an airy exhalation.

Nancy glared into that alien face, willing him to see reason. No one wanted a massacre. Joda's antennae splayed wide in aggression, began to quiver, then swiveled down. He lowered his blaster a fraction.

"Nancy, be reasonable. Their weapons—"

"Are only out because they feel threatened," she finished for him. "Let them eat."

Captain Luftew pushed over to stand by Joda. "How do you know?"

"It's obvious." Nancy frowned in confusion. "Isn't it?"

"We wait." The calm, breathy voice echoed from her wrist device as if from many mouths.

Nancy took in the silent insects, half of which now swayed in place, then cocked an eye at her translator.

"We commune directly," the voice echoed.

"Tele…pathic?" Nancy stuttered.

The captain stepped closer. "I've heard of races that mind speak, but never met any, let alone the likes of these creatures."

"Lokii," the voice supplied.

"Pipe down there! We're strategizing." He glared at the translator before continuing. "If they—"

"Sorry." The ghostly voice from Nancy's wrist had the captain's antennae vibrating as his shell darkened a shade.

"If they continue—"

"The Lokii…" More echoes, more quivering antenna.

"If the Lokii"— Luftew paused to glare from the translator to the foremost mantis, daring him to add something. The silence stretched for a second. The translator hissed softly as if to comment, sputtered, then fell silent. The captain nodded and continued—"don't want a confrontation, there need not be one." He stepped out to face the lead insect. "I am Captain Luftew. We were breaking the sunflower trap, when your swarm descended."

Nancy coughed pointedly.

"Yes, well," the captain continued. "We appreciate your help. Thank you."

The burly crustacean turned back to Nancy. "Satisfied? But we're still at a stalemate here."

As if reading his thoughts, which they probably were, the Lokii lowered their weapons and clipped the strange tubes to their belts.

The captain's antennae lifted in surprise. "Joda, stand down."

The big security officer seemed about to argue, then turned to bellow orders. The crew stowed their weapons and set about gathering food packets, reassembling crates, and seeing to the wounded.

"Shouldn't have needed any help," Joda grumbled. "I'm sending a sled back for heavier weapons."

Tensions eased quicker than Nancy would have thought possible. Perhaps this new race truly was telepathic and helped calm things. That would also explain her earlier certainty that they didn't want a fight, even if the Lobstra had not been so sure.

She joined Captain Luftew as he approached the lead mantis. Joda and Reemer followed close, the latter oozing along and leaving a foul slime trail. Two insects drifted up to bracket the presumed leader. The three aliens swayed as the captain's group approached, serene reeds in a summer breeze.

"I am Hassaam. I now lead." Her translator had no difficulty interpreting the Lokii movements and whatever else they were broadcasting.

Captain Luftew introduced his people, surprising Nancy with the title of War Engineer. He gestured at the insects to either side of Hassaam.

"I am Hassaam," the translator expertly layered two voices together.

She exchanged a look with Joda, shrugged, and studied the insects devouring flower heads, hoping for some unique feature to distinguish the three Hassaams. The Lokii seemed to be exact copies, with triangular heads, stubby antennae, and quad-hinged mouth parts. The similarity to Earth's praying mantis was startling, except for the sheath of green armor that rose over each delicate head like a halo. And, of course, they stood a head taller than her and wore identical tool belts.

Nancy rubbed her throbbing temples, thankful that she'd stopped sweating and the smoke had cleared away. When she turned back to the three Hassaams, her translator spewed out clicks and buzzing in Lobstra. Her annoyance flared at being excluded. Stupid machine.

The three Lokii stood placidly, almost regal in the face of Captain Luftew's obvious agitation. No, regal wasn't the right term; these were not imperious beings. The three radiated quiet resolve, steadfast as Buddhist monks. That calm bearing made them easy to pick out from among the rest of the Lokii. Funny that she hadn't noticed before.

"You imprinted us," Reemer sputtered out the words before Nancy could comment. "Your ugly puss kind of glows."

"Indeed." The three turned to Reemer, who had reared up in indignation. They nodded solemnly, again reminding her of robed clergy. "You obsess over individuality. We have obliged."

"I don't need an oversized walking leaf in my head!" Reemer's squelching and flatulent speech shifted to a rolling growl.

"That's great, isn't it?" Recognizing the prelude to slimy projectiles, Nancy mustered false cheer and hastily stepped between her companion and the Hassaams. "No more guessing. Thank you."

Reemer deflated and noisily swallowed the phlegm he'd been amassing. Joda turned away with a disgusted grunt, which seemed to mollify the little guy. One antenna quirked to watch the big officer shudder.

Without the tension of drawn firearms, discussions with the Lokii proceeded smoothly. The alien leaders conversed through Nancy's translator, but by the end of the day, she doubted the device was necessary. The insects' swaying, head jerks, and arm movements conveyed ample meaning, which only made sense if mild telepathy was at work. Nancy adjusted the translator to show an amber light when transmitting and a green when "listening" to the Lokii.

The newcomers proved uninterested in the Lobstra's quest, which baffled Captain Luftew. The Hassaams brought their people lightyears simply to forage on the varied vegetation Fred had to offer. She got the impression the swarm would multiply during their visit.

"Sir, I dislike this," Joda cautioned during a break. "We should not leave so many aliens along our back trail. They could overwhelm us without warning. Or worse, take control of our ship."

"The Hassaams are sincere." Luftew spoke carefully. "But you have a valid concern. Activate the ship's wartime protocols. It will be safe cloaked and airborne. Anyone approaching without the proper security key will be vaporized, but I suppose that is unavoidable."

"And the Lokii behind?" Joda pressed.

"Have faith." The captain pulled himself up straight, antennae swiveling horizontal in what amounted to a sigh. "It is the one thing I would change about you. A little faith, old friend."

They feasted on the many food packets that split under the sunflowers' heat. The Lobstra ate to the point of bursting. The insects grazed, but also presented fruit, leaves, and flowers they had gathered. Nancy surreptitiously ran a few toxin test strips over her meal before filling her plate with fishy granules and fruit.

"You integrate well with the crew," Nancy's translator echoed as she chomped into a purple net fruit. Hassaam number two leaned forward over a small pile of seeds and cocked its head in curiosity.

"Our arrangement suits me," Nancy replied.

"But you are…different. We understand individuals vary within a species, but you are no Lobstra. How do you cope?" Curiosity and confusion radiated from Hassaam.

"Look, it's no big deal. You just adjust. Why?"

"HaSSaam needs to know."

The emphasis on the esses was a new distinction her translator had not captured during earlier talks. In fact, she didn't think it was catching it now. The device echoed the conversation, but the communication felt more direct, more natural. As an experiment, she switched off the device.

"Well, HaSSAAM might have to be disappointed."

"HaSSaam is swarm dynamics and cultural interactions. There is no HaSSAAM."

Ah, his curiosity made sense now. "Ha-SS-aam, people are different, races are different. But if you focus on individuals, we're all very similar. Even Reemer, a disgusting little twerp, is a decent enough guy deep down."

"Deep down," HaSSaam echoed. "We are not used to…different."

She felt pensiveness as he drifted away, antennae shifting with a faint undercurrent, a seed, of understanding. Linguists said eighty percent of communication was through body language, but this was so much more than interpreting facial features or stance. Words from the Lokii flowed directly into her mind.

"How?" she blurted out. "How can we talk with no translator?"

HaSSaam turn back, his gaze flicking to her wrist. "A marvelous device, though slow and imprecise. We emulate its functions and improve them."

"Telepathy?" Reemer was right, they were poking around in her their heads.

"Aptly put, but fear not. We do not literally read minds, just thoughts directed at us as deliberate communication. Most species have a latent ability. Activating the loci in your mind would be quite straight forward."

HaSSaam offered to unlock her latent telepathic abilities, to establish pathways for communication. He said it would be like a sixth sense, that he could implant the core linguistic algorithms from her translator, accelerating the creation of neural pathways to deal with new languages. She saw in the Lokii's intent how perfectly natural and non-invasive such a thing would be. It would not alter her personality or influence her thoughts. An old musical flashed to mind.

"If I could talk to the animals, just imagine it…" She let the lyrics trail and lifted her chin. "Do it!"

The alien laid the combs of his right arm across her forehead. One minute her mind clicked along wondering at the possibilities, concerned that she'd made the right decision. Then her perception shifted. Like the car that appears just before a crash, voices and less recognizable impressions crowded her head. Sounds were richer, overlaid with meaning, and she found they made sense.

"It worked," she whispered as HaSSaam withdrew his feathery forearm from her face.

"Acclimating may take a few days, but this will be far less cumbersome than your translator."

Anxious to try out her new skill, Nancy headed for the dining pavilion. She found Meinish in animated discussion with Herman, a young Lobstra with short primary antennae. The clicking and bubbling made sense! Beyond that, minor gestures she rarely noted—the flip of a pincer, the shift of a mandible—carried incredible nuance.

The old Lobstra shed his grumpy demeanor as he lectured about the role of lead searcher. He wanted Herman as an apprentice. She marveled at the exchange as Meinish discussed the nature of random chance and its divine influence. But it was all too much. Her head buzzed and she jittered with tension reminiscent of a caffeine high. The press of people and noise turned smothering and she stumbled away to escape.

The symptoms eased on the walk to the enclosure she shared with Reemer. Sweat turned the tepid evening wind clammy against her cheeks. She slipped through the magnetic netting, fell onto her cot, and covered her face with both hands, willing the world to stop spinning. The pillow felt cool, but also wet. Her eyes watered and her sinuses clenched in response to the smell of old sardines. Nancy sat up, but the noxious pillow clung to her head. She slapped it away and kicked a spongy lump by her feet.

"Watch the antenna, sister!" Reemer hissed out foul air. "I'm sleeping here."

Mucus trailed down her right cheek. She sucked a bit into the corner of her mouth, gagged, and lunged for the flask of water on her makeshift nightstand to purge the bitter taste that spread across her teeth and gums. It helped, but residual stink rose up the back of her throat.

"Reemer!" Her entire cot glistened and sparkled under the dim nightlight. "Why are you in my bed?"

"Better! Mine feels wrong."

She flipped on the lantern and immediately regretted it as pain lanced behind her eyes. Reemer's small cot was neatly made, its rubbery slime-resistant sheet taut across the surface.

"You haven't even tried it. Get the hell out of my…" Her recriminations died as she took in Reemer's state. The slug's hide was dark green, nearly black, like an overripe avocado. Mottled gray blotches oozed a milky substance that made his normal slime seem wholesome by comparison. The hiking boots the Lobstra made her poked out from sallow folds along his skirt. "Aw, not my new shoes."

The comment kindled a trace of the alien's usual snarkiness. One antenna dipped in a halfhearted caress of a boot.

"Nice and soft now." His gaseous laugh petered out into a sort of moan.

"You're sick."

"You're thick and ugly," Reemer countered. "Mix some seawater, and I'll get off your precious bed."

Nancy rummaged beneath the bed for the salt and water canister. Reemer's mischievous pranks and painfully foul moods were legendary among the Lobstra. Captain Luftew eagerly handed over every trace of salt from his stores in hopes of improving the slug's disposition. Daily soakings helped steer the Squinch back to his normal, marginally acceptable wise-assery.

Nancy sprinkled a handful of pinkish crystals onto Reemer's cot, then sluiced it with water. A lip around the edge of the rubbery surface contained the shallow puddle.

"There you go." She turned to stow the containers.

"Too weak." There was a wet rustling as Reemer shifted.

"I'm not falling for that again. Get your butt moving." There was more rustling and when she looked back, Reemer's head hung over the bedframe. His antennae hesitantly felt at the floor, then went limp. Nancy huffed out a sigh. "Oh for Pete's sake!"

She picked up the little alien, trying to keep his body from contacting her jumpsuit. He would wiggle around to slime her clothes or spray her with some nasty concoction, then guffaw while bathing. She steeled herself to not give him the satisfaction of reacting.

Without so much as a snide comment, Reemer let himself be eased into the water. He lay motionless. Nancy scooped water over his back and smoothed his blotchy hide with her hands. Several minutes passed before he spread his skirt wide and splashed about like a beached ray. When he gathered the skirt back under him, the puddle was gone except for a few slimy patches.

Nancy stripped her sheets, wiped her hands on the dirty bedding, and sat to examine her boots. Thankfully the mucus hadn't gotten inside. Some scrubbing would bring them back to life. She started in with the corner of a sheet. Reemer's drama took her mind off her head, and thankfully the buzzing and dizziness subsided.

"Better?" Nancy asked as she finished with the left boot and scooped up the right.

"Better," he agreed.

Reemer curled onto his side to look at her. Much of the blotchiness disappeared, but a few patches persisted on his flank and near the top edge of his skirt. His hide remained a darker shade of green than usual.

"Will you be all right?" Nancy pressed.

"Just too long away from the sea. I'm good now." Reemer's response was slow and measured, then he brightened sounding more like his old self. "Hey, you're making more sense than usual."

"Thanks, slime ball. The Lokii gave me a boost." She tapped her temple, then the dark translator. "Might not need this anymore."

"I'd swear you had secondary mouths and everything. A little formal and prissy, but good diction. You let those bugs into your head?" He shivered, healthy slime rising on his skin.

"Just HaSSaam, the cultural lead. He sort of switched me on for interpreting. The Lobstra were loud and clear." She recalled the buzzing jitters from dinner. "Too much sometimes. I'll get used to it."

"You can get into their heads, find out what really riles the shellbacks and other races." Reemer's eyestalks gleamed with anticipation. "Splatting and spitting is fun, but I can do more. Meinish enjoys things too much. He thinks I'm some kind of oracle."

Nancy rolled her eyes. Wait…others? "More aliens?"

Naval surveys classified Fred as primitive. The crew of the Endeavor had not expected to run across anyone else during their three-month exploration. They knew merchants occasionally bartered with the Squinch, but the galaxy was vast and inter-species encounters uncommon.

"Sure, lots more. Always happens." Reemer paused in slurping the residual slime off his cot. "Aliens…funny term."

"Always happens?" Nancy sat forward, her boots forgotten.

"Shiny flying ships everywhere when the jungle wakes up. Squinch pod leaders clamor to get in some good trading, but they never want to have any real fun."

"You don't help your pod groups?"

Reemer pulled himself up straight. "The mayor himself gave me an important role this cycle. 'Reemer, go find an island to guard,' he said. But you found me, and this is more fun."

"Why now?" Nancy stifled a laugh at the mayor's directive.

"The cycle starts every five years, and they come." Reemer shrugged, a sort of rippling of the thick hide below his neck. "The rest of the time the jungle's pretty boring. That's why I don't bother going inland much. First cycle was dull, but I got into some good trouble last cycle."

"How do the Squinch manage to talk to these visitors?"

"Mostly by pointing and piling up the things we want to trade. Some people know the common trading language or just sort of make sense to us, like Meinish and the Lobstra. His clicks sound like bubbling, and I usually get the gist of what he says. These Lokii are new and—well, you know—sort of make you understand them. Others hiss and squawk and just sound weird." Reemer considered, then offered a rare disclaimer. "No offense."

"All for a few ounces of precious nectar," Nancy mused.

Fred came on the navy's radar—as it were—only three years ago. That probably explained their wildly inaccurate records. If the bureaucracy had investigated further, or not scheduled the Endeavor's visit exactly on top of a cycle, her crew might still be alive.

A percussive explosion boomed from the north, shaking the enclosure and toppling the water and salt containers to the floor. Nancy rushed outside as a great WOOSH erupted to her right. Light painted the underside of the cloudy sky as flames leapt above the treetops. The wall of fire was perhaps a mile away, on the opposite ridge overlooking the sunflower plains. It blazed for a minute before dropping back to hug the treetops. Captain Luftew strode from the pavilion bellowing orders. Nancy hurried over.

"Lightning?" The cloudy night sky seemed an unlikely source, but it was all she could think of.

"Incendiaries." Joda came up behind them.

"Aye," Luftew agreed. "Someone's having a fracas. Nectar hunters do not get along all that well."

"The Lokii seem easy to work with." Nancy watched the fire expand to a thick crescent.

"Phaa!" the captain spat. "Aren't really hunters now are they? Here for the buffet, not the nectar. No stomach for it. Look around, they're almost gone already."

Nancy spotted HaSSaam and a couple of Lokii scouts near the edge of camp. Droves of the creatures had been dining when she'd turned in, not an hour ago. The cultural lead waved his forelegs in a regretful goodbye before slipping off into the dark.

"Orders, Captain?" Joda asked.

The Lobstra raised his bandaged claw to his eyes, studying the distant conflagration through a squat black device. Nancy had initially worried he would lose the appendage, but it mended quickly. She'd seen others re-growing lost limbs and was glad he didn't have to endure that. Losing a main claw carried a stigma of weakness that just didn't suit the captain.

"Nothing moving in the valley. The conflict must be beyond the ridge." Luftew looked from transport sleds to pavilion where four crewmembers frantically stowed the remains of the feast. "Get ready to move. We'll stay the night, but get the sleds loaded. I want a squad down there." He pointed to the valley floor. "And roving scouts. If no one bothers us and the wind keeps the flames at bay, we stay out of it and move on in the morning."

The captain turned away and headed for his enclosure. He stumbled sideways in an awkward lurch, but Joda was beside him to lend support.

"The claw?" Joda ask as the pair continued away from her.

"Just dizzy," Luftew said. "My head is buzzing like a gem wasp nest."

10. Bad Habit

"IT STINKS," Reemer complained.

"Really? You think it—" Nancy wrinkled her nose. He wasn't wrong. "Something nasty's burning, like a pile of old gym socks soaked in vinegar."

The fires kept to the far side of the valley and burned out before morning, but that stench kept the crew up half the night. This morning, everyone shambled about in a sullen haze with much antennae and head rubbing. They moved out quickly, gave the burnt area a wide berth, and headed for the plateau Meinish selected for their next search.

The group perked up as smoky plain gave way to rolling hills filled with broken rock and stubbly brush. Eroded cliffs of what looked like sandstone loomed in the distance. Horizontal bands of red and slate blue stone painted the distant walls. Off to the right, a carpet of trees ran along the edge of the plains to the base of the cliffs. A shimmering river separated forest from plains, its source cascading down the plateau into perpetual roiling mist. The humidity had dropped noticeably since veering away from the swamps, a move that significantly improved their odds of finding the Szooda.

Nancy sighed. She'd argued for bypassing the plateau and heading into the dessert, but fate wasn't to be denied her chance to lead the Lobstra. At least they moved fast across the open territory. Nancy and Reemer rode on their hoversled, while most of the crew trotted along on spindly legs, eating up the miles.

Captain Luftew called a halt when one of his advance scouts limped back toward the column. The sleds pulled into a circle, and the crew took station around the perimeter. Nancy hopped down and walked to where Luftew and a small group gathered around the hurt Lobstra. The captain held a spikey brown golf ball covered in long dense spines with the metal tongs clutched in his lesser pincer. The scout had several of the giant burrs stuck to his shell. A light-tan Lobstra rivaling Joda in size gingerly poked at two burrs lodged under the scout's right flank.

"Hold still, Wispa," Drissa chided when her patient pulled away. "They're still burrowing."

"Can I take a look?" Nancy asked.

The captain rotated the forceps so she could examine the burr.

"They start two miles to the northwest." Wispa seemed eager to focus on something other than the prodding. "Only a few at first, but they get thicker fast."

"From a thistle of some sort?" Nancy asked.

"Didn't see any plants—" Wispa broke off with a gasp and annoyed clicks as the medic plucked a wriggling burr from under his front leg. "These were scattered on the ground. We'll have to cross a dry riverbed packed with them thanks to storm runoff. The rocky slope on the far side looks clear. I tried to make a path, but the buggers stick. Those spines just sink in and—ow! By the Lady that hurts."

"That can't be good." Reemer appeared out of nowhere and leaned forward to peer at what Drissa held with her forceps.

The second burr had come apart. Several spines jutted from the smooth white plates of Wispa's underbelly. The medic gripped one with tweezers, but the spine jerked away, fine barbs flexed along its length, and it burrowed into the shell. The other detached spines wriggled in place, disappearing into the scout's belly. Wispa gasped and dropped to his side. The burrs along the Lobstra's back vibrated weakly, but the shell was thick enough to keep them at bay.

"We'll get pain killers into you, then sort this out." Drissa rummaged in her satchel, withdrew a gray tube, and pressed it to Wispa's belly.

"Thanks, Doc," Wispa muttered. "But it's already stopped hurting."

Drissa exchanged a confused look with Nancy. Burrs and spikes could be defensive protection or used to propagate the species. Since these detached from the parent organism, they must carry seeds. When seed pods were ready to disperse, barbs attached to passing animals that would transport the next generation to areas with less contention for good soil and nutrients.

But rather than just hitching a ride, these burrowed—odd evolutionary behavior, especially on a planet with no indigenous animals. Then again, Fred's flora was highly mobile, so the burrs could have been meant to engage other native species.

"Wispa, think hard." Nancy knelt by the scout. "Were there any plants at all around, maybe clinging to the rocks?"

"Wispa!" The captain's voice cracked like a whip when the scout failed to respond. "Answer the question."

Wispa's antenna sprang straight out and his eyestalks swiveled to his commander, then to Nancy. "Yes, Sir. Tubes, green tubes with short needles."

"Succulents." Nancy nodded. "Cactus class or Cactaceae family at least."

"Guess so." Wispa's burst of attention faded and his head drooped to the sandy dirt. "All tangled up in the rocks and crevices."

"Rooted to the rocks or into the soil?"

"Let the lad sleep." Captain Luftew waved two assistants forward to help lift Wispa onto a small hover board, then turned to Drissa. "Will he be all right?"

The big medic's clicks held agitation and fear. "How should I know? I'll get some images, see what those things are up to, and let you know."

"Ideas?" Luftew turned to Nancy as she studied the remaining two-inch spines that hung loosely from the section of burr they'd removed.

"I'll work on it. Just don't let anyone touch these things."

"Bad," Reemer said. "Plants that get inside you don't come out nicely."

"We'll spread the word," Luftew said. "Work with medical. Even at half speed, we'll be at that ravine by day's end. I need options."

The cautious pace allowed Nancy to stretch her legs and think. She examined the flora as she pondered the burr problem. Not surprisingly burrs and needles became more prevalent as temperatures rose and the climate dried. She sat down on a weathered rock and looked west at the receding carpet of thick forest. The remains of her expedition and the Endeavor's shuttle were back there. She vowed to return to the site someday, but first there was work to do.

She carried the cracked burr in a specimen container and examined the flexible ring at the base of the spines. Magnification revealed each barb had a mechanism allowing the things to grip and burrow. She opened the container and used the forceps to pull at the white spaghetti-like tendrils inside the main body. The material held water as expected in a succulent offshoot, but the fibers were longer and separated by a slick film. Despite the color, it resembled primitive muscle tissue more than plant matter. She pushed the slimy fibers apart looking for a kernel or seed core.

"Can I have it?" Reemer's glistening head pushed up between her hip and arm to prod the burr.

"What!" Nancy jumped in surprise. "No, I need it."

"Smells delicious. I like those nuts." He nestled into her side, fouling her tunic with mucus.

"I'm trying to figure out why this broke off in Wispa." She held the carcass to the side opposite her insistent friend. "You don't even travel inland. How can you know these taste good?"

"Rain washes them downriver." Reemer gave up trying to push past her and scrunched into a compact oval, sulking. "Tastes like scared fish. There are plenty more at the med platform." He stretched his head forward, antennae scissoring toward the delicacy. "Sooo good."

Though fixated on the damn burr, Reemer was in a good mood for a change. His saltwater bath seemed to be holding. Plus, he was right. The meds had other burrs she could dissect.

"Fine."

Nancy had barely set the container down when Reemer's digestive organ fell wet and heavy across it and her hand. The wriggling white worms appeared instantly, and her hand stung as if plunged into ice water. She pulled away, an edge of the stomach clinging to her fingers before snapping back to the rocky surface.

"Jeez! That hurt." Nancy clutched the dripping hand to her chest.

"Mmmm. Scaredy-fish can't run away now," Reemer cooed, ignoring her.

The rest of his purring didn't translate to anything except rapt contentment. She stalked off toward the medical sled to get cleaned up and look for a new sample. The formation stopped for the afternoon meal, so she didn't have to jog to catch up. Still, the bit of exercise felt good.

Reemer's content muttering faded behind. She'd heard of playing with your food, but talking to it seemed a bit much. And how did food taste scared? Maybe adrenaline or whatever hormone triggered the flight response in fish added flavor. If a meal of scaredy-cat—fish in this case—turned the Squinch on, he'd go bananas over Earth rodents and birds, which were hardwired to flee danger and probably packed with the cowardly flavor. Nancy's foot landed wrong and she stumbled as a thought hit her.

"It can't be." She shook her head at the irony, but it made perfect sense and laughter burst from her, raw and uncontrollable.

She tried to think of something else, deadly spines, dead crewmembers, but Reemer's words kept center stage. Air whooshed out until her stomach ached. She managed a breath as a yellow shape approach through her streaming tears.

"What's wrong, missy?" Meinish grasped her shoulders, concerned eyestalks searching her face as she wheezed and wiped her eyes.

"He thinks they—"she dissolved into sobbing laughter, grabbed Meinish by a skinny foreleg, and forced the words out"—taste like chicken!"

When her outburst faded, Nancy asked a confused Meinish to take her to the medical sled.

"You can use my laser scalpels and test equipment." Drissa happily handed over a jar of dead burrs packed in alcohol. "I'm running a toxicology scan on Wispa's blood. Something's suppressing his system, keeping him unconscious. I found three spines in him. Two are lodged near his heart, but one is creeping toward his brain."

"Can you remove them?"

"I'd rather not. When we pulled the protruding spines, they discharged a neurotoxin that nearly killed him. A dose deep in his tissue would be fatal. The captain wants to stay put until we know how to handle these things." Drissa withdrew a small white box from her station and handed it to Nancy. Something scrabbled inside. "I kept three alive."

"Let's pool our resources." Nancy stepped to the second raised workstation while Meinish settled back on his tail.

Two hours later, Nancy scrubbed her eyes and rolled her stiff neck. The searcher perked up at the sound of snapping vertebrae. Didn't he have work to do? A dozen tissue samples in various states of dissection adorned her workstation. Drissa helped her save sketches annotating muscle fibers and nerve analogs to the Lobstra database, then carefully pressed their next test strip down on a live specimen.

A victim's movement triggered electrical impulses in the burr and spines. A spine detached and burrowed using the hinged barbs for propulsion. As the sugars in the tissue were depleted, the spine ran out of energy and came to rest. Pulling them out was problematic, because flexing the barbs backward triggered venom release. The term venom usually referred to toxins injected by animals, but these plants used similar delivery mechanisms and were so much more than simply poisonous to touch or ingest.

"Damn," Nancy cursed as spines penetrated the hardened synthetic material. "They poke through just about anything short of metal."

"We've made solid progress." Drissa pushed away from the tabletop. "I can use an embolic probe to encase and remove the spines in Wispa without triggering a release."

"But we can't have everyone who steps off the sleds falling into a coma."

"Keep trying the chemical inhibitors. We won't need armor if you can shut down their ability to sense vibrations. I'm going to work on Wispa."

Two assistants followed the big medic off toward the enclosure at the other end of the sled. The old searcher sidled up to take her place.

"I know you don't hold much stock with our Lady Luck, but giving her a spin might be something to consider," Meinish said.

Nancy bit down a surly reply and counted to five. A random selection of chemicals or boot fabric certainly was not going to help find something resistant to the burrowing burrs. It was fine for the old guy, the entire crew really, to waste effort praising unplanned accidents and arbitrary good fortune, but time was short.

She needed these deadly pods in the conquered pile, hamstrung and lifeless. Their construct made no sense. With no actual seeds, the internal tissue might root and grow as an offshoot, but she thought it unlikely. The entire mechanism for burrowing was counterproductive, sending the spines too deep to grow outward and capture life giving sunlight. They might kill the host organism, but the plant was unlikely to rise from the fallen carcass. Still, the old Lobstra was trying to help. She took another calming breath.

"It isn't that simple. I need to eliminate what doesn't work, assess viable alternatives, and formulate a solution using protective clothing or a clearance strategy. This isn't a case where I can just line ten things up and throw a dart to pick one."

"Ah." His antennae wilted. "You need faith. That lad Herman might make things clearer." He pointed a claw over the rail extending from her workstation. "Or ask Reemer. For the love of…what's he doing?"

Reemer headed toward them, sort of. He was perhaps fifty yards away, body stretched to its full length as he made for the ramp. But his tail put on a burst of speed. He shrank to a ball and shot off to the right, only to have it happen again sending him left. His body shrank then stretched with each maneuver, similar to his travel on forest paths, though he'd never done the accordion thing and there weren't any diagonals to avoid. If Nancy didn't know better, she'd say…

"He's drunk! I bet it's the burr venom."

"Did the boy get stabbed?" Meinish asked.

"He ate my first sample. No wonder he made all those happy little sounds. It got him high."

Reemer made it to the foot of the ramp, pinballed aboard, and headed for the workstation. Blotches again covered his hide, but for once he didn't seem to mind.

"Hi, ya all," Reemer called loudly as he stretched toward her samples, mucus happily spraying from his mouth and bubbling from beneath his skirt.

"You've had enough, cowboy." Nancy pushed him toward Meinish.

She sighed at the mess on her hands, wiped them on her jumpsuit, and considered just wearing clothing made of slime.

"All this work is gonna make your skirt bloat. Eat 'em all! That's what I say." Reemer spun in a wild circle, then made another try for the table, but Nancy rapped his sensory antenna with her forceps.

"First off, no eating the burrs," she said. "Second, if you eat more, you'll overdose and die. You're wacked out after just one."

"Why ain't he dead already?" Meinish asked. "He's way smaller than Wispa."

"Maybe Squinch have a natural immunity." Or the digestive process itself might neutralize the plant's toxins. "I'll need samples to analyze for reagents, then—"

"Coming right up!" Reemer reared tall, hacked, and spit a wad of digestive goo onto the deck.

His antennae and skirt undulated wildly, and he fell backward into the storage shelves. He thrashed and laughed, trying to right himself. Nancy had only seen Reemer's underbelly up close when examining him after the net vine attack. It had been scored and swollen from his encounter, but looked relatively healthy. Now, scars and ridges covered his belly. The blotchiness continued underneath too, covering the area in dark green bruises that must be incredibly painful. No wonder he snapped and complained. Reemer finally rolled upright, revealing a crushed white container covered in slime.

"Nobody move!" Nancy lunged forward and picked through the smashed box with her forceps. "The burrs are loose. Watch your feet!"

Her voice rang out, bringing the Lobstra on the sled up short. Joda, Drissa, and three others froze, eyestalks sweeping the deck. Nancy's cheeks grew hot under the security chief's glare. The three burrs couldn't have gone far. They moved slow and deliberately, much like sea urchins. A sick turtle with a broken leg could outrun them. The area around her workstation was clear. Damn it, we have more tests to run!

"Uh, missy?" Meinish pointed at Reemer.

Even in his dopey state, the slug took her command seriously, propped himself up on the table's edge, and scanned the floor. Three spikey balls clung to his back.

"Reemer, do not move." Nancy bent for a closer look.

The outer spines of each burr rotated weakly. Two were stuck just behind Reemer's head, while the third clung to the middle of his back. He twisted and stretched his eyestalks, trying to see.

"Stop it! Three burrs are stuck on you." She opened the forceps, but hesitated.

"That's bad," Drissa said as she and Joda joined them. "We scraped them off Wispa's shell, but the Squinch's soft hide has no protection at all."

"Bad?" Reemer squeaked and again tried to crane around to look.

"Shhh!" Nancy whacked him on the head, then turned to the Lobstra. "Any ideas? I'm not a doctor. I've only practiced on corpses."

"What!" Reemer drew in frantic, raspy breaths.

Nancy huffed, set down the forceps, and took one of Reemer's eyestalks firmly in each hand. She pulled his eyes level with hers and glared.

"I swear to God, if you don't hold still, I'll—"

Plop…plop…plop.

Behind Reemer, three slimy burrs lay immobile on the deck. There were no visible punctures on his back, just glistening blotchy skin and a thick coat of slime.

"Ack!" Reemer croaked as her grip forced his eyestalks to hyperextend.

"Oh, sorry." She let go, and his eyes retracted to rest tight atop his head.

"They're dead." Drissa held up a burr. "The spines along one side just melted into limp grass."

"What's this mean?" Joda asked.

He leveled his blaster at the burrs, apparently ready to scuttle the entire sled to take out the alien spores. She looked from Reemer to what Drissa held. Some substance in the slime incapacitated the burrs, destroyed them. Between that and the potential of a toxin neutralizer in Squinch stomach acid, a plan began to form.

"It means we have a chance." She patted Reemer on the head and grinned.

"Thanks to me," the slug added smugly.

"That's another thing," Joda said. "Why can we understand the Squinch now? The captain told us the Lokii worked on you, but now all of a sudden he—" Joda jerked the blaster toward Reemer, looked abashed, and holstered the weapon. "Suddenly we understand him perfectly."

What was this? Nancy hadn't activated her translator in days. Reemer spent so much time with Meinish, who he'd always gotten on with, that it hadn't occurred to her he might talk to other Lobstra.

"Reemer?" Nancy asked.

"Yeah, we talk fine now," Reemer answered her implied question. "It got easier for me after my salt bath and that killer headache subsided. Meinish had a head buzz too a few days ago."

Come to think of it, the captain and several of the crew mentioned buzzing irritation. She was about to ask Joda about that when someone shouted.

"Contacts inbound!"

The camp exploded into well-rehearsed motion, crisp orders rang out, and Joda shot off to help. Nancy hurried to gather the dead burrs, Reemer's stomach juices, and slime samples from the now giggling alien as the sleds jockeyed into their defensive ring.

Joda reappeared after the medical and command sled parked at the center of the formation.

"Hostiles coming up our back trail. Humans."

11. Keep Your Friends Close

"THEY SHOULD be friendly." Nancy squinted through the ballistic shielding, trying to make out details among the dust clouds. "Our expedition was purely for scientific research."

She urged Captain Luftew to prepare a hospitable welcome, but the gruff leader kept them penned up on the command sled and put a dozen crewmembers in the high rocks along the edge of the plain. The setting sun made it difficult to pick out details. The golden orb was similar to Earth's old Sol, but carried a blue tinge. Meager rays pushed through the thickening cloud layer piling up against the distant plateau.

Nancy's heart raced. If enough of Endeavor's crew managed to survive to resume their mission, she'd have a lot of explaining to do as to why she abandoned her post and now helped an alien race destroy the native species. Harry's frightened eyes looked through the roots of the needle tree in her memory. Others may have survived, but not her friend. She rubbed at the stains on her hands as they waited.

Shadows stretched across the sparse vegetation from the rocks to the west. Perhaps Commander Gunthall repelled the attack and launched Endeavor. Systematic rescue of survivors would take time, especially with only the one transport. Travel on foot was obviously too dangerous for the ill-prepared group of scientists, so she expected to see the shuttle or even the round hull of the good ship Endeavor itself come over the horizon.

Instead, two columns of dust crested the horizon followed by a low-flying ship with flat wings, perhaps a quarter the size of Endeavor. The Lobstra forward guards blocked the newcomers' progress with a pair of heavily shielded weapon pods—part of the bigger, badder armaments Joda had retrieved from the Lobstra mothership after their run-in with the sunflowers.

Two security people manned each pod and the gun that bordered on comical in size. The long-barreled design mimicked their handheld blasters. Each gun crew stood in a semi-circle of gray material encircling a panel of targeting controls. The sections along the enclosure's top edge and around each gun barrel were made of transparent ballistic shielding similar to the four-foot-tall bulwark that now rose from the edge of their sled.

The advance stopped a hundred yards out, and the dust settled to reveal a hoverbike to either side of the main craft. Two people rode the left bike, and one rode the right. Landing struts extended from the flying craft as it settled to the ground with a high-pitched whine.

Pain fluttered deep in her stomach. It had been stupid to get her hopes up. These people were not from Endeavor. Nancy ran a hand across her eyes and wiped the wetness on her pant leg. Her fingers and hands itched in a gummy sort of way, so she scrubbed them against the material, then each other. Two figures emerged from the ship and walked to where Captain Luftew joined the gun turrets.

The captain exposed himself while Joda, the big bad security officer, waited safe on the command sled. She'd assumed Luftew was in one of the deck houses, not out confronting this new group. She edged over to Joda's workstation. The Lobstra didn't use chairs, so the big alien hunched over a u-shaped console of displays, instruments, and dials. An embedded screen showed a close-up of the captain as the two strangers approached. One was tall, certainly over six feet, while the younger man was shorter and scrawny by comparison.

Each man on the screen was overlaid with red squares, while the Lobstra had green circles. Hash marks, lines, and indecipherable alien script littered the display. Her new translation ability did nothing for written language, but this was clearly a monitoring and targeting arrangement. Larger holographic displays above the workstation showed an overhead view of the shuttle, hoverbikes, and surrounding area with more green marking Lobstra concealed among the rocks.

"Ship is back in orbit." Joda pointed to the bird's eye view. "We have plenty of firepower. Are these your people?"

Nancy stopped scrubbing her hands and squinted at the image as Captain Luftew waved to the nearest gun turret. The massive weapon dipped to train on the ground. The taller man swung his arm out, flat palm clenching into a fist. A line of ports on the bow of the shuttle slid closed, and the left bike flipped the twin guns protruding from under its front cowling up into the stowed position before settling to the ground.

The other rider didn't respond until the tall man again gestured. With an angry jerk, the big square-of-a man riding the second bike lashed out at his steering column and his guns also flicked skyward. The leader turned back to the Lobstra captain with a disgruntled and apologetic look that was so intrinsically human it made her chest ache.

It seemed like ages since she'd seen another human. The leader was striking and rugged, not handsome, but nor was he ugly. His brown hair was close cropped along the sides with long luxurious curls on top and across his wide forehead. Chestnut brown skin gave his broad cheeks and squat crooked nose a healthy glow. Except for his beefy build and height, he might have been a Pacific Islander. Maybe the man just had an incredibly deep tan, or perhaps a touch of Samoan ancestry.

The boy was a few inches shorter and of lighter build and skin tone. The soft curve of his cheeks made him look young and nervous. He juggled the equipment bag on his shoulder and took notes as the other two spoke. A curl of black hair fell across his cheek. He brushed it back revealing an adorable little half-smile and shining blue eyes that tended more toward gray. Nancy upgraded him to a young man in his twenties, the kind who looked boyish even after gray hairs made an appearance.

"I don't recognize them." Nancy shook her head. "The captain was smart to be cautious."

"That's why he gets the big bonus. They have the feel of hunters."

Joda manipulated controls topped with colorful tufts of hair. The design allowed him to use his pointed secondary legs instead of pincers to make fine adjustments. Nancy had the sudden urge to draw little faces on the flesh-toned knobs. She imagined the massive alien presiding over a sea of troll dolls with spikey hairdos that he reached out to affectionately ruffle.

"Interference from the shuttle is blocking our sound," Joda said as she forced down the image of him playing with ancient dolls. "There, that's got it."

"… figured your crew knew where it was going," the larger man finished.

"Or you are following us, Captain Gekko." Luftew said.

"Well…yes and no." Gekko smiled apologetically. "We had a bit of a clash with some nasty Snakes the other night and needed to put distance between us and them."

Captain Luftew's antennae tilted up. "Snakes?"

"Long sinewy fellows. Young Mister Farnsley here got quite the nasty bite. Venom hit hard, nearly killed my best tech." The captain clapped the younger man on the shoulder, staggering the poor fellow.

"I've dealt with Esha before. Competent negotiators with twisted agendas." Luftew pointed a claw at the young man. "You are fortunate, Mr. Farnsley."

"Call me Jake." He looked apprehensive, as though he'd never talked to a seven-foot-tall lobster before. Nancy could relate.

"Fortunate indeed, Jake," Luftew said. "My people are immune, but I've seen others succumb to Esha bites. You must have excellent medics, Captain."

"That and antivenom we received in trade." The human shrugged in deference. "I like meeting the competition. We can't collaborate on the hunt, but side trading can be mutually beneficial. The Esha wanted nothing to do with us, but perhaps you are interested in a little bartering?"

Nancy followed the conversation easily despite the unfamiliar words. They used an abundance of hard consonants and clipped phrases, a limited vocabulary exploiting common phonemes from both races.

"What language is that?" She asked Joda.

"Trader's voice. Most can manage the sounds for simple discussions and transactions."

The emotions her newfound ability usually supplied was largely absent, perhaps because they listened remotely or simply due to the language's terseness. Still, the human captain came across as a conflicting mix of honesty and someone trying too hard. His speech and gestures held an undercurrent of uncertainty, like a salesman hawking a product he's been assured is superb but has never used. He could just be nervous dealing with a new race. She just couldn't tell.

"He's lying about…something."

"Certainly," the security chief replied smoothly. "Hunters compete. His interest in trading sounds plausible on the surface, but is not the whole truth. More likely they were estimating our capabilities, strengths, and weaknesses. The captain will know how to deal with them."

In the end, Captain Luftew agreed to a short détente. Perhaps the shrewd leader was abiding by the old adage about keeping your enemies closer. Within an hour, both groups established well defined camps separated by a commons area with dining pavilions.

Nancy took advantage of the extra time to work with her samples. She and Drissa analyzed Reemer's excretions and assigned the Lobstra's staff to develop synthetic equivalents. By mid-evening, Nancy found herself with little to do but wait. Her grumbling stomach urged her toward the dining tent, while Drissa opted to catch up on paperwork.

Reemer made himself scarce, so Nancy ate with Herman. To date, she'd barely exchanged a dozen words with the would-be searcher apprentice, but found him excellent company with a wealth of knowledge and a refreshingly sensible outlook. She took advantage of his openness to ask about the whole "worshipping Lady Luck" thing, which quickly led to discussion of Herman's potential career moves.

Searching was a respected traditional career, but Herman longed to join the scientific league attempting to prove the existence of Providence through experimentation. Apparently, the belief system built on Lady Luck—what Nancy saw as an extreme form of chaos theory—stood on the brink of evolution. They were deep in conversation when she realized two humans loomed over their corner table.

Both men wore green pseudo-military uniforms equipped with an impressive arsenal of loops, lanyards, and pockets. A handgun hung gunslinger-style from each man's belt, thin barrels pointing toward pant legs tucked firmly into the tops of dingy tan boots. One was a block of a man with a broad scowling face and bushy brown brows matching his close-cropped hair. The other was older, a wiry whip of a fellow with a long craggy face and eyes gleaming with anticipation.

"Told ya there was a woman with 'em." The lanky man bobbed his head and leered. "Consortin' with the crawfish."

The big man's scowl actually deepened, something she'd thought impossible. His cold black eyes glittered, and his right hand rested casually on the pistol as he caressed the trigger with his index finger.

"You should think before opening your mouth." The words were a dangerous purr laced with threat aimed at his oblivious companion.

"Just saying, Urneck. She's a bug lover. Gotta wonder why."

Nancy felt more than saw the larger man's eyes slide over her. Weapon and hand were at eye level, giving her an up-close view of scarred knuckles and neatly manicured nails. His fingers twitched again, then rested along the pistol. She rolled her eyes. Fixate much?

"Pete has a point." The beefy man, presumably Urneck, jutted his chin at Herman in a dismissive gesture. "You on one of them stupid spacer rotations? Helping out the bugs instead of real people?"

Nancy was not in the mood. She'd seen too many people hurt and killed in the last few weeks to put up with bullies. Their attitude was doubly annoying because these jokers were the first humans she'd seen since losing her own crew. Plus, she felt Herman's confusion. The Lobstra didn't know how to react. That alone made her furious and ashamed. She forced herself to stay calm and kept her voice light.

"Stop playing with yourself and act civilized." Nancy lifted an eyebrow at his caressing hand.

Urneck's face darkened, accentuating his ruddy complexion. He leaned over, pushed close to her, and growled, "Watch yourself, little girl. Grownups don't like brats."

Her stomach clenched. She might be physically smaller than this arrogant pig, but he couldn't be more than forty. She wanted to laugh in his stupid face, but pushed up from the table, forcing a grin that probably looked ghastly. In fact, she rather hoped it did.

"I don't see any grownups. I'm Nancy and this is Herman, a Lobstra, not a bug or a crayfish." She glared at Pete's smirk. "It has most definitely not been a pleasure, so if you will excuse us?"

Urneck started forward as if to block her, but a heavy hand landed on his shoulder and pulled him up short. He grabbed his pistol, started to draw, but stopped when he realized the newcomer was his captain.

"Good of you to make introductions, Mister Urneck. Negotiations are complete. We'll be trading a block of calcium permanganate and a few other compounds for some cryo-rounds. You should be able to retrofit them to the kinetic guns in your armory. Please see to the arrangements. I will take up the social mantle in your absence." The human captain turned to her and Herman, a clear dismissal for his crewmen. "Captain Veech Gekko at your service."

The captain spoke in standard, his voice gruff but courteous. Nancy shook the hand he thrust out, happy to see him include Herman with a nod. He didn't go so far as to offer his hand, which the alien probably wouldn't have understood anyway.

"Dr. Nancy Dickenson," Nancy supplied as he released her hand. "This is Herman, assistant searcher. Pleased to meet you, Captain."

"May I?" Captain Gekko gestured to the stool next to Nancy. She nodded and they sat, while Herman simply settled back down on his tail and clacked his claws on the table. "Please, call me Veech. Medical doctor?"

"Botanist. Some advanced biology, but I'm no surgeon."

"Pity. We've got a few ailments among the crew. Med computers are wonderful, but a second opinion, especially from a pretty lady, can go a long way to easing concerns. Robots have little empathy." Nancy started to comment, but the captain forestalled her with a raised hand, scratched his blunt chin, and rubbed a finger alongside his mildly crooked nose. "I'm only going to do this once ma'am, but I do apologize for any inconvenience my lads may have caused. Some of the crew are rather opinionated. I don't encourage such behavior, but have little say in the mission ashore. Shipboard things are different."

Nancy trusted her first impressions. He had a few rough edges, but Nancy liked the captain, an extreme counterpoint to her feelings toward the other two who had thankfully slipped away. People were transparent, and so many harbored agendas. Captain Gekko just wasn't that complex. He held back details in his discussion with Luftew, but was easier to read in person. Something inside her relaxed. If his ship arrived after the attack, they might even have news.

"Have you received any navy transmissions about the survey ship Endeavor?" she blurted out.

"Can't say that I have. Navy doesn't come this way. We track fleet movements, but space is a big place." Veech scanned the pavilion and waved to the young man who'd accompanied him earlier. "Jake, over here."

Jake broke away from Meinish and wound through the Lobstra relaxing under the pavilion. The rest of the human crew clustered at the far end where they had been joined by Urneck and Pete. They looked wary and had pulled four of the tables into a defensive arc facing the open space between themselves and the alien crew.

"Yes, sir," the man said as he arrived tableside.

"This is Jake Farnsley, my technical officer," the captain said. "Jake, meet Dr. Dickenson."

Jake nodded and extended a hand. "A pleasure, ma'am."

Enough with the ma'am stuff! She couldn't be more than ten years older. Nancy self-consciously touched a hand to her head, as if she could cover up the bits of gray.

"Please, just Nancy." Jake's grip was pleasantly firm and warm.

His long fingers wrapped around hers in a comforting way. She looked into his boyish face and smiling eyes, felt a blush start to rise, and dropped her hand. Christ, she'd been more articulate with the two psychos.

"Right, Nancy." He studied the ground.

"Jake does most of my comms logging too," Veech said. "Have there been any naval dispatches on the ship Endeavor?"

"A couple of navigation advisories came in, sir. I don't recall the details." Jake gave her an apologetic shrug. "Real-time comms is Ray-Jay's job, but I end up doing most of the stuff they're too busy for. I can pull the records. What ship class is the Endeavor?"

"It's an independent research vessel. We were—are—under a navy survey charter. Ran into trouble a couple weeks back."

"Not a fleet ship." Jake nodded, and the captain lifted an eyebrow "More to look through, but there are other avenues for that. Give me an hour."

"Let the doctor know what you find, but I'll need a written report. Best to be aware of any military interest." Captain Gekko dismissed Jake with a wave then turned back to Nancy. "What kind of trouble?"

Nancy recounted the attack on Endeavor and summarized the events that had led her to join the Lobstra. Veech commiserated with her situation and exuded a sort of tightly controlled empathy.

"Hell of a time to start a survey. Brass should've known better." He scowled, lost in thought for a moment. "You took up with a Squinch of all things! How's that been?"

"Very…interesting, Ree—" Something wet and heavy slapped her knee.

She glared under the table. Reemer clung to her right leg. Though water resistant, the material of her pants was not up to the challenge of Squinch slime. Goo seeped into the fabric, annealing it to her calf. From the knee down, it felt like she had been dipped in warm honey—foul-smelling, putrid, warm honey. Reemer's saltwater therapy was wearing off again.

"Not my name. No names!" Reemer hissed.

Nancy looked across her knee to see Captain Gekko's face bobbing under the table and splitting into a crooked smile.

"There's your little vixen. Quite the…" he fumbled for the compliment that had wanted to roll off his tongue. "…looker."

"He's…ow!"

Reemer bit her thigh, eyestalks pleading. That vague "trouble" he got into last cycle apparently left him desperate to remain anonymous.

"He's usually better groomed and less clingy. Being away from the sea is hard on him."

"A bit yellow for a male, but if he's been sick, well—" Veech straightened and met her above the table. "Hope the little guy feels better soon."

Commotion erupted from the human-occupied tables. Two hulking men argued with Jake and blocked his path back to the ship. Pete's cackling laugh cut through the tumult. Lobstra fell silent and eyestalks swiveled to watch the heated exchange.

"If you will excuse me?" Captain Gekko sighed and heaved himself to his feet with an apologetic half-salute.

As the man stalked toward his crew, the wet clenching pressure on her calf subsided. Reemer whooshed out a sigh and preened his antennae, ignoring her. She reached down and grabbed him by the scruff of the neck.

"Hey!"

He wriggled, but his illness made the slime tacky. Keeping hold was easy, but she'd be up all night washing the stench from her hands. She needed to scrub again tonight anyway. The phantom pinch of drying blood and faint red flecks along her forearms—and there, under her nails—attested to that.

"We're going to have a little talk, mister."

She half carried, half dragged the sputtering Squinch to their enclosure.

12. Out with It

R EEMER TRIED to keep calm as Nancy pulled him toward their sleeping quarters. Talking was not a good idea. There were too many things the human would take the wrong way. Running into human hunters complicated matters. A cover story and fake name would help him go unnoticed. He wracked his brains—both of them—for something to tell Nancy that sounded believable and downplayed his role in last cycle's unfortunate events.

Every part of him already hurt, and being stretched and pulled made thinking difficult. His hind-brain busily keep his skirt flowing, but their dizzying path threatened to scramble his fore-brain. Reemer frantically worked his skirt ridge, forcing his back half to keep up in spite of the woman's refusal to walk in a proper line. How she always managed to stop at the right spot in spite of these insane maneuvers remained a mystery. His neither regions made valiant attempts to head for their destination while the human jerked his front end left and right, as if the tent might dart away if approached directly.

With a final unceremonious thrust, the world lurched to a stop and cool rubber caressed him. Vile clumps clogged his lower orifices. He sputtered bits of soil onto the cot, coiled around to groom, and froze under Nancy's glare. It didn't take any newfound communication skills to see that further delay was not in his best interest.

Her odd mode of travel aside, the human was an ideal companion. She always led him into situations rife with opportunities for fun mischief. Friends were hard to come by among his own people. They were always so worried about foraging, trading, and of course procreating. Not that there was anything wrong with those activities, but his people were just so boring. Squinch rarely explored inland, but the jungle called to him; even its rocks tasted interesting and vibrant.

When he tried to share his adventures, no one would listen— let alone participate. The human hunters he found last cycle were marvelously responsive to jokes and playful antics. Squinch barely reacted to flatulence, wads of slime, and foul odors, but humans and other races responded very well indeed. Nancy was no exception, but their relationship had grown deeper and he genuinely cared for the human. They helped each other. She had saved his life twice. All of which made it even more difficult to fabricate a story about last cycle, but it had to be done.

"The humans…" he hesitated. "Uh…the other humans may know me."

"I gathered that much. What did you do, and how mad are they?"

"Not all of them." He cringed under the undeserved glare. "The captain and Jake seem nice. I'm certain they weren't here last time. But some of the others were." He shivered at the memory. The big twins, Ray and Jay, got hold of him shortly after the incident. They'd started cutting off pieces. When he didn't respond properly, they brought out salt. "There was a misunderstanding. Some of the crew got very…cross."

"So, your pranks backfired." Nancy nodded and sat down, her sunken little eyes unreadable.

"Well, sure." He needed to make this good. "I just laid a few slime bombs in unexpected places, but they ended up fouling the main drive a bit."

"Oh my god. You didn't blow up a ship, did you?"

"Nah, they kept it from going critical. I headed for deep water, just to give them room to work." He kept his voice light and upbeat despite the memories. "A simple misunderstanding. They eventually stopped looking for me. Mucus under the current now."

"That's why your people got you out of the way, to avoid a repeat of last cycle."

He didn't like the way this was going. That floating island was Mayor Breem's favorite place to bring his mates. If Reemer hadn't been there to discourage hunters from using it, there was no telling the problems they might have caused. Even Nancy could have made a mess of the place if not for him. He'd only left the island because the hunt had moved well inland and his job was complete.

"The Mayor needed his island safe. It was low profile but important work."

He puffed himself up, which made his back itch because the damned blotches blocked his lubricating slime. Those spots pulled and stretched painfully, but Nancy looked suitably impressed, and seemed willing to concede the point.

"Fine, but will they recognize you, arrest you?"

The term "arrest" was new, but painted a picture in his mind similar to being cast out, only in a confined area. The ultimate Squinch punishment of being driven away and an outcast didn't faze him. Solitude left time for exploration. But to be locked in a small space, kept from going anywhere, doing anything…he shivered. But Ray-Jay wouldn't confine him for long. The twins just didn't have patience for something like that.

"The last crew tried to get Mayor Breem to turn me over. They know my name, but we all look the same to you folks—plus my colors are way off."

"Sounds like you need to stay out of sight until we move on in the morning."

Reemer bobbed his head and turned to his grooming, happy to omit the more awkward details of his prior adventures.

13. Help is on the Way

MORNING TURNED to afternoon before Nancy and Drissa were able to offer viable protection from the aggressive burrs. The med team did a wonderful job weaponizing—or rather armorizing—the Squinch secretions. Nancy tested three synthetic equivalents to the slime coating against a live burr. Two recipes worked well, rendering coated boots and clothing effectively invisible. The burrs couldn't sense articles coated with the compound, even when moving and interacting with the burr directly.

Developing an antitoxin from Reemer's stomach juices proved more difficult. She couldn't run live trials, so introduced spine toxin to her own and Lobstra blood samples. The medical equipment let them monitor reactions at the cellular level. The synthetic formula bound to ninety percent of the pathogens, but the few markers that could not be neutralized attacked hemoglobin and other essential proteins. It was a start, but more work was needed to come up with a fully effective medicine.

"We can keep the spines off," Nancy reported to Captain Luftew.

She held a large box containing her last live burr and had a canister of neutralizer tucked under her left arm. The captain stood at the helm of his command sled, watching the human party stow its gear and make for their vehicles.

"Show me."

She set the box on the deck, then sprayed her right boot and pant leg. The mist smelled like ocean fog with a hint of dead mouse—the faintest whiff you catch when the wind is just right. The spray evaporated quickly, leaving an oily residue on her clothes. Nancy swallowed her anxiety, flipped back the lid, and stepped in. The burr ignored her, refusing to activate even when she nudged it with her toe.

"Impressive." The captain's antennae bobbed. "But we do not cover ourselves with fabric."

"Drissa added a binding agent that clings to your exoskeleton. The treatment is hardy, but she recommends reapplying every few hours."

Captain Luftew thrust his battle claw out, nearly conking her nose and giving her an up-close view of his wounds. The bandages were gone. Fresh, blue-white chiton filled the finger-wide fissures, welding sections of good shell together. If the aliens molted like terrestrial invertebrates, the ugly scars would eventually be cast off. Still, Nancy found it hard to believe he was willing to subject his claw to potential further abuse.

Nancy sprayed on the neutralizer, thoroughly coating the proffered claw. The captain lowered his claw into the box and hit the burr like a golf ball, putting it from side to side. He gurgled in satisfaction and squashed the burr flat.

"We don't have an antitoxin yet!"

Nancy grabbed the claw with both hands and heaved. It was like picking up a bag of cement. The burr was a mash of broken brown spines. White tissue squished out between its cracked shell.

She breathed a sigh of relief. It hadn't activated. Even the intact spines were quiescent.

"That was a stupid stunt." She inspected the underside of the claw and rummaged in her bag for forceps to pull two spines from the lower claw hinge. "Those spines are still sharp and can pierce your shell. These didn't go deep, but watch for numbness or anything out of the ordinary. Wispa isn't back on his feet yet. We don't need you down too."

"Do Lobstra even have testosterone?" she muttered under her breath while bagging the spines.

Nancy regretted her words—but damn it, that was childish. Though easy going, the Lobstra's militant hierarchy might deal harshly with insubordination.

"Scouting is a messy business. I needed to see how effective your treatment was." He examined his claw and nodded in satisfaction. "Spray everyone, but we'll load up the carts and keep foot scouts and guards to a minimum unless there's trouble." He turned back to his console. "Good work, Nancy. You've given us a real chance. Convey my thanks to Drissa and her team."

Nancy felt a smile tugging her lips as she hummed and hurried back to the med sled. Her good mood wasn't just because of the praise. The captain never addressed her by name. He usually called her doctor—or nothing at all. How odd that the bubbling clicks of her first name put such a pleasant ball of warmth in her stomach. She glanced back at the hulking leader's vigil and frowned. She'd gotten so busy with the neutralizer compounds that she'd forgotten about Jake's search for information on Endeavor. As the human's craft lifted, her heart sank.

Joda declared them ready to move as the sun crossed its zenith in a sky painted with wispy gray clouds. The day wore on, the sun's brilliant halo lowered toward the horizon behind them, and the leading edge of the plateau rose ahead. Nancy kept to the med sled and helped Drissa recoat crewmembers as they rotated off watch. There were so many protein compounds in the protective spray that it glowed bright under a black light. Drissa rigged up two darkened booths to help ensure complete coverage. Nancy bent to secure one of the handheld ultraviolet lights as her sled accelerated, then lurched to a stop. She cursed as her head smacked the enclosure's support pole, picked herself up, and headed to the front of the sled.

"Stupid no-shell," the driver, a Lobstra with blue tiger stripes along his back, swore as he settled the hoversled back to the ground.

A security team member with his shell hunched in threat pointed his blaster over the side.

"Sorry, sorry." The human voice drifted up from below.

Nancy peered over the rail. Jake Farnsley slid off the back of a hoverbike. The driver was a hard-looking blonde with her pageboy hair pulled back in a tail. She sat astride the bike, pointedly ignoring the fact she had just stopped in front of a moving vehicle several times her size.

"Um, sorry for that." Jake froze when he saw the gun. "Is Dr. Dickenson aboard?"

"It's all right." Nancy put a placating hand on what passed for the guard's shoulder.

The shell was dry and slightly warm. Lobstra exoskeletons didn't sense pain, yet did provide rudimentary tactile sensations. The guard relaxed and raised his gun to point over the humans' heads.

"Dr. Dickenson!" Jake waved a small silver pad in greeting. "I have your report."

Nancy searched the waist high bulwark for the forward ramp controls. The guard grunted, snapped on his weapons safety, and reached under the rail to her left. A four foot section of bulwark retracted, and the forward ramp extended.

"Five minutes," he said and turned away to speak into the radio hanging from his left breastplate.

Jake hurried up the ramp as soon as it touched down. His untidy uniform gave the impression of crumpled leaves. He stopped and gave a little half bow over the datapad clutched to his chest. His storm-gray eyes sparkled, clear and eager from within yellow-black circles of fatigue.

"Call me Nancy. I'd given up on you." She found herself smiling.

"I didn't forget, but Urneck had me working on gear all evening. He can be…insistent."

Nancy waited, but Jake just kept studying the deck. Strangely, it was more of a comfortable than uncomfortable silence, but time was short. "And?"

"Success!" Jake snapped his head up, grinned, and pushed the pad forward. "Three messages reference the Endeavor mission."

Nancy took the silver pad. The appropriate memory segment was open, and she scrolled through the messages. The navy prided themselves on daunting and cryptic message formats. The bulk of the text in each contained header information, addressees, and field formatting. Appeals for more natural language missives always went unanswered by fleet command. She was passingly familiar with the pedantic structure, but still found it hard to pinpoint subject lines and the meat of each message. Two looked to be basic space advisories. The third was titled Science Mission Endeavor Status and several pages long, discussing crew roster, mission goals, and—

"The first one, there." Jake bent in to point at the small screen, then jerked away when his chest touched her back. "Um, that just recaps your flight plans from a couple months back. Mentions your trajectory, host ship drop point, and return sail plan. The second—" he leaned in, hesitated, and settled for pointing at the device. "That's an old advisory from when they lost contact with your crew. The fleet declared Endeavor missing and asked for immediate reports of any contact."

His verbal highlights helped her quickly pick out the relevant passages in the confusing jumble. Then she returned the display to the longer message. "This last one looks more specific. A lot of mission background, crew information…" she trailed off as she scanned the report.

"That's the money one! Navy is sending out another ship." He looked over her shoulder again, his proximity curiously comforting as he reached across to find a section labeled recovery options. "Yeah, there it is. SS Bernard will be here in two weeks. They were closest, but the general advisory also asks local merchants to divert if feasible. Course navy won't pay, but I guess compensation claims can be filed for fuel and resources. Phttt, good luck with that."

The words blurred as her eyes brimmed with moisture. They were coming! A weight in her chest eased. She swiped her eyes clear with thumb and forefinger, hoping it looked like she had a headache. She'd been coping well with so many strange situations that finding a tangled ball of emotional stress lurking just below the surface came as a shock.

Her position with the aliens was tentative at best, especially given the psychotic plants that gunned for them around every corner. The promise of true safety among her own people made her throat clench. She sniffed and snot crashed to the back of her throat, making her cough and hack.

Jake jumped back, the warmth of his closeness disappearing. "Are you okay?"

"I—"

"Dr. Dickenson, we need to move," Joda's voice boomed from the control panel behind them. "Now, if you please."

"Got it, thirty seconds," she called back to the sled operator, took Jake's hand in hers, and squeezed. "Thank you." As an afterthought, Nancy planted a quick kiss on the young man's cheek.

"My pleasure, really." Jake flushed scarlet and pushed the pad back as she tried to return it to him. "You'll want the specifics. You can return it next time we meet."

He hurried down the ramp and scrambled awkwardly onto the back of the bike. The driver gave her passenger and Nancy a contemptuous smirk and gunned the bike forward, raising a dust plume from the sudden down thrust of hover jets.

As the sleds got moving, Nancy settled into a corner where she could watch the landscape slide by and read. She puzzled over why the Bernard was authorized to expend munitions, when a wet slap sent the data pad spinning from her hand. It hit the deck hard and slid toward the overboard scupper drain. She dove after it, slimy hands slipping on the deck. Her head cracked into the upright support of the bulwark, and stars danced in her vision.

"Ha! Serves you right," Reemer spat as pain exploded in her head.

"Reemer! What the hell?" Nancy probed the knot above her right temple, then realized she was kneading truly putrid slime into her hair. No blood at least.

"Keeping you sharp, puny human. You missed dinner."

"So you figured you'd ruin my gear?" With a start she sat fully up and looked to the deck drain.

The pad teetered on the edge of the scupper, jiggling with the sled's motion. She reached for it, but Reemer swept his tail in an arc, slapping the device overboard like a puck through a goal. Nancy watched helplessly as it tumbled to the ground below the sled. It hit with a muted clack. She marked the location…there, near the flat red rock with burrs poking from the jagged edge and a tuft of spiny grass. Reemer broke into ugly sputtering laughter.

"What is wrong with you?"

She glared at the Squinch and gasped. He looked horrible. Rather than just blotchy, his skin puckered around bloody lesions. His sensory antennae were ragged with strips of skin dangling as if from rotting flesh. His eyestalks crinkled like brittle cellophane and a milky film covered pupil-less eyes that jerked from side to side.

"What? Can't take a joke and late for…" He trailed off, tilted his head, and fell sideways. Messy ichor bled from the edge of his skirt as he convulsed and flopped like a fish out of water.

"Drissa!" Nancy dove forward to wedge herself between Reemer and the stanchion he bludgeoned with his flailing head.

It was all Nancy could do to keep him from pulverizing himself against the topside equipment. Drissa hurried over, then disappeared for what seemed like an eternity. Nancy held Reemer's tail between her knees. Sickly fluids and blood coated her from head to toe. The med tech returned with a jet injector and pushed the silver tube against Reemer's neck. The translucent green fluid within its sight glass disappeared with a hiss. In moments, Reemer's body relaxed, his spasms dwindling into mild twitching.

"What was that?" Nancy eased out from under the slug and wiped slime from her face with an even dirtier hand.

"Mild narcotic," Drissa said as she stowed the injector in her belt pouch, then threw a silky towel to Nancy. "I saw how the Squinch reacted to ingesting burrs, so added a touch of spine venom to the tremor reducer I make from needler tree sap."

"Wasn't that risky?"

"Perhaps." Drissa shrugged with her claws. "As an invertebrate, his physiology should respond to our medications.

Calculating the venom based on body weight was straight forward. I already had low dosage extract available from my experiments."

"Sola dosis facit venenum," Nancy said as she toweled off. The oddly soft rag magically wicked the mess away from her face and arms.

"What?"

"The dose makes the poison, or the cure in this case."

Drissa helped set up a saltwater bath in one of the application booths. They wrestled Reemer into it and carefully sponged the healing water over his abused hide. Although he remained unresponsive, his skirt stopped bleeding and healthy green flushed the skin around the lesions on his back and sides. Drissa eventually had to return to her duties, but dispatched an assistant to help get Reemer below decks.

Only the command sled and medical sled had rooms below the main deck. They were small and cramped, but several storage areas had been cleared out to provide lodging while the crew was sled-bound. Reemer stirred as they laid him on the cot, his head raising ever so slightly.

"Can you hear me?" Nancy rested her hand between his eyestalks. The skin felt feverishly warm, but at least he was breathing normally.

"More water…need—" he slumped, exhausted.

Their salt supply was dangerously low. Nancy mixed a saltwater bath and considered their predicament. It was odd how easily Reemer and his pranks became a constant in her life. His humor was disgusting at the best of times, but it was genuine. This new mean streak cost her the data pad and messages from Earth. Reemer the prankster wouldn't destroy something important to her. He had to be hurting—a lot. The little guy might not even pull through. Just one more thing this damned planet—no, those bastard plants—were trying to take from her.

Drissa sent for Nancy when the scouts rotated off watch at sunset. Reemer dozed and Drissa's assistant, Breena, promised to check in on him, so Nancy went topside. Despite their neutralizing compound, three scouts managed to get spines stuck in shell joints. Thankfully, the thorns didn't burrow or release venom.

Nancy got to work, reapplying compound to the oncoming watch and inspecting those rotating off duty to see how well the coating held up. Thin spots developed on each scout's primary legs, along the lower abdomen, and the underside of the tail fins, all areas that repeatedly touched ground. Fortunately, enough compound remained to deter the burrs. Drissa made up a special batch of neutralizer, adding a weak epoxy to provide a kind of rubberized undercoating on high contact areas.

The Lobstra commander again displayed his penchant for traveling at night, and the caravan rolled on into darkness split by dazzling headlights. When a light drizzle finally decided to fall from the starless sky, the watch rotation increased. Nancy's world narrowed to a succession of inspections, applications, and spine removals, but she managed to catch cat naps between shifts.

She jolted awake, surprised to see sheer cliff walls looming over the sled. The western edge of the plateau drew a dark outline, blocking the lightening sky overhead. The rain fled with the darkness. Pre-dawn light filtered through mist evaporating off the ground, rocks, and even the sled itself. They stopped abruptly, and the other vehicles again formed a defensive ring around them. The command sled hovered off to her right, black smoke rising from its aft section. She snapped fully awake as shouts echoed through the damp air.

"Alpha Team, get those blasted fires under control," Captain Luftew roared.

"Heavy salvo incoming!" Joda called from the command console of the nearby sled. "Going to miss. Stars, they're not targeting us." Joda's voice boomed from the med sled's announcing system. "Medical Team, take cover! You have incoming projectiles. In ten, nine…"

The topside workers scattered for shelter. Nancy took two steps toward the application booths, but saw three Lobstra heading there and backpedaled toward the pilot house.

"… two, one."

She dove inside and huddled among a tangle of white spiny legs. But there was no explosion, no violent rocking of impact. Instead, a light pattering sounded for a few seconds, like meaty wet hail. All fell silent, until the screams started.

14. Pain Urchins

N ANCY TWISTED as a fleeting pressure crossed her right
calf. A splotch of brown slipped into the sea of legs
crowding the console. That couldn't have been a burr—too big
and with hints of green. She grabbed the cool metal railing running
along the rear of the command enclosure and pulled herself up.

"Drissa, something's on the floor!"

The three Lobstra turned from the console. The driver was
flanked by the sled's big security officer, Malka, on his right and
Drissa on the far side. They backed to the controls and scanned
the floor. Nothing moved. It hadn't been her imagination.

"Lady!" Malka hissed and slapped at his shell.

The big Lobstra scrabbled at his sidearm, trying to draw the
gun. Drissa slammed the door closed at the far end of the small
space and spun back to calm Malka. He wailed and thrashed,
sending the smaller pilot crashing back into his controls. The deck
canted wildly, and it was all Nancy could do to keep her feet while
the pilot clung to his panel and worked to bring the sled under
control. Shouts and a splintering crash from outside trailed off into

grinding vibration that rose through the balls of her feet as the sled lurched to a halt.

Nancy couldn't take her eyes off Malka. She'd never seen a Lobstra in this much distress—never felt such anguish. The aliens were absurdly stoic. Even with cracked and broken shells, torn off limbs, and worse, they didn't cry out—not like this. His shrill wheezing shrieks clawed at her heart, begging for the torment to end. Other cries pressed in from outside. So hard to think.

"Got it." Drissa rose from Malka's tail section with a wriggling green-brown lump clutched in her fore claw.

The foot-long cactus struggled within thick cloth, but the medical officer held it tight. The bulbous green head tapered into a brownish body. The shape and needle placement reminded her of the magnimamma cacti of Mexico, except of course this one twisted and turned in an attempt to snag Drissa. Evenly spaced pear-green cones with a wicked yellow needle protruding from each made up the skin. Needles and cones moved independent of the thrashing body, more like a sea urchin than a plant.

Malka stopped thrashing, but remained crumpled by his console, whimpering and incoherent.

"It's in his bloodstream." Nancy searched for a container.

A crate beneath the controls held fire extinguishers. She dumped the canisters on the deck, and Drissa shoved in her squirming catch. Nancy slapped down the lid and secured the odd latches on either side.

"Give him something, doc." The pilot's controls were dark, but the floor still slanted left.

Drissa hurried over to Malka and swept open her med kit.

"He's delirious." Even Nancy's newfound abilities couldn't make sense of his rambling.

"His body temp has skyrocketed. Something is overstimulating his pain receptors," Drissa said. "The meds are back at my workstation."

"What do you need?"

"We have to see what's in his system. Grab the scanner hanging by the comms console. The big case under my desk has emergency applicators. And bring all the green vials. A locally derived med should help."

Drissa turned back to her patient and ran a small cutter—similar to Nancy's own—along ragged punctures grouped low on Malka's tail. The shell around each hole had already turned an unhealthy-green. Drissa sliced away the jagged edges and pressed a pad slathered with cream to the nearest wound. Nancy scooped up a fire extinguisher and swung the foot-long canister, measuring its heft. Better than nothing.

Outside was chaos. The deck adjacent to the pilot house remained clear of the bastard plants, but five or six green-brown lumps moved between her and the medical enclosure. Off to the right, the three Lobstra who took her first hiding spot writhed on the deck. Two others danced about at the far end of the forty-foot vessel, trying to dislodge cacti latched onto their legs.

Blowing smoke had her blinking back tears as she picked her way downhill and kept a wary eye on the nearest cacti. Beyond Drissa's workstation, the underside of the command sled rose like a breeching whale. Topside equipment lay sandwiched between the two crafts, and sparks dripped from a gaping tear where their sled had rammed the other. Smoke billowed thin and wispy from the front of the command sled, but the fires were under control.

Movement on her left pulled her gaze from the wreckage. A pair of vermin shot across the deck. These were not the languid sea urchins of Earth, nor the largely immobile burrs that required direct contact to latch onto prey. She squeezed the base of the canister, blasting a powdery stream across the creature coming in from her left and painting a white crescent on the deck.

The creature stopped dead, reacting to the chemicals or the cold. She skipped past, heading for the med deck door, but the second one came at her from the right. She mashed down the extinguisher's feathery trigger. A jet of fine powder shot from the nozzle, then stopped as the canister ran dry. Before she could leap back, the creature swarmed over her right boot. Nancy swung the canister like a club, but the thing scurried away before she connected. It scuttled to the deck edge, quested blindly until it came to an opening, and then disappeared over the side. Curious.

Nancy darted inside, collected the items for Drissa, and made it halfway back to the pilot house before more foot-long cacti dropped from the sky. They hit hard, two dozen pot roasts plummeting to the deck. Impossibly, the impact barely phased them. Spikey green heads swiveled in search of prey. Nancy leapt over a pair and pirouetted away from another, putting rusty childhood ballet to good use. But her form was flawed, and her left foot brushed a green head. Hot bright pain washed through her leg. She stumbled, medical supplies scattering.

The thing curled around her left boot, needles digging into the sensitive arch—bright agony. She fell, right leg scissoring with the aborted dance move and catching the cactus mid body. It let go and she twisted to keep from falling face first onto the creature. Vivid yellow needles whirled and glistened inches from her face, then slowed to a stop as the thing righted itself. The fleshy cones along its body undulated and the cactus trundled away like a millipede.

Nancy struggled to inhale against the scanner strap pulled tight across her neck. Her leg and hip screamed as she sat up, groped for the med kit, and scooted on her butt toward the control room. Twenty feet of hell later, the door opened. Claws grabbed her shoulders and hauled her inside. They should have felt sharp and hard, but it was more like giant foam scissors pulled at her. Her left side felt sort of soft too. The agony hadn't left, but it danced along the cloudy pillow that was her leg and side. Soon her entire body lay on soft cushions and the world faded away.

Clicks and bubbling squeals drifted through the darkness and stringent medicinal odors. Her left side ached, and her fingers tingled against the cool hard surface she lay upon. At least the biting pain was gone. The sounds resolved into voices as her head cleared.

"Not going to make it," Drissa said, sadness tingeing the alien's thoughts.

"Nothing can be done?" The Lobstra leader's thought-voice was a sonorous balm.

Where had Captain Luftew come from?

"Too much toxin," Drissa said.

Nancy's eyes refused to move. The effort sent a spike through her temple, and a moan escaped her cracked lips. A wet sponge dabbed her forehead while something hard stroked her hair, both soothingly cool. The pain receded, and she managed to crack an eye open to pale blue light.

Drissa hovered blurry and too close. Her words from a moment ago sat bitter in Nancy's stomach, but it was comforting to see a friendly face, to have the nearness of someone who cared. Not long ago, waking to that giant insectoid face would have torn a scream from her. How odd to truly understand these were people like her, just living their lives.

It was easy to assume you'd treat others fairly, without bias or bigotry. But that idealism rarely survived first contact. She was lucky to have lived and worked with these people. Knowing she had come to understand and accept them brought peace. She looked into Drissa's adorable black eyes, at the cute little ridge of horn that swept up between her antennae. Here was a good person. She sighed, accepting her fate.

"Dr. Dickenson, we could use your expertise if you don't mind." Captain Luftew's face replaced Drissa's. She wasn't an expert on Lobstra expressions, but it felt like he was scowling.

"Captain?" she managed to croak.

"Poor thing's dehydrated," Drissa said. "Breena, some water, please."

"Ladies, though the situation is currently under control, time is short." The captain's scowl turned on the medical officer. "Perhaps the good doctor can drink and advise simultaneously?"

Drissa nodded, then offered her slender primary claw to Nancy. "Can you sit up, dear?"

Nancy took the offered appendage and let herself be pulled up. She had been lying in a corner of the small medical bay. He stomach went queasy and her head swam to the point she had to brace against the bulkhead. A water canister pushed into her hand. Drinking helped clear her head. She rested the canister on her thigh. Her left pant leg had been sliced open and that boot was gone. Neat white bandages wrapped the foot and continued up over her ankle. It ached, but was bearable.

"But you said…" Nancy trailed off, following Drissa's gaze toward the facility's two beds.

One of Joda's security personnel lay propped up and quietly conversed with Breena, the med tech who had brought her water over. The specialized blaster, gun belt, and communication harness he sported were dead giveaways. His right side was burnt, and blistered shell flaked off in several places. A curtain partially encircled the other bed. A Lobstra lay draped over the cushioned surface, legs and claws hanging to the floor. His eyestalks made feeble little circles and his antennae hung flat along his chest plates.

"Oh no." Nancy dropped her gaze.

"One of the cursed plants got in here during the attack." Drissa whooshed out bubbles as she spoke. "Wispa was recovering nicely, but the burr poison traumatized his system. Anaphylactic seizures. I tried to—" Her voice broke. She wiped bubbles away from her mandibles, but couldn't go on.

"Lad's beyond help." The captain clacked his narrower cutting claw softly on Drissa's back. "He'll go to join our Lady soon."

Even with the captain's not-so-gentle urging, it took half an hour for Nancy to pull herself together. Drissa brought her up to speed, while Nancy got cleaned up. The missing boot fit over her bandages. Although she still limped, it was vastly better than clumping around in one shoe.

Drissa's updates continued as they headed for the command sled. Although the crew managed to drag the medical sled out from under it, the captain's hoversled had been badly damaged by the collision. Crews welded the two vehicles together to compensate for broken lift units. The collision and ensuing chaos led to numerous minor injuries, but five Lobstra managed to get poisoned during the attack. Drissa administered low dosages of her burr anti-toxin, which had worked wonders on everyone except Wispa, who quietly died a few minutes after Nancy woke.

"But where did they come from?" Nancy asked.

"They hurled themselves from those cliffs." Drissa pointed skyward.

Though preternaturally swift and resilient, the small cacti did not stand up well to blaster fire. Many had been reduced to decorative smears before Joda screamed at the crew to stop blasting holes in the deck. Fortunately, someone noticed Nancy's trick with the fire extinguisher. An organized sweep of the vehicles let them daze, capture, and dispose of the creatures. Drissa kept several to examine and use for synthesizing her medicines. They'd used up most of those extinguishers clearing the sleds.

"Once sprayed, they seem blind and just stop in place. I hope to confirm that the powdered chemicals clog the cacti sensory organs."

Deadly threats excited the medical officer, made her eyes shine with the kind of enthusiasm Nancy herself used to feel in her discoveries. Drissa's experiments offered a panacea of medicinal possibilities. Nancy should be right alongside the Lobstra sharing in the fervor, but her enthusiasm wouldn't rise. She couldn't escape the memory of Harry's desperate eyes, Greg's lifeless torso dangling from the radish-thing, and now Wispa's limp form. It had to stop. She no longer cared about classifying and cataloguing. The things on this planet killed indiscriminately and didn't deserve to live. All creatures had weaknesses, things that were anathema and deadly to them, those were what Nancy needed to focus on.

"I thought the cold jet of propellant might have helped too," Nancy said. "But my canister went empty. The second one hit me and just turned away."

"Found better prey?" Drissa asked.

"No, it moved slow and walked overboard, right off the sled."

During those first few minutes of the attack, when she was on the floor of the pilot house, a creature scuttled over her right leg without latching on. The one that walked overboard also refused to attack her right foot—even when she punted it. She studied the bandage peeking out from the top of her boot, comprehension dawning.

"The neutralizer!" Nancy grabbed Drissa's bony elbow. "I doused my right leg to show the captain how it worked. The Cacti react to it too, just differently than the burrs."

"Checking if it repels them is simple." Drissa's antennae bobbed with excitement. "I'll have it done before we move." She stepped toward her enclosure, then waivered as if uncertain. "Can you let Joda know? I need to confirm this in the lab and get the team producing more spray."

Nancy nodded, and Drissa hurried off, leaving her to continue alone. The slim metal ramp that now joined the two sleds felt solid, but she couldn't help fixating on the ground below. A handrail would have been nice. She wrenched her gaze up to the far side and hurried across the short gap. She burst into the command bridge to find Meinish arguing with the captain and Joda.

"It's time to move on to the blasted plateau." The old Lobstra thumped his revered map for emphasis, no doubt urging another random cast of his search algorithm.

"We can't leave these creatures on our back trail," Joda shot back, then turned to the captain. "Let me eradicate them."

"Your proposal?" The captain waved Nancy closer.

"One sled, blasters, and thermite. There must be a nest directly above us. We can't simply press on. Something like this stalled the last mission. We don't have the luxury of losing this time." The big officer folded his formidable claws across his chest plates and glared at Meinish. "Let me crush these things."

"Ooka," Nancy declared, surprising herself.

"Dr. Dickenson?" Captain Luftew raised a quizzical eyestalk.

"That's my name for these little cacti. It means pain urchins, and I like Joda's plan. Wipe them out while we have the chance."

"I don't favor risking more crew on a side objective. Security scans can't pinpoint these…urchins. That cliff is riddled with tunnels."

"Drissa can treat—"

The captain cut Joda off with a waved claw. "I won't risk our lead medical officer in a tactical raid."

"You don't have to." Nancy stepped up beside Joda. "Coat the team with burr neutralizer. It drives the Ooka off and leaves them disoriented. Drissa will have the specifics soon, but I saw two turn away from my treated leg."

The captain scratched at his mandibles. "Joda, was anyone coming off patrol attacked?"

"Don't think so." Joda scrolled the tabletop display. "No, not one of them, and none of the oncoming watch either."

"Low risk, if it works," the captain muttered. "How long would you need?"

"An hour to equip and treat the team," Joda said. "The cliff has two major ledges on the way to the top. I recommend three stages. Let my people clear a ledge, then bring the main sleds up while we clear the next section. The whole evolution might take four hours to be safe. Could go faster."

"Now hang on, sir!" Meinish's spines and antennae bristled. "Other teams are closing in. Providence sent us this way. With the enemy so thick, we must be close. Don't throw away our advantage. Let the Lady guide us from here."

As a scientist, Nancy couldn't afford to believe in blind luck, even in the form of the Lobstra's Lady of Providence. Still, she felt for the old searcher and envied his conviction. Her life's work had been to bring new species forth, honoring their unique habitats and adaptations. But her conviction was a bitter, fickle thing. She still catalogued and recorded new specimens, but her legacy was now a combat manual, logging not just physiology, but vulnerabilities, eradication techniques, and personal recommendations to ensure the monstrosities she discovered did not survive. Her datapad bulged at the seams with such findings.

By comparison, the old Lobstra's motivations seemed pure and wholesome. Even Drissa's medicines were ultimately altruistic. She too left a wake of devastation, but from a planetary perspective it was insignificant. Nancy wanted them all dead, every shambling, whipping, needling piece of garbage that dared to kill should reap what they sowed—death. She rubbed her hands, scrubbing the cuff of her sleeve across the backs.

"Are you with us?" Captain Luftew's question cracked across her thoughts like a whip.

"With you?" Apparently the conversation had continued.

"Will you help Drissa prepare the neutralizer and prep Joda's team?"

"Yes, of course." The tips of her ears felt hot, but she nodded eagerly.

She followed Joda out of the enclosure. He paused, turning to her with barely audible clicks like nervous coughs.

"Thank you."

"My pleasure." Nancy smiled and continued toward the ramp.

"You did get your datapad?" Joda called after her.

Nancy's hand whipped to the pouch at her side. She kept her notes close, both for ease of recording and to ensure their safety. The familiar rectangular outline bulged under the waterproof fabric.

"It's with me always, why?"

"Not your notes. Reemer told Breena about the pad you dropped. My scouts found it back along our track. Dusty and beat up, but I'm sure it's serviceable. I left it in your quarters with Reemer."

The messages on Endeavor and…Reemer! She'd totally forgotten about the little guy and hoped Drissa's assistant had been checking in on him. Hopefully he hadn't gotten caught up in the attack. Abandoning her friend was unforgivable, even if he had been acting the ass lately.

"Haven't had time. Wonderful of you to retrieve it." She rushed over and hugged the "man"—yes, it was right to think of him that way. The gesture was awkward, like wrapping her arms around a big porcupine wearing armor and carrying weapons, but it felt right. She released the startled Lobstra and bustled to the med sled. Her work with Drissa still came before Reemer and that datapad.

The first stage of the ascent went like clockwork. They treated everyone accompanying Joda, not just his team, but the sled driver, technicians, and backup personnel waiting in ready reserve should things prove difficult. Only a handful of the small urchin-like cacti clung to the boulders and crevices along the first hundred foot rise. These were quickly dealt with. Before the bits of stony debris finished raining down, Joda sounded the all clear and the remaining vehicles lifted off in sequence, heading for the lowest ledge.

The hoversleds handled the nearly vertical ascent with ease. In addition to the antigravity generators that allowed the bulky vehicles to bob along in the caravan, each sled was equipped with thrusters. Repairs complete, the command sled decoupled and rose smoothly on roaring columns of air that smelled faintly of ammonia. The adjacent crew danced and shimmered in the downwash as they prepared to launch.

The med sled made the climb last. As the engines revved to a steady whine, Nancy braced against the railing. But the rock wall slipped quietly past the deck edge with only the barest hint of acceleration. She loosened her death grip and examined the eroded cliff face. Cornerstones formed ledges sprouting grass and the occasional shrub. The latter held still, as any self-respecting plant should, although they passed plenty of pocked blast marks and two scorched ledges where Joda's people must have wiped up residual Ooka.

They landed on an outcropping the size of a football field. Tall, gently-swaying grass carpeted the ground, surprisingly uniform for a wild landscape. Strict orders kept everyone confined to the sleds while Joda's team cleared the next section. Nancy helped Drissa use the supply boom to pull grass for analysis. The hardened forks pushed into the thin topsoil like a hot knife through butter. The tufts thrashed violently, but fell still when their root ball pulled free. These plants would no doubt have something nasty in store for trespassers.

Nancy assessed and categorized while Drissa separated samples and fed them through her analyzer in hopes of finding medical applications. Each clump of pale green grass sported wispy fronds along the individual blades. Nancy touched her scalpel to several of the small bulbs sitting at the intersection of the delicate feathers. Each sprang open, revealing a flash of pink before snapping shut again. The motion left her scalpel coated with a clear yellow resin that she scraped onto sample plates.

The Lobstra spectrum analysis was damned near instantaneous. The fluid contained a bizarre protein ring. Her digital references correlated several of the more prominent markers. The stuff was a Psoralen compound, a potent one. Poison parsnips and other plants back on Earth produced a weaker form of the defensive juice. It bonded with the skin's cellular DNA. Ultraviolet light caused burning and blistering phyto-photo-dermatitis—plant induced skin inflammation accelerated by sunlight.

If memory served, those compounds could be useful in treating psoriasis and other dermatological disorders. But the Lobstra didn't have skin, so perhaps Drissa could exploit the DNA reaction. Nancy considered the seemingly harmless clump of grass and shuddered at the thought of someone blithely walking through this field and stepping into the sun. Plants back home caused acid-like burns, but these would do much worse. The thrashing grass would ensure effective delivery of the compound. A human without protective clothing wouldn't survive the walk.

She needed a way to quickly kill this stuff. If she worked fast, they could confirm her findings and use the boom to go after the field below. Nancy rubbed her hands in thought and started her data entry under the taxonomy of the high plains grass family Poaceae. She added a new binomial describing the plant's behavior, Dormientes acidum or sleeping acid, and logged the common name as "acid grass." The entire entry went under the new order name all of Fred's species had earned, Diabolus.

As supporting data flowed from the spectrum analyzer, a blur of green crashed into her sample table. Bits of grass flew to the deck. Nancy slapped away the featherlike blades that landed on her arm. A spikey head rose from the grass tufts awaiting examination. The pain urchin turned to Nancy and charged.

15. A New Discovery

NANCY SWUNG her datapad, catching the advancing urchin on the side of what passed for its head. It spun off the table, hit the deck with a hollow plop, and whipped back toward her like a tenacious terrier. Her foot still throbbed from the last encounter as she backed away from the plant. A fist-sized chunk had been burned off its side leaving blackened skin that oozed ichor. Its movements were labored, and the thing slowed and finally stopped as fluids puddled out beneath it.

Frantic activity broke out by the pilot house and along the far side of the sled. Security reserves dashed about firing off their handheld canisters of neutralizer to clear the deck of urchins splatting down from above. She grabbed a sample container from under her work area and bent to scoop up her dead urchin. The acrid stench made her nose itch and brought back childhood memories of salsa cooking lessons and the blackened remnants in Mrs. Sosa's big skillet.

Her hands shook from pent up adrenaline, but she finally wrangled the sealed container and datapad back to the exam table. Gouges across the back of the pad caught on her sleeve, but the screen was intact. The expensive navy devices were tougher than civilian models like the one Jake gave her. She shoved the pad into her belt pouch and looked around. Security had the fallout from Joda's operation above well in hand.

"Ah, crap." Cursing herself as a horrible person, she rushed aft toward their improvised cabin to check on Reemer.

Nancy swung around the backside of the research enclosure and skidded to a halt. The door to their room stood ajar. Her eyes watered, and a sour pain rose behind her jaw as she approached. Just inside lay a rotting clump of meat. If this world had flies, they would have mobbed the putrid remains. Brown spines stuck out in several places. Three chunks of urchin lay within the translucent mound.

"Ah, Reemer." Nancy knelt.

The half-digested mass was the Squinch's final act of defiance, or maybe just an attempt at a last meal. She scooped up the remnants of Reemer's eye stalks, which had dissolved into the general goo, and numbly cleared away the slime from the gelatinous mess that should have been her friend's head. Tears blurred her vision and dripped from the end of her nose, mixing with snot and saliva. Some cold analytical part of her wondered at how effectively emotions overrode sensory inputs. For the moment, the stench didn't threaten to make her retch, but she would have traded that in an instant for the deep ache and emptiness.

If the captain hadn't tied her up prepping the assault force, she would have checked on Reemer sooner. Then there'd been the acid grass analysis, which was obviously lethal and needed to be dealt with. But wiping out a single field on an isolated cliff face wouldn't matter for squat on a planetary scale. They lacked the manpower to deal with the vast territory occupied by these devils. This world needed an inoculation, or better yet a genetically engineered virus to purge it of the offensive species. An infectious and deadly transgenic construct could spread across the globe and do the work for them. Impacts to the native ecosystem would be difficult to predict, but the alternative was to let the Diabolus plant kingdom reign supreme. Nancy was willing to risk upsetting the natural order. Otherwise, no one was safe.

Slime oozed between her fingers as Nancy paused her absent stroking. She looked down at the eyeless stalks and barely discernable features of what had once been her best friend on Fred—the only true friend the geeky, middle-aged botanist had made since leaving Earth. The ache squeezed the air from her lungs as she realized an ugly truth. Her negligence hadn't been the captain's fault, or Drissa's, or even the acid grass. Eagerness to make the mission successful and pay back Fred's flora had consumed her. She could have made time to check on her friend, could have visited him after the first urchin attack rather than obsessing in her role of judge and executioner. And a courageous little alien had paid the price. She hugged the mess, juggling to hold onto bits and gobs that fell off the loose remains as deep wracking sobs took hold.

The mass quivered, a bit of goo splashing onto her side. Her hopes soared as she peered into the mess. Could he still be alive? No, just a blob, some residual nervous system spasm—a false hope. She sagged.

Something heavy and wet splatted against the back of her head, slapping Nancy's tear-stained face down into the goo.

"Slime lover!"

She came up sputtering and spitting bitter gunk. A mottled yellow form curled on top of the shelves. It rumbled with a wet hawking growl and reared to spit another wad. She looked down at the translucent mess then back at the all too solid form and let the dissolving mass slip to the floor.

"Reemer!"

Nancy rushed to the shelf and swept the sickly Squinch down in one deft motion, causing him to choke on the wad of slime he'd been preparing to launch. She didn't care. The little guy felt solid and wonderful. How had she mistaken the pile of goo for her friend?

"Careful!" Reemer sputtered.

Nancy looked into the cloudy eyes, taking in his unwholesome appearance. Reemer's skin was blotchy yellow like a rotting banana. Sores and fissures covered his hide. He oozed bloody pus from several splits and looked to have lost maybe half his body weight. She gingerly sat him on the bed and dove under the cot in search of salt and water.

"None left," Reemer said, bringing her up short. "Wasn't helping much anyway."

"Breena's been here?" The medical assistant must have been seeing to Reemer's needs. There had been a double-handful of salt left just the other day—perhaps enough for two more baths.

"Nice gal." Reemer sighed. "Been by a lot, not today though."

Relief and annoyance came on the tail of hearing the Lobstra had been caring for Reemer. Nancy certainly wanted him looked after, but should have checked on him herself. She felt nauseous.

"Jealous?" Reemer asked.

"What? No!" Was she? "Of course not." Well, maybe a little. It didn't sit well that someone else had stepped in to replace her. And the fondness in his voice was unmistakable; Reemer liked Breena.

"She's not fun like you. Wouldn't even flinch when I bubbled up my last bath. Spattered her good with nice sticky foam. Nothing. But you? You were great, blubbering and sobbing. And when you spun around, I thought you'd die."

Wet-raspberry laughter filled the small room, but Nancy just glared. Reemer regained control and pushed his head into her palm with wide, guileless eyes and his mouth puckered in that little O shape that somehow conveyed childish innocence. She couldn't help but pet the top of his head, scratching lightly between the eyestalks and careful to avoid the open sores on his neck. The damned guy was an enigma, disgusting and rude one minute, cute and charming the next.

"You just like grossing me out. So that glob there"—she pointed to the mess on the floor—"was just to get a rise out of the next person to check on you?"

An eyestalk swiveled toward the deck. "No. The spikey thing crawled in here earlier today. It was hurt but still sort of fast. I thought I'd see how it tasted because the burrs make me feel better. You know?"

"Yes, I've seen that," Nancy said drily.

"That thing tasted the same, but I started feeling sick and it thrashed about when it should have been done. I coated it again and again. It finally settled down, but things started spinning and I just had to get away. Don't know how long I was sleeping up there before you came in. Still woozy."

"Or just addle-brained, like a Slurg," Meinish clicked from the doorway. Soot smudged the old searcher's shell from the battle claw hinge down, leaving a gray area along the length of his side. "Captain's ready to move across the plateau. He wants you with us to cast the lottery. Can't say as I mind. You've helped a lot so far, missy." He limped into the small room and bent to examine Reemer. "By the Lady, you look terrible. I've thrown up handsomer things than you, boy."

"At least I'm not a dried up old pincher, with…" Reemer puffed up as he answered the insult, but then sank down flat. "Not worth the effort."

"He's out of saltwater," Nancy said in response to Meinish's questioning look, then pushed the searcher toward the door. "Get some rest, Reemer. I'll have Drissa check on you while I'm on the command sled."

"Breena!" Reemer managed to put a lusty note in his voice.

"Okay, Breena."

It was a good sign that he had the energy to try to get under her skin. Meinish burbled and coughed, but let himself be hustled outside before speaking again.

"Saw a Squinch once before who got landlocked. Died looking better than that."

"I know!" Nancy nodded as they hurried toward the ramp. "I need to get him back to the ocean."

Six sleds made the final ledge and set up in their standard defensive ring. Joda's security sled had moved on to clear the final leg to the top. Their portside ramp extended directly onto the command sled, crossing over barren dirt and rocks.

"Tough one." Meinish broke the silence as they approached the command center. "Mission comes first. There's too much at stake for detours. Even random…" Meinish trailed off at her scowl.

She wanted to grab him by the antenna. Her friend was dying—his friend was dying! Of course the mission was important. Cataloguing and destroying these abominations of nature was important. But if saving Reemer was as simple as getting to natural saltwater, couldn't the mission and her twisted agenda be paused for just a day? The sleds might not be the slow, plodding vehicles they had at first seemed. The ascent up the cliffs was testament to hidden capabilities. All those deck anchor points and railings weren't just excessive design features. Nancy opened her mouth to argue as they stepped inside.

"All clear to the top," Joda's voice boomed from the overhead speakers, demanding everyone's attention. The captain and an officer whose name she'd forgotten stood over the planning table, while Herman, Meinish's young would-be-apprentice, hovered near the panoramic window. "Big field of Dr. Dickenson's acid grass up here. I've got the lads burning it back to make a landing zone. We'll be ready in five. No urchins, but we've got a line of bigger things standing like statues just past the grass, maybe three hundred yards in."

"Hostile?" Captain Luftew asked.

"Have to assume they aren't friendly, sir. I count twenty of them just standing there. Look sort of like the urchins, but taller, maybe four feet. Those branches off either side of the middle almost look like arms."

"A good sign." The captain dipped his head in acknowledgment as she and Meinish joined him. "The last mission sighted similar things with their remote drones, but never reached them. The Esha slipped through first and took the prize. Our people found only barren rock. Doctor, should we handle these as we have the urchins?"

"Tough to say." Nancy shrugged. "I'll consult with Drissa. Some pictures—even better, a specimen—would help us understand what we're up against."

"Copy that, Captain. I'll see what I can do. Joda out."

Fifteen minutes later, Nancy was back on the med sled with Drissa. The image of what resembled a short saguaro cactus floated above the medical display. It had the same colorations as the little urchins, but was obviously much larger.

"There, that's got it." Nancy set the last sample plate on the desk.

Joda wouldn't risk his sled and the newly secure landing sight to capture a full specimen, but he managed the next best thing and acquired a thumb-sized sample from one of the plants standing sentinel. It was a little scorched around the edges, but had dermis, deep tissue, and vascular layers to examine.

Drissa fed the next plate into her equipment. As before, the machines made short work of the samples, and Nancy scrolled through the graphic displays. She relied on Drissa to read the Lobstra language, but the magnified images, chemical compositions, and DNA sequences were familiar enough.

"Same ambulatory mechanisms we've seen before." Nancy rubbed her eyes. "Subcutaneous vascular system for hydraulic muscle motion; surface sensory receptors, probably for detecting prey; and a heavy toxin profile if I'm looking at this one right. Read me the specifics?"

Drissa's foreclaws flew over the controls. "Yes, a neurotoxin compound like we've seen before. Too much damage to pinpoint the delivery mechanism, but we have venom off the scorched needles. Those security goons are blaster-happy heathens!" She huffed, but continued to scan. "Here's something. Not a toxin— something new. Long carbon chain, bunch of hydrogen. This is a pheromone profile."

"Lucky hit. Those don't usually present outside the flowering stage." Nancy bit her lip. "Though on this planet, pheromones might be more than just an aid to pollination and reproduction. We'd need to experiment."

Drissa bobbed, the gleam in her eye saying, "bring it on" to Nancy's heightened senses. Or perhaps it was just the way her stalks swayed, the angle of those antennae, and Drissa's general facial features. The aliens were becoming as easy to read as humans. People always talked about having twinkling, angry, or cold calculating eyes. Except for pupil contraction, the eyes themselves never really changed. Cues for those emotions came from the structure around the eyes and facial expressions.

Yet there was definitely something about the eyes, as anyone who held your gaze beyond the comfortable social norm knew. She'd love to know if her Lokii-enhanced abilities were pulling more than words from the speaker or if she was just getting used to the medical officer's expressions.

"Whoa! Here's an exact match." Drissa frantically worked the controls as Nancy leaned in for a closer look. "And another."

"What?"

"DNA profile panels. We've got exact matches for three—no five, five phylogenetic markers. Exact matches with both the urchin and burr samples."

"That would mean they are the same taxon, maybe the same species."

Nancy had keyed an entirely new entry for this plant into her datapad. If its genetic material was identical to those other two, she'd have to reconsider. It wasn't unusual for terrestrial plants to look different in spite of having identical markers, but this variation seemed extreme. She hadn't come up with the new name because she generally linked the common names to observed behavior or habitat. On Fred, that usually meant seeing how a plant attacked. If these things turned out to fly or do something else really bizarre, she could always change it later. She kept the cactus family and keyed in a new entry for Vigil Dolor, pain watcher. Vigil in Latin could just as easily mean guardian or sentinel instead of watcher. It fit for now.

Nancy tucked her datapad away and stood. "Holler if you want more help. I need to check on Reemer."

Her belly clenched in vertigo as the cliff face slid past the railing. The sleds had begun their final ascent.

＊ ＊ ＊

"Don't go in there," Breena advised.

The medical tech pressed her face to the bulkhead outside of Reemer's quarters. Her head rested on the joints of both claws and her body shuddered as she spoke. Was that sobbing?

"What did he do?"

Nancy patted Breena on the back. The tech stood perhaps five feet at the eyestalks, not nearly as large as Drissa.

"He—" Breena choked. "I try to ignore his antics—I really do—but there are limits. You deal with him."

Breena flashed an apologetic look and stormed off. Nancy pushed the door open a crack. The room was well illuminated with soft white light radiating from the walls. Reemer was on his cot, looking just as bad as the last time she had seen him. He lay curled on his side, deathly still, vulnerable, and innocent—too innocent. She pushed the door open.

"What did you do to Breena?"

"Who's there?" Reemer's moan sputtered into a cough. "Father?"

That brought her up short. Stuttering hiccups and gasps broke his shallow, erratic breathing.

"God," Nancy whispered as her anger dissolved.

An eyestalk swiveled to look back, satisfaction flickering across its milky surface. Again with the eyes! Dark humor and smugness radiated from the seemingly dying Squinch.

"How could you?" Nancy felt her face flush. "That woman has done nothing but worry and take time from her duties to help. And you repay her by playing dead?"

Reemer rolled upright so that his skirt was again in full contact with the bed coverings. "I am dying!"

"Not fast enough," Nancy muttered and paced the small floor. "God, the drama. Father? Seriously? Are you a closet Shakespearian actor?"

"I don't shake my hunting spear at people." His voice grew hurt. "Even I don't do that."

"What? No, he was a playwright—oh never mind." Nancy plopped down on her cot and glared into his stupid face. "Why must you always push? Just be normal."

"You mean boring?" Reemer preened at the thick mucus of an antenna that dipped toward his mouth, which he'd formed into a fleshy beak. "Fine! I'll be as interesting as day old fish. Done."

Nancy let the silence stretch on, but that seemed to be all he had to say. "Okay. We're almost to the plateau. How are you doing?"

"Dying."

Again Nancy waited before prompting, "can you elaborate?"

"I'll be dead in four days, maybe five."

"Don't be melodramatic." But she felt the honesty in his words. It hurt him to speak so directly. Humans covered up pain with humor. Maybe that wasn't such a bad thing, to a point at least.

"Hey, you want normal, you get normal. Five days tops. We aren't barbarians. I have an education in the core disciplines. See these sores?" He pointed an antenna at the red rents in his hide then flicked his skirt up to show more ringing the orifices beneath. "These happen when we're away from the sea too long. They compromise my slime coating. In a few days dry air will be in contact with my skin and invisible little critters will get inside me. The flesh will shrivel, rot, and drop off. Poof."

He finished with a raspy breath and muted sputtering from under his skirt. His words settled over her like a lead blanket. The mission neared completion—she could feel it—but she'd let Reemer down. He looked on the verge of shuffling off despite his endless capacity for pranks. Even now, his breath rattled so badly that she could imaging it stopping at any moment.

"Are you sure you have that long?"

"Yeah, it's just that normal takes too many words." Reemer splayed his antennae and sucked in a wheezing breath.

"Hang in there. I'll see what I can do to wrap up this mission and get us back to the coast," Nancy said as she stood to go. "Will anything help in the meantime?"

Reemer perked up then drew in another ragged breath. "Tell Breena I need to see her before I take the final swim." He withered under her glare. "Really, I want to thank her, and say… " His words trailed off in a mumble as he wheezed and sputtered.

"What was that last bit?" Nancy snapped.

Sad eyes looked through wilting antennae. Nancy tapped her foot and held the pitiful gaze until Reemer finally looked away. "Okay, fine!" Miraculously, he had plenty of breath again. "I want to apologize."

For once the little cretin was sincere.

16. Side Trip

T HE LOBSTRA planned, and the pain watchers…well…watched. Sentinels really seemed the more descriptive term, and Nancy made a note to update her files. The silent ring of sentinels looked on as Nancy joined the command team for a strategy session.

The plateau was huge and roughly teardrop shaped, stretching forty miles across the arid landscape below. Joda's little hand-launched drones worked on building a detailed map because orbital reconnaissance provided only the roughest of outlines—in deference to Lady Luck rather than due to any limitation of the Lobstra instrumentation. Apparently making things too easy would be cheating.

The surface proved more irregular than Nancy expected, with valleys, streams, and several cave entrances. The landscape around the landing site was not barren. Copses of trees formed a sparse forest further in from the edge, dark green masses in contrast to the rocky tan and red strata of the eroded edges.

The expedition huddled in a black bullseye, the charred remains of acid grass that had proven remarkably flame resistant.

Joda expended precious fuel getting just the immediate clearing to burn. The grass had gone wild, flinging acid in all directions. Fire turned the liquid attack into a caustic cloud that took down two of his people. Drissa was optimistic they would recover, but their lungs and airways had been badly compromised with a form of chemical pneumonia.

As the topological and atmospheric data flowed in, the map image in the command room took on more defined features. Areas of lower humidity would appeal to the Szooda. She pulled those map sections and worked with Meinish to seed his search algorithm until they were both satisfied. It was trickier than it seemed because the environmental data often showed low moisture directly adjacent to a waterway and humidity spikes in the center of what should be arid valleys.

Meinish assured her that the readings were accurate, but the anomalies multiplied the options rather than narrowing them. And this was just the first elevated land structure. Mountains rose above the western rim of the plateau, towering to heights she supposed would rival the Andes of Earth. Though distant, the scattering of white along their skyline must be snow. Their quarry certainly wouldn't be up there, but the sight served as a reminder of how vast the planet really was. And the old curmudgeon hopes to find this queen plant by sheer luck?

"It's a good pattern," Meinish declared after laying out the last set of parameters for the captain. "Lady, bless our course."

The devoutly arbitrary searcher had quickly accepted narrowing his field of consideration based on her scientific analysis. It seemed totally contrary to his espoused desire to let random chance—Lady Luck—determine the next step. When she asked about it, he had a ready answer.

"Missy, our lady only suffers fools for so long," Meinish explained. "A searcher has to ask the right questions, not just in our Szooda quest, but in the larger sense of things." He'd waved away her smirk. "I know I resisted your help at first, but then I asked myself something. 'Old fool,' I said, 'where do you think this little soft thing came from? Did we plan to meet her, or she us? No, the Lady brought us together.' So you see, your presence and all you provide for our search came to us by random happenstance. Lady Luck at her finest! I'd be a darn fool to waste a casting like that."

This was the scientific method turned upside down. Meinish asked questions and conducted research to gather his parameters. The closely guarded algorithm could be thought of as his hypothesis, and acting on the output was his experiment. The weak analogy made her smile. Despite the searcher's professed love of all things random, he did a boat load of work to facilitate Lady Luck's divinations.

"Anything to add, Dr. Dickenson?" Captain Luftew asked.

"No, sir. Meinish knows his stuff. If we knew where the creature was caught five years ago, it might help with the local terrain parameters, but we used the older information from the successful Lobstra missions so that will have to do. I just appreciate the opportunity to help."

"Please proceed." The captain relinquished the control panel to the old searcher.

The algorithm readily pumped out a search pattern for scouring the roughly five-hundred square miles of elevated landscape. Nancy still had her money on high desert to the north for finding the Szooda. Drissa found DNA records from the last batch of captured nectar closely resembled the sentinel and urchin DNA. The tests and equipment from ten years ago had been different. Hard conclusions were difficult to draw, but chances looked good that they were on the right path. After the timetables were roughed out and crew assignments made, Captain Luftew departed for a tour of the sleds while Meinish and Joda worked out the details. Nancy hurried to catch the captain.

"Sir, may I speak to you?"

Captain Luftew looked up from the datapad a young Lobstra handed him just outside the command center. It seemed that regardless of race, a captain's time was never their own.

"Certainly. What is it?"

"Reemer has been away from the ocean for too long, sir. He's dying."

"How bad?" His antennae quivered at half mast, the most excited he seemed to get outside of an active battle.

"We're out of natural salts for his medicated baths, and his skin is rapidly deteriorating. He says he only has five days left at the outside. Can we detour back to a waterway?"

"The shoreline is too far." Luftew looked east. "Would a river do him any good?"

"The brackish water near a delta might do, but at that point we'd almost be back to the sea anyway."

"I may be able to detach a small dart-class sled. It would be dangerous without a proper escort. Give me—"

"Esha!" The shout rang from the sled closest to the cliff edge.

The captain cursed and strode back to his command center.

"Red team to sled four. Flying squad muster for damage control," Joda called over the topside announcing system.

Nancy found herself alone as the Lobstra rushed to engage the snakelike aliens that had boarded sled four. She stepped to the railing and watched as two sleek black Esha flanked a Lobstra about thirty yards away. The Lobstra struck with its big battle claw, collaring an Esha a third of the way down its body. It seemed like a good grip, but the snake managed to wriggle out of the crushing grasp and struck back over its body at the claw. The second invader sank its fangs into the tip of the Lobstra's tail, where the shell was thinnest.

The Lobstra was a technician with no weapon. Meinish described the Esha as sinister with deadly venom, which fit right in on Fred—more literal snakes in the garden. Joda's red team swarmed onto the distant sled's deck carrying black tubes with white tips that looked like magic wands. The third guard had a bulkier device cradled in both claws. The two Lobstra brandishing the wands forced the Esha away from the technician, then the third guard brought the big gun to bear. Cables shot out of the cannon to entangle the snakes. The Esha wriggled and hissed, but were stuck fast. They crashed to the deck and out of sight behind the bulwark.

Nancy shuffled left to get a better view and her foot snagged on a mooring cleat. She tried to jerk her boot back and met the gaze of an Esha whose head rose over the side. It had a blunt nose with deep nostrils and odd flat depressions just above each eye. Its body scales smoothly overlapped, but the face was made of craggy plates with visible cracks between. The thin slit of its mouth extended far back behind the eyes, forming a perpetual grin. The black vertical pupil set within a gold iris looked on, cool and emotionless, as the rest of the creature slithered sidewinder-fashion over the edge and coiled on the deck.

Her academic mind took inventory, while her primitive brain screamed for her to run. But Nancy couldn't look away, and her foot was still stuck fast. The snake's head would dwarf a Doberman's and when it shifted Nancy caught a glimpse of her boot. An eight-inch fang skewered the tip and pinned her foot to the deck. If she hadn't moved at the last second, it would have driven straight through the top of her foot. Boots were damned hard to come by out here, and Drissa had gone to great lengths to have this pair made. This stupid snake was not going to ruin them!

Concern for footwear trumped mesmerizing gaze. Nancy yanked out her datapad and jabbed the corner into the snake's eye. A squeal sent pain spiking through her temple as the Esha thrashed and dropped back over the edge. The fang remained, a bloody knob of raw flesh at the top where it had been ripped from the snake's mouth. A mighty yank tore her boot free, and she sprinted for the command center as heavy bodies hit the deck behind her.

Screeches and shouts filled the air. Nancy hunkered down on the command bridge where she watched Esha slither aboard and the Lobstra move to defend. Two Lobstra worked with the captain to monitor video feeds and vectored security to intercept dozens of invaders.

The attacks on the outlying sleds were brief and focused, making a path to the command sled. Twice, the snakes managed to set charges against the doors of their enclosure. The first was swept away at the last moment by security. An explosion rocked the sled as it discharged off the port side. The second left Nancy's ears ringing and tore the starboard door off its hinges. Fortunately, it had been a shaped charge and the force hurled the door and part of its frame aft, rather than inward where the shrapnel would have killed them all. The Esha charged the broken doorway in pairs. The snakes were fearless, but not immune to blasters. After a time, the assaults changed to feints designed to draw the defenders out.

Commotion on the far side of the ring of sleds drew her attention to the monitors. Six Esha took control of the smallest supply sled, and the twenty-foot vehicle surged straight toward them.

"Brace for impact," Captain Luftew bellowed.

The deck heaved and bucked as the other sled rammed them amidships. Metallic fingernails screeched across a chalkboard made of dueling tomcats and bubble wrap as the smaller vehicle ground its way up under the command sled. With a popping burst all fell silent, and red lights flared across the controls.

Nancy studied the ceiling and made it to her feet on the second try. She clung to the console to keep from falling backward on the severely slanted deck. Curls of gray smoke rose from the rear of the supply sled that now peeked out from under the forward railing, wedged tight much as the med sled had.

Joda's teams reclaimed control of the rogue sled, and the Esha retreated. But the damage was done. Over the next hour, six dead Esha were piled onto the med sled and Drissa saw to injured Lobstra. Nancy thought their battle claws should have made short work of the serpents.

"Hard to catch 'em," Meinish said when she voiced the thoughts. "They wriggle and sway so much it's hard to track and anticipate them." He pointed to the body of one of the snakelike aliens. It appeared intact, except the kink that set its head off at a severe angle. A few black scales had been pried up in a line across the unnatural bend to show their silvery undersides. "Joda himself got that one. Crushed it good. But those others caught a blaster or got their heads bashed, didn't they?"

The old searcher was right. The two nearest bodies ended in bloody gore. The eyes of one were ruptured and still oozed yellow gel down its snout. Black-red blood caked around a lower jaw that hung limply away from its face. Her stomach clenched. These were spacefaring beings. Was the reward really worth this much bloodshed?

This nectar must be astronomically valuable to warrant the risks and to bring out such vehemence in their competition. At least the Lobstra didn't resort to treachery. They—and she herself—visited destruction on the local wildlife, but of course the plants weren't sentient. Her head throbbed, and exhaustion swept in. It was all she could do to nod politely at the searcher. She scrubbed her itching hands on her pants, then turned away to find her room.

✳ ✳ ✳

Nancy drifted through a sea of feathery caresses. The activity around her felt industrious, moving, stowing, fixing, but all she knew was the tickling cool touch of hundreds of white limbs longer than normal Lobstra legs. They trailed off into the distance, growing from a roiling mist. She felt oddly comforted by the attention, happy to forget her duties and just luxuriate. Something nagged, an important task. The claws moved faster, pulling and raising welts. Then she was falling. Wind roared, and the smell of rich earth rose from the planet below as she plummeted toward its green surface.

"Time to go, missy."

"Meinish?" Nancy blinked at the blurry Lobstra hovering over her cot.

"Getting young Reemer ready to move. Boy looks like a wad of used snot. Similar personality too." The old searcher stepped back to give her room to sit up.

"I hear your dusty old mandibles clacking, but I…" Reemer's voice drifted in from the door, but trailed off.

"Move where? Why?" The cot opposite her was empty, the bedding stripped.

"To the sea so your foul-mouthed friend can get back on his…err…feet." The smell of burnt metal and oil drifted in with the booming voice and big Lobstra. Meinish pressed against the wall to give Joda space. "That is what you wanted, correct?"

"Soon, yes. But I just asked the captain." The acrid machine-shop odor rolling off Joda woke her faster than his words. "And the search has to continue. We're getting close."

"By the Lady we are close," Meinish agreed, though his antennae wilted. "But repairs are gonna take days, missy. The slug doesn't have the time. We'll get searching again soon enough."

"Meinish keeps tabs on the lad," Joda said. "I've worked this out with the captain. We're loaning you a landpod. It has basic navigation, a small measure of weaponry, and is loaded and ready to go once you verify we packed everything you'll need. You should be able to make it down to the coast in a day and a half."

"I didn't think you—" The big security officer always seemed so aloof. "Thank you."

She climbed to her feet and wrapped her arms around Joda. He went somewhat rigid—quite a feat given his exoskeleton—and nimbly passed her off to the irascible searcher who accepted the hug with slightly more grace.

"We'll leave a communication relay at the edge of the plateau if we move before you return. Keep us apprised of your intentions. I want my pod back in one piece, Dr. Dickenson."

∗ ∗ ∗

Not only was the landpod loaded, it sat idling with a soothing whine on the deck just outside her room. The car-sized transport rested on six stubby legs, but the flat edged skirt around its perimeter was similar to those of the larger sleds. The ubiquitous Lobstra construction material shone dull gray, hard as metal without being cool to the touch. That was about where the similarities to the rest of the fleet ended.

Rather than open to the weather, the pod was enclosed in a transparent dome that stretched ten feet back from its nose. Behind the main dome was a smaller secondary cockpit about half the size, its dome open on the near side. Reemer lounged among Lobstra controls, on a circular cot. Several closed ports ringed the aft edge. The sled tapered toward the front, making the vehicle more narrow and streamlined than the larger sleds. Molded stabilizing fins swept down each side to merge with ailerons protruding from the aft edge. The vehicle looked sleek and fast. The largest transport sleds could probably hold several of these below decks. A familiar Lobstra waved from the pod's main cockpit.

"Ready to go, missy?" Herman fiddled with something on his controls and the dome retracted three feet to form a window.

Nancy raised her eyebrows at Meinish as the old Lobstra emerged from her quarters.

"He's a fine pilot." Meinish shrugged. "No time to teach you, and the lad needs to get out on his own a bit, find himself as it were." Nancy ducked back into her room as Meinish scowled up at his would-be apprentice. "That's Dr. Dickenson to you, Herman!"

Her meager belongings were indeed already aboard. She grabbed Jake's datapad then her own and winced at the dented edge. The last few odds and ends went into her pouch with the laser cutter, and she made a mental note to reach for it instead of her pad in the next crisis. She looked around their tiny room and drew in a stale lungful of Squinch stench before heading to her ride.

The pod proved fast, maneuverable, and somewhat terrifying. Herman either had a death wish or a blatant lack of respect for the crushing forces kinetic energy, inertia, and gravity could synergistically muster. By the time they reached the base of the plateau Nancy was white knuckled, having just watched the cliff face and the better portion of her life flash by during the too-brief descent.

"That was exciting." Herman beamed as he stopped and punched in ground level coordinates.

"Are you suicidal?" Nancy rasped.

"Orbital plot shows a shallow bay to the southwest," Herman said, oblivious to the fact Nancy was just shy of going into cardiac arrest. "Most of the route backtracks over our path, so we have good details and know what to expect. Tomorrow though, we skirt the swamplands to the south."

"You didn't answer my question."

She eased up her death grip on the improvised chair that had been welded in front of the right-side console. Herman used the more typical leaning post, a sort of padded tee that rose in front of his console like a thin podium. It fit snuggly between the base of his forelegs and let the young Lobstra rest the bulk of his weight while driving.

"What?" Herman finished with the controls and his eyestalks swiveled up to the left, a pose that she had come to associate with contemplation. "Don't think so, missy. The pod is fully stabilized and has loads of built in safeties. Crashing would take real effort and—"

The pod bucked to the left and plowed straight down into a rock outcropping. Nancy's harness snapped taut, nearly strangling her. The engines cut out, and all was silent for a moment as a pattering of debris settled across the dome. Herman's small claws flew across the controls, checking and adjusting.

"So that's what that lever does." Reemer's thin reedy laugh bubbled from the intercom, but dissolved into violent coughing.

"I feel so very safe." Nancy dangled in her harness, then flopped back against her seat as Herman nosed the pod out from the rocks. "I take it there are controls back with Reemer?"

The pod launched smoothly forward as the Lobstra turned a bashful eyestalk her way.

"I just disabled them. Don't you worry, mi—" Her glare cut him short. "Er…Doctor Dickenson."

"Nancy works fine, Herman. I know you look up to Meinish, but it sounds silly when you talk like an old coot. Learn to be a searcher, not a curmudgeon."

"He really is a surly old lump." Herman nodded and a Lobstra smile spread across his features. "But he's been a lot better since you two showed up."

"Hell of a guy," Reemer interjected over the intercom. "Hey, my controls are broken!"

"Better? You're kidding." Nancy ignored the indignant Squinch.

"By the Lady it's true. Makes me wonder if I really want to be a searcher. Then you come along and suddenly he's surly likable Meinish, which is loads better than nasty Meinish. Magic."

"You'll get there." Nancy sensed his desire to talk. "You speak of the Lady often."

When there wasn't an immediate reply, she watched the landscape roll by. The pod could surely go faster, but the broken rocky terrain made it difficult. The little vehicle moved at a hover without raising the massive dust clouds traditional thrusters kicked up. But the pod flew only a foot or two above the ground. They constantly skirted boulders and underbrush the larger sleds would have coasted over. All in all, they traveled at a pace amounting to a healthy jog.

"The Lady is real!" Herman's exclamation held emotional pain. "But everything can't be left to Her. I can't live on faith alone and hope things go well. We have responsibility for ourselves and others."

"Meinish may seem fanatic. But I see all the work he does, the mapping and computer set up. He doesn't just wait for inspiration from the Lady."

"He doesn't, but others do. Entire enclaves simply exist, trusting that good fortune will arise without lifting a claw. The

Grand Matriarch is one of them." The last was a whisper. Herman swung his eyes forward and fell silent.

"The medicine you seek is for your matriarch?" Nancy asked.

"Yes."

It was a tough dilemma. If the leader of Lobstra nobility simply sat back and waited for things to happen, their society would stagnate. And if healing compounds synthesized from the nectar prolonged life, such a leader could be in power for a very long time.

"How old is your matriarch?"

"Three hundred and seven cycles." Herman kept his eyes on the path ahead even though the pod's navigation handled all but the trickiest maneuvers.

"That's incredible. How long does a typical Lobstra live?"

"One hundred and thirty years."

A monarch whose reign outlasted her citizens' lifespan was hard to comprehend. On old Earth, royal families held power for generations, passing titles down their bloodlines. In more recent history, royal families were mere public figures, rallying symbols for national pride and traditions. Parliaments and congressional bodies did the real work, managed laws, taxes, and regulations. The system was antiquated, but it certainly could work. Progress hadn't stopped just because of a royal family's credentials.

"Wow. Over twice the average and still going strong. At least, presuming more nectar can be found and the medicine produced. Surely there are governing bodies, coordinators that help guide and control the regime?"

"You misunderstand. The Matriarch celebrates with the five-year bloom and is over three hundred cycles old. Records show she has been in power nearly fifteen hundred years. The Lady's Council administers the will of the Matriarch as it intersects with divine Providence. It is true that some factions try to provide a path forward, a modicum of growth." His antennae drooped low. "It's just too long."

It didn't make sense. The Lobstra showed only the barest understanding of the flora of this planet. If they had been coming here for thousands of years, why was the search still so difficult and uncertain? By now they should have had everything down to a science. Drissa's constant discovery of new medicines and uses for the wildlife would be old news. There shouldn't be anything new under the slightly blue sun. And what of their space faring capabilities? Lobstra technology was only slightly ahead of the navy's. How long had they been stuck at the same level? Hundreds of years? Thousands?

"I see how that could cause problems," Nancy murmured.

Herman gave the equivalent of a human nod and dropped into what felt like a moody silence. Nancy watched the scenery roll by for a while. Enclosed in the faster vehicle made traversing the unpredictable terrain much simpler. They really didn't have to worry about much. The pod passed over the blanket of burrs and acid grass without issue. Soon the taller vegetation of the forest proper rose on the horizon, and the landscape shifted from sand and rocks to prairie. The forest line grew ever so slightly as they approached, an indication of the large distance they still had to travel before cutting south around the swamp. Reemer slept fitfully most of the morning, and Herman maintained his brooding silence. Boredom settled over her, and she pulled out Jake's datapad.

Jake left the naval messages under a conspicuous icon on the device's main page. "Nancy's Stuff" hung under a winking yellow smiley face that made her lips quirk up at the corners. When selected, the face looked shocked then outraged before settling back into a knowing wink and displaying the information. Herman glanced sideways at her cough of laughter.

Jim Stein

She reread the original advisory, noting the large number of recipients. They included merchant, exploration, and military vessel contingents as well as outposts and satellite communication networks. Of course, the vast majority would be in distant sectors nowhere near Fred. Space was a big place.

Paging through the longer third message had her hopes soaring. If the schedule was correct, the SS Bernard would arrive in ten days. She was not forgotten. Warmth spread through her chest, followed by a chill of realization. How would they find her?

The Endeavor would have beacons and plenty of mass for orbital sensors to detect. The navy would focus on the science mission's landing site. They would see evidence of the carnage, but there wouldn't be any bodies to count thanks to the jungle predators. The searchers might scour the planet for survivors, or they might simply conclude that all hands were lost.

With all the encroaching alien vessels, it seemed likely the Bernard would interrogate the hunting parties. Surely Captain Gekko's crew would let them know she was alive. That thought gave her some comfort, but she would have to talk to Joda and Captain Luftew about contacting the ship when it made orbit.

Planet Fred

17. A Relaxing Bath

T HE POD coasted to a halt in the shadow of a small hillock among sparse prairie grass. They were beyond the areas thick with burrs, and the grasses looked to be a normal, non-deadly variety with the occasional wildflower poking up on a scraggly stem. Many Lobstra had been on foot at this point in their trek, their signs of passage further evidence the region was safe.

"Health and comfort break," Herman announced as the pod settled on its landing gear. He peered outside and drew his blaster. "Looks quiet. A cluster of burrs off to the right there at the base of the hill."

"I see it. Shouldn't need neutralizer. The rest of the flora looks safe enough, but watch your step."

Reemer snoozed on in spite of Nancy hammering on his dome, so they decided to let him sleep. Stretching her back and legs eased the knots. A coffee stand with dark Columbian would be wonderful, but this was a no-frills rest stop. She sighed and conducted a mental inventory of the grasses and occasional broadleaved sprouts, all of which already held a place in her log. Nothing new and thankfully nothing in the Diabolus order. No

165

Diabolus, no Diabolus. The litany helped her refrain from using crush and twist steps to smash plants as she paced around the pod. Not everything on Fred was evil.

Suppressing the primal urge to stamp out this treacherous planet had her skin prickling with pent up energy. Nancy sanded her itching palms on her pants, then the scratchy flap of her travel bag. Hunting through the bag produced a towel, which she used to wipe her fingers and wrists until the needling itch subsided. They looked clean, but the feel of cloying residue told her she'd missed some spots. By the time she climbed back into the pod, Herman was finishing up his status report.

"We'll stop for the night just shy of the forest," the Lobstra said into the comms panel. "Expect to make the coast after midday tomorrow."

"Keep us apprised," came the terse reply, though it was harder to make out over the radio.

"Affirmative." Herman shut down communications.

"Any news on the repairs?" Nancy asked as she settled back into the embrace of her harness.

"Progressing. Another day or two before they can think about continuing. Meinish is having a fit, said that the Esha don't count when it comes to Providence and wants the captain to get a move on things. But maintenance says the damage is extensive." Herman's eyestalks swiveled to look at the secondary cockpit. "Little guy okay back there?"

"I'll check."

Nancy slipped out onto the little walkway connecting the cockpits. It sloped down from the forward area, then immediately up to the higher aft one. She slid the door open and gagged. It smelled like something had died. She leaned in to try and rouse the Squinch and retched her lunch out onto the seamless floor next to Reemer's hammock. With eyes streaming and sinuses closed in self-defense, Nancy lifted her head to find two milky eyes hovered inches from her face.

"Aren't you going to finish?" Reemer wheezed and raised his head a few inches in anticipation before he sagged back down.

"I'll clean it up." Nancy spit the words out with an acidic glob of mucus.

"Yummy."

The sick Squinch might digest his food externally, but he couldn't think she would—that she could. Nancy made the mistake of looking down at the mess and promptly added more. Thready laughter drifted from the cot as she tried to recall when she'd eaten spinach.

"Well?" Herman asked as she plopped back into her seat.

"He's alive. Barely."

"That bad, eh. Another hour and we'll make camp just outside the tree line. Less than a day and we'll have him frolicking in the surf." Herman lifted off in a smooth spiral, and the pod raced onward.

"Good, then I can kill him," Nancy murmured and promptly fell asleep.

Making camp for the evening was simply a matter of finding a good parking spot that sheltered their small craft from a rising wind and any aggressive plants. Herman left the outbound Lobstra track and pushed southeast for an outcropping of rock thirty yards from the trees. He swept the area with a low-power beam before landing. Far less dramatic than blasters, the weapon simply sizzled away the few bits of flora along the base of the rocks.

Beyond camp, the transition from rocky prairie was abrupt, with only a few small trees venturing past the edge of the forest. Soil conditions or a severe climactic gradient must separate the regions—not unheard of, but unusual given the transition didn't occur along an elevation change. They walked and stretched before dining on surprisingly tasty rations.

The mild evening provided a wonderful opportunity to retract Reemer's dome and air things out. The prevailing winds quickly carried his concentrated stench back toward the open plains. Regrettably, that same wind carried an ever-increasing number of biting seedlings from the forest. Nancy slapped at the mosquito analogs, her annoyance doubling when she realized they couldn't bite through Herman's shell and refused to even approach the sick slug.

Reemer skipped dinner, attempted a few half-hearted insults, and retired early to his puddle of slimy water. Though they were flat out of salt, a bit of fresh water on his cot eased the slug's discomfort and reduced the number of insults he hurled.

She and Herman spoke at length about the Lobstra matriarchal society. The Lobstra seemed relieved to share his concerns with someone who wouldn't judge, and Nancy grew convinced that something in their society was desperately and dangerously broken. They sat against the rocks as the discussion turned more chatty than philosophical, but the seedlings were thick as flies.

"No more for me." She scraped the green-red remains of a small attacker from her neck. "They're eating me alive." Her knees popped and complained as she stood, a sign of too much sitting— not her age.

"Early start tomorrow," Herman agreed and began to rise. He was a lefty and sort of reclined on his left side with his head propped up on his narrow cutting claw, like royalty lounging upon a settee. His feet scrabbled, sending small stones skittering. "What's this?"

Under the dim light washing from the pod, yellow tendrils crisscrossed Herman's abdomen and wound up over the first pair of legs at his lower thorax. The vines trailed up and over the rocks, pinning Herman's lower body. Nancy flung her pouch open and frantically rummaged for the datapad—no, the cutter. She jerked it from its securing strap, took two steps, and froze.

Herman laughed the Lobstra's clicking gurgle, leveraged himself around to examine his predicament, and calmly slid the thinner edge of his cutting claw between the vines. He sliced with the satisfying sound of holiday wrapping paper being cut to size. The severed ends wriggled, their sap-blood black under the colored light as they retreated over the rocks. The breath she'd been holding escaped with a relieved sigh. The net vine, or Piscandi vitem as she had classified the thing, might be a major problem for soft creatures like Reemer, but was no danger to a being with cutting claws and an exoskeleton.

"Shall we?" Herman asked as he walked past.

Nancy stowed her cutter and headed for the safety of the pod and a good night's sleep. The latter proved elusive thanks to howling wind and her racing mind. Herman slept poised over the glowing panel, resting on his T-chair with claws hovering over the controls and looking exactly as he did while driving. Rather than sleeping with closed eyes and slow breathing, Lobstra just stopped moving and any legs not supporting them simply dangled.

She finally turned on Jake's datapad to flip through the messages again, but found no new information. As she backed out of the files, another area caught her attention. The icon was a fat smiling cat perched in a tree. At a tap the cat's green stripes faded away, followed by the black ones, until only the smile was left.

The screen blossomed to life as a parade of photographs swept onto the screen, faded, and were replaced by others. The first pictures showed a ramshackle farmhouse, neat but in disrepair. Pics of cows and pigs were interspersed with a long-coated yellow dog happily yapping at chickens and shaking off water by a reedy pond. The theme shifted from animals and landscape to people. A middle-aged woman wearing round glasses worked at a terminal near the kitchen, her long black braid draped across her clavicle as she stuck her tongue out at the camera. People flicked past sporting business suits, casual wear, and lab coats. Then the dark-haired woman was back with a handsome man in a button-down shirt. His round boyish face smiled down at the baby the woman cradled. The baby grew into a boy of ten or so, with his father's round features and mother's raven hair. Nancy watched Jake's first baseball game, a failed attempt at bull riding, and on through his jubilant entry into the engineering program at Quantum University. Then a crashed plane, two gravestones, and young Jake shipping out on a star freighter.

The screen returned to its standard listing of files. In addition to pictures, there were data files and video clips. Quantum engineers were in high demand. Nancy wanted to learn what had happened to him after leaving Earth and how he ended up on Fred. But at the same time she felt a stab of guilt for invading Jake's privacy. Sleep snuck in while she wrestled with her conscience.

Vague images drifted through a nondescript landscape. Nancy knew it was jungle, but nothing was clear. Blurs of green and brown replaced shrubs and trees in a cartoonish backdrop for nightmare creatures that paraded onto the scene. The indistinct shapes growled and clicked as they scuttled across the stage, never touching her, never really interacting—an insane beauty pageant for monstrous plants, aliens, and ghostly apparitions that faded out of focus with the pattering click of high heels, leaving only vague impressions and a kink in her neck. Something insistent poked her arm.

"Time to get moving," Herman said.

Nancy sucked in a trickle of drool and sat up. Herman worked over the controls as light rain tapped a steady cadence on the dome of their cab. Behind them, Reemer poked at a rations cube on the edge of his cot. The insistent rain made certain morning routines a priority, which she attended to while Herman called in his status report and gathered breakfast.

The constant drizzle and close confines of the forest slowed their progress. On the open plains Herman rarely needed to take manual control, but today he was a full-time pilot actively negotiating trees, deadfall, and thickets. The hilly terrain flattened and grew easier to navigate close to the swamps. The pod rode easily over the still pools scattered across the lowlands, but areas dry enough for a quick stop grew few and far between.

Things moved in the sluggish waters. Nancy thought the wind and rain whipped up those little wakes until they dipped a bit too low and charcoal-green vines shot from the surface, and a heavy wet appendage slapped onto the windshield near her face. The dark central vine sprouted flat green leaves, a cross between seaweed and old spinach. The thing stuck fast on the translucent dome, and the pod jerked to the right. Herman turned into the dragging weight as more slaps sounded against the hull. He flipped open a bright blue cover and tweaked the controls within. A high-pitched whine replaced the slaps as the vine covering her windshield went rigid and fell away.

"Guess we better get a bit more height and nose back over land." Herman swung them smoothly away from the water as if he dealt with swamp kraken every day.

"That was awesome!"

Herman's thorax darkened as blotches of red blossomed on his shell. She hadn't realized that Lobstra could blush.

The rest of the trip proved incident-free. The distinctive odor of seawater and sweet rotting vegetation greeted them an hour before sunset as trees and swamp gave way to tidal marsh. Herman pressed on past the grasses and reeds and settled the pod on a sandy stretch of beach.

The gray sky held low heavy clouds that spoke of continued rain. Although waves crashed quietly off to the left, the sandy point sheltered a calm inlet where Reemer wouldn't have to contend with the surf. They climbed down and checked for hazards. The only signs of plant life were the occasional patches of dead seaweed that sat in globs just beyond the waterline. Ripples rolled across the water's surface, driven up onto the wet sand by the steady wind. A few small crustaceans scuttled across the sandy bottom, and tiny silvery fish flashed along a stretch of rock poking through the sand. The rocks were dark brown and coated with swaying green fronds. Reemer would be familiar with anything underwater, but Nancy pointed it out to Herman. The bottom sloped slowly away and was clearly visible to about twenty feet out, where it abruptly dropped off into the deeper channel.

"Nice day for a swim." Nancy eyed the sky, and a fat raindrop splashed across the bridge of her nose. "Let's get him out here."

Herman keyed a device that hung near his blaster. The dome over Reemer retracted and a short ramp extended from the hull. Fortunately the prevailing wind swept inland toward the distant dunes and scrub, allowing her to approach the pod with only mild nausea.

"Wakey, wakey, little buddy. Time for your bath."

Reemer looked like a moldy, half-melted stick of butter. His morning meal sat near his head, swamped in stomach excretions and half eaten. Nancy fought down her gore and poked him. "Reemer, we're here."

A listless eye stalk swung to look at her before falling back. Nancy sighed, leaned over the edge, and wedged her left hand under his head and her right under his skirt. Or at least that's what she tried to do. She hadn't expected him to be firmly stuck to the rubber cot. She adjusted her grip and tried to force her fingers under him like a spatula. Something tore and blood oozed out from under his skirt.

"Ah crap." She looked to Herman. "We've got a problem."

While they worked on trying to pry Reemer off his cot, Nancy flooded the surface with seawater to jumpstart the healing process. In the end, Herman unbolted the cot. It was a lightweight polymer, but the Squinch was four feet of pure bulk and had to weigh at least a hundred pounds. Nancy didn't know how they were going to wrestle the awkward thing down to the water without tearing Reemer's skin off. Amazingly, Herman simply grasped an edge of the cot in each of his main claws, lifted the entire arrangement clear of the cockpit, and scuttled down to the water where he gently lowered bed and Squinch into the lapping waves.

They took turns standing waist deep in the tepid water as the clouds let loose. A firm hand was needed to stabilize the partially submerged cot so it wouldn't tip. Nancy managed to gently lift Reemer's head and propped it on a pillow of empty ration wrappers. Squinch could breathe underwater, but she didn't know how badly his bodily functions had been compromised. The rain subsided quickly, and the setting sun bathed the landscape in brown hues at odds with the gray skies.

During her second turn in the water, Herman made a report and prowled the shoreline, blaster in claw as he peered across the dunes through the darkening gloom.

"Crew's on the move," he called back over his shell. "Captain moved to the med sled, and they're towing the command sled until repairs are finished."

"Great."

Reemer had her worried. Little bits of skin and mucus washed over the edge of the cot. Finger long fish flashed eagerly forward to take advantage of the unexpected feast. Sometimes they nipped at her calves. Nancy stood in the water wearing shorts and a light top, having stripped off her working uniform to keep it dry.

A flash of something larger off to the right made her gasp in surprise and look back at the cot. In addition to the smorgasbord the fingerlings enjoyed, a steady stream of blood billowed from the edge of the cot. Hopefully that wouldn't attract anything with sharp pointy teeth.

"Herman, are there predatory fish on Fred?"

"A few." He scratched the base of an antenna with his battle claw. "But they won't bother a Squinch. Little guys can back down even the big nasties."

"What about a sick Squinch?"

"Good question."

Herman sidled up to the water's edge, shifting his vigil from looking inland to watching the water. Nancy wasn't certain if that made her feel better or not.

18. Open Invitation

"**Y**OU'VE GOT to be kidding." Jake couldn't help wondering if this was another prank on the new guy. "There's nothing out here."

"Ray-Jay logged a blip down here and Urneck wants it checked out," Angie called over her shoulder as the wind whipped her short sandy-blonde hair against his cheek.

Angie, short for Agnes but never call her that, leaned back into him suggestively as they continued along the dunes on the hoverbike. She gunned the engine, forcing him to grab her full hips tighter just to keep from pitching off the back. He caught the hint of a smile on her profile as she studied the path ahead. Even through the light riding jacket, her firm body felt nice as she pressed back. Ray would be furious if he saw her being such a tease. The big blocky twin would be even less pleased if he thought Jake made a play for Angie.

She certainly wasn't interested in him, but maybe making her dead-eyed boyfriend jealous added spice to their relationship. He'd have to ask Captain Gekko to stop sending them out together. The bike lurched around a dune, he grabbed a handful of overly soft flesh, and his cheeks blazed—hopefully pulling blood from even more embarrassing paths.

"East of that inlet I think." Angie wiggled her hips delightfully as she consulted the heads-up display on the windscreen. "Only got one reading, maybe an hour inland. We can cut along the swamp."

"Okay," Jake said, though his soft words probably blew away before reaching her.

Hopefully they wouldn't find anything. The position marker Ray discovered had been generic, without the unique identifiers that correlated to the hunting groups they planted tracers on. That was because Jake had modified this particular tracker. They never should have picked up a signal from the chip installed in his datapad because he'd set it to passive mode. He could search for the device with an orbital scan, but it never should have broadcasted a signal to QUEN.

Dr. Dickenson must have mucked around with the pad. He'd hidden the software activation toggle among some personal files so it wouldn't be obvious he'd stolen a tracker. The spunky little doctor, Nancy with the raven hair, must have checked out his stuff. That made him grin. Her warm, firm handshake had sparked his interest. Aside from her nicely contoured bod and cute little nose, the woman was smart with a healthy dose of common sense. He got the feeling she liked him too—or his stupid ego had decided to make one of its rare appearances.

He'd wanted to keep tabs on her—and his equipment—thus the extra tracker in his datapad. Lobstra search parties never split up, so perhaps she'd struck out on her own. How the woman managed to put so much distance between herself and the aliens was a head scratcher. Hopefully, she wasn't in trouble.

Jake clung tight as the bike skidded around a dune covered in waving oat grass. Maybe they wouldn't find anything. His pad only stayed active for a short time and the single data point wasn't much to go on. Nancy would be long gone by the time they reached the spot.

He was more or less just along for the ride. Angie held the specifics of her orders close, but as the bike turned inland Jake's confidence that they wouldn't find anything rose. The ride with Angie was a nice distraction, and he wouldn't have to deal with any inquisition over borrowing the tracker.

"What's that?" Angie looked back over her shoulder and slammed on the inertial dampeners.

Jake thumped into her back, clonking his head against hers as the bike lurched to a stop.

"What the heck?"

He blinked back tears and carefully probed the bridge of his nose. It didn't feel broken, but blood dripped onto his palm. He tilted his head back to keep it from dropping onto his shirt and Angie's back.

"Something in the rearview." Angie pulled field glasses from her jacket.

The woman was a mass of contradictions. One minute she was charming and normal, the next, well…her utter lack of concern for his bleeding nose was in character for those darker moments.

A dull gray lump squatted near the waterline on the far side of the dunes. Two figures stood at the water's edge or maybe in the water; it was hard to tell from this distance.

"There we go. A Lobstra and their human doctor." Angie lowered her binoculars with a nod. "They have a Squinch in the water on some sort of platform and are just standing there. I'll call it in, but no way will Urneck pass on getting the doc's help. You best get comfortable, cutie. Looks like we'll be spending the night." She gave his cheek a seductive caress, heedless of the smeared blood, then backed the bike behind the dune.

"You do realize that Ray would literally kill me if he thought something was going on out here?" Jake dismounted, wiped his face, and pushed a small wad of tissue between his upper lip and gums to help stop the last bit of bleeding. Rather than waiting for an answer he unloaded the overnight gear from the saddlebags and trunk.

"We'll see," Angie murmured.

Baffling. Why hadn't he stayed in school? Engineer or auxiliaries officer on a reputable freighter would be so much better than dealing with a crew of questionable mental stability. Dad had always said it's not who you work for, but how well you work. But there were limits some days. The last thing he needed was a misunderstanding with the big angry communications officer and his twin.

On the best of days, the Ray-Jay brothers were cool, aloof, and only mildly terrifying. Jay was marginally more easy-going, but agitating either one triggered sullen anger in both. Not even the captain was immune to their barely masked disrespect, bordering on open hostility.

Jake shivered. The landing shuttle was large by most standards, but not big enough to avoid the twins' animosity. The same went for Urneck. Unlike the twins, malice didn't radiate from the weapons officer, but Urneck would casually—almost gleefully— point a disintegrator or micro inhibitor at people. He pretended it was a joke, but behind the wink and smile lurked…an eagerness. The man wanted a reason to spatter someone's brains across the bulkhead. Yet Urneck was the de facto leader of the shady crew and landing mission. The captain was technically in charge aboard ship, but without a second in command Urneck usually stepped in as if he owned the mission, the ship, and the people. It was an unusual arrangement, and Jake needed to be careful.

"Angie, tell them the signal is from my datapad." He firmed his resolve with a cough and nod. "I installed a tracker when I gave Dr. Dickenson the messages. Captain's orders."

Angie lifted and eyebrow. "That might have been good to know before we left, honey."

* * *

Gray sky and the distant crash of surf melted into hazy dreams where Jake repaired some giant device. As he activated the beast for one final test, the distant rumble made him wonder if he'd done something wrong. He tried to turn toward his controls, and the blurry outline of the machine faded, dissipating like smoke. Jake blinked up at solid gray cloud cover. Warmth against his left arm had him scooting back from Angie, who had somehow managed to wiggle her sleeping pad close. They'd started off several feet apart, and he had snapped pictures to prove it.

"Morning, Slugger," Angie purred and gave him a wicked little grin. "What's your rush?"

He shook his head and avoided eye contact while pulling himself together. They broke camp quickly, and after a brief argument Angie agreed to stay behind the dune with the bike. If he approached alone, Dr. Dickenson wouldn't see him as a threat. Even so, he took his time walking down the beach to give the big Lobstra a chance to see him coming.

Their orders were to bring Nancy back to the shuttle using whatever means necessary. A directive like that wouldn't come from the captain, and out here Angie called the shots for Urneck. Lobstra were stubborn, so it was unlikely this one would divert from its mission to visit with humans. But he might entice Nancy to come back to talk with Ray-Jay about recent communications with the navy. The twins sent out his reply to the emergency advisory via subspace relay. The message contained the little he'd gleaned about the scientific mission's fate and the fact there was at least one survivor. Interstellar coms were tricky, dependent on relay beacons and the dynamic network of vessels capable of faster-than-light travel. If all went well, a reply from the navy's inbound ship could be waiting back at the shuttle.

Wet sand clung to his boots as he stomped up the beach and waved in greeting. The Lobstra spun from studying the water and raised his blaster in clear warning. Nancy sat in the surf next to the Squinch, who looked half dead as he languidly rolled with the gentle waves. Their vehicle squatted on its landing pegs, covered in drying clothes and…undergarments. It was a tiny vessel, and from the looks of things, they had slept in the cockpit.

"Hello," he called in his best I've-just-been-out-for-a-stroll voice.

"Jake? What the hell are you doing out here?" Dr. Dickenson patted the sickly Squinch, stood, and waved away the big alien's gun. "It's all right, Herman."

The Lobstra lowered his weapon as she waded out of the water. It would be too much for them to believe he had been wandering about and just happened across the small group. Most of the species on the planet had technology to thwart orbital observation, but this small craft was unlikely to have such capability. Still, something urged Jake to be honest—mostly honest.

"I can track my datapad and got worried when it turned back toward the coast. Since our camp is just south of here, we came to investigate."

"You were spying on me?" Her tone made it clear how inappropriate that was.

"What? No, I just—" his ears burned.

"No, they used you to track our progress in the hunt." Herman again raised his weapon and looked beyond Jake. "How many others?"

Jake went very still, his blush reversing course as blood drained from his face. The massive crustacean rose to his full height and quivered with menace. Even discounting the gun, it was all too easy to imagine those massive claws crushing bone and cutting tendons. With no weapon, Jake suddenly felt very small.

"Answer the man." Nancy's prodding snapped him out of his stunned silence.

"Just one back with our hoverbike." Jake blinked at the massive alien and small woman. "Hey, I understood you both without a translator!"

"Yes." Nancy nodded. "That seems to be going around."

"But how?"

"Later. For now, get your friend out here so there's no misunderstandings."

Unlike him, Angie had a gun, several guns in fact. Her laser rifle would currently be aimed at the Lobstra.

"Angie." Jake spoke into the mic in his collar. "Come on over, so we can sort this out."

It took coaxing from him and Nancy to get the others to agree weapons were not needed. Once the guns were holstered, they all breathed easier and entered into more civilized discussion. Oddly, Angie couldn't understand the Lobstra and quickly developed a blinding headache trying to follow the lopsided conversation. Although Herman's meaning was clear to him, there was no mistaking the clicking words for standard.

"It's the Lokii," Nancy said in response to Angie's frustrated question. "Their ambassador triggered some latent telepathic ability, and it's spreading. I bet after your headache clears you'll be able to understand them too."

"Insane." Angie rubbed her temples and turned away to study the dunes.

"That explains why so many crewmembers had headaches after our last meeting," Jake said. "We thought it might be a pollen bloom, but med screens couldn't isolate the culprit. Thinking back, everyone who complained either spent time talking to you directly or was in a Lobstra negotiation session. Sort of spreads like a virus."

"Freaky." The slug splashed his way out of the shallows and plopped down between Nancy and Herman. "Years of mangling the galactic trade standard to make half-understood deals and the stupid bugs had a solution all along."

Nancy introduced Reemer and gave a quick recap of how the little group split off from the main Lobstra mission to get the Squinch to the sea. The little alien had been too long inland and needed a few more days of regular bathing to recover. That explained the sickly yellow hide covered in raw pink sores, as well as the small fish that had flashed through the water feasting on skin and mucus that sloughed off. The Squinch looked too exhausted to say much, and Jake saw an avenue for convincing Nancy to return with them.

"Come back to camp. We'll set you up in a temporary shelter. You can stretch out and relax while Reemer recuperates. There's a pool in the shallows that's perfect for your friend."

"We'll have to discuss it." Nancy shot a glance at her companions.

"Talk it over. If you come back, we can comb through the communications log for updates from the navy." Jake took Angie by the elbow and walked the unsteady woman back to the dunes. "You okay to drive?"

"Just hard to concentrate. I'll be fine."

By the time they recovered the hoverbike and returned, the others had decided to accompany them. Nancy seemed to have made the decision with reluctant support from the other two—a refreshing display of loyalty. Jake breathed a sigh of relief. Angie had stayed out of things for the past few hours, but he had no doubt she would have had a backup—likely unsavory—course of action in mind if the trio had refused their offer. Life on a freighter couldn't be this complicated. It would be so nice to be in a crew with at least a bit of esprit de corps.

19. Calling Home

"WHERE ARE WE?" Reemer slurred from the shallows, then shot off toward the rocks after something he'd stirred up.

Netting between the black basalt closed off the natural pool to anything bigger than flatfish. Occasional salty spray geysered over the natural breakwater, bringing a surge of warm foam. Nancy jogged along the pebbly beach, pacing Reemer as he moved across the bottom. He surfaced after about thirty yards and spun toward her.

"The human compound, with Captain Gekko and his crew," Nancy said, though his memory had been spotty all day so he had probably forgotten his question.

After arriving at the shuttle, which was nearly half the size of Endeavor, the Squinch spent a listless day in the pool. She'd feared the worst, but Reemer rallied near dusk and took to scuttling across the bottom in search of food. By evening, he'd caught and—in an increasingly greedy and messy display—devoured five sandy-brown flatfish.

The nastier sores had closed by mid-morning, and his damaged hide sloughed off to reveal smooth golden skin. Although his general coloration had shifted from green to yellow-gold, Reemer looked decidedly better. His poor memory and slurred speech still worried her, but those would probably clear up in time. Reemer came ashore, this time towing a flapping black ray along on the end of his hunting appendage.

"Gekko, you say?" His voice gurgled as he spewed digestive compounds onto the gasping sea creature.

"Yep. We spoke with him when they traded with the Lobstra, just last week. Remember?"

"Gekko," Reemer mused as he poked at the dissolving fish like a little kid who couldn't keep his fingers off the birthday cake. "Well at least they aren't—" Both eyestalks contracted in concentration, then shot straight up to their full length. "Humans? Grint and his psychopaths? Nancy, we shouldn't be here, they'll be looking for me." Another thought seemed to strike him, and those eyestalks stretched impossibly high. "They know my name!"

Nancy thought back to the dining pavilion, when Reemer had stopped her from introducing him by name. She'd certainly used his name with Jake and Angie, having forgotten all about Reemer's desire for anonymity. Last night's conversations with Captain Gekko, Jake, and the surly weapons officer, Urneck Grint, were a blur. Upon arrival, her first priority had been to get Reemer back in the water. By the time she'd slogged ashore, changed, and eaten it was late and conversation fleeting with a promise of more tonight. She cudgeled her memory, but only recalled Reemer being referred to as "the Squinch."

"What aren't you telling me?"

Reemer rolled in the putrid puddle that was his meal, slurped noisily, and sighed.

"Huh?" He lifted his head and streamers of goo dripped from his tiny mouth.

"You were just—" Nancy threw up her hands in disgust as his attention drifted back to his meal. The boy just wasn't all there yet.

"Eating is an ugly business with this lot," a tenor voice commented from behind her.

She spun around to find a muscular man in a para-military uniform. Though of the same stout build as Urneck Grint, his blond hair was cut close to his scalp. And the man's features were more rounded, befitting his broad face better than Urneck's angular cheek bones and oft broken nose. A smile would be charming beneath those blue eyes.

"No kidding. I barely keep my own food down when we eat together." She extended her hand. "Nancy Dickenson."

"We know who you are." He stood with left hand behind his back and the right draped casually over a pistol holstered at his hip. "Angie said you had a Squinch named Reemer with you."

He studied Reemer, looked at Nancy's outstretched hand, and cocked his head as if confused. Just as she was about to drop her arm, he shrugged and shook. His grip was firm, not crushing. The calloused fingers weren't something normally found on spacers, but the edges of his mouth turned up in a brief smile that actually touched the man's eyes.

"Jay O'Brien, Comms and Ops. That Reemer?" He released her hand and jerked a thumb toward the feasting Squinch.

Nancy hesitated, but the beans were already spilt. "Yep, that's our Reemer. Still recovering and eating like a horse. Guess we were away from the ocean too long."

She held her breath, as confusion again pinched the man's features. Whatever Reemer had done to warrant hiding from the crew must have been a doozy because the man seemed at a loss on how to respond. But his eventual reply was a pleasant surprise.

"Huh, common name I guess." Jay gave another shrug and turned to leave. "But I needed to see for myself. Catch you later."

"Wait!" Nancy called. "Jake says you might have replies from your report on the Endeavor. Messages or relays?"

"Don't think so." He turned back before stepping out again toward the camp. "Better talk to Jake. He met with my brother Ray this morning—looks like me but with a Mohawk. He can fill you in."

Nancy slapped her thighs in frustration as the man walked under the garage area and stopped to look over the two hoverbikes parked there. The structure was little more than a rainfly stretched between the shuttle and a group of interconnected temporary structures. An extra room had been erected for her, Reemer, and Herman, but the Lobstra opted to stay with his landpod.

Their quarters measured ten-foot square, a semi-ridged structure of dull green fabric ribbed with ultra-light struts every few inches. The interior walls were sturdy enough to mount a small table, shelves, and a bunk along each. The Squinch had spent last night at the water's edge, but would want his own bed tonight. Herman had the cot and rubberized pan soaking in the far end of the lagoon where the stench wouldn't bother anyone. The wave action would have it clean enough to install by afternoon. Reemer should spend the rest of the day in the pool, but she needed to find Jake.

"Will you be okay down here?" Nancy asked.

Reemer paused in his slurping. "Tasty fish. Warm water. I'm good."

"I'm going to find Jake and check for messages. Herman is working on the pod, but ought to be down shortly to set up your bed."

"Okie dokie."

His slurring grew less noticeable with each meal. He'd fully recover in a few days, but the humans might not stay put that long. Those other hunting parties were constantly on the move, so it would be no surprise if this group left soon. Stretching out in the housing units was nice, but they could always go back to pod sitting at night.

She hadn't made any friends among the humans. Aside from Jake and his captain, the crew was either dismissive or openly hostile, which made sense if Angie spread word of Reemer. But Jay thought their grudge was with a different Squinch by the same name, so why had her Reemer been so worried?

"Are you sure these are the humans you crossed? Jay doesn't even know you."

Reemer took a moment to slurp up the last of the swirling goop and squirming digestive components. He did it with much less gratuitous gulping than usual. She found her breakfast simply swirling about in mild agitation instead of actively clawing its way up her esophagus and thanked whatever deity was responsible.

"Who's Jay?" Reemer asked.

"The man who was just came down to take a look at you."

"Nice of him. So where are you off to?"

Reemer slipped back into the water, sighed, and disappeared beneath the surface. She waited a good three minutes. He didn't surface, so she headed for the shuttle, vowing to get some answers out of the forgetful little creature this evening.

The shuttle was a cramped and confusing catacomb of small compartments. Jake said he'd be in the auxiliary equipment room on deck four all morning, which was somewhere amidships. It had taken months to grow used to maneuvering around the Endeavor, which by comparison was laid out with admirable logic. Here there were no central passageways, no frame number markings, and virtually no rhyme nor reason to the numerous dead-end passages.

It was as if the little ship was designed solely to maximize space usage without concern for traffic flow or ease of movement. Thankfully, the deck system was the same as naval ships, with the deck number increasing as she descended. The entry ramp brought her in on deck two. Access to the vessel must surely be electronically monitored, but wandering around without an escort was disconcerting and felt like sneaking—especially during her great restroom hunt.

Nancy came to the end of yet another corridor and glared at the symbol above the doorway. She'd covered deck three several times over without finding a ladder down. Poking into rooms made little sense, but there was no one around to ask. The crew must be up on the command level or working down below. She knocked, heard no reply, and cycled the door open.

Dazzling white light and the overpowering scent of disinfectant had her blinking back tears. Three sliding white doors with viewports lined the left bulkhead. On the right side of the narrow room, two windowless doors stood open. The small compartment behind each held a gleaming stainless steel toilet—or perhaps they were made of something lighter.

Nancy sagged with relief, thankful no one was on the commode or showering in the adjacent stalls. The far end of the room opened on sinks, a mirrored grooming station, and several small lockers set just inside another door. She hurried through and emerged in an alcove with a ladder leading down. If the designers of this vessel were forced to live onboard for a month, stupid layouts like this would change in a hurry.

Just as she stepped onto the top rung, clanging sounded from below. A scraggly head of gray-yellow hair surged up the ladder, the person underneath not bothering to look up as he climbed and hummed to himself. Nancy jumped back. Pete wasn't a large man, but as he emerged his shoulder caught her under the arm and spun her off balance. She staggered back two steps and plopped down hard.

"Oho, the accommodations are improvin' here 'bouts." His scowl turned to a gap-toothed grin that puckered the scar on his left cheek as he finally noticed her.

"Mr. uh…Pete," Nancy stammered and scrambled to her feet.

"Yep Pete, just Pete." The old man's reedy voice grew shrill as he pulled a sheaf of papers from under his left arm and poked them into her face. "Whatcha doing here, little lady? None of them lobsters with you is there?"

"You might at least apologize for knocking me down. And stop that!" Nancy swatted the papers aside. No not papers, a glossy magazine.

Too much tan, beige, and other skin tones showed on the cover. Nancy felt her ears redden. Pete laughed—more of a cackled. The man was such a stereotype.

"Sorry, no one usually up here this time of day." It was a reasonable apology, but his eyes gleamed with some inner amusement that made her wary.

"No harm done, I guess. Jake's expecting me in the Auxiliaries office. Down a deck, right?"

"Yep, straight off the bottom. Auxiliary is fourth or fifth door on the left. Gotta big pump mounted outside. Can't miss it."

"I'll watch for that. Thanks."

Pete stared for an uncomfortable moment, and Nancy edged closer to the ladder, worried he would decide to escort her. She just didn't want the disturbing old guy behind her. Maybe he was younger than he looked, but his demeanor and unkempt appearance made him seem ancient. His cloudy gray eyes lingered on her. Instead of focusing on her chest or mouth, he leered at her forearm and boots. Creepy.

"Times a wasting," Pete declared. "Gotta go. Ya know, go?" His snicker escalated through a giggle to a full-blown laugh as he turned and cycled open the door to the facilities.

Nancy hurried down the ladder. The pump was a red-finned spider sitting in a tangle of piping outside the heavy blast door. Knocking bruised her knuckles and made the barest of sounds. She reached for the flat wrench in a bracket near the pump, thinking it would make a good knocker. But the door opened, revealing Jake with an electronic clipboard held loosely in his left hand.

"Dr. Dickenson." Jake's boyish smile felt genuine and somehow clean after her encounter with Pete.

"Finally! This shuttle is confusing, especially having to go through the bathroom to get down from deck three."

"Aw, sorry ma'am. I should have mentioned that. It's a quirky design and probably not what you're used to." Jake stepped aside and motioned her into the compartment. "Ray hasn't answered my request for info, but we can dig into the records directly if you have a couple hours."

Nancy stepped through the doorway onto an area ringed with consoles and status panels. Machinery sprouted from the walls and dropped away beyond a safety railing. Ladders plunged down either side of the elevated platform into a maze of equipment—like being inside a giant bakery full of vats and ovens. Waves of hot, dry air carried the pungent chemical odor of material on the bitter edge of burning.

Jake strolled over to a standard computer console nestled amongst the alarm panels and adjusted the controls. The display sprang to life. She liked the way he hummed under his breath while zipping through the electronic material. His speaking voice was a clear baritone, and his wordless tune resonated with the drone of machinery. The song was one of her favorite old power ballads.

"Here we go, ma'am. We can build a query ourselves and pull results from the database." He typed words into the blank search field: Endeavor, Greenorb, and Fred. "Who the heck names a planet something like that? It's embarrassing."

Nancy gave a noncommittal shrug. She'd pressed Harry about the planet's name on several occasions. He always supplied a cagey grin in place of an explanation, but something about the name definitely tickled her friend.

"They have slugs, so I bet we find earthworms too," Harry had said when last she'd asked. "I call dibs on naming those. Of course they'll be fredworms. And if there's geologic instability, we're talking fredquakes. Most species will be fredbound, but boy do we have some fredshattering discoveries ahead of us. Just think—"

He'd have gone on if Nancy hadn't pelted him with synthmeat cubes from her sandwich. They'd dissolved into laughter too easily, blowing off anxiety in a last bit of fun before things turned ugly. The commander probably knew more about the silly name, but she'd never gotten the chance to make an end run around Harry's stonewalling.

"Oh, add in Gunthall, he's our commander. And Roving Darwin is—was—our mission name."

"Anything else, doctor?" Jake asked as he typed.

So formal and respectful—and annoying. Nancy tried to put a lid on her rising temper. She should appreciate his deference, especially among this crew where a lack of manners and courtesy was the norm. So why did she want to throttle this guy? Because she needed a friend, a fellow human to talk to, commiserate with, and simply be herself around. His formality added unnecessary distance.

"Stop…calling…me…doctor." Nancy bit off each word. How old does he think I am? "It shouldn't be too hard to call me Nancy. I could really use a little human kindness. The rest of your crew is surly or downright creepy, and I'm pretty sure everyone from mine has been killed. I've been traveling with aliens for weeks without even being able to speak standard."

"I didn't—" Jake tried to inject as she sucked in a ragged breath and wiped away a hot tear that insisted on rolling down her left cheek.

"And I swear to God, call me ma'am one more time, and I'll clobber you with my walker." The anger and loneliness receded, leaving a sort of sick embarrassment. She scrubbed away another tear, turning to hide her face and feeling a fool. Just perfect.

His silence gave her time to compose herself. When she risked a glance, Jake blushed and his ears burned red. His boyish, pale complexion made a fireworks display of his anxiety. Mannish, she chided. Can't get mad at him for making me feel old and then turn around and do the same thing.

"Um…" Jake clearly searched for a way past the awkward moment, then pointed at her waist. "Why do you always do that?"

Caught off guard, she looked down to find she scrubbed both hands along her beltline. The bit of moisture from her tears was long gone, and her knuckles were raw from the continued abuse. She dropped her arms, but they rose back of their own accord, so she crossed them in front of her, exasperated with the nervous habit.

"Trying to get them, you know, clean." What the hell was wrong with her?

"Just curious, and Nancy works for me." Rather than push the topic, Jake gave a smile of apology and understanding that made her feel warm inside despite her outburst. "After we get this data call submitted, I'll pull up the report we sent the navy."

He turned back to the console and scooted sideways to leave an open spot on the small bench. She ran a hand through her hair and joined him. By the time they were ready to submit the query, it contained several dozen keywords.

"That'll probably net us too much stuff, but it's easier to sort through excess than track down missing messages." Jake waved at the console. "Care to do the honors?"

Nancy nodded and clicked the submit button. Jake laid a gentle hand on her shoulder for just a moment before pulling up the outgoing messages. The contact felt warm and reassuring, even though it was gone all too soon.

"I don't get it," Jake said after ten minutes of searching. "I can't find our response to the advisory on your ship. My draft is here, but not the official transmission."

"Just let me read the draft." Nancy waved a placating hand as he frantically scrolled on. "Could the captain have taken some logs, for himself?"

"Maybe." Jake's fingers hovered over the keyboard. "But he usually just pulls a copy, which wouldn't lock out the original—unless he was making corrections."

Nancy perused the draft that Jake opened on her side of the display. His concise message simply stated that something had happened to the Endeavor crew and a survivor was still on Fred.

"It would have been good if we'd worked this up together," Nancy said. "I've got the coordinates of our last site on my datapad and could have added more mission and crew details."

"No problem." Jake peered at her screen, then made a selection on the embedded menu. "Go ahead and add what you want. We can send an update through QUEN's uplink."

"QUEN?"

"Our freighter, or at least the artificial intelligence running the ship systems. Sort of becomes one and the same thing after a while. She's still in orbit and does the actual broadcasts. Come to think of it, I can ask QUEN to look for that original message. Our update will need to reference the timestamp and other data that gets appended at transmission."

Jake typed in a request to the orbiting ship. Moments later, a feminine voice purred from the console, "Naughty, naughty. Does Veechy know you're slipping notes to me?"

"Damn it, not voice comms, QUEN." Jake slapped at the console, his face scarlet. "Text only."

"I wanna talk." QUEN's voice turned pouty—if such a thing was possible for an AI. "You know the lady is always right, Jakey dear. If you're nice to me, I'll download something special for you when my Veechy isn't looking. I know you like—"

"No need for that. Voice it is." The young man's nervous laugh had Nancy blushing in sympathy, though the exchange piqued her curiosity. "This is an easy one. I need our outgoing report on the science ship Endeavor. It should have gone out five days ago in response to an emergency space advisory. I'm uploading that and the draft message for reference. I'll have a new outgoing message for you shortly. We want to update the original"

"We, is it?" A red light blinked on above Nancy's console next to a small lens that irised into focus. "Hmm, nice to meet you Dr. Dickenson."

"Ah, and you too, QUEN."

The flat black lens regarded her, studied her—an all too human scrutiny. QUEN's voice conveyed a wicked smile, disconcerting, but an AI was by definition a thinking entity. Some went further than others in emulating human mannerisms.

There had been an international lab back on Earth with an embedded intelligence program that had basically gone postal when it felt under appreciated. The operation closed for months while they worked to undo the effects of progressively nastier pranks executed by the computer. That entity had been operating with limited access to the facility's systems. This one seemed playfully opinionated, but Nancy imagined QUEN could be quite a handful if you got on her bad side.

"And thank you in advance for helping with the messages. It's been a lonely few weeks and it is so nice to speak to people again."

"You see, honey!" The presence jumped back over to Jake's side of the console. "That's how you treat a lady. Like a real person, not your servant."

"Sure thing." Jake rolled his eyes. "Would you please stand by for an updated status report on Endeavor?"

"Will do, lover." The feline quality returned with purred vengeance.

"Stop calling me…" Jake trailed off as the cameras went offline, leaving them alone again.

Over the next hour, Nancy consulted her information and rewrote the message while Jake split his time between monitoring his equipment and avoiding eye contact. The latter was rather annoying. Despite the telepathic abilities the Lokii unleashed, there was comfort in spending time with another human, and here he was ignoring her. Hopefully that didn't make her prejudiced.

Nancy prided herself on treating individuals with respect and common courtesy. Her time with Reemer, the Lobstra, and the Lokii had to count for something. Though, she wasn't above casting judgement on people like Urneck and Pete. She might not be perfect, but she certainly outshined those Neanderthals when it came to civilized behavior.

Nancy gave her changes one last proofread and found Jake sprawled across the deck plates, head dangling over the floor edge while his hair danced in the hot wind from the equipment below. He tapped at a coupling and craned to consult a digital readout mounted to his right. Modern equipment shouldn't need such ministrations. He was either giving her time to finish or avoiding her, a notable accomplishment in the crowded space.

"I've added the info I think will be useful." She pitched her voice to cut through the hum of machinery.

Jake jerked upright and banged his head into the bottom of the railing he'd been peering through. "Crap."

Nancy winced in sympathy, then thought better of it. "Serves you right!"

"What's that supposed to mean?" Jake rubbed his head and shimmied out from under the railing.

"If you weren't acting like I was radioactive, you wouldn't have been poking your head around where it was likely to get smacked."

"Wait…what?" Jake stuttered. "I'm just giving you some space, ma'am."

Ma'am? How old did he think she was? The recent stress and living outdoors had likely weathered her a bit, but did ten years make such a difference that he wasn't even willing to be around her? She longed for conversation with someone who didn't have slime or antennae as prominent facial features. She'd welcome joking around a little, not the disgusting, potty humor Reemer excelled at, but just goofing and cracking inane puns would be wonderful.

Captain Gekko was the only other person in the crew who acted within the bounds of civility, but he was understandably consumed by his responsibilities. Here stood her best chance at some comradery, his adorably perplexed expression saying better than words that Jake was unable to comprehend casual exchanges with a person as old as she.

Nancy had been his age not so very long ago, a newly minted botanist in her early twenties conducting doctoral research. Even senior professors and established experts in the field were companionable and approachable, except of course when she was in the throes of defending her thesis. Her entire life had been spent in easy going, collaborative environments. Maybe things were different for Jake, perhaps the independent spacers made life harder, expected more class distinctions, or required extreme deference. But as a casual observer, it didn't look that way to her.

Jake stared at the floor, wearing a wary expression and those ridiculously distracting dimples. He clearly just didn't see any reason to interact more than was strictly necessary with someone as ancient as herself. What a goddamn awful attitude! Nancy backed away and waved at the console.

"Just send the update," she said, her voice a mere whisper.

"Oh, okay." Jake rushed to the terminal. He edited in silence, merging her information into a standardized format, then opened a channel to the ship. "QUEN, Jake here." There was an awkward moment of silence during which Nancy willed—well dared really—him to turn and look her in the eye. But he kept his gaze locked on the controls.

"Oh, Jakey, I'm so glad you came back for more." QUEN's breathy reply sounded more like panting after exercise than the sensuous murmur it was clearly meant to be.

"Uploading now. Get this out soonest, please."

"Now that wasn't so hard was it?" QUEN dialed down the gasping, getting closer to the mark. "I would, but—"

Her words cut off, the room went dark, and the ever-present hum of machinery ceased. A split second later, red lights flooded the compartment. With a distant clunk, half of the console came back.

"You have a problem," QUEN said, all trace of playfulness gone. "Low-grade energy signatures are disrupting shuttle systems and corrupting data faster than error correction algorithms can adjust. I show cascading casualties, but I'm locked out of diagnostics. Only emergency backup systems and lighting until I can sort it out. Jake, you have lifeforms inside the hull, upper decks. No readings from the machinery levels, but internal sensors are going haywire. You and the doctor don't even register."

20. Layered Defense

D RISSA SAT back on her tail and finished dissecting yet another variant of the walking cacti. It was amazing how a species with the same genome could propagate such diverse subclasses. If only she could access medical logs from prior missions. Others must have encountered these creatures and developed theories.

Dr. Dickenson's unique perspective helped immeasurably. Her incessant push to identify the root genetic sequences and correlate their findings into a clear taxonomy went well beyond Drissa's job of assessing the vegetative compounds and collecting those with potential medical applications. Nancy pushed the data collection to new heights. No one knew why plant life on Fred produced so many unique compounds, but Drissa was starting to see a pattern in the data she and the human compiled.

The whip-like cactus pinned to her exam table stretched half the length of her antenna. The outer skin covered in tan nodules was peeled back to expose the vascular structure beneath. Genetic analysis put this in the same family as the pain urchins and watchers. Its internal structure mirrored those others despite the plant being more slender and propelling itself with snakelike movements.

Each variant had extensive vascular hydraulic capillaries to act as a crude musculature. The dermal structures held arrays of sensory cells around the spines—nodules on this specimen—with denser clusters at the crown of each plant. They all bore a defined root system, though the snake cacti roots were vestigial. And of course, they all produced copious amounts of defensive toxins.

The compounds would be invaluable in treating neuromuscular diseases and other ailments. This wasn't the panacea of long life that the Szooda nectar yielded. But gathering the toxins in quantity meant widely available medicines to ease the suffering of countless individuals instead of a privileged few. She had Joda's ground forces harvesting specimens. Her lockers were nearly full, and her team worked around the clock extracting the toxins and recording empirical data—data that needed to be shared with future expeditions instead of locked away for posterity as her predecessors had done. She clacked her cutting claw in annoyance.

"That's a pretty picture, snapping at the locals." Joda threw his battle claw up as she spun to face the security chief. "Whoa there, no threat here, Drissa!"

She forced herself to relax, backed up, and lowered her claws. It wouldn't do to accidentally initiate a duel just because she was overwrought. But the situation was so damned frustrating!

"You're part of the senior command staff. Why are records from prior missions incomplete and redacted? That information could help," Drissa demanded.

Joda's antennae flicked left and right in confusion, but he relaxed his stance and took several bubbling breaths. "You know it isn't done that way."

"Yes, but why?"

He must have access to more information than a lowly medical officer. His antennae drooped low and spread wide in disapproval, though she was uncertain if it was with her question or the answer he was about to give.

"Apparently, Providence should not be unduly influenced. The records are locked away by the Matriarch herself in order to…keep the search pure."

"But it's in her best interest to share prior data. That information would improve our chance of success, and finding the nectar prolongs her reign."

"All things come to an end." Joda let out a wet sigh. "She supports the Lady."

Hot rage filled her at the audacity, the presumption.

"The Lady be damned!" Blasphemy, but she couldn't help it. As a scientist, Drissa was already a pariah to the main sect of Providence. "People have died. Foreknowledge could have prepared us, could have helped avoid those attacks. We're scratching in the dark. If not for Nancy's help, I'd only have produced a fraction of the medicinal compounds we've managed so far. It's time to help ourselves."

"I recommend you keep those sentiments to yourself." Joda pitched his voice so it did not travel to the med techs working the stores. "I can't fully disagree with you, but such thoughts are blasphemous. I don't want to see you sent home."

Joda sidled closer and placed a comforting foreleg upon hers, their antennae nearly touching. The fins of her abdomen fluttered at his closeness, but also at the realization she could be sentenced—perhaps put to death—for her idealism. She always admired the big officer's strength and determination, but now there was compassion and understanding. The intimate contact made her head spin and suggested a possible future. She leaned into his touch, just enough to let him know she didn't mind, then gently broke the contact and turned back to her work.

"I suppose you are right. Thank you for hearing me out and for the warning. I will be careful."

Joda relaxed, but stopped short as he turned to go. "Almost forgot, searcher needs your help. These things"—he pointed to the specimen staked out on her table—"are flowing out from the cracks and crevasses ahead. Meinish says his search pattern played out and we need Dr. Dickenson's inputs for the next plateau search. Captain told him to get them from you."

"I have the doctor's notes, and we worked closely on building the last parameters. I can provide something." Then a thought struck her. "Are we still in communication with the pod?"

"Herman reports in daily." Joda's antennae bobbed in the affirmative. "I can patch the frequencies into your sled's control room if you like. They've linked up with the human hunters on the coast while Reemer recovers."

"Interesting. Set me up with those and give me an hour. Then I'll need Meinish over here to work out exactly what he needs. If we can raise the good doctor, she can double check our work."

"I'll make it happen," Joda said. "We're still trying to decide if it's worth plowing through the critters ahead. If we skirt around them, it will take at least the rest of the day and maybe tomorrow to clear the grid. Can I tell the captain that a new search will be ready tomorrow?"

"Meinish has to answer that question." Drissa rummaged through her work area for her notes and Nancy's data wafers. "I'll work my side as quickly as I can. Even if we can't verify with Nancy, that part will be done today."

Joda bobbed again and turned toward the loading area. Sunlight peeked through the thinning clouds and glinted off his shell, making his face and claws shine. He really cut quite the figure. She'd noticed before in a sort of detached fashion, but now her fins tingled. And he'd taken the time to hear her out, to warn her.

"Joda?" Her call stopped the big security chief in his tracks. "Thank you for…everything."

He waved his antennae in acknowledgement, and she caught a glimpse of his mandible flicking out in a pleased arc before he hurried off. Her eyestalks swiveled to track his departure, but there was no time for idle daydreams.

Nancy's data wafers contained more information than expected. It took half an hour to find the section containing search parameters. The human hoarded information, partially formed theories, copious notes, and of course her scientific taxonomy for the indigenous flora. There was even a section cataloguing virus and bacteria strains, with a note that Breena was working on a side project. Drissa would have to ask her assistant what that was all about. She had given Nancy free reign with her staff, but needed to be cognizant of everyone's workload. She could ill afford a poor evaluation for losing control of her people.

Fortunately, Nancy's notes concerning Meinish's work were consistent with her own, though in addition to variables like temperature and humidity, the doctor pieced together connections between plants with common genome markers. Nancy suspected her Dolor species line had increased in toxicity, mobility, and general aggression as the mission progressed. There were placeholders for more variants she expected to find along the same family line and predictions that each would be more agile and aggressive than the last.

Although they had encountered plenty of aggressive species that did not possess similar genome sequences, Nancy's reasoning suggested the Lobstra were swimming upstream against a set of increasingly capable lifeforms of the same species wearing radically different forms.

Drissa snapped her delicate under-claws in thought. She was no dedicated student of random happenstance and divine Providence. Her tentative belief in the Lady embraced providence as a guiding concept rather than a driving force in her life. Sometimes things simply worked out for the best, which made it difficult to totally discount Lady Luck—even while railing at the short sightedness of the current administration.

But Providence aside, what were the chances that they encounter two distinct versions of Dolor creatures in force? She glanced at the long slender cacti on her dissection table. That made a third variant to attack as the search progressed, each more formidable than the last. She had overheard one of Joda's team liken the cacti snakes to whip worms, highly aggressive mindless swarms that latched on and died rather than lose their quarry. Two scouts had been hit, in spite of careful precautions and use of their neutralizing agent.

Drissa looked at the placeholders in Nancy's hierarchy once more. Beyond the one or two additional variants that Nancy theorized, there was a space reserved for an apex Dolor. The implication was that the snakes, watchers, urchins and perhaps other types descended from this one. Nancy's notes were in the margin.

Aggressive; toxic or other offensive capabilities; highly mobile; progenitor?

"Meinish is ready for you." Joda's voice made her jump.

"Sorry…again," Joda said with a hint of amusement. "Studying defense in depth now?"

"What?"

"Your diagram there." Joda scuttled closer to peer at her display. "Well, from a ways back that pyramid looked like the layered defense diagram we train to. You know, lots of weak outer ring defenders, with each subsequent ring or layer having fewer defenders, but with more firepower. Then at the top is your prime objective, a battleship or command center."

"Hmm." Drissa tilted left, willing herself to view the hierarchy from a different perspective.

"But I see all your magic medical notations and symbols now. Your stuff, not mine. Meinish is in your control booth, and they're trying to raise Herman and the doctor. Ready?"

Drissa nodded absently, closed the files, and gathered her things. She walked with Joda to the enclosure, her mind still processing his words. Every biological system had something akin to his layered defense concept. Immune systems and repair mechanisms both had some early form of pervasive defense like fever and swelling, which if ineffective escalated through processes designed to eradicate illness or injury in the most efficient way.

Could the model apply to an entire species? Nature evolved for survival, and the Dolor line had several unique classes designed to defend. Nancy's notes flashed through her mind, the word progenitor lodging there. If the plant they sought was of the dolor genome, the fact they clawed through ever stronger creatures— defenders—would indicate they were on the right track. More than the right track, given the concentration of snake cacti. They could very well be nearing mission success.

21. Unwelcome Guests

O UTSIDE OF the auxiliary room was chaos. Dim red emergency lighting bathed the passageway, and Nancy's ears rang with the whoop and blare of multiple alarms, each of which cut off abruptly only to be replaced by a different tone. She and Jake stayed close to the bulkhead and made their way by feel toward the ladder. Blasts of steam and other less savory gasses randomly vented from safety valves along the route.

"QUEN says the shuttle systems are shutting down." Jake consulted the headset he'd donned as they left his equipment room. "She's trying to override and stabilize the damage, but someone's taken control of our systems."

"Where are we heading?" Nancy yelled as a stringent siren sent pain spiking through her temple.

"Control nexus on deck three." Jake rummaged through the satchel at his hip and pulled out a small black tube that sent a dazzling beam of white light down the passageway. "I'd rather have a gun, but at least we aren't blind."

His light sliced through the eerie red haze. Cables and pipes ran down either side of the overhead and plunged into the bulkhead just beyond a skirted opening in the ceiling. Ladder rungs glinted through the steam and disappeared into the opening overhead.

"Looks clear," Nancy said.

They crept forward, and Jake shined his light up the ladder well. The door to the bathroom, or head as it was called shipboard, stood ajar. But there was no sign of whatever intruders QUEN detected.

"Me first."

He scurried up the ladder and shined his light down as she climbed. Just as she stepped into the small alcove at the top, a clunk and rasp sounded from behind the doorway. Rather than the smooth, sliding doors that recessed silently into the bulkheads in most of the vessel, this was a heavily hinged arrangement. It looked to be some special blast- or vacuum-proof boundary.

Jake spun toward the sound as the door slammed open. The heavy edge clipped his temple, snapping his head to the left with a dull thwack that barely slowed the door. Nancy grabbed his belt and managed to swing him away so he didn't tumble headfirst down the ladderwell after the flashlight.

"Gotcha!" Pete leveled a handgun at them from inside the bathroom, his eyes wild in the red emergency lighting.

"It's just us," Nancy snapped as she helped Jake sit up against the wall.

Blood trickled from a gash just in front of Jake's right ear. His head lolled to one side, then the other in semi-consciousness, but at least he breathed normally.

"Identify yourselves!" Pete cackled. "Intruder protocol is—"

"You idiot!" Nancy wanted to throw something at the fool, but her hands were full of moaning junior-technician, and not in a good way. "Stow the gun and give me a hand."

Pete blinked, lowered the pistol a fraction, and scowled. "You can't—"

"Now!" Nancy roared.

She fixed the startled man with a glare that caused smoke to curl up from his scraggly beard, or that could have just been a stray puff of steam. Pete's mouth dropped open, but he shoved his elongated pistol into a hip holster and hurried forward.

"No need to get all bossy." Pete stooped and slid a hand under Jake's right arm.

They levered the young man to his feet and helped him stagger to a stool by the sinks. Nancy cleaned his bloody face with the wet towel Pete offered. The wound ran from his hairline to below his cheekbone, a nasty vertical line of dark crimson bruising. The actual gash that bled with the gleeful abandon of any head wound was less than an inch long. Hopefully he didn't have a concussion. Pete staunched the blood flow as she rummaged in her pouch for a bandage. All botanists carried a decent first aid kit. Even discounting deadly flora bent on murder, thorns, scrapes, and poisonous nettles were occupational hazards.

"What the hell were you thinking?"

"Something's onboard." Pete sounded like a petulant four-year-old. "I thought you might be one of those cactus things."

Nancy found what she needed, pushed the towel away, and spread a thin paste over the gash. The medicine turned pink, and the blood flow stopped a few seconds later. She applied an adhesive bandage, pulled the activating strip off the back, and watched it draw the wound closed. When the contraction finished, she affixed a sterile surface bandage and snapped her fingers to get Jake's attention.

"I'm fine." Jake slurred his words and gave her the languid smile of a happy drunk.

"How many fingers?" Nancy waved her right hand with index and middle fingers extended.

"Pretty." His eyes tracked the peace sign.

"Fingers, Jake. How many?"

Jake smiled for a moment longer, then his face screwed up in concentration. "One, two…two."

"You'll live." Nancy backed away, only to find Jake had stealthily intertwined the fingers of her left hand with his. She pulled, he held on, and she decided to ignore it for the moment. "Pete, what have you seen?"

"I was in here doing my business when all hell broke loose. One of them walking pricklies was down the passage a ways, so I ran and got Gertrude." He pointed to the far door, then patted the gun at his side. "By the time we got back, the thing was gone and I heard you two on the ladder. That's about it."

Nancy sighed, tugged her hand out of Jake's, and closed her eyes. Dealing with this madness was getting old and making her feel old. The constant alarms helpfully added a splitting headache to take her mind off the fatigue. What was she even doing in this hellhole?

Her life-long goal of cataloging enough species to go down in the obscure annals of botanical history alongside Darwin and Sir Joseph Banks was a pretentious daydream. Even her burning desire to eradicate the species that killed her crew had burnt down to a low guttering flame. Perhaps Breena would finish the designer virus they'd started and cleanse this world of the Dolor species—that would be one down.

At this point, the Lobstra were on their own. All she wanted was for Reemer to recover, the navy to arrive, and to go home. But her feelings and wants didn't matter. This stupid planet and its insane ecosystem insisted on getting in her face. She hauled out her datapad, brought up a picture of a Dolor watcher cactus, and spun the screen around to Pete.

"Is that what you saw?"

Pete scratched at the wispy hairs on his chin and squinted. "Nah…well, sort of, 'cept it weren't so clean. Had a lot of bumps and growths all over. Size looks about right based on your scale."

"How about the color, green-brown with big yellow needles?" Nancy prompted.

"Hard to say under these darned lights, but I think so. Only saw prickers on the bumps, sort of like whiskers on a witch's mole. Rest of it seemed smooth and sleek, didn't have all those rows of needles." He ran a surprisingly well-manicured finger along the length of the watcher. "Keep in mind, I only had a quick look."

"We really need to get to the control node." Jake stood on his own but looked wobbly.

"You okay to continue?"

"Just don't make me do jumping jacks or anything. We've got to assess the damage and make repairs so QUEN can reestablish control."

There was no sign of the watcher as they crept into level three's main passage. Pete took point since he had the only real weapon. Jake had retrieved the light along with a large wrench. Nancy gripped her sample cutter, but whatever was on the ship would have to get way too close for the little tool to do any good. They paused at an intersection just as the alarms went silent. The absence of sound pressed in with steady, phantom ringing.

"That was QUEN," Jake said into the thick silence. "She's still locked out, but managed to reset the warning systems to operations mode. Alarms are visual only, so we'll be able to hear ourselves think. QUEN's uplink must be damaged too. Bandwidth is low and data packets are rerouted almost as fast as she can transmit. The control room is down on the left."

"Hold up." Nancy pulled him back as he started forward. "Shine your light on this thing."

She pointed to a dark mass nestled into the corner of the ceiling, just out of reach. It looked like insulation on the cables, but she swore that it had just moved. Back down the way they had come, two other small shadows clung to the overhead and another sat halfway up the wall.

Jake swung the light up to the ceiling above Nancy where the ever-present cables and pipes ran in parallel bundles. A drab green lump the size of her fist nestled among the strands of a cable. Bulbous lumps covered the irregular egg shape, and a cluster of fine yellow needles curled out from one end like a tuft of hair.

"That's one of those warts from the shambling cactus." Pete stood on tiptoe to poke at the thing with the end of his pistol.

The creature pulled back from the gun and hissed despite it lacking any sort of mouth. Pete collided with Nancy as he backpedaled with a squawk. Satisfied, the thing inched back to its original position and curled around a cable. Those hair-thin needles probed at the wire then wrapped tight. It held fast for five seconds, relaxed, and the needles reached out to find the next foothold.

"The parent plant must drop these as it moves." Nancy watched the needles probe at the next wire in the bundle.

"What are they?" Jake flipped the light back down the passage, confirming the distant blobs were also invasive plants.

"Offhand, I'd say they're offspring, baby cacti." Nancy studied the little plant above as it quested with its needles—or were those roots? "Odd they separated from the parent down here. And why try to root in the overhead?"

"Leave 'em," Pete said with a nervous chuckle and scowl. "Just leave 'em be. We can clean the little freaks out after QUEN has things in hand. Control node?"

"Yeah, let's do that first," Jake agreed.

They moved down the passage to an alcove lined with equipment racks. The embedded components boasted a complex array of lights, readouts, and gauges that reminded Nancy of an old-style airplane cockpit. And standing right in the middle of the whole arrangement was the shambling cactus.

"Shit on a shingle," Pete cursed as he pushed her and Jake against the wall. "Should I shoot it?"

"Might not do any good," Nancy said. "Not sure where it's vulnerable. Center of mass?"

Standing at three feet, the plant was of similar shape but shorter than the watchers the Lobstra encountered. Pete was right about it not having the precise needle rows that ran the length of watchers. The skin of this variant was a sickly yellow-green, smooth, and riddled with shallow holes, which would have been left by the detaching offspring. One remaining lump near the top pulled itself free and scuttled up the face of the computer equipment, with the faint rustling of dead leaves blowing across concrete. A half-dozen other lumps poked out of the gear of the control node.

"Why the hell is it having pups here?" Pete turned a dial on the back of his weapon before sighting on the big plant. "Dispersion setting will pummel it, maybe without beating up the gear too bad."

Something was off. The two upright arms sagged like a half-deflated balloon animal. Jake's light reflected off runnels of wet sap seeping from the perforations along its body. The central trunk—where the head of an animal would be—sagged against a stanchion between equipment racks. The off colors and general appearance were signs every greenhouse expert recognized.

"It's already dead," Nancy said more loudly than she'd meant.

Jake crept forward and poked it with his wrench. The thing had been precariously balanced and half sank, half folded to the floor.

"But those are still alive." Jake waved at the infant cacti poking from random crevices in the computer equipment. "And those yellow roots are jabbing into the panels. That's gotta be what's messing up our systems. This one's fouling the network diagnostics port."

He jabbed his wrench at the nearest green mass. The creature hissed and stretched like a blob of goo, then reeled itself back into position by the roots embedded in the small rectangular opening.

"QUEN, we're at panel three alpha seven," Jake said into the headset dangling around his neck. "There are half a dozen little plants clinging to the equipment. Looks like maybe their roots are gumming up your data feeds."

"Well isn't that interesting, sweetie." QUEN's voice shifted back to playful as it came through the small speakers. "Show me exactly where."

Jake stepped over the parent cactus to examine the equipment. He described the location of each plant and reeled off equipment designations that meant little to Nancy. "I'm uploading a few images from the headset. Should we just pull them off?"

They waited under the pale crimson light for the computer's response. Although the little cacti were largely inert, they occasionally shifted position as if to get a better grip. Between adjustments, the skin of each pulsed at odd intervals. The warning lights on the computer racks were no less frenetic than the other alarm panels they'd passed. Most flashed amber or red, interspersed with an occasional green that more often than not gave in to peer pressure and reverted to a more disquieting color.

With a start, Nancy realized the cacti pulsed in time with those occasional green lights, or their pulsing could just be easier to notice in the glow of a green indicator. The only concentration of steadily burning green lights formed a triangle around one of the creatures who clung to the face of an ankle-high panel at the back of the alcove. That cactus was nearly apoplectic, shifting to such an extent that it resembled a beating heart.

"Why's that panel got so many green lights?" Nancy asked Jake.

"Comms and alarm system hub." Jake looked past the heap of plant sprawled on the deck and shrugged. "Just shows QUEN has silenced the audibles. Green down there doesn't do us much good, but it saves our eardrums and keeps us sane."

"Do you think—"

"Something down there is pushing my buttons, sweetie." The AI's sultry voice cut Nancy off. "Go to rack A74 module B. That houses the uplink error correction algorithms. What do you see?"

"Red." Jake stepped over the dead plant to look at the panel. "Can we move this thing?"

"Should be safe." Nancy grabbed what had passed for an arm, which felt curiously dry except for the goo drizzling from each golf-ball-sized hole. "Pete, give me a hand."

Pete grinned and made as if to clap, but stopped short at her glare and hurried to help. They dragged the inert mass out of the alcove and propped it up against the wall under an emergency light. It was good and truly dead, but for a crazy instant Nancy imagined the thing wearing a sombrero and taking a siesta under the red glow of a setting sun.

"Showing red link status, red packet integrity, and looks like ten to the negative second bit error rate," Jake reported.

"Oh, that's not good at all," QUEN said. "Let me shoot down a calibration and synch signal. Tell me what changes."

A quiescent little lump of green nestled among the red lights just below the tiny display screen Jake watched. Two lights to the right of the display quietly turned green.

"Error rate is dropping," Jake said. "Ten to the negative three, now four."

The surface of the small creature affixed to the panel pulsed, gently at first, then more rapidly. The green lights flickered on the edge of yellow.

"Increasing gain," QUEN reported.

The yellow flashes slowed momentarily, then sped up again.

"Errors escalating," Jake said as red flickered into existence on both indicators. The lights strobed between yellow and red for a few heartbeats, then burned steady crimson. "And now we're back to negative two."

The little cactus had swelled and shifted during the brief light show. Its roots wriggled like worms where they disappeared into ports and crevices. Now that the indicators were back to red, the creature again grew still.

"It's the cactus." Nancy's voice went high and squeaky with excitement. "The baby plant went all pulsing and squiggly. I think it squashed QUEN's signal. Now that things are shut down again, it's quiet."

"QUEN?" Jake poked at the small plant, but jumped back when it hissed.

"Interesting. Hang on. I'll issue a quick synch packet."

There was a momentary flash of green in the upper light to the right of the display. A spasm shot through the little cactus and the light flipped back to red. The cactus relaxed. Jake relayed what they'd seen.

"Very interesting." QUEN sounded intrigued. "Biomechanical interface, organic computing. Or at least enough to intercept data streams and muck about with my signals. Give me the list of components within a meter of each creature. I need to run a revised diagnostic routine."

Jake dutifully read off information from the front of each piece of gear. The highest plant up near the ceiling was apparently an overachiever. It sat between the racks, with needle roots extended out to either side to infiltrate two different components.

They stood back and watched the light show resulting from QUEN's diagnostics. Indicators flashed and went dark at a seizure-inducing rate. Nancy's head hurt, and buzzing filled her ears despite the silenced alarms. When the display subsided, red still dominated the panels.

"Smart little devils. Quick adaptation and now they've spread into my backup pathways. I can't circumvent them."

"Daft machine, just pull 'em off." Pete put action to words and strode to the nearest cacti before anyone could stop him.

"Wait!" Nancy yelled, but it was too late.

Pete jammed the barrel of his gun up under the creature and pried it loose. The needles stretched and began to slide out with the main body. The whole thing came loose with a ripping sound as several needle roots parted. Others slid fully free and whipped back against the gun. Pete threw the weapon down and clutched his right hand to his stomach.

"Bastard stung me!"

Jake unclipped one of the ever-present fire extinguishers from the bulkhead and advanced on the cactus-entwined gun. He brought the butt of the canister down three times with a resounding thwack, then gingerly pulled the gun away from the oozing mass with the tip of his wrench.

"See! That did the trick!" Pete cackled, then sucked air in through clenched teeth. "Damn, that stings."

The man was an idiot. Yet, most of the lights near the creature's perch now burned a steady green.

"Let me see your hand," Nancy said.

"None of your uppity analysis crap." Pete's strained laugh turned into a wince.

He scowled and extended his hand. Three long red welts crossed the knuckles where the needles had raked. The palm swelled like a balloon, and his fingers trembled.

"Stupid move. We've got to keep the poison from spreading." She fumbled in her first aid kit for a numbing agent and the antitoxin cream she and Drissa developed. "If this doesn't help, you'll need an injection. I have an anti-venom that should work, but need a syringe."

"Not a problem. Got a med locker on each deck." Pete relaxed as she slathered his hand, a bit of his cocky attitude returning. "Give me my gun back, greenhorn, and go get a longer stick to pry off those other critters. Stop making things so hard."

Pete snatched his weapon back from Jake, but fell silent when a series of dull clunks echoed down the passage. Nearby hissing made it sound like they stood amidst angry snakes. Red lights blossomed back to life where Pete had removed the cactus.

"Emergency fire suppression activated," reported a smooth, mechanical voice reminiscent of the ship's artificial intelligence, though it came from hidden speakers along the length of the passageway.

"QUEN?" Jake's voice cracked. "Override! Override!"

"Sorry, lover. No can do. Still blocked out."

"What is it?" Nancy asked.

"Nitrogen purge." Jake rushed to a red panel on the last equipment rack and flicked switches with abandon while avoiding the cactus squatting on the panel's face. "Flushing the area for fire suppression. Those distant thumps would have been airtight fire-doors closing."

"Who puts that kind of thing on a shuttle?" Nancy cried.

"Nothing worse than a fire in space," Jake shot back, then sagged and flipped one last switch. "It's a last-ditch effort for unmanned areas, but they've overridden the safeties."

"Two minute warning." Even QUEN's voice sounded strained.

"So bonehead here"—Nancy dropped Pete's hand in disgust—"triggered a defensive response."

"Hey!" Pete fell into sullen silence at her glare.

"Guess so," Jake said.

Little bits of root protruded from a port near the red lights. Their ends still twitched, directing things deep inside the equipment.

"They function without the plant. We have to remove the roots completely. Judging by the intact strands that stung Pete, the ones left might go back a foot or more."

"Front panels come off easy," Jake said. "But what then? Pick them out with tweezers? There's not enough time."

"Minus twenty-seven till snoozeville," QUEN added helpfully.

"Will the nitrogen put them to sleep too?" Jake asked.

Nancy shook her head. "The gas will displace carbon dioxide as well as oxygen, but the species here get a lot of their energy from intra-tissue sugars. We'll succumb long before they go dormant. We'd need an extra ten minutes, then maybe they would peter out and QUEN could take control again."

Jake spun to face Pete. "Run to the nearest repair locker and bring back emergency breathers. Go!"

Pete sprinted down the passage—really more of an awkward loping, but he was trying. She bit her lip. Ten minutes was only a guess. For all she knew, the things would be able to function for hours in a nitrogen environment. They would eventually go dormant, but there had to be another solution. She fingered her pouch. With the excitement of Pete getting stung, she'd neglected to secure her sample cutter and it rattled around in the bottom. The first aid kit also had spilled into her usually neatly organized bag. Even the small canister of neutralizing agent was loose.

"One minute," QUEN said. "Still no control from here."

The neutralizer had proven effective on all of the Dolor family they had encountered so far. It just might work here too. But given the response Pete's attack elicited, she was hesitant to spray them with something noxious, it might cause an even worse reaction. Did shuttles have self-destruct systems and overload settings like in the movies? Better to calm them down first, knock them out if possible. Her head buzzed as if full of bees. Was it getting hard to breathe? An idea slogged its way out of her jumbled thoughts. She clutched the sample cutter, blinked stupidly at its controls, and fumbled for the right setting.

"Freeze 'em," Nancy slurred and pushed past Jake. "They sleep, QUEN aborts, we live."

"Brilliant!" QUEN said. "Twenty-two seconds until nitrogen purge complete."

Nancy waved the little device across a panel. Frost formed on the composite surface, coating the small silver switches and black dials. Jake grabbed her arm and wrenched her away. Stupid kid thinks he has to be in control.

Well, she didn't want to die. She struggled, and her free hand connected with the side of Jake's head. Her wrist throbbed, a dull ache that made her dimly aware she'd just punched him. Jake shook his head, but rather than release her arm, forced the cutter toward a different panel.

"Controls fire suppression," he gasped. "Do this one first."

"Oh, right."

Her head drooped, but she let him guide her hand. As frost formed on the new panel and different plant, her eyes drifted shut. Sleeping would be so nice—fluffy pillows and soft blankets, a warm embrace and bodies pressed close. The man behind her whispered something. His breath tickled her ear, and she giggled. Then his sultry voice turned…feminine?"

"Got it!" QUEN called over the speaker system—not just the headset, but the hidden shuttle speakers too.

Nancy's head throbbed against the cold floor, but comforting warmth pressed along her left side. She blinked and wondered why so many switches and knobs had sprouted from the floor. The nearest was an inch from her nose, while others marched off into the distance in neat little rows.

Lifting her head seemed like too much effort, so she shifted her gaze down and found a green bulk encrusted in ice. Her world shifted ninety degrees with a nauseating flip. She'd blacked out and crumpled against the equipment racks, not the floor. The right side of her face was plastered to the controls. Well, more like frozen to them.

As up and down sorted themselves out, Nancy pried her chin and lips free of the frozen drool without losing much skin. The heavy warmth lying across her hip shifted as Jake levered himself up and turned bleary eyes on her.

"All good?"

They gently pulled the frozen cacti from the panel. The surprisingly tough roots slipped from the gear like long strands of pasta now that the plant was dormant. They nearly exhausted the power charge on Nancy's sample cutter, but worked along the equipment, freezing and removing the nasty intruders. Jake opened the front panel where Pete had torn the first creature loose and drew each root out by the severed end.

"Reestablishing control," QUEN said as they finished with the last panel.

"Is that all of them?" Jake asked.

There was no answer, but after a couple of minutes green flooded through the indicators in the alcove. The red lights along the passageway flickered into the normal harsh white just as Pete careened around the far corner and skidded to a halt.

"Got 'em!" Pete wore a clear plastic hood with a chemical oxygen generator dangling down either side of his face like white mutton chops.

Straps were looped haphazardly across his shoulders and a half dozen pouches containing emergency breathers flopped on each hip. He blinked at the white lights overhead, then at the green panels. His triumphant smile drooped as he pulled off his hood and shrugged off the breathers in a noisy clatter that masked the approaching footsteps.

"Hold it right there." The command full of menace came from one of the two large men who stepped around the corner opposite Pete.

Eyes still adjusting to the white lights, Nancy blinked into the glare and found herself staring down the barrel of a gun. This was not another overlong pistol like Pete's. The newcomer nearest her had what looked at first like a big log resting on his hip. The weapon's maw was ridiculously wide; a curious cat could get its head stuck in there.

The powerfully built men wore green para-military uniforms, though the second—Jay, whom she'd met down on the beach—carried a standard disruptor pistol that was thankfully aimed at the deck. The twins were remarkably similar, except the one pointing the cannon at them kept his thick blond hair in a tight Mohawk instead of a simple flattop and his features were somehow hardened—as if he trusted no one.

"Ray, it's okay. QUEN's back in control," Jake said as he screwed the panel face they had been working on back in place.

"Never pegged you for a saboteur," said the man with the cannon. "But Urneck figured something was up when you bugged the dame's datapad."

"What?" Jake turned to study the men, and his face grew tense. "We fixed the control node. The plants were disrupting things, so we froze them. Look!" He waved at the small pile of creatures they had removed.

"Or maybe"—Jay lowered his pistol and worked through his thoughts aloud—"your botanist girlfriend with the pod full of samples convinced you to bring them aboard."

"Why on Earth would I do that?" Nancy had barely exchanged a dozen words with these buffoons, but saw why Jake called this pair the granite twins. Why on Earth would she want to incapacitate their shuttle?

"Way I see it, you've been working with those lobsters and bugs." Ray snapped the business end of that cannon up a fraction. "They must know we're tracking them and sent you down to disrupt things. Figured we wouldn't catch on to a pretty, helpless woman nursing a sick slug. Played us for suckers."

"I'm telling you," Jake said. "Just freeze the little cacti and they pull right off. It's clear here, but we saw plenty more going after the cable runs. We can help. Just ask QUEN for god's sake." He spoke into the headset. "QUEN, tell them."

Jay seemed to consider the suggestion, but his brother cut in, gesturing with the big gun. "Captain grabbed control of QUEN's interface just after she broke through your locked fire boundary. He has her busy looking for other compromised equipment. We'll cool the two of you off in the brig. You know where it is; get moving."

Jake and Nancy turned to Pete, who stood among the nest of pouches looking dazed. His eyes shifted from them to the twins, and an ugly resolve settled onto the man's face.

"Yeah, get a move on!" Pete plastered on his signature grin, though his eyes lacked their typical mad shine.

Jay looked to Pete. "See any more surprises below?"

"More cacti in the overhead. They spread them out good. Came running through the airtight doors soon as I could."

"What's with all the breathers?" Jay scowled at Pete's feet, then shook his head. "Never mind, I don't want to know what goes on in your noggin. Just go see Urneck. We need to sweep the shuttle clean."

22. Brig and Cookies

"I DON'T know where she is." Herman leaned into the cockpit as he spoke.

Reemer wished the Lobstra would just go get his bed. He felt much better, but a long nap would help settle his stomach after that questionable rockfish. But Herman would rather stay with the pod and argue.

"Listen, young'un, we need her to confirm the new variables." Meinish's complaint rang from the pod's speakers.

It was good to hear the old searcher's voice. Reemer swallowed the wad of slime he'd been readying and scooted closer to the forest of spindly white trees that were Herman's legs. Things had been pretty confusing when they'd left the Lobstra main party. He'd hardly interacted with the old curmudgeon in those final days and now felt a pang of longing for the old searcher's company. Meinish always presented exquisitely tempting targets.

Well, opportunities would present themselves. In fact, a bit of slime set just right would cause the young searcher-to-be to lose his grip on the pod's sidewall. An additional bit of mucus behind Herman's tail might send him skittering into a backward slide with a belly-up skid in the wet sand at the lagoon's edge. Possibilities and potential outcomes swirled like colorful puzzle pieces. The tableau crystalized into a chain of cause and effect, the outcome an absolute certainty.

What's the point? Reemer swallowed the expulsion needed to set off that chain of events and nuzzled up against Herman's forelegs. The action should not have felt satisfying and cozy, but an odd warmth flooded his belly. Perhaps he wasn't fully recovered after all. He felt strange and off balance too, as if things inside had shifted around.

Herman looked down as Reemer made contact. "You haven't seen Nancy, have you?"

"Not since this morning. She spoke with one of the big guys while I hunted flat tasties. Probably went into the ship."

That couldn't have been just this morning. Each delicious flatfish restored a measure of health and cleared away the fog. But time flicked fitfully from one meal to the next, making it difficult to put events in the right order. Those jumbled thoughts had finally settled down to normal, discounting the fact he couldn't seem to stop nuzzling the Lobstra.

Nancy had gotten them here just in time and was stuck here on account of him. Not everyone was cut out to be a carefree adventurer. The human was tough and resourceful, but would have been dead a couple times over if it wasn't for a certain Squinch with the fortitude to venture inland and counter the angry forest. Reemer stretched to the side and used the shorter tactile antennae to preen each eyestalk in reflection.

On the other antenna, perhaps traveling and adventure were overrated. It might be nice to stay put for a while. A cozy little den would be nice, close enough to shore that the receding tide left pools for the little ones to splash about and explore.

"Wake up!" Herman emphasized the words with a poke from his foreleg, snapping Reemer's thoughts back to the present. "I could use some help. Go find Nancy."

Reemer shook out both antennae to stop the incessant grooming and pushed away from Herman. No more adventure, settling down? What a weird daydream.

"Yeah, yeah. I'm going." He left a trail of slippery mucus behind the Lobstra—not his usual well-placed prank, but chances were good Herman would take a spill while he was gone.

"Tell her to come out and talk to Meinish. They're ready to close in on the nectar."

"Sure, gotta have that nectar," Reemer muttered as the ramp to the human ship came into sight.

Odd for them to leave the doors wide open. Anything could just wander in and leave a gooey trail for the uppity humans. Reemer tried to muster excitement at the prospect, but the usual antics just didn't seem interesting today. Tricking the nastier crewmembers from last cycle would have to suffice. Reemer looked down at his glistening pale-yellow coat and nodded as understanding blossomed. Father might not be pleased with the change, but that maniac Urneck would be looking for a handsome green fellow. Reemer could glide right under the bully's nose without being recognized. That was sure to be fun!

Reemer slunk through what seemed like half the shuttle before encountering anyone. It took forever to work up to the top deck and sneak toward the commotion coming from the cabin just off the command bridge. Alien voices—oddly choppy, but perfectly understandable—came through the closed door, and Reemer shimmied up the wall to the observation port.

"Do you think this is funny?" Captain Gekko yelled at one of his big security people. "You can't just lock up the only other human on the planet. Especially when we reported her status to the navy's rescue ship."

Captain Gekko was easy to recognize from the Lobstra trade meetings. The other man was surely one of the twins that always did Urneck's dirty work, like trying to jettison a certain slug over a simple prank gone wrong. Like their mentor, the big men had no sense of humor. Sometimes, that made for an even funnier—if dangerous—outcome. Reemer had vowed to steer clear of this group, but the thrill of temptation sent a shiver through the Squinch's skirt. The thrill of being poised in a perfect position, an untraceable shadow, the invisible stalker—

"What the hell is all this slime!" bellowed an angry voice.

Urneck Grint rounded the corner. He seemed shorter than Reemer remembered, though to be fair, the human's head was down as he followed the slime trail. And of course Reemer was suspended above the deck, trying to melt into the doorframe. The door slid open and the captain rushed out. Gekko stood taller, but Urneck was beefy and wide. Their collision brought both men up short with a mutual grunt.

"Grint!" The captain recovered first. "Ray told me an interesting story. Get in here and explain why your men have detained Dr. Dickenson and my tech specialist."

"News to me, captain." Urneck forced joviality, but glared at Ray as if challenging the other man's right to speak to their superior.

The subtext had to be courtesy of the Lokii's translation ability because reading human expressions was usually frustrating. At least Urneck seemed to have forgotten about the slime. Reemer just wished the man would step fully into the room. As it was, he stood only couple of feet away. Just close enough for a wet thwack on the back of the head and—Reemer pushed down the thought and concentrated on being one with the wall.

"It isn't that bad," Ray interjected. "The navy don't know anything, and we saw them taking the control node apart. They had a pile of cactuses ready to plant inside."

"Cacti," the captain replied absently, then his eyes narrowed. "What doesn't the navy know?"

"Ray." Urneck snarled a warning.

The man gulped and looked from Urneck to Captain Gekko, clearly unwilling to explain.

"Fine, you tell me." Gekko turned to Urneck.

"Well, it's embarrassing. In the confusion of planting all those trackers and setting up camp, the response to the navy's advisory never went out." The captain's face flushed red and Urneck continued in a rush. "QUEN just figured it out today, when Jake and the girl were working an update. Might be a good thing. If they are sabotaging the shuttle, we can't trust their messages."

"They are not saboteurs." Captain Gekko's flat tone did not invite argument.

Urneck wisely fell silent, but Ray had missed the finality in his superior's voice. "But, sir, we saw them—"

"Enough! They have no motive. Plus, QUEN located the three big walking plants that spawned those baby cacti. For god's sake, you told me that there's even a dead one at the control node. Coincidence?" The captain half turned to Urneck, then spun quickly back to Ray, leveling a finger at the man, "Do not answer that! We're going to the brig."

The three men streamed from the room and the door hissed closed. Reemer breathed a sigh of relief as Ray—the last out—strode passed.

"And lock my door," the captain called back over his shoulder.

"I'll lock your freakin' door, old man. Last time I try to help," Ray grumbled as he glared after the others and slapped his hand down on the wall panel adjacent to the doorway.

Fat calloused fingers thumped Reemer squarely on the back. Gouts of milky yellow fluid erupted onto the offending hand. The sticky defensive ejection was eye-wateringly foul to ward off nasty ocean predators.

"Jesus!" Ray snatched back his hand and gagged.

The big man wiped his mouth with the back of his slimed appendage, doubled over, and vomited. The impressive volume and gooey consistency presented a riot of mingled hues, a truly admirable ejection.

While Ray majestically spewed, Urneck threw a fire blanket over Reemer and drew the ends together. The next few minutes were a blur of jouncing, jostling, and trying to untangle foot, face, and skirt. Although Squinch did not find their own defensive secretion nearly as repugnant as others did, it proved unpleasant in the close confines. Reemer was forced to reabsorb most of the material, and the reclamation process was not exactly enjoyable.

Fifteen minutes later, Reemer found Nancy. Unfortunately, taking pride in the accomplishment was difficult while thumping against Ray's backside.

Reemer had managed to poke an eye stalk out as they bumped down a ladder, but one passage seemed much like the next inside the human vessel, especially without the trail of pheromone-filled slime. Ray finally strode into a white room, while the captain and Urneck stayed near the door. Beyond the human's fat head, Nancy and Jake sat in what could only be the brig. The operations officer hauled Reemer inside, the sack slung over one broad shoulder. Reemer took smug satisfaction in the fact that saliva still dribbled from the corner of the man's mouth, and he held his left hand away from his body as if it were contagious. Serves him right!

Reemer's stomachs dropped as the floor rushed up and slapped against already sore skirting. The Squinch scooted over to Nancy and glared at Ray. The man smirked, made a rude gesture with one finger, and wiped his nose in contempt. But his eyes widened, the smug expression vanished, and he bolted through the doorway. Reemer nodded at the sounds of retching, then turned to Nancy.

"Hi there! Meinish needs to talk to you."

* * *

"Um, you're yellow." Nancy marveled at how much better Reemer looked, but his skin no longer held any green.

"Yeah, well no time for chit chat." Reemer shot a nervous glance at Urneck. "Come on, Herman has a comm link open."

"We aren't exactly free to go." She looked up as Captain Gekko stepped into the cell. "Are we?"

"Not at the moment." He looked embarrassed. "I need to understand what's been going on, but I don't have time right now. My ship is still in jeopardy. I'll be back to hear your side of the story."

"But, Captain—"

"Not now." The man was infuriatingly calm as he held up a hand to silence her. "I want to know what you are after, why this Squinch was spying on me, and why Mr. Farnsley was mucking about in the equipment racks."

Captain Gekko strode out the door, which slid shut with a hiss and blocked off Urneck's smiling face. It was in no way a friendly smile. Nancy sighed at the injustice. She'd just started to feel comfortable with Jake, maybe even with that crazy bastard, Pete. Now, they were accused of espionage—more like framed for it. Urneck couldn't possibly believe she and Jake had been trying to disable the shuttle. The man had a hidden agenda that put her, and by association Jake, on his hit list.

Jake sat a couple of feet away on the padded bench, and Reemer looked up expectantly. At least it was a nice cell. The small suite had a private bath and an adjoining room with bunk style beds molded into the walls. Hopefully, Captain Gekko would be reasonable and ignore whatever poison his second in command spewed.

"What's with Urneck?" Nancy asked.

Jake jumped then slumped back, elbows on knees. "He's mean, ornery, and pretty much controls the crew."

"What's he got against me—and you for that matter? What's he hope to gain?"

Jake was silent for a full minute, then surprised her by actually answering "Greed, I think. And control. The nectar is valuable. Like, buy a small planet valuable. He almost had it five years back, but some Squinch rooked him out of it by fouling his engines. The ship was mortgaged to the hilt, and he ended up losing it. So his disreputable crew signed on with Captain Gekko, mostly for the ride."

"The Lobstra use the nectar as a potent medicine," Nancy said.

That much was probably common knowledge. She omitted Drissa's description of how it prolonged the life of their matriarch. The human crew was clearly in competition with the other races, and disclosing privileged information wouldn't be wise.

"Hmm, could be," Jake replied. "I haven't given it as much thought as I should. No matter what the use, it must be damned near the rarest stuff in existence. One harvest funds a fully manned expedition, pays crew bonuses big enough to live on for years, and still leaves a whopping bankroll for the expedition lead."

"Is that the captain?" Nancy asked.

"I think it's Urneck Grint. The captain mutters about how little control he has on the ground. I get the feeling he's in it to pay off his ship and only gets a small bonus. Grint is really in charge down here."

That didn't bode well. Her expression must have turned somber to match her thoughts.

"Hey, it's not all bad." Jake forced some false cheer into his voice and sat straighter. "They're not going to dump you in a ditch or anything. Urneck wants something, probably your expertise. PhDs don't usually team up with the kind of crew we've put together. Maybe he wants to see if the plants can be cultivated off-world or something. Who knows, might make you famous."

"Oh god."

The last thing on her mind was how to propagate the species. She was much more interested in eradicating them, at least the Dolor family. She and Breena had already gene spliced several native virus strains, hoping to have one ready for release before the Lobstra left. With five years to thrive and spread, the next cycle might prove clear of the deadly Dolor variants. Hell, there might not be a cycle at all. Then the navy could sponsor a safe scientific survey.

Intellectually, Nancy understood the delicate balance of nature and how losing a single niche species or nuisance animal could have devastating repercussions. Earth's history was rife with examples of well-intentioned eradications and introductions that had gone wildly awry. But that didn't mean the Dolor shouldn't pay for the deaths and mindless violence.

"It'll be okay." Jake scooted close and put a comforting arm around her shoulders.

She huffed out a breath, let go of the anger and pain, and leaned into his warmth for a long moment before pulling away to think things through. Obsessing was no help, but she would have to come to grips with the potential impacts if they chose to unleash their virus.

Why did the Lobstra and humans find her so…what? Interesting, useful, threatening? Rather than actively hunting for the nectar, the human crew preferred tracking the alien groups. Yet staying put seemed to have made the human hunters a prime target. The other plant attacks had been defensive or in response to intrusion.

Oddly, Endeavor's destruction had been more disorganized and savage than the attacks on the Lobstra and the human shuttle. Unlike the hapless scientists, Captain Gekko's crew carried firearms, and seemed eager to put them to use. But the recent attack was more sophisticated, making brute force defenses less effective. Entering the ship and pinpointing the data systems was much more than a triggered defense response. An intelligence guided the assault. The puzzle pieces were not all there, but Nancy was willing to bet the breeders and their rooting offspring were Dolor specimens.

An hour later, Captain Gekko still hadn't returned to cast judgement, and the silence grew into a morbid, brittle thing. Jake rummaged through the desk for pencil and paper and sat down to draw.

"Low tech," Nancy commented over his shoulder.

He sketched out what was clearly an electrical schematic, but in addition to the angular circuits and familiar components, there were several squiggly lines that snaked through the picture, joining at the top of the page.

"Helps me think," Jake said absently. "All the software in the world can't let your mind free-form images like a pen or pencil."

"So what are you thinking?"

"Damned plants are smart. Here's where the roots from the cactus Pete tore off ended." He touched the tip of the pencil to where the ends of each curving line merged into the more formal representations of the circuitry. "The more I think about it, the less it looks like the random damage you might expect from a tree root growing into underground equipment. At the time, I was focused on removing the loose ends, not studying the thing, but damned near every strand found a critical component, a memory chip, or a buffer. Don't know what they were doing at the data nodes, but they sort of wrapped around the optic junctions in a way I'd swear was a passive tap, like they were reading the information flows for god's sake."

"Is that possible?" Nancy asked.

"You tell me, plant lady. Designers use taps all the time to pull info, but organic ones?"

Talk about sophisticated! There were plenty of examples of plants adapting to the stressors and manmade habitats. Root tip sensory capabilities allowed them to steer away from toxins and impenetrable substances, or toward beneficial nutrients. Some roots even sought out water flowing in sealed piping, as though they heard the liquid. But how could species that evolved on a planet devoid of technology adapt to do what Jake suggested? Darwin's head would explode.

Jake's sketches made her head spin. A solitary doodle in the lower left corner looked like an upside-down cactus. The roots came out of the top and cascaded down either side toward a rounded double-u. But the cactus had a smiling face. Happily attacking some sort of resistor, maybe.

"What's that?" Nancy pointing at the little drawing.

"Oooh." Reemer materialized beside her, both eyestalks craning over Jake's other shoulder. "Naughty."

"N-Nothing. Just doodling, it helps me think." Jake's left hand slid down over the image.

"She's not quite that top heavy," Reemer said. "Maybe if you added—"

"Ha…well. Damned plants," Jake cut in. He pulled open the narrow drawer, swept the desktop clear, and slammed it shut. The pencil gripped tight in his right hand tapped the plastic surface, a chattering, nervous sound. "Geez, the captain ought to be back by now. Don't ya think?"

Jake's neck turned red, then his cheeks and the tips of his ears. If not a cactus, then….oh. Oh! Heat radiated from him, or maybe her own face was getting pink. She grabbed the pencil to stop the agitating noise.

"A game!" she winced at the volume of her voice as she knelt to draw a board on the floor. "Tic, tac, toe. You've got to see Reemer play."

All three were laughing about strategies and the nature of diagonal lines when the door slid open. Even Reemer seemed to be thoroughly enjoying himself and had tried a number of antics to see the openings for a corner to corner win. Nancy looked up, expecting the captain, but Pete crab-walked sideways through the door, carrying a wide tray.

"Dinner." Pete set his burden down on the desk. "QUEN got the synthesizers reset."

"Where's Captain Gekko?" Nancy stood and examined their meals.

The smell from what looked like a stroganoff on two of the plates was enticing and the sides were real veggies and potatoes. A dead flatfish glistened from atop the third plate, detracting from the overall presentation.

"Caught it myself," Pete said proudly as she eyed Reemer's plate. "Cap's still going over damage reports. Watch the drinks. QUEN gets a little heavy handed with the alcohol."

Something slithered onto the table, skewered the fish, and withdrew. Nancy gave an involuntary shiver as Reemer dug into his meal. She focused on Pete, having seen more than her share of the Squinch's dining habits.

"You're in a good mood."

"Party night!" Pete's huge smile set brown and gray whiskers bristling from his apple cheeks. "Brig has the best vid display and tables out front. Whole crew's here." He pointed at the still open door. "More food and dessert where that came from, so stick your head out if you want any."

He swayed ever so slightly, his merry eyes glassy and somewhat vacant. She pointed at his bandaged right hand, thinking they'd overmedicated him for the cactus sting.

"Did you get anti-venom for that?"

Pete wiggled his fingers in front of his face, lost in thought for a moment. "Don't hurt none. Computer gave me a shot of anti-something."

He turned his palm toward her so she could see the wagging fingers poking from the white gauze. Without another word, he spun and headed back out to the common area, leaving their cell door wide open.

"That was odd." Nancy picked up a plate and headed for the bench.

"Not as strange as you might think." Jake grabbed the other meal. "Don't worry. QUEN monitors the medic stations. I'm sure Pete got what he needed. Those baby cacti were new, but she's got a complete analysis of the known local flora."

"That would be interesting to peek at."

Nancy and Jake ate in companionable silence with the bench angled away from Reemer. But that did little to block out the slurping and less savory sounds from the Squinch. In the main room, Pete joined Angie and one of the twins, probably Ray since Jake said they were a couple. The three sat on small white stools, and Pete leaned eagerly forward listening to someone out of sight.

A muffled male voice rose and fell with emphasis and animation, and the trio outside the door burst into guffawing laughter. Angie fell off her stool. Ray caught her arm as the beautiful blonde's butt plunked onto the floor. She laughed harder and pawed at Ray's arm, trying to regain her seat, which she finally managed after a couple of tries.

Pete gaped, an open-mouthed grin splitting his profile as he passed something between thumb and forefinger over to the couple. First Ray, then Angie raised the small tube to their face. Angie passed it on to someone out of sight. Nancy looked to Jake.

"See, not so strange, considering…" he spread his hands and shrugged.

"They're stoned!"

"That's a rather hippie way of putting it."

"Fine." Nancy scowled. "They're neurologically impaired on purpose. I didn't think spacers did that?"

"Spacers don't, but this group does. Don't worry. You won't catch the captain or me out there."

"It's not him or you I'm worried about."

Nancy was appalled. Her navy escorts and the science team knew the dangers of having impaired individuals working shipboard. Crewmembers were pulled from the watch rotation if the doctor put them on even a mild narcotic. The ramifications of poor judgement in space were just too extreme, the risks too high to take chances. Planet side was a little different. Even her expedition had held the occasional birthday or social gathering, with food and alcohol in moderation. It was a matter of degrees, she realized as she sipped at the vaguely mango flavored punch QUEN had prepared. "What are they using?"

"Hard to say." Jake put his empty plate on the bench. "I need something sweet. Wanna go check out the desserts?"

Seven people sat in the circle outside. The laughter and side discussions dwindled into silence as Nancy and Jake stepped through to the outer room. The crew sat in an oval with Urneck poised at the far end as if presiding over the gathering.

"Doctor, welcome. Did you enjoy the meal?" Urneck spread his arms wide, the benevolent monarch of his small realm.

"Yes." Nancy frowned down on Pete.

"You pompous, little—" Urneck grated out the words, trailed off, then plastered his fake smile back in place. "—darling. I see you're enjoying QUEN's mango mojitos. Care for a chaser?"

He held up a dull silver tube the size of a lipstick canister. It was what had been passed around the circle. Like makeup, there was a core stick of tan material poking from the end. With a smirk, Urneck closed his left eye and drew the stick across his eyelid as if applying eyeshadow. He considered for a moment and did the same to his right eyelid.

"Take it easy, boss," cautioned the woman to his left. "It's a new formulation."

"You worry too much, Dianne. I trust you cut it right."

The woman preened under the compliment, but bit her lip as Urneck held the drug out to Nancy with a challenge in his eyes. Dianne was lean and short, maybe five six with flaming red hair. A trim athlete to Angie's Slavic, muscular build. Nancy eyed the little tube, but made no move to reach for it.

"No, thank you. Don't want to mix my vices." She took a sip of her mojito, which really was delicious. A pleasant glow spread in her stomach, making it difficult to stay focused. She could really use some of those sweets Jake mentioned. "What's in it?"

"Your little cactus friends." Dianne said as Urneck nodded and lowered the tube. "Well, their venom at least. I separated out some of the nastier proteins and refined the remnants. Had to cut it way back with an inert base, added a little topical dilator, an absorption transmitter, and voila. Potent stuff, almost like the—"

"Enough!" Urneck rubbed his forehead, and Nancy wished him a killer headache. "Just go get some cookies."

Jake beat her to the dessert plate. Rather than traditional round cookies, the substantial pile of treats were cut neatly into two-inch squares. The dense little pound cakes had been liberally infiltrated by chunks of chocolate and peanut butter candy. Heaven!

23. Take a Hike

N ANCY STUDIED the subtle spiral pattern molded into the white ceiling of their prison. With the lights down low, she imagined drifting through swirling distant galaxies. The food and drink had provided a brief respite from her troubles, and the bit of alcohol let her fall asleep long enough for Jake and Reemer to finish arguing over the other bed. The posturing and name calling subsided to a peaceful quiet punctuated by Reemer's steady breathing. The Squinch lost the battle and curled up on the floor next to her cot. The sounds he made in sleep would have been embarrassing a few weeks ago, but now she found them as comforting as the heavy breathing of an old hound dog, albeit a gassy, slimy one.

The fact that Captain Gekko had not returned worried her. The crisis was past, or the man never would have let his crew party. That the captain hadn't joined in the frivolity and drug usage was a good sign. Harvesting natural compounds for recreational use was nothing new. The indigenous peoples of every continent held spiritual ceremonies centered on the use of mushrooms, peyote, curare, and many other substances. Herbalists and hedge witches had relied on wild plants to speed healing and soothe symptoms long before written histories were kept.

The Lobstra did the same thing with more advanced techniques to transform the local flora into medicine. Nancy thought of Drissa's pained description of how their matriarch's life had been artificially extended—an unnatural and unhealthy extension. The medical officer took a big chance speaking out against the monarchy's status quo, but Nancy had been a receptive audience who understood the dangers and addictive nature of potent medicine.

The glassy-eyed wanton stares of the crew last night were a perfect example of misuse. Thinking back on Grint's actions during the trade meeting and the wistful, haunted expressions that had flashed across the faces of the others at odd moments, Nancy wondered if the effects of their homemade entertainment ever really subsided. The humans acted like skittish street addicts going through the motions and wanting nothing more than the next fix. If it wasn't just her imagination, the situation was more dangerous and unpredictable than they'd thought.

The party used diluted compounds from the everyday nasties on Fred, and the mysterious nectar was powerful enough to lure numerous species across interstellar space. The casual term used for the prize originally had her thinking of the nectar as some sort of sugary ambrosia, perhaps prized for some religious significance. Its allure made more sense if the prize was a wildly powerful organic compound capable of yielding a fountain of youth drug or the quintessential narcotic. The Lobstra clearly sought the former to keep the current ruler in power. But trying to envision how potent the latter drug would need to be to draw people like Urneck Grint into this game made her head spin. A swish and hiss interrupted her train of thought.

"Psst." The sound came from the door. "You awake in there?"

"Lights," Nancy said and squinted against the glare until she could make out a grizzled face poking through the doorway.

"Geez, too early for lights." Pete shaded his eyes with his right hand and a sack of silvery cloth hung from his left. "You need to get up and get going."

"What're you talking about, old timer?" Jake asked through a drawn-out yawn.

"Ain't so hard to understand. Look, I brought you food too." Pete held the sack in front of him, a thin smile touching his lips. He looked back over his shoulder briefly, then nodded encouragingly. "Door's open, just take it and get out while you still can."

Nancy swung her feet to the floor and immediately regretted it when her bare soles touched down on Reemer's wet back. She ignored the sudden urge to disinfect her feet, crossed her arms, and glared at Pete. The wiry man flinched, but managed to look her in the eye.

"We're waiting for Captain Gekko," Nancy said. "He'll see reason and realize we were not the ones trying to disable this ship, no matter what people have told him."

Pete dropped his eyes, then tried to look back up but seemed incapable of meeting her gaze again so turned to Jake. "You know I'm not one of them, not really. I did you wrong, but Urneck wasn't going to listen to me. If I bellyached, I'd just have landed in here with you. They're all going to be sleeping it off, but the ship's moving this afternoon. You gotta git!"

"We'll wait," Nancy said.

"Ain't no captain coming down to listen!" Pete wailed, turning back to her. "The fools got out of control last night. Gekko's gone. Grint's taken over, and he's gonna keep you caged up 'till he needs you."

"They killed Captain Gekko?" Jake jumped to his feet.

"Nearly as bad. Run him out into the wild with nothing but the clothes on his back." He turned back to Nancy, forestalling the question she was about to ask. "Yeah, they ran off your lobster friend too. The situation got pretty tense. That boy is hardy. I thought he was going to make a fight out of it, but he got smart before things turned ugly."

Nancy slumped, her hands dropping to her sides. Cool dampness pushed under her left palm, and she absently stroked the top of Reemer's head. With Herman and the captain gone, where could they go? Grint would just round them up again at his convenience.

"There's a message from your friend in here." Pete's glare softened and he stepped over to the cot. "He insisted on that much. Grint tossed it into the recycler, but I grabbed it when they turned in. I put a decent pistol and first aid kit in here too."

He pushed the sack into her lap. The bulky weight was oddly comforting, and dangling straps let it be worn like a backpack.

"Nancy?" Reemer poked at the pack, eyestalks beseeching with puppy dog eagerness.

"Where would we go?"

"Plan later, move now," Pete said, as if she had made a decision. He glanced over his shoulder again, then pulled a datapad from his pocket. "Doors are on override for another thirty minutes. It's the best I could manage."

Nancy looked from the Squinch to Jake and nodded.

"I need a few things from my shop." Jake pulled on his shoes. "And more of those cookies."

By the time they wound through the sparse coastal forest, pale purple light blossomed over the water. Each sported a pack of sorts. Under Pete's constant urging to hurry, Jake had frantically stuffed a rucksack with a random assortment of gadgets, tools, and equipment from his workroom. Reemer wore a harness that Jake had cinched around the Squinch. Several small pouches hung from the webbed material, and three handheld lights were hooked through loops across his back. As they moved away from the human's shuttle, thick sallow mucus welled up around the harness, fouling the silver grip of each light. There would have to be a pretty compelling need for illumination before she'd be grabbing one of those.

Pete stayed behind, claiming he would be fine due to his "damned near ironclad alibi." He'd wished them well, and even given Jake a hesitant pat on the back as the three headed off along the trail the captain had supposedly taken. Pete was skilled enough to follow in the other man's wake with ease, but stoutly refused to join them, saying, "I'll be damned if Urneck's gonna run me off!" Then he'd erupted into his disturbingly gleeful cackle and promised to cover their tracks to slow any pursuit. The three made good time despite Reemer returning to his habit of pin-balling from one side of the trail to the other.

"What's he doing?" Jake finally asked, as they cut across a wide-open swath of ground and Reemer shot out to the left, hit the natural rock formation that roughly outlined the area, and then careened far to the right.

"Believe it or not, he's following us," Nancy said with a grimace. "Remember the tic-tac-toe game? Same thing. He just isn't wired to see or move on diagonals."

"But he didn't do that in the ship."

"I think it depends on his perception." Nancy shrugged. "Manmade passages can fool him. If his brain doesn't think the diagonal is there, then he doesn't see one and therefore needn't resort to using right-angled paths."

Chew on that, techno boy! She grinned at how well that statement came out. Jake's jaw worked open and closed, but the poor guy couldn't muster a response. He was pretty when flustered. Mark one up for the older woman. Jake gave up with a shrug, which made the well-muscled cords along his clavicle stand out under the olive-drab pack straps. Slightly older, she amended, stifling a laugh—just slightly.

They headed north, rapidly putting distance between themselves and the humans. The thin deciduous tree line coalesced into thick tropical forest. Most of the trees were benign. They did have to skirt a solitary needler tree that stood along Captain Gekko's path through the woods. At the outset, they couldn't have been more than a few hours behind the man. The occasional footprint and smashed bit of underbrush made it hard to tell if they were gaining, but following should be faster than breaking trail. The man didn't seem to have a destination in mind. His path wandered east and west, as if he searched for something.

Just past noon, they heard a distant rumble and hurried to the crest of the next ridge, carefully skirting the purple flower field of a net vine. A shuttle rose above the treetops to the south and moved off to their left, heading toward the plateau.

"They're running late." Jake took a swig of water, then offered the bottle to Nancy.

Pete had packed plenty of food along with some basic survival stuff and the pistol, but he hadn't thought to ensure they had potable water. Luckily, Jake had grabbed a few self-filtering canisters. Nancy took the bottle. The tepid water was bland and oddly dry, the taste apparently filtered right out of it.

"We've come what, maybe ten miles?" she asked.

"Twelve according to my handheld. I get fixes from QUEN. Captain probably doesn't have that luxury, but it looks like the old man finally figured out where he was."

"Why do you say that?"

They pushed to their feet and walked along the ridge to the point where the captain's trail came up from below. It crested from their right and immediately dove back down the far side to the left.

"Sorry, thought you noticed." Jake pointed along the line of crushed vegetation. "After resting at the last rise, he shifted course. Captain's been traveling straight along north by northwest ever since. So I figure he finally got his bearings."

"Lucky he hasn't run into something nasty in the underbrush. Where's he headed?"

"Salt marsh, if he circles the inlet shallows." Reemer pushed past the humans into the underbrush, forcing them to follow in his wake. "And it isn't luck. The forest always settles down when the hunt moves inland."

That welcome news opened up a big question. How did the forest track the hunt's progress across such a vast and varied landscape? Although many of the aggressive plants fell into the Dolor family, there was no indication they or the other species formed a communal organism. Large single organisms like the vast mango groves in equatorial regions were suspected of conveying information on climate conditions and fires across thousands of square miles using rudimentary neural pathways in their underground root system. But the hunt moved to arid high plains, a region too dissimilar to the forest and swamps to have any chance of a common system of roots.

"Why would Captain Gekko head into a swamp?" Nancy wondered aloud. "Sounds like hard traveling, unless he plans to raft across the inlet."

"No, wait." Jake stopped in his tracks, and Nancy nearly plowed into him as he stared at the map on his screen. "He's heading for Endeavor! Your original landing site is about fifteen miles beyond the inlet and swamp. If he doesn't cross at the ocean, he'll have to ford the river somewhere along the way."

Her old team's site? Nancy's stomach clenched. Early on, she'd tried to find survivors because there just wasn't anywhere else to go, but now the thought made her queasy. Had the rains been enough to wash away the blood?

"Makes sense." Nancy spoke her thoughts aloud. Anything to keep the memories from welling up. "Endeavor will have supplies and equipment. He might even be able to get off a distress call if the communications gear still functions."

"Shortest path is across the inlet. My money's on him crossing there. Cap's crazy about water. Says it's just like zero-g, except with resistance to swim."

"That will be interesting." Reemer giggled with dainty little puffs and only a light spray of mucus, an almost pretty sound compared to his usual guffaws and spurting slime.

"What are you talking about?"

The Squinch continued to chortle. His newly acquired yellow hide grew vibrant, contrasting with a network of darker striations along his head and neck. The pattern resembled the cracks and fissures in elephant hide, a pleasing effect that accented the rich golden hue.

Nancy's question went unanswered for the better part of the afternoon until the landscape made a final fitful climb to a ridge overlooking the inlet. The landscape flattened out a hundred feet below, sweeping forward as the ever-diminishing trees and scrub reluctantly gave way to reeds and grass. The inlet shimmered turquois blue, the water color fading to dark green then finally brown off to the right, where the river mouth drained from the swamp. A crescent of sandy beach swept off far to the left.

The tang of open saltwater warred with earthy vegetable odors from inland. Whitecaps blanketed the blue water, out of place given the gentle breeze and interspersed with green and yellow bodies. What Nancy had mistaken for wave crests continued well up onto the sugar-white beach.

"What the heck is that?" Jake squinted at the scene below.

"The Gathering." Reemer sighed and scooted along the rise to the right. "The captain must have headed into the swamp after all. The river has shallows a few miles north, we'll probably catch him there."

"Hold on." Nancy hurried to block Reemer's path as he picked up speed. "Are those Squinch down there?"

Reemer shot a casual glance at the water far below, then to the left and right as if working out how to bolt around her. For once, his inability to shoot off at a random angle worked in her favor.

"Like I said, it's The Gathering." Reemer shifted left and huffed when she moved to block him again.

"I've got him." Jake pointed to the sand spur separating sea from inlet. "That bigger dark blob. He's wearing camo."

"Good eye. Gotta be the captain." Nancy's glare had Reemer wilting. "If I didn't know any better, I'd say you didn't want to go down there."

"Whaaat? N-No," Reemer half wheezed, half stuttered. "I just didn't see any humans." He reared up and extended his eye stalks. "Just trying to save time, but I see him now. Lead on, doctor!"

She'd never had cause to question the alien's eyesight. Then again, she and Jake did have a distinct height advantage. At her nod, Jake headed down the slope, carefully skirting clumps of feathery brown sea grass. Reemer bobbed his head, but waited patiently for Nancy to go next.

"After you," she said with a shallow bow.

Reemer looked like he might protest. But his skirt rippled, and he bounced from left to right down the slope, grumbling about humans refusing to walk straight.

The narrow spit of sand sat a half mile off and divided the marginally rougher water from what would normally have been a calm inlet. At that line of demarcation, the whitecaps changed, taking on multi-colored hues. The sheltered water teamed with Squinch, thousands of them.

The beach held half again as many slugs, a riot of green and yellow against the sand extending to the seagrass covered dunes below. The shimmering press of bodies thinned out toward the ocean, but a knot of green with one notably larger upright form stood at the base of the sandy point. A massive dark-yellow Squinch stood with the half-dozen green slugs surrounding Captain Gekko.

24. Prodigal Daughter

"A PRISONER has no rights," the yellow slug said as they approached the spit of sand.

Galactic Trade Standard wasn't the best language for expressing complex ideas, but it was one that both Squinch and humans could manage. Deep in argument, the group didn't notice them approach. Nancy pressed up behind Jake as she strained to make out the accusations being flung at the solitary human by the slugs blocking the narrow patch of sand. She looked around in mild panic, but Reemer was close on her heels.

"Please be reasonable, ma'am." Captain Gekko turned his palms skyward. "I just need to get across the water. Then I'll be out of your hair...uh, out of your slime."

He crouched, putting his eyes on a level with the Squinch that had drawn itself up tall and exuded a curiously haughty air. The captain addressed it as ma'am, and there was an underlying female quality to the imperious tone. She was dark yellow, nearly orange, with sensory antenna of burnt sienna that jabbed accusingly at the bedraggled human.

The captain may have avoided major predators, but the underbrush had not been kind. His fatigue-style uniform resisted rips and tears, but dirt and burrs clung to sleeves and pant legs. Gekko's waves of black hair were a rat's nest of confused curls over a weary face. Scratches, gashes, and grime covered his face and hands. Despite the dark circles under them, his gray eyes sparkled with suppressed amusement. She couldn't tell if he'd spotted them coming up behind the slugs.

"Very funny." The female Squinch didn't sound amused. "Trespassing on a sacred ceremony is punishable by…by…" she fumbled to a halt and looked to the olive-green slug on her left. "Herbert, what have we done with prior interlopers?"

Herbert rubbed his sensory antennae in front of pursed lips, as a human might wring their hands. His eyestalks arched down to watch the motion as he answered. "We've made them bring fresh fish for everyone, barred them from playing pick-the-shell—oh, last cycle I gave a stern talking-to to that Benny, morose lad. Do you know that he once made a motion for us all to start building houses? I asked him what a house was, and he prattled on about odd dwellings that humans made from…" he trailed off, finally noticing the annoyed glare the female had turned on him. "And there's always—"

"Death! Yes, of course." She nodded as if in agreement with her befuddled cohort and swung her gaze back to the captain.

"Now, Belinda, there's no call for that," Herbert cried, seeming to regain his mental bearings. "I'm the mayor, and I won't be killing any humans over an accident. It would be bad for business."

"Excellent point!" Captain Gekko smiled.

"Now don't go trying to cozy up to the head slug. He's far too busy to see to a proper punishment." Belinda bulled toward the human and swept her eye stalks back to Herbert. "Nothing says we can't get ourselves a new mayor."

"If I may?" Jake called out as he strode between the startled guards and stopped just short of Captain Gekko.

The guards had been focused on the exchange and seemed thoroughly unable to decide if letting more people onto the spit of land was acceptable. Nancy followed Jake's lead with an apologetic smile for the poor fellows. Reemer tried to slide in the opposite direction, but she grabbed the harness and hauled him along. After a moment of initial resistance, he followed, flapping his skirt loudly and giving the guards a smug little glance. The baffled group whispered amongst themselves, but Nancy kept her attention glued to the pair in front of her.

"Why hello there!" The mayor bubbled with cheer, happy for the distraction.

"No, no, no," Belinda cried, her leathery mantle turning crimson as she whipped her head between the new arrivals and the captain. "These are closed proceedings. The sanctity and reverence of The Gathering must be maintained. I will not allow—"

Wild laughter, three intertwined bodies, and a geyser exploded from the surface to their right. The Squinch's declaration cut off as buckets of slimy water crashed down, drenching them all. The guards were far enough back to avoid the fallout. They erupted into guffaws that quickly subsided under a wet, angry glare from Belinda. The oblivious revelers moved off without a backward glance.

"I am certain our trespass is quite upsetting, and recompense is due." Jake continued without missing a beat, fished in his pack, and offered two round mirrors to the angry Squinch.

Belinda's demeanor changed in an instant. Her entire body flushed, replacing the angry orange tinge with pale gold similar to Reemer's coloration. Even the mayor's hide lightened several shades. He inched forward, oohing and ahhing over the gift until Belinda slapped at his reaching antenna with one of her own.

"Well, this changes things." The female Squinch giggled, ignoring a hurt look from the mayor. She grasped each small round mirror with a sensory antenna and turned them left and right to get a better view of herself. "Yes indeed!"

The gift allowed Jake and his captain to rationally discuss crossing the inlet in a way that wouldn't incur the wrath of the mighty Squinch nation. The Squinch frolicking and games had more in common with a college frat party, but Belinda insisted The Gathering was a reverent event and that the humans wait a day before crossing the inlet or its headwaters. They could head north into the swamp and cross the river inland, but the passage would be difficult and take even longer. In the end, Captain Gekko agreed to camp out, build a raft, and stay out of the water so as not to disturb the proceedings.

Reemer remained notably absent during the negotiations for safe passage. While Jake erected a sun shelter near the dunes—really just a hyper-thin reflective tarp stretched over a depression and propped up by driftwood—Nancy plopped down near her subdued friend. She couldn't sit too close, because Reemer huddled in the center of a glistening circle of slimy sand.

"Why so glum?" Nancy asked as she watched Jake work.

The tech had stripped to the waist. Rather than the average build she'd expected, his uniform hid broad shoulders, a flat stomach, and even a bit of a discernable swell to his biceps. His too-pale skin soaked up the sunshine. He caught her watching, gave a nervous half-smile, and turned away to finish laying rocks along the trailing edge of the enclosure.

"Just don't like being here," Reemer answered wetly.

"Why not head down to the water and talk with your friends?" Was he pouting?

"I better not."

Reemer sounded wistful, but shivered as he watched the cavorting tangle of Squinch at the water's edge. Dozens of slugs dozed on the nearby beach, but those swimming were active and playful. Couples and small groups dotted the surface, splashing, laughing, twining around each other, and generally having a grand time. More would be underwater. Nancy was uncertain if the slugs had gills, but she'd seen Reemer stay down for an hour with ease.

Her friend seemed to have fully recovered, but lacked the enthusiasm and gusto she had grown to expect. Although learning to appreciate his humor and modes of expression had been trying, she preferred that to dealing with a brooding, miserable Squinch. There had to be something she could do to cheer up the little guy.

"Almost ready," Jake called over his shoulder as he knelt to drive a couple makeshift stakes into the sand.

Jake's bare back was to them, his waistband riding a bit too low and providing an exceptional target of opportunity. Maybe it was time for one of those well-timed Reemer attacks. Nancy elbowed the Squinch, ignoring how it slimed her sleeve.

"Bet you can't hit that," she whispered.

"Ooh?" Reemer's eyestalks swiveled to the unsuspecting man, mucus gurgled, but the sound trailed off and the slug's antennae drooped. "Na, poor guy would freak out."

Reemer sighed and went back to making circles, smoothing the sand into a flat gooey mess with his tail end.

"Are you okay?" Nancy asked.

"Drop it." With an angry shake, Reemer trundled along the perimeter, expanding his gooey area and forcing Nancy to roll out of the way.

"You don't have to bite my head off." Nancy stood and dusted sand from her butt. "Come on, Jake. The captain's going to need help with the raft."

They found Captain Gekko near the far end of the inlet where the water turned murky. He worked to untangle a giant pile of driftwood the swamp had disgorged. The wood sat high and dry, presumably driven onto the shore by storm surges over the years. There didn't seem to be any living wood, which was a relief, but some of the branches were so brittle that they snapped and sent up billows of dust.

Over the course of an hour, the three separated branches and logs by length and diameter. Jake produced a cylinder of industrial-strength twine. The captain tied a rectangular frame together, and they all helped lay in cross pieces to build a rough deck and support braces.

"Beautiful!" Jake proclaimed as he secured the last branch.

"Really?" Nancy eyed the end result with skepticism, trying to envision the four of them paddling the awkward thing ten yards, let alone half a mile to the far shoreline.

"Well, there's plenty of room and the logs are solid." Jake hauled the nearest corner a few inches off the ground to prove his point. "It's wood, so it ought to float. What's not to love?"

"How do we steer?" Nancy asked. "Or even get it to move for that matter?"

The raft measured eight feet long by five wide, or—more precisely—that's about what it averaged. Without power tools, they had simply matched up the best logs by length and snapped off as many excess branches as possible. Nancy's sample cutter trimmed the occasional springy branch, but was useless on anything bigger than half an inch around and it ran out of juice fast so needed time to recharge. The result was a ragged monster-raft with deck planks of varying length that resembled the jagged teeth of some sort of carnival aberration. The craft would probably spin in circles all day long.

"Just need to get her launched and out a ways with these." Captain Gekko threw two skinny poles onto the deck. "The mayor agreed to tow us across."

Unfortunately, they couldn't even test out the vessel's stability because of their promise to not set foot in the water. As evening approached, the humans retired to Jake's accommodations to brainstorm ideas and play a few hands of a timeless classic, spacer poker.

"The science mission will have line-of-sight satcomm gear." The captain raked in chips from his winning hand and dealt the next.

He fired the cards like bullets from a machine gun, each skidding to a stop with suspicious precision in front of a seated player. The game was five card draw. Nancy didn't know if Captain Gekko's voracious appetite fueled his winning streak, but it was going to be difficult to tally things up. They played for nutro-chips, and the man was crunching down nearly as many as he bet. The tiny brown crackers tasted of salt with a hint of caramel and were magically satisfying. So far, no one had ventured to bet one of the delicious cookie bars. Once that happened, the game would officially be high stakes.

"I'll take two." Jake pushed his discards back to the dealer and accepting new ones. "Line of sight won't be useful until the navy ship is nearly here. We'll need to run out some sub-space messages first. The advisory response is a priority, otherwise they could end up on the wrong side of the planet."

"Forget the navy. LOS gets me QUEN," the older man replied.

"Oh, right." Jake frowned down at his cards. "But Grint will have security lockouts in place by now."

"I'm good." Nancy waved away the need for new cards. "Captain, we have to contact the authorities. The navy needs to look for other survivors."

"Just Veech, Nancy. I'm not the captain of anything right now. Look, we have an ace in the hole. Young Jake here can crack through any roadblocks on my ship's computers. But if the long haul communications gear still works, we'll send out your status. I promise. Cards?" This last was to Reemer.

"I dunno." The Squinch's eyestalks stretched and swiveled, examining his hand from every conceivable angle.

"You're gonna wear the spots off!" Jake blurted out. "Man up and play."

"What's that supposed to mean?" Reemer shot back, eyes pulling in tight against his head. "Oh, right, the game. Pass."

"And a lucky one for me." Veech drew one blue diamonded card from the top of the deck.

A rustling at the low doorway caught Nancy's attention. Two figures oozed into the tent, blocking the fading sunlight. Jake flicked on his portable lantern, casting the two Squinch into harsh relief.

"Oh, this looks fun. A game?" The mayor leaned forward to examine the chips and cards spread across the silvery blanket serving as their table.

"A game of chance," Nancy said. "Mindless fun. We could teach you."

"Yes, yes, dear." The golden-toned female called Belinda cut her off. She still clutched one of Jake's mirrors in the prehensile tip of her right antenna. The Squinch paused occasionally as she spoke to eye her reflection. "Just checking up on you. Mayor Breem and I are a bit too old for the ceremonies of The Gathering. We did scoot down to the contraption you built, very impressive."

"Thank you." Veech pried his way into the one-way discussion. "Will towing it be a problem?"

"Not at all." Belinda gave a vague wave with her free antenna. "Herbert will take care of the details."

"Quite right," the green slug agreed after a moment's hesitation. "The festivities should conclude by midday tomorrow."

"Sacred ceremonies," Belinda corrected.

"Of course, of course." The mayor wrung his antennae together. "A little rest and the lads will get you three across before dark. You can count on us." He puffed out what passed for his chest in pride, and Nancy grinned in spite of his count being off.

"There's four, sir. You haven't met—" Nancy waved at Reemer to make introductions, but his spot at the makeshift table stood empty except for a slime trail, stack of chips, and five cards face up, four queens and a deuce. "Well, we also have a Squinch with us."

"That is highly irregular," the mayor blustered. "Some poor nomad from a distant colony, I'd wager. Haven't had visitors here in forever. Have we, dear?"

The mayor looked to Belinda, who Nancy was starting to suspect actually ran things in the Squinch kingdom. But his companion had gone back to preening in her mirror.

"Well he's around here some place," Veech interjected. "Nice fellow, by the name of—"

"Reemer!" Belinda cried.

The female slug spun around, releasing a spray of mucus that slapped wetly across the humans and mayor, although Nancy doubted the latter noticed. Nancy blinked through the slime. Reemer was halfway out the door, having skirted around the shadowy edge of the enclosure. Belinda had spied him in the mirror as he tried to sneak out.

Reemer cringed and slumped under the other slug's gaze. "Hi, Mom. Hi, Dad."

"My baby!" Belinda rushed forward to lay her head across Reemer's neck.

"When you said the mayor had you guarding that island, you never mentioned he was your father." Nancy had to wonder at the way his mother cooed and fussed.

Those early days after the attack remained a blur, but she'd gotten the distinct impression watching the floating island had been an excuse to get her socially awkward friend out from underfoot. But the spineless mayor seemed more of a figurehead. Belinda must have come up with the assignment to keep Reemer away from trading sessions with the alien visitors. So why was she so happy?

"Didn't want to brag," Reemer managed around the fussing… What, first lady—first slug?

"Here, dear, your skirt needs to fan out more, and do try to arch your neck gracefully, it's ever so much more attractive. Oh, I have a salve that will help heal those dry patches. Watch how it's applied." Belinda pushed one of her prized mirrors at him.

"Finally, some breathing room." The mayor sighed with relief. "Belinda's always wanted a daughter." Tension drained from the Squinch, softening the lines of his torso and neck as he turned languid, happy eyes back to the game table. "What do you call this?"

"Poker. It's a card game," Nancy said as his words sunk in. "Wait, Reemer isn't a girl."

"Not much of one." The mayor waved dismissively. "Still cringes and pouts like a boy. But fear not, Belinda will whip Reemer into shape. Not in time to mate tonight, of course." He poked at the jack of spades with his right sensory antenna. The card stuck fast, and he held it in front of his face a moment before deciding to gnaw at its edge. "I'm surprised he changed so young, but it's probably for the best. Reemer was an exasperating son, always off exploring, trying new ideas, and generally being far too pushy. He'll make a wonderful daughter."

Species capable of changing gender were rare, but not unheard of. Still, the thought of her crude and rude friend as a girl just felt wrong. Thinking back, Reemer hadn't been his old jovial self since recovering from the brink of death. He'd—or rather she'd—been subdued, less interested in juvenile antics, and increasingly introspective. But then, hormones would do that to a girl.

"He almost died, you know." Nancy couldn't help defending her friend. "We went inland for a couple of weeks and it hurt him. Nightly salt baths weren't enough, so we came back to the ocean."

"Ah, that could well have accelerated the change." Mayor Breem nodded—a ridiculous gesture with the playing card still plastered to his antenna. "Like I said, the boy never had much common sense. Tell me about your adventures."

The Squinch leaned forward expectantly, the sodden jack hanging forgotten from the end of his antenna. For someone who condemned Reemer's adventurous nature, the mayor certainly seemed ready for some vicarious thrills. Nancy looked to the doorway where Belinda merrily, but firmly, hustled Reemer outside to get a better look. Jake and his captain moved off as the game stalled out and pawed through their meager gear. There was little else to do, so Nancy sat opposite Mayor Breem and did her best to weave a tale of wonder and adventure under the glowing lantern.

The Mayor's rapt attention and coaxing pulled Nancy through everything from her Earth-side training to the quirk of fate that brought the Lobstra in contact with the Lokii's strangely infectious telepathy. Though thoroughly enthralled, the mayor was no ignorant savage. He pressed for details about the various Dolor sub-species and confirmed that the physical stress to Reemer's system likely triggered his sex change. But she nearly choked to death on a nutro-chip when Mayor Breem offered a shockingly graphic hypothesis about Urneck Grint's formative years and over-compensation issues.

Nancy woke late. Jake still snoozed on the far side of the gaming blanket, so she hustled outside to scrub her teeth and take care of other pressing business. Captain Gekko bent over the distant raft and double checked the bindings. Squinch lay along the shoreline like washed up seaweed, but there was no sign of Reemer.

She smiled at the memory of last night and headed back to their makeshift tent as hundreds of Squinch stirred into sluggish wakefulness. Green bodies disentangled themselves from the lighter, yellow slugs and made their way to the water. The creatures had settled into pairs or groups of three, always with a single yellow female. One larger group of five males fell asleep entwined around their chosen mate. Lucky girl. Nancy enjoyed the idea of the harem concept turned on its head for a change.

The aliens' internal clocks were well synchronized. The slow awakening rapidly turned into a virtual stampede as nearly every Squinch moved toward the water. Down the beach, a dark blob sat low just off the shoreline. Captain Gekko had launched the raft, and it sped toward her. The man clung to an upright spur and waved frantically.

"We've got company!" Jake burst from the tent, backpack slung over his shoulder and a beeping gadget in his hand.

"What is it?" Nancy rushed to meet him.

Jake pressed the pistol into her hand and returned his attention to the device. "A pod's coming up from the south. Grint's found us."

Wind played across the dunes, making the tall grass sway and point the way inland. Morning sun slanted down the sparse ridge standing quiet sentinel above the sand. Behind them, splashes punctuated the burbling chatter of hundreds of Squinch as the aliens entered the water en masse.

"Nothing there," Nancy said.

"Listen." Jake cocked his head to the side.

The low whir of a single engine rose above the noise, and a dirty smudge above a break in the rocky ridgeline resolved into a rising column of dust. The device beeped faster until the frantic warning blended into a single tone.

"Definitely one of our pods." Jake flipped off the alarm.

"Why would that drive the Squinch off the beach?"

The abrupt cessation of the alarm left them listening to the crash of bodies hitting the water, the distant engine's whine, and a whumping thud like a load of bricks being dropped over and over.

"Get off the beach!" Captain Gekko yelled and pointed off to their left where the rocky ridge jutted out into the dunes.

His raft slowed to pick its way through the fleeing slugs. Water churned along the aft edge of the ungainly boat, an outboard engine made up of four Squinch with eyestalks poking up just above the deck. How on Earth did they see where they were going?

Another whump had them backing toward the water across a suddenly empty expanse of sand. A blaring bugle-call rolled across the beach as a large mottled form oozed around the rocks beyond the dunes. The Slurg spied them and barreled forward on a wave of slime that left shells and sand suspended in gelatinous tracks to either side in its wake. Dealing with the last giant slug she'd encountered had taken a lot of firepower. Their lone pistol was next to useless, but maybe a couple well-placed shots could blind—

The thought died as another massive form slid around the jutting rocks, followed by a third. Her feet splashed in the shallows as the three Slurg bore down on them.

25. Back to Square One

T HE RAFT bobbed thirty yards away. Captain Gekko yelled over the stern, trying to coax the Squinch closer to shore. They refused.

"Take a shot." Jake danced in waist deep water trying to keep his backpack dry.

The trio of Slurg crossed half the distance to Nancy and Jake in a mad, bugling dash with eyestalks tucked in tight to their heads. With a rifle, she might blind one. But they came on too fast to possibly get them all, and the pistol didn't have that kind of accuracy. A fourth shadow emerged from behind the rocks. Just what we need.

But the dark gray vehicle hovering above the sand was no alien mollusk. A gout of flame shot from the nose of the squat vessel, impacting with a whoosh behind the trailing Slurg and singeing the beast's skirt. Judging by the burst of speed the creature put on, running wasn't an option. The raft floated off to her right, the terrified Squinch floundering in confusion despite the captain urging them closer.

"Guess it's time to go back to the brig," Jake said. "That pod's loaded with a weapons package. It's a slower configuration, but plenty fast enough to catch us—even on the raft."

"If we don't become slug food first." Nancy backed farther into the water and sighted on the lead monstrosity's skirt. She didn't have the pod's firepower, but maybe a hotfoot would drive them off.

"They don't swim." Jake waved her to deeper water. "We can wait with the captain."

The thought of going back tasted sour. They'd never get another chance. Even if they did, having been so easily rounded up again would keep them from taking it. She stopped and turned as Jake waded on, sighted down her pistol, and took the shot.

The energy pulse distorted the air in a straight line of turbulence that terminated on the lead Slurg's undulating skirt. A patch of rubbery skin the size of her fist crinkled and turned black. Licks of smoke rose from the spot, and the creature bellowed. She shot again and again, but the Slurg charged on. Two people sat behind the pod's windshield, Grint's men.

Nancy lowered the gun in disgust as yet another bulk shot onto the beach. That little spit of cliff was way too prolific. The newcomer darted up behind the pod, then past it. This second pod was fast, sleek, and manned by her favorite crustacean.

Herman came on like a linebacker with cockpit dome open and antenna waving in the wind. His passage startled the Slurgs. They slowed, their trumpeting taking on a querulous note. Energy beams lanced out from Grint's weapons pod. Some went wide of Herman, while others fizzled short. The rearmost slug took a shot in the back of its head. The smoking hole would have killed any other creature, but the Slurg simply grew confused and trundled off toward the dunes. Grint's team couldn't be that bad of marksmen, especially with a computer guided arsenal. Herman clearly had countermeasures and maybe a dampening field protecting his flank.

The Lobstra pod slid to a stop at the water's edge, her silver chariot. Nancy looked to the raft where Captain Gekko was just pulling Jake aboard. Water streamed from his open pack. Hopefully his equipment hadn't been ruined. The human's pod roared as it expelled a bright, hissing object that streaked into the side of Herman's vehicle and exploded. The Lobstra's pod lurched violently under the impact, and Herman waved for her to hurry. There was no time to get the others back ashore.

"Get going! We'll draw them off." Nancy yelled, hauled back, and threw the pistol out to Jake.

The sidearm was light, feeling like a toy compared to the antiquated 9mm style the navy had her use to qualify. The gun spun in a long arc toward the raft as she shuffled through the water toward Herman. Grint would have his people chase her. She'd seen the hungry look in his eyes. The madman wanted her help in the hunt and to synthesize drugs. She'd endured enough white knuckled rides with the young Lobstra to trust his piloting skills and the speed of his craft. Herman could keep them distracted while Jake and Captain Gekko crossed the channel and disappeared into the jungle that came down nearly to the water's edge on the far shore.

"No!" Jake cried from his perch on the raft.

She didn't know if he was arguing with her decision to split up or bemoaning the fact that the pistol plunked into the water, having only sailed two thirds of the way to the raft. Nancy didn't wait for clarification. She sloshed up to the pod and swung herself inside, making shooing motions toward the other men.

"Belt in," Herman said, and the pod leapt into motion.

The humans changed course immediately, accelerating in an attempt to cut them off. But the Lobstra pod was too quick, and the other vehicle settled in behind. The hulking Slurg turned as the chase moved up the beach. The beasts seemed at a loss for how to handle the new development. The largest animal followed for a few yards, then stopped alongside their abandoned tent. The temporary shelter had stood witness to a surprising array of revelations and stories in the past twenty-four hours. At some point in the morning, one edge of the tarp had pulled free of the ground.

The slug bent to snuffle at the material, which gently flapped in the steady ocean breeze. Then it proceeded to ooze overtop of the low-slung tent, enveloping first the loose edge and then the entryway under its crushing bulk. The Slurg wrapped itself around the weakly protesting material, as a huge translucent appendage snaked out from underneath the slug and stabbed at the tarp. Thankfully, an energy bolt exploded against the rear shielding, forcing Nancy to look away. *What the heck is so romantic about this beach?*

"Low power shots." Herman's feathery arms flew across the controls, sending the pod into an evasive serpentine. "They're trying to disable us. This crate's build for speed, not battle. Should we circle back for your friends before the shields collapse?"

Nancy shook her head. "Just keep heading inland. Make them chase us. Jake has a job to do."

"I better put some distance between us then," Herman said as the next blast snapped her head back.

With trial and error, they zeroed in on a comfortable lead that allowed the rear shields to absorb the occasional blast without buckling and spinning them off course.

"They're putting all their power into the engine," Herman said as another flash of light threw his control panel into stark relief under the slanting afternoon sun. "The shots are to keep us awake."

"Thank you for buying them time."

Nancy laid a hand on the segmented plates along his back. Herman's carapace was cool and damp under her fingers. The feathery edge held a kind of gentle sharpness. When this was all over, she'd love to sit down with Drissa and discuss physiology.

"It's nothing." Herman studied his controls, but Nancy "heard" the blush in his voice. "But I feel like a cuttlefish."

"Cuttlefish?"

"Sure, bouncing back and forth on a long rubbery arm, like a cuttlefish in the surf zone. They latch onto the rocks, get pulled out to sea, and spring back with the next wave. Captain Luftew sends me to deliver you, but the humans drive me off. Then I get this mystery signal on my tracker, the captain says to turn around, and now we're being chased back to the plateau."

"Like a yoyo!" Nancy imagined the poor guy bouncing back and forth. "Cuttlefish on your planet must be different. Ours just jet around like a stubby little squid. They don't have any really long arms. But I understand your point."

Herman retraced their outbound journey as the humans pushed them onward. They plowed through swampy fringes, forest, and finally emerged onto the open prairies preceding the more arid desert plains. The plateau rose above the horizon, looking delicate and surreal in the distance as rays from the setting sun lit the weathered cliff face.

"We can lose them after dark," Nancy said.

Herman drove on in silence for a full minute before answering.

"They know that too, so why not gambled on a few high-power shots?"

"Maybe that's still coming," Nancy suggested.

"But it's obvious they can't catch us. The longer they wait, the less energy is left for a disabling shot."

"I hadn't thought of that. Maybe they want to see where we're heading, although at this point that's pretty obvious." She pointed to the distant plateau. "And they already know where the Lobstra expedition is hunting."

Another flash of energy hit the rear shields.

"Still weak. It's like they're trying to keep us running." Herman studied his readouts, flipped a few switches and grew silent again.

Could Pete be aboard and trying to help? That seemed unlikely. The old codger might have been able to hide his involvement in their escape, but Grint would have put two of his most trusted people on their trail while he attended to more profitable business. If Herman was right and the Lobstra were truly closing in on the nectar, the bastard would want to get there first. She looked from the horizon to the pursuing pod, a terrible thought blossoming.

"Not just running," Nancy said. "We're running blind. Speed up! If they've called for support—"

Herman was quick on the uptake. The pod lurched forward, snapping her head back against the seat. He gripped the controls, inarticulate bubbles rising as the carapace strap pulled taut under the acceleration. Another jolt of energy punched into them from behind, notably stronger, but they pulled away fast. Their own shadow stretched ahead, flickering across the scrub brush and rocks jutting from the dusty ground.

Blinding violet light blossomed across their path, flattening bushes and rocks alike just before her eyes slammed shut. Light and pain lanced through the lids like hot pokers. The deafening roar hit a split second later, and she flew forward against her restraints. It felt like they'd hit a wall, but the pod must have ground to a halt or they both would have been turned into bloody pancakes.

Nancy blinked away purple-white afterimages as the landscape reluctantly swam back into focus. Ringing in both ears replaced the reassuring whine of the engine. Herman slumped forward in his harness. Translucent blue liquid oozed from below his legs where the cracked shell exposed white flesh. Nancy fumbled to release her buckle and help him.

The thin whine of several engines grew louder as a sleek little pod settled to the ground on their left and the pursuing pod pulled up behind. A significantly louder roar sent up clouds of dust and rattled her teeth. The main shuttle majestically dropped from the sky and landed directly in front of them. An access ramp extended from its side and spit forth a smiling Urneck Grint.

Nancy worked at the clasp and glared at the pompous ass. The Lobstra pod sat nose down, so she fell forward onto the gauges when the mechanism gave way. Herman hung limp in his harness. Unbuckling him might exacerbating his injuries. Although the controls were dark, the forward and rear canopies slid open when she toggled the emergency release. Nancy scrambled over her seatback and grabbed Reemer's spare bedding from the rear section. The rubbery material was bulky enough to wad into a cushion that she stuffed against the panel before releasing Herman.

She held tight to the points of his shell and eased the unconscious Lobstra onto the bedding. His powerful claws hung limp to either side, as did his legs. His breath gurgled a steady rhythm, but an alarming amount of blood coated his tail. Plasti-skin might patch his cracked shell, but Herman needed real medical attention.

"Come down from there." Grint had the gall to chuckle as he waved—the bastard.

The flutter in her belly at his careless attitude turned into a hot prickling that spread to her shoulder blades and played across her neck and ears. She clawed through her pouch for the first aid kit and skin sealant. The tiny can was meant to cover small cuts. She emptied it across the gaping wound, but the elastic compound did little to staunch the oozing blood. Her fingers clenched into fists, itching for the lost pistol.

Grint slapped the hull and called to the burly twins as they emerged from the pod. His words were lost beneath her rising anger and pounding pulse, his tone mocking and amused.

"Get a doctor, you pig! Herman needs help!" The words tore from her throat, a distant screech as if someone else screamed and ranted. She went on, degrading the man's heritage and integrity. Whatever she spewed hit a nerve.

"Get the girl."

The smile slid off Grint's face, and rough hands hauled Nancy from the cockpit. Her feet hit the ground hard and at an awkward angle that sent a lance of pain through her left ankle. She sputtered and fumed, but Ray-Jay held tight, an iron grip on either arm. They marched her past Grint and a third person, Dianne. The woman gave the twins a haggard frown.

"Help him," Nancy urged as her feet clanged on the shuttle's ramp, sending a fresh jab of pain up her leg.

"You heard the lady!" a new voice bellowed from the wrecked pod. "Get your ass in gear and help the Lobstra. Or feel my wrath!"

All eyes turned toward the order. Nancy got a good view as her escorts spun around. The familiar voice burped and wheezed with an improbable note of authority. The underside of the Lobstra pod distended. A dark blob detached from the hull, oozed to the ground, and reared high as it approached, an avenging giant storming out from the pod's shadow.

Jay released her right arm and hurried to the cockpit as though intent on helping Herman. But the big man stopped dead when the approaching silhouette moved into the light and the spell of authority shattered. The forbidding figure resolved into a yellow slug, a Squinch hunched up on its hind end. Its glistening body spread impressively wide, a cobra's hood without the underlying arsenal of fangs and venom.

Further eroding Reemer's imposing visage were the ribbons and bows of seaweed threaded along her skirt and around the base of each eye stalk. Belinda accessorized well. The red-green vegetation created a beautiful flowing accent, but totally undermined Reemer's quiet menace, turning it into an awkward implausibility—much like a cute bunny making demands of a lion.

On top of all that, the ends of those pretty adornments were tattered and frayed. Reemer herself looked much the worse for wear. As she deflated, skin stretched beyond its intended elasticity hung in bags around her glistening foot, and her eyes streamed thick mucus in an attempt to dislodge crusted dirt and grime so thick it was a wonder she could see.

How long had she been clinging to the underside of the pod? The only point in their mad dash that would have left an opening to board was the minute or so it took Nancy to wade ashore and hop in before Herman rocketed inland. She cringed at the image of the poor Squinch plastered to the hull beneath her feet and weathering energy blasts, slashing underbrush, and flying debris all day.

Nancy's chest swelled with pride. Reemer looked much like her mother, radiating a quiet authority and coasting toward Grint. But the hours of desperately hanging on for dear life took their toll. Reemer's sagging skirt tangled, and she fell forward into the dirt. The last vestiges of regal intimidation flickered out, leaving only a bedraggled young slug squinting up at the human mutineer.

"Get a box for the slug." Grint's ugly smile was back as he motioned Jay toward the weapons pod and turned back to Ray. "Make sure she gets her own cell this time."

"I'll look after the lobster," Dianne said in a near whisper as Ray hustled Nancy to the shuttle.

There was no rancor or sarcasm in the woman's voice. The athletic redhead headed for the Lobstra's pod with a sad smile. Jay was the reasonable twin, so it made sense that his girlfriend would be the compassionate one. Dianne carried a case of med supplies and leaned into the ruined pod to examine Herman. Nancy wanted to stay and make sure he would be all right, but Ray hauled her up the ramp and into the cool interior.

26. Misery Loves

"PIG!" NANCY spat the curse as Urneck Grint shuffled past absorbed in reading the datapad he held balanced atop a silver mug.

Her favorite insult rolled off the man. Over the past several days, he'd grown inured to her taunts and now only spared a dismissive wave before crossing to the gleaming desk that squatted like a spider in the center of the open bay. She'd woken up here in her new cell with a headache and vile metallic taste in her mouth, clear indications of being drugged. The sterile white walls reminded her of the brig, but the space was grander. A workstation sat to either side of Urneck's desk, forming a horseshoe around a raised platform.

Though not quite cavernous, the space was larger than she would have thought possible aboard the otherwise space-efficient craft. The area around the control center was a hexagon with her cell forming one side, a ten by ten foot cube with a transparent wall facing the controls. The arrangement made her feel exposed. Her only modicum of privacy came from the small bathroom set at the rear of the room, a door-less alcove that thankfully put a solid wall between herself and prying eyes in the control room proper. The ceiling was a standard eight feet, but rose outside to a startling fifteen with ducting and struts visible in the overhead.

Nancy spent her time studying the layout and trying to discover what was in store. The common area had one door off to her left through which Urneck came and went. Dianne had also crept in one day to say Herman was better and had been released. Giving up leverage was out of character for Grint, so Nancy wondered what else the man had up his greasy sleeve. The woman seemed sincere, but was tight-lipped about further details, preferring to steer the discussion to more personal topics—as if Nancy was her bestie forever. She'd learned way more about Dianne's love life and dreams of settling down behind a mythical white picket fence than she had about the injured Lobstra.

That brief exchange had been her only conversation in days. Urneck showed up sporadically but had no inclination to be civil. Food was dispensed automatically through an alcove near the front of the cell, so there wasn't going to be another Pete-inspired escape. But Nancy would have traded her next meal for a few minutes of conversation with the crazy old coot simply to alleviate the boredom.

The other four walls of the main room would hold cells similar to hers, but the bits of wall to either side she could see were blank white panels. Directly opposite her and to its right stood empty cells that were dark except for light spilling from the central space.

Her captor stood at the control center, sipped his coffee, and took a big bite out of a danish covered in glistening sugar and sticky fruit topping. Urneck's every movement grated on her nerves. Steam rose from his mug, and saliva flooded her mouth in response. Her rations didn't include coffee, tea, or anything remotely pleasing. When the insufferable man did show up, he always had some sort of treat with him, an insidious torment.

"I hope you choke on it!" Nancy slammed her palm on the translucent barrier at the front of her cage. "When it's your turn on this side, I'll be sure to visit."

Hopefully Jake and Captain Gekko had made it to the Endeavor and gotten a message off to the fleet. Barring catastrophe, they should have been able to cover the remaining distance in a day, two at the outside. Daydreams often brought a handsome admiral who coolly watched his men clap Urneck and his people in irons before shoving them into a dark pit to rot. Sometimes the admiral was young and lean, with wavy black hair and an easy smile. Jake would make a good officer; he was dedicated, smart, and—she imagined—good at many things.

"The navy has notoriously bad food," Nancy added. "Even what we had on Endeavor tasted like swill compared to the delicious fare I get here. You'll spend years eating dry ration cubes in some forgotten high-security prison at the edge of nowhere."

It was a blatant lie. Navy grub, even in space, was amazing, but the statement finally got a rise from the man. He stiffened and turned with a scowl that gave way to a smile as he chose his words.

"We'll never know because I don't plan to go to prison. I have QUEN blocking all interstellar signals." He turned away and fiddled with the controls as his tone slipped into feigned concern. "I hope you weren't counting too hard on any messages getting off-world."

He grinned. She couldn't see it, but his smug posture and the haughty way he turned from the controls and strode to the door without looking at her made the fact infuriatingly obvious.

"Pig!"

The doors slid shut on his laughter, leaving Nancy to her thoughts. Even if he was telling the truth, the navy rescue team should still arrive soon. Surely the most technologically advanced organization on Earth would have a way of finding their research site. Then they'd get the whole story straight from Jake. They might even be able to scan the planet for human life signs. She wrapped herself in the comforting thought, needing to believe help was on the way. Her mind drifted back to the image of Admiral Jake dressing down a cringing Urneck Grint.

Boredom was the worst part of things at this point. Nancy pushed to her feet and went back to studying the room's layout and controls as best she could from her vantage point. If she had her satchel and datapad, she could have taken notes, would have recorded the numbers and symbols visible on the displays. At least she'd memorized the keypad sequence that opened the main doorway when Dianne visited.

Wait! Something on the controls had changed. A new panel section was lit, showing similar displays and readouts as the two that were already active. And the cells on the far side of the room were now fully illuminated, as if standing ready to welcome new visitors.

Nancy cracked her eyes open at the sound of voices and commotion outside her cell. She lay on her cot for a minute, squinting at the blurred shapes shuffling past the control console to stop in front of the empty cells.

"Get a move on it," Urneck bellowed.

The swine leaned back in his chair with feet carelessly propped on the workstation. The burly twins hauled a gray metal crate across the room. The corrugated cube had to be eight feet tall, and despite the wheels they strained to get it positioned squarely in front of a cell door. Lobstra hoversleds would have saved them considerable effort—not that she wanted things to go easy for these pirates. Urneck could rot for all she cared. If the opportunity ever presented itself, she'd see to it that he did.

The man was absolute scum. His crew wasn't much better, especially the sweating brutes that latched the face of the container flush with the cell door. They used an airlock mechanism, and only a small crescent of the cell showed to either side of its bulk. Of the two men, Ray was the worst. Jay seemed to think for himself once in a while, like when he tried to help Herman. Although he was prompted by Reemer's command, Nancy held out a glimmer of hope for the man. But his brother was a total write-off. Brutish and cruel, Ray didn't deserve any more second chances than his bullying leader.

Urneck looked over his shoulder as if sensing her glare. She huffed and mouthed an obscenity at his leering smile. The cretin simply shrugged, pulled his legs off the desk, and leaned over to flip a switch. There was a clunk and whir from the container, but nothing else.

"Don't just stand there, imbeciles. Use the prods," Urneck snarled.

Ray and Jay pulled long metallic wands from brackets on either side of the container, then slid open access ports on the back side of the box they had hauled in. Just as Ray lifted the forked end of his prod to his opening, something green flashed out and stabbed the back of his hand. He howled and backpedaled as the four-foot-long tentacle slapped blindly trying to connect again. The deep-green appendage was three inches across with white highlights on the top edge of a continuous spiral, as if a length of flattened seaweed had been twisted to form a flexible arm. There were likely spines along the white ridges.

"Get back." Jay jabbed his prod through the other access panel. Flashes lit the opening as he worked the length of the pole in deeper, clearly connecting with something inside.

The tentacle went rigid and retracted. Ray lunged, thrusting his rod forward using only his left hand, while his right hung at his side. The nearer opening gave her a limited view of the container's interior. A great bulk shifted and retreated from the miniature flashes of lighting. Thin smoke curled from both access ports, bringing the scent of burnt pine and spices.

"Together, fools," Urneck roared.

The twins jabbed, a mighty spark cracked, and something spilled into the cell. Or perhaps many things retreated from the prods. It was difficult to tell with the container blocking her view.

"Payday!" Urneck mashed down a red mushroom-shaped button and threw another switch. The locks along the edge of the container clunked open, letting the cube roll back as an audible thrum of energy sparked the cell's barrier wall into place. Jay rolled the container clear to reveal…a monstrosity.

A single creature filled a good portion of the cell's interior. Of course it was a plant—after all they were still on Fred—but this was a Frankenstein monster of stitched-together parts that offended her botanical sensibilities. Its twin trunks consisted of wide green ridges much like a Saguaro cactus, similar to the pain watchers and the walkers that had invaded the shuttle. Each trunk was perhaps two feet wide and tall enough that the thing occasionally smacked the ceiling as it shuffled around testing the walls of its enclosure. If Nancy focused on the center of mass, it was easier to imagine the creature as just another succulent, probably of the deadly Dolor variety.

But the trunks were festooned with odd appendages and growths that jutted out at spurious intervals along its height. The left trunk tapered toward its peak, then split into a nest of dark green spirals that occasionally twisted around to prod at a recess in the wall or the folded cot. It had eight twisting arms like the one that tagged Ray. The top of the other trunk fanned out into a broccoli-like crest four feet across.

Little green and red growths sprouted from the crown of its head like a warty hairdo. Instead of spurious growths, that trunk had holes or dark lesions along its length. She counted three, but there could well have been more on the other side. Down by the foot of the creature, a group of spurs jutted out horizontally. The stubby cylinders ended in blunt pink caps like erasers jutting from a fistful of pencils.

The creature shuffled to the back of the cell. Instead of turning around, it simply scooted backward. She was surprised it didn't topple over. Fans of vegetation swept out below the pencils, each a cross between romaine lettuce and a cactus paddle. Those clusters swept front to back and side to side to propel the creature. The leafy feet sprouted from the base of both trunks, but the creature should be too top heavy to keep its balance. Perhaps the upper half was hollow. If so, the great expanse she thought of as its head might in fact be nothing more than a leafy display.

"Nancy!" A familiar voice bubbled from across the room.

"Drissa?" Her heart raced at the sight of a familiar face.

She had been absorbed in trying to make sense of the creature and hadn't noticed the Lobstra being escorted into the room. Ray pushed Drissa into the cell next to the giant plant. Rather than the energy screen used to contain her neighbor, Drissa's cell door was similar to Nancy's own, a modified transparent polymer with a normal-sized doorway that clicked closed to seal the Lobstra inside.

"I'm sure you two will have plenty to talk about." Urneck grunted as he stood, scanned the controls, and walked to the exit. "Extractions will start in the morning."

Ray and Jay filed out behind their leader, and the door slid shut with an air of finality. Nancy desperately wanted to hear news, but didn't relish yelling across the open bay. Of course, the entire space would be monitored, so even a whispered conversation was likely to be overheard or recorded. Nancy gave an inward shrug and pitched her voice to carry.

"How's Herman doing?" She'd meant to ask about the creature, about how Drissa had been captured. But apparently her subconscious had more pressing priorities.

"He's fine. The humans did a passable job patching him up." Drissa's bubbling voice carried more readily than her own, but rose with a note of skepticism. "They said you were in an accident?"

"Sure, you could say we accidentally ran into an energy beam that stopped us dead in our tracks. I don't know if the pod will ever fly again."

"I thought it might be something like that." Drissa's antennae drooped. "Yesterday, the humans brought Herman to the plateau asking for our help. Officer Grint said they had been attacked by some sort of walking cacti and needed someone who knows Fred's aggressive plants to identifying the poison. Captain Luftew wanted to talk to the human captain, but Grint said his leader was incapacitated by the attack. On the surface, it seemed plausible. After I examined Herman, the captain sent me to look in on the human victims."

"Let me guess, there weren't any."

"Just one irascible man. The wounds on his soft little hand were almost fully healed, but he pouted like a hatchling when I asked him about it." Drissa paused in thought. "Now that I think of it, he reminds me a lot of Meinish."

"Old news and half-truths. There was a major attack last week, but we dealt with it and were arrested for our troubles."

"Makes sense." Drissa nodded, an awkward movement that looked like a shallow bow. "They showed me a pile of rotting vegetation. The plants all tested out as Dolor species, but the creatures had clearly been dead for a while."

The walking cacti and their clever little pups had been Dolor nasties after all. Good riddance! Grint wouldn't have wanted an expert just to analyze the attack on the shuttle. But he might want help to deal with this new prize specimen.

"Then he just happens to find this thing." Nancy pointed to the giant plant creature that now tested the seams where walls, floor, and ceiling met by the lavatory.

Drissa wouldn't be able to see to the back of the adjacent cell and the common wall between was opaque. But she certainly had seen the massive plant as they marched her in.

"Their timing was impeccable. Our capture team had just cornered the creature. I think that's why Captain Luftew was distracted and let me go aboard their craft. I was led into a small room and asked to wait. I went a little crazy when the ship lifted off." She held up her battle claw.

Nancy gasped. Even from a distance, she saw that the claw was scored with gouges and abrasions. The med tech might have radical ideas when it came to the governance of her people, but Drissa was as mild mannered as they came.

"Are you all right?"

She gave one of those odd little Lobstra shrugs. "At first, I didn't worry that they had locked me in, but when gas hissed out of the vents, I tried to smash my way out. It's a blur, but I finally passed out. You know the rest."

"They scooped the queen out from under Meinish," Nancy concluded.

"Presumably. We've seen enough of the inhabitants to know that this thing"—she waved at the adjacent cell—"is special. I haven't had the pleasure of testing it, but I'd bet my bonus that a death-cheating elixir could be tickled from it."

Bitterness mixed with a note of satisfaction rode beneath the Lobstra's words. From Drissa's perspective, the fact that the humans had stolen the prize out from under her crew might not be the catastrophe it seemed, thanks to her disdain for the artificially extended reign of the current dynasty. If another race stole the nectar from Captain Luftew, it would mean a loss of face and bonus money. But it might also move the Lobstra society one step closer to a new monarch. She tried to recall if Drissa had let slip how much potion and time their reigning matriarch had left. Could the dynasty last until the next cycle, or would a younger sovereign rise to power in the next five years?

"So Grint rounds up the best people to help extract this precious nectar, and maybe gets some leverage against the other groups in the process," Nancy mused.

The man had no morals. He took and took, and people got hurt in the process. At least Herman was recovering thanks to Dianne. Hopefully Reemer was too. It seemed oddly sexist, but she worried that the Squinch had become delicate and vulnerable in her new persona. The brash antics of the old Reemer could have just been a front to hide his insecurities, but she doubted it. Her friend enjoyed causing mischief too much for it all to have been an act. She tried to push down the unpleasant image of Reemer curled up in the corner of a cell, frightened and alone. Worrying over where Grint had stashed her would not do Reemer any good right now. Grint might be a misogynist bully, but he hadn't killed anyone.

Fragmented memories of Harry and the science team rose unbidden. She thought of Jake and Veech picking their way through the carnage, searching for a working radio. She saw the broken shells of Lobstra she had known and Breena's grief at the loss of a friend. Humans hadn't done all that. That was Fred. That had been the plants.

Nancy glared at Fred's apex creature. Her gut told her this was the Dolor queen. These were the mutations that killed. She pounded the door of her cage until her fist hurt, trying to draw the thing's attention. These were the mindless and indiscriminate murderers. A rational part of her knew it was just instinct, some misguided reaction to the environment or need for certain nutrients that drove them, just like the few carnivorous plants of Earth. But another part of her seethed at the wanton loss of life, wondered how many cycles had passed with alien soil drenched in blood. Had other innocent research expeditions unwittingly set foot on Fred, hoping to advance their knowledge of the universe only to be slaughtered?

She scratched her itching palms before wiping them against the smooth fabric of her blouse once, twice, three times. She looked up at a muffled wet slapping, the sound of stalks thrashing against stone. The creature had moved forward and bent low. Its leafy headdress smacked the front wall, occasionally brushing the containment field, which added the electric buzz of a bug zapper. The spiral tentacles crowning the thinner trunk coiled and thrust at the front corner of its enclosure—the great white shark of Fred, always moving, always hungry.

Grint would want her and Drissa to help classify and extract the nectar, but Nancy would happily give it more than a simple DNA work up. If she got the opportunity, she'd dissect the thing to find out what made it tick. With a little more insight, she and Drissa could finish cultivating the virus and put an end to the aggressive cycles on this planet. Preserving the natural balance was laudable, but the Squinch and the galaxy would be better off.

27. Insurance Policy

"AHHHH!"

Reemer cringed and snapped awake at the inaudible cry, which made no sense, so perhaps it had been a tattered remnant of a dream. She stretched and flowed from cot to cool floor. Her skirt and foot produced a faint sucking squeak as they propelled her across the pristine white room to the food station. It seemed a little early for dinner, but maybe her captors finally deigned to net some live fish.

The synthetic cubes of mush she'd been subsisting on were truly revolting. So much so that she had barely managed to regurgitate onto the last few meals. Even her digestive symbionts, the little wriggling creatures that took delight in preparing her food, grew apathetic and did an increasingly poor job of breaking down the meals before she had to slurp up the bland mess. Lately, the entire process grew tedious and gruesome, more so without decent fish. Still, she listened hopefully at the depression in the wall. Nothing.

"Ahhhee!"

The sound that wasn't a sound jangled her nerves instead of vibrating against her antennae, making it difficult to pinpoint the source, but it definitely hadn't come from the meal slot. Reemer inched up to the wall she considered the room's entrance. It was the only one that was truly blank, a smooth white surface, lacking the bed, wash basin, and sparse features protruding from the other walls. Unless she'd been dropped in from above, it stood to reason that a doorway existed, and this wall seemed the obvious choice.

The wail came from beyond that presumed doorway. Reemer couldn't say exactly how she knew. There was a kind of pressure in what she perceived. Similar to the way you felt a big rock coming up, even with eyes closed. Maybe that was the brain interpreting water pressure building against the skin. This felt similar, a thought with a hard edge.

It all seemed so familiar. She'd definitely encountered something similar recently, not just the pressure, but the mild buzzing and confusion of hearing while not hearing. That happened a lot with Nancy. Come to think of it, with Meinish and Herman too. This new sensation reminded Reemer of the pesky interpretive lag when conversing with outsiders.

When Nancy first showed up on the floating island, listening to the woman's garbled speech and waiting for her translator to catch up had been great fun. After the rampant dizziness and headaches brought on by the damned Lokii's interference, the human no longer needed her talking computer. But there was still a barely perceptible delay—just a split second. Concentrating on it made her brain hurt. It was easier to pretend the others spoke true Squinchish and ignore that moment's hesitation when meaning pressed in on the mind. Yes, that was the same pressure she had just felt from somewhere outside her prison.

She strained her senses, picking up the ever-present hum from the lighting, a faint vibration of distant equipment that translated through the floor, but no true noise. The room was either soundproof or isolated by a dampening field. Still, the pressure came in steady waves conveying little more than a jumble of emotions: anger, fear, and perhaps desperation. Why could she pick up those inarticulate calls at all? It stood to reason that Nancy and Herman would be held nearby, but the presence hadn't felt like either of her friends.

Reemer pushed up onto her haunches, transferring the bulk of her weight to the tail of her foot. The telltale glint of monitoring lenses reflected near the ceiling in each corner of the front wall. A few short weeks ago, launching a nice wad of corrosive juices would have seemed like a good way to send her captors a message.

But Mother had spent the night before their capture coaching her newfound daughter on the proper way of behaving and handling tricky situations. She'd been so proud that Reemer found herself soaking up the advice, which turned out to be astoundingly logical. So instead of spitting or defecating on the human's equipment, Reemer wrapped herself in solemn dignity and gave the cameras an imperious glower full of meaning and portents. Let them stew on that for a while; she would handle the men on the other end of those cameras soon enough.

"Did you see that?" Jay squeaked, an uncharacteristic sound from the big man.

His twin jabbed his index finger at the screen, started to comment, then compressed his lips and bounced the outstretched finger in a thoughtful jiggle.

"It's nothing, just a stupid slug," Ray finally concluded.

"Mama bear's angry," Angie said from her seat at an adjacent console. She grinned at the image of the giant plant on her own monitor. Dianne was just approaching the front of the cage.

Urneck's leg was draped over the arm of the chair to her right as he worked the controls. "She's gonna get you!" she sing-songed, gleefully taunting both men.

The twins were big and bad, but Angie knew them both intimately. She'd dated Jay briefly before hooking up with Ray. It had been good for comparison purposes, in addition to feeling deliciously wicked. Angie had seen the granite twins in more than a few compromising positions, but never unnerved by an alien.

"Nah." Ray grunted, but the sentiment lacked conviction and seemed to wilt under the glare radiating through the surveillance equipment. "The thing's just hungry. You saw it waiting for dinner."

"Yeah, that's it!" Jay sounded relieved. "Hey, didn't Pete load a crate of flatfish he caught in the channel? Let's give her one of those."

* * *

"DNA sequence confirmed," Drissa called out. "It's a Dolor."

Nancy wasn't surprised. She'd already entered Dolor as the species and Diabolus for the order into the database on her handheld. No sense rushing the rest of the classification. Inspiration would undoubtedly strike as the work continued. She thought of her dead crew and injured friends. If this turned out to be the queen of the species, there was a fitting name for a royal pain. With a malicious smile, Nancy entered a temporary family and species of Interfectorem Gloria, Killer Bitch.

It had taken days of complaining and cajoling to get her datapad back. She felt whole again with the device and familiar weight of her satchel. But they'd taken the laser cutter and cracked open her little computer, looking for hidden surprises. When Urneck gave it back, he'd held up a tiny crystalline component on a metal pin. It looked much like a small diamond earring.

Apparently Jake put trackers in everything he got his hot little hands on. She supposed the little crystal had transmitted the signal that Herman followed to the Squinch mating beach. With the device removed, no one would be charging to the rescue this time. But the computer still worked, so at least she could help with the analysis.

Drissa huddled over a larger bank of equipment that had been brought to the front of her cell. The portable console held a medical scanner, spectrometer, and who knew what else. During working hours, it blocked the cell's entrance. Drissa worked from inside, while Dianne and a young blond man poked and prodded at the creature with retractable syringes, sample cutters, and other devices jabbed through the containment field.

The creature hated it, of course. The process was painful to watch, not so much because she was worried about the Dolor, but because Dianne didn't really know what she was doing. The woman might be competent with first aid and synthesizing drugs, but if it was truly a nectar they were after, carving off bits of the plant's epidermis and pulling core samples wasn't the way to go about extracting the substance.

The spirals along those flailing arms also held venom delivered through fine hair-like needles making up the white ridges. Nancy got a chance to meet the blond man up close one day. His name was Craig Finkle, and after he had been tagged by a spiral arm, the left side of his body collapsed into paralysis. Dianne had half-carried him over to Nancy, made introductions and pretty much begged for help. That was when it became clear the woman was out of her depth.

So, likely in accordance with his plan all along, Urneck gave Drissa her own equipment, reunited Nancy with her meager gear, and let the three women work up an in-depth analysis of the aggressive plant.

"Bingo." Nancy pulled her thoughts back to the present. "If you have any good ideas for a full classification, sing out."

She pulled up the sketches and scans they had done on the prior, perhaps arguably less evolved, Dolor specimens. A comparison with their current subject unfolded as the wireless node transmitted new findings from Drissa's station. Data flowed in on soft interior tissues, epithelial scrapings, and deep organ-like colonies of specialized cells. The DNA was indeed conclusive. Significant overlap of complex molecules, sugar profiles, and a variety of acids were also present. In fact, it was starting to look like this plant comprised a superset of all the compounds and components they had encountered to date on Fred, and then some. Cross-correlation and a little deductive reasoning would let them pinpoint the undiscovered sub-species she'd hypothesized, other killer plants wandering the planet.

"Do you see the peptide chains?" Drissa asked.

"Sure do, and that's another common denominator across every variant. Those could underpin external hormonal signaling, almost like a communications network." They needed to put their heads together, or this analysis was going to take forever. Urneck already chafed over the delay, but they hadn't been able to recommend a method that would force the thing to bloom or whatever was needed to release this over-valued nectar. And her throat was raw from the long distance talking. "Urneck, this is ridiculous. I'm not going anywhere. If you want to solve this riddle anytime soon, you've gotta let us work together, not just yell across the room."

The jerk didn't even respond, just sat there fiddling with his controls and looking miserable. Served him right for being such an ass. Nancy blinked when the transparent door to her cell clicked open, then shrugged, slung her satchel over her shoulder, and strode out.

"Just don't get any bright ideas," Urneck warned as she joined Dianne at Drissa's console.

"Why not?" She was done being scared of this bully.

The thought must have been painted across her face. Urneck smiled his crocodilian smile and did something on the console. Behind him, the blank wall adjacent to Nancy's cell changed from opaque white to clear, revealing a cell similar to her own. Standing dead center was a startled yellow blob. Reemer quickly regained her composure, but rather than call a greeting, she pulled herself fully upright and glared at the man. Urneck actually faltered, as if forgetting the words he had been about to spew. But the man was nothing if not bullheaded.

"I have an insurance policy," Urneck grumbled, managing to tear his eyes off Reemer.

Relief and irritation flooded her in equal measure. The Squinch had been right next to her all along while she'd worried and fretted about her safety. Grint must have been laughing his head off. Bastard. She tried to put it out of her mind and turned back to watch Dianne prepare another round of samples. The woman carefully typed pertinent information into the database, but when she stood to prepare slide smears, she turned clumsy, spilling as much sample material as she successfully corralled.

"You're exhausted." Nancy took a titrate tube from the other woman's shaky fingers. "Let me finish these. You need a few hours of sleep."

Dianne smiled, but cast a nervous glance at Urneck. "Thanks, but I need to stay involved."

"Tell you what. You stick to data entry. I'll prep."

"That works." Dianne sat down and shifted her attention to the keyboard.

They worked in silence until Nancy dropped the small vial of solution she'd rendered into the centrifuge carousel.

"We still need molecular analysis and gas spectrometry on this one, right?" Nancy sliced a thin layer off the edge of a dark green skin sample. The meat beneath the bumpy outer layer was striated, a tan layer with white underneath.

"Yep," Dianne answered through a yawn. "That will complete the panels for this round."

She stretched the layer of tissue out and neatly pinned the corners. The computerized laser microdissection routine would carve off delicate layers and batch them through DNA and RNA sequencing. The process could isolate molecular components more accurately than a human with a microscope.

"Not sleeping well?"

Nancy kept the question casual. She suspected the woman suffered from an attack of morals. Maybe Dianne hadn't realized the kind of riffraff she'd signed on with. Getting the woman to open up might help cultivate some rapport.

Dianne started at the question, but immediately relaxed. "Just too busy."

"At night?"

"Sure. The boys are rather demanding."

"Oh, sorry." Nancy's face grew warm, and she cut away a frayed corner of her sample.

"No, nothing like that." It was a relief to hear an earnest laugh escape the woman. "It's just that my day job hasn't gone away. I'm still on the hook for a quota of product. I'll be going full tilt after we're done here. The boys like their drugs, but they like having them ready for sale even more."

"Ah." Nancy was certain her face was turning even brighter red.

"Doctor has a dirty mind," Dianne teased in a good-natured way.

"You doing okay over there?" Nancy looked to the Lobstra.

"Data on the last batch is almost collated." Drissa's antennae peeked over the top of the equipment as she glanced up. "I'll be ready to run your new samples in half an hour."

At the end of the day, they rolled the workstation off to the side and Drissa retreated into her cell. The system would continue dissecting and processing the last round of samples overnight, so they could expect fresh data in the morning. Nancy asked Dianne for any information they had on the nectar itself. Although humans hadn't acquired the substance in recent memory, she agreed to see what QUEN could dig up. The situation was exasperating. How had they expected to get at the stuff if they didn't bother to understand what they were after?

Once the workstation was happily cranking away on its analysis, Dianne sheepishly escorted Nancy across the room to her own accommodations and wished her a good evening. At Nancy's prodding, she promised to get some real sleep and to be fresh in the morning.

The magnetic lock snapped shut on her cage, and Dianne shuffled over to the central controls. The rogue chemist was clearly intimidated by Urneck, but managed the man well as she spoke softly and reached around to massage his shoulder where he'd apparently slept wrong on the unyielding desk. Urneck glared over at Nancy a couple of times during the quiet discussion. In the end, he simply shrugged, grumbled something, and locked down his workstation for the evening.

The athletic woman smiled and waved, looking rather pleased with herself as she walked out. Nancy couldn't think why until she spotted a clear panel that had resolved near the front of the cell. A four-foot section of the wall adjoining Reemer's cell had turned translucent. She blessed Dianne's thoughtfulness and rushed over to peer in on the Squinch.

"Reemer?"

In addition to being transparent, the wall section allowed adjacent prisoners to speak with one another. Reemer slid off her cot and moving to the opposite side of the panel. "I was worried I'd never see you again."

"You've been here all along?" Nancy put her hand flat to the window and the Squinch did the same with the front of her skirt.

"Yep, and it sucks. White walls, no communication, bland food. At least they gave me a real fish yesterday."

"Herman?" Nancy asked.

Reemer swung her head from side to side, a gesture she'd only recently picked up. "Never saw him. Insane driver though, thought I was going to end up splattered across the rocks there for a while."

"Sorry about that." Nancy coughed. "If we'd known you were clinging to the hull, we'd have pulled you aboard."

"No you wouldn't have, dear. There just wasn't time," the Squinch chided. "I do understand, but it was still harrowing."

Nancy tried to ignore the uncomfortable feeling that she talked to her mother. "Looks like you came through it okay."

Remnants of the ribbon still decorated Reemer's skirt, tail, and head. The Squinch had trimmed off the frayed edges and rewrapped the bows back into tidy decorations. It gave her a Victorian air, like the gingerbread woodwork of a grand mansion unconcerned with the passage of time, regal and proud. How had she ever imagined her friend as frightened and helpless? Maybe a bit more reserved, but certainly not helpless.

"Well enough," Reemer replied. "Now let's talk about you."

And they did, well into the night. It felt more like an interrogation, but Nancy was happy to fill the Squinch in on recent developments. Now that she had her datapad back it was easier to keep track of time. They'd been captive for a week. Reemer spent most of that time in strict isolation and must be starved for mental stimulation. So she told her as much as possible about the situation, of how Dianne had helped with Herman, and even about the recurring dream where leaves sprouted in her hair and roots poked from her boots.

* * *

"Pin it to the wall!" Dianne shouted.

"Trying," Craig said through clenched teeth.

The plant heaved sideways, slamming the beefy man against the energy field again and almost breaking away. Craig grunted, but managed to hang onto the controls strapped to his forearms and joining him to a pair of robotic arms. His exoskeleton arms extended through the force shield and held the thrashing Queen Dolor. "Any day now, Doc!"

Nancy blinked. That last was directed at her, and she hurriedly keyed in the start sequence. The full body spectral scan had been her idea. With the morning coffee, Dianne had brought exciting information about the nectar's chemical makeup. Humans had never captured the thing, and races that had were highly secretive. The Lobstra succeeded in the crazy quest more often than not, but the matriarch's security was nigh invulnerable—no surprise given the nectar kept the aging monarch in power.

So QUEN had dug deep for pirated information from an old archive and one moldering data file in particular. The transmission had been intercepted fifty years ago after a race called the Zebreena made a surprise appearance and absconded with the coveted substance. Their initial report went out on a subspace channel, protected by only simplistic encryption and their unknown language. Subsequent interactions with the race had produced a sound translation of the language and the key to decoding the old message.

Their information was sparse, consisting mostly of mission log entries with time and date stamps. Their rudimentary analysis was based on electron microscope observations, but the alien's version of electrophoresis allowed them to separate molecules in the genetic material. Nancy was startled to see a large concentration of haploid cell remnants in the supposed nectar's makeup. A true nectar would have presented mostly sugars and trace chemicals. With the predominance of dangerous plants on Fred, she had long suspected that the prize would turn out to be a particularly nasty blend of toxins. But if the old data file was accurate, the substance they were looking for primarily consisted of reproductive building blocks.

Haploid cells roughly correlated to animal gametes, cells that each contained half of the genetic material needed to form a fertilized egg and propagate the species. The data showed three distinct haploid compositions, making it possible that rather than combining into diploid cells consisting of two different halves, these alien creatures might combine three or more sets of DNA and RNA as they reproduced.

Their spectral scan would use multiple frequencies to image internal structures and help them localize the creature's reproductive system. If they were lucky, the process would pinpoint where mitosis and storage of these cells occurred.

"Nancy?" Drissa quivered with nervous energy.

"Scan starting," Nancy said as she finished initializing the program.

The energy barrier along the near edge of the cell drew away from the wall far enough for Dianne to push the scanning mechanism up against the creature. Servos in Craig's robotic arms whined as leafy appendages slapped and writhed. He pinned the bouquet of stinging spiral tentacles against the trunk, making it safe to complete the procedure—if they were quick. Nancy and

Drissa monitored the equipment and called out the time remaining in the procedure. If the creature broke away from Craig, Nancy would reestablish the containment field while Drissa helped Dianne get clear. But Craig held on tight, despite the occasional colorful outburst that warmed her ears.

"Done!" Dianne pulled her equipment back, and Nancy snapped the energy wall into place with an electric thrum.

28. Eyes Open

J AKE STARED down at the brief message that had finally come back over the cobbled-together equipment they found aboard the science team's ship.

SUBJ//RE SS ENDEAVOR MISSION STATUS//

REF//MSDID DTG 190723NOV2212Z//

NARR//REF RECEIVED. USS BERNARD INBOUND YOUR LOCATION. ETA TO FOLLOW.

BT//

Typically cryptic and exceptionally uninformative, the reply left out little details like when help would arrive, how the navy viewed Captain Gekko's involvement, and protocols to establish a secure communication channel. At least the return message had come in on one of the standard line-of-site frequencies, so he had a fairly accurate bearing on the approaching vessel and wouldn't have to waste power broadcasting in the blind next time.

It had taken him a full day to get the transmitters aligned and chase down a break in the outgoing waveguide. The inside of the Endeavor had seen better days. There were rotting piles of vegetation everywhere, and a good deal of the equipment had been wrecked in a standoff between the crew and the native plant life. He and the captain found piles of discharged weapon cartridges, mostly fitting handheld pistols or non-lethal tasers. The expedition lacked heavy weaponry. But, judging by their dead adversaries, they'd put up a good fight.

Occasional splashes of dried blood decorated the ship's interior. Thankfully, there weren't any bodies. During their trek, the captain made it clear they would dig graves for the casualties. Jake was relieved he didn't have to haul around decaying corpses.

"Pretty damned vague." Captain Gekko scowled down at the reply.

"We could clean out a couple of staterooms and settle in to wait." Jake figured that would be better than dealing with the jungle.

A thump sounded through the bulkhead, and he exchanged a look with Captain Gekko. All was silent for a few seconds, then a series of tapping, tentative footsteps came from the passage outside. Jake grabbed his pistol off the desk. Nancy's throw to him at the inlet had been abysmal, but one of their Squinch escorts had retrieved the gun as the Lobstra pod led Urneck's goons away. Though waterproof, he'd stripped the thing down to let it air dry, and the weapon was none the worse for wear.

The captain readied his own firearm, a low-powered Endeavor pistol with a modified stock that allowed it to be aimed like a rifle. Highly accurate, but even with the refurbished power cartridges Jake had over-charged, killing anything bigger than a rabbit was unlikely. The shuffling grew louder as the thing in the passageway drew close.

"Come on, give me a target." Jake aimed at the feathery green branch feeling its way around the open doorway.

The rapid, agitated chittering outside turned softer, and then—impossibly—resolved into words. "Peace, human. We are not your enemy."

Despite the mild statement, Jake kept his gun trained on the figure that emerged with the branch—or was it an arm? The creature had a triangular green head with bulbous eyes that shifted between green and brown. Eyes on a plant didn't make sense, but then little on Fred did. The thing stepped into view on a pair of spindly roots, and its tapered body was backed by long translucent leaves extending nearly to the floor from the tall figure. It fixed him with a serene gaze and stood swaying in a non-existent breeze, waiting. His mind took a moment to catch up to his eyes. This was no plant; it was a giant insect. Jake lowered the pistol.

"Why are you here?" Jake asked.

The mandibles and tiny appendages along the creature's pointy mouth worked furiously, like the palsied fingers of a banker contemplating his profits. The motion produced wet clicking that he somehow understood.

"I am HaSSaam of the Lokii. We have a common purpose."

A headache buzzed at the base of his skull. Great, more aliens.

* * *

"You're hurting her," Reemer insisted.

"It's just a plant." Nancy had enough to deal with without her friendly Squinch going off the deep end. "And a killer plant at that. This might be the progenitor of all the nasty variants we've encountered, and probably a few more we haven't seen on this peach of a vacation."

There was a downside to having the access panel open between cells. Nancy spent much of her time out in the common area working with Drissa and Dianne. Reemer was still stuck in the small cell to ensure Nancy's cooperation, and the confines made the Squinch moody.

The Dolor was fascinating. Urneck didn't need to worry about her skipping out at this point. In fact, he'd have to pry her away if it came to that. They were so close, not just to extracting the nectar—or more accurately the reproductive fluids and solids—from the Dolor, but to understanding what made this murderer tick.

"Wait, what's a peach?" Reemer asked, then slapped her skirt up against the clear divider. "Never mind. Can't you hear her?"

Wonderful, a hormonal slug. Nancy clamped down the unkind thought. Reemer needed time to adjust to her new physiology.

"Don't personify it. We've been calling it the queen, but these things are asexual, or more accurately hermaphroditic. They carry both male and female genetic material. Think about that net vine that nearly hauled you into a grave. If we can figure out what's going on here, you won't have to worry about that kind of thing happening again."

Nancy had been too busy working on the current problem to speak with Drissa about the virus they'd cooked up, but genome information from the queen could further refine the viral targeting and propagation paths. With an effective delivery system, this planet could be monster-free in just a couple of years. Wiping out the Dolor wasn't the legacy she'd imagined when joining the Endeavor, but would be a fitting memorial to the fallen crew.

She used an alcohol wipe to scrub at the faint stains on back of her hands and watched Reemer's hide darken to rich gold. Changing from male to female couldn't have been easy. It really was possible the poor thing was dealing with a chemical imbalance.

"You don't understand. This isn't a species, there's only one." Reemer stabbed her eyestalks toward the far cell. "She's unique. I just know it."

"All the better," Nancy said.

The hunting races were required to return the queen plant after extracting their prize. She had no idea who created the rule or how they enforced it, but even Urneck intended to comply. She had figured they would all have been in deep space by now, any rules of engagement forgotten once the goods were in hand. But the stricture bound the winners to return the creature as soon as possible to where it had been captured.

A simple solution would be to just jettison the thing after harvesting its treasures, but that offended her sensibilities. Long before a botany degree had been a glimmer in her eye, it had torn at Nancy's heart to see Mom sit an unwanted poinsettia or philodendron outside in the snow. Nothing deserved such a slow painful death. Then again…these were Dolor.

Nancy tried to pinpoint the paragraph she'd been reviewing on her datapad, but looked up at a sharp, drawn-out squeak. Reemer slid down the panel, a living squeegee that fouled the material instead of cleaning it. She spared a glance for the twin-trunked horror across the bay. It sagged against the back wall of its cage. Of course it wasn't a thinking being, but the scan sent everything from x-rays to ultrasonic waves into it. The process may well have damaged tissue, but it would recover.

The drooping red leaves on a particular Christmas plant her mother had exiled to the backyard sprang to mind. An eight-year-old Nancy rescued the poor thing and nursed the plant back to life under a glow light in the basement. Then one night Flash, their big orange tabby, decided it was a chew toy. Flash grew lethargic and started vomiting the next day. In a fit of fear and anger, little Nancy threw the poinsettia into the backyard creek. But the cat got better after hacking up some red bits along with a big wad of fur. Unlike the monstrosities here, the houseplant was only mildly poisonous. Nancy had cried all day, ashamed of killing the plant.

She scrubbed until her hands stung, threw the still white wipe into the recycle bin, and glared at the Dolor, refusing to feel sorry this time.

"Hit it again," Dianne said from her seat at the control console.

Craig pushed the cattle prod into the vee where the Dolor's trunks split and ran the device slowly upwards, making the ridged skin twitch and crawl. He paused to caress each of the three protruding arms at the plant's midsection, where tan needleless tips thrust out like giant erasers, or perhaps a disturbing parody of a woman's chest.

Their work done, Nancy and Drissa watched from the open doorway of Nancy's cell. They had identified two concentrations of haploid cells in the main trunk. There were three distinct cell types in a reservoir near those midsection protrusions and three others collecting beneath the leafy crown. Normally, the cells would only be combined and released as part of the parent plant's flowering cycle. The internal structures seemed to be primed and ready, but Nancy couldn't predict when exactly things would start to move naturally.

Her graduate studies included researching electro culture, the use of electricity to stimulate a plant's growth and natural processes. With Craig's help, they modified the prods, lowering the current and upping the voltage to create portable electrostatic generators. It had taken some trial and error, but they were now into the third day of successfully collecting nectar.

Each morning, Craig used his robot arms to corral the Dolor into a harness set in the wall. Then he would take up one of the prods and start the tedious process of coaxing forth the valuable materials. The conductive bands not only held the creature still, they also helped distribute the static charge across its skin receptors.

Milky fluid dribbled through the tubing connected to funnels on each protrusion at the plant's midsection. A soft suction helped keep liquid flowing and regrettably bolstered the impression that they were operating a giant three-headed breast pump. Certain shapes and forms were more efficient than others, so it made sense for flora to mimic those found in the animal kingdom.

Craig's device lingered among the outthrust appendages, tickling and coaxing. When the flow of liquid dwindled, he moved to the crown. Figuring out how to collect the material from that bushy mane had been more problematic. All across the head of the creature, small red tongues had emerged in response to the static charge. The tip of each spun out sticky powdery strands like cotton candy. Collecting the stuff was troublesome, especially since they could not fully immobilize the plant's head. They finally settled on an electrostatic brush mounted on the end of a mechanical arm. It combed back and forth across the thrashing headpiece, sweeping up the material as fast as the writhing red tongues could produce the stuff.

"Efficient." Drissa scuttled over to lounge against Nancy's cot.

"Stop...you'll kill her," Reemer droned, his voice devoid of inflection.

"Give it a rest," Nancy said.

Reemer sprawled across the front of the isolation panel, her back to them. She barely lifted her head to speak and had clearly given up hope that the others would heed her warning. Yet she still seemed compelled to make a token effort. The Squinch people, and Reemer in particular, had never shown much affinity for the jungle species. So why the change of heart?

Nancy was all for following your gut. Insight and instinct were hallmarks of many great scientists. Reemer's continued insistence that she "just knew" they were hurting the plant and that bad things would follow had almost been enough to make the botanist second guess their course of action—almost. But it was a moot point. They were all captives, and the sooner the extraction was over, the sooner they could send the plant back and get on with more important work.

"Drissa," Nancy whispered so that Reemer couldn't hear. "I've got ideas for the…vaccine."

Back on the medical sled, Breena had come up with the euphemism to refer to their designer virus. Drissa's assistant was happy to help and quick to isolate natural infection agents in the Dolor specimens. Like Drissa, the small Lobstra had little love of their matriarch. But Breena reminded them of how offended the devout would be with their undertaking. Talk of creating a lethal virus would raise more than a few eyebrows—well, antennae. Vaccines often contained live virus cells, so the term proved appropriate; they would inoculate the planet against the deadly Dolor plaque.

"Wonderful!" Drissa replied. "We can make a new formulation. Breena has already…"

Drissa trailed off and looked past Nancy. The main entrance stood open, and the granite twins marched in dragging a third figure between them. Urneck Grint strode in on their heels. They'd grown used to having the run of the detention area. Urneck only showed up in the evenings to check progress and lock them back in their respective cells. Nancy hadn't seen Ray and Jay since they brought in the Dolor. This time, they dragged one of the Lokii across the room and dumped it into Nancy's cell. The giant insect staggered a few paces, then crumpled to the floor.

"Say hello to your new roomie," Urneck told the room at large.

Although he tried to sound cavalier, the man was clearly not amused. He clutched a blaster in his right hand. Dark stains marred his uniform, and a cut above his left eye seeped blood.

"Does hurting people make you feel manly?" Nancy asked as she hurried across the chamber.

The Lokii's wings were canted at an unnatural angle, and green liquid oozed from several blaster holes on its thorax. A nasty gash ran between the bulbous eyes. It clearly wasn't a threat right now. She glared at Urneck.

"Don't get all high and mighty!" Urneck shot back, though he did have the decency to holster his weapon. "A dozen of them attacked us, no doubt trying to steal the nectar, but it was a joke. The bugs don't fight worth a damn. When I clobbered their general here, the others just scurried away. Figured hanging onto him was good insurance."

"Yeah, you're a natural underwriter, and I hope you choke on your collateral someday."

She carefully unbent the crooked wings and smoothed them back along the Lokii's abdomen. At least they hadn't broken, but she had no idea how to deal with the lacerations. The deeper holes were seared around the edges from energy bolts. She gagged when she found two that had burned clear through the poor creature.

There was no practical way to treat those wounds, but she grabbed a clean cloth from the lab station and gingerly tried to staunch the flow of blood from a cut below the antenna. The wheezing Lokii radiated a familiar aura of calm.

"HaSSaam?" Nancy whispered.

There was the barest bob of the head. Grint wasn't as smart as he thought. He'd indeed captured one of the Lokii leaders, but HaSSaam was a cultural lead, not their general—that would be Hassaam. The distinction didn't make much of a difference. The Lokii were a strange bunch, but alien as they were, they were peaceful, even helpful. They'd saved the Lobstra and her from getting fried in the sunflower field, and their gift of translation certainly made things easier. Rather than the Lokii attacking humans, it seemed more likely that Urneck made a preemptive strike against the gentle foragers?

"You wrap darkness about yourself." HaSSaam cocked his head to peer around the cloth, his mental voice serene and amused, but too weak.

Nancy pulled her gaze away from Urneck and the twins who retreated into a hushed conversation with a nervous-looking Dianne. She studied the delicate face, lost herself in those depthless orbs. Under the lights, HaSSaam's eyes took on a rusty tinge, reddish-brown with shifting black flecks replacing the vibrant green she'd seen on her last meeting. The flecks and half-seen patterns shifted in a soothing kaleidoscope. She puffed out a breath and forced her clenched hands to relax.

"Just tense. We need to patch you up."

"Here you go." Drissa set down a med kit. "Human first aid, but there's a sealant and patching compound that works well on Lobstra plating, so it should do for him."

"This is HaSSaam." Nancy stood, relinquishing the Lokii to Drissa.

"We've met." The Lobstra brusquely set about cleaning the worst burns.

Drissa moved on to apply a clear salve to the deepest hole, squeezed in a purple paste, and swirled it around with a little spatula. As the components mixed, the paste turned milky white and hardened, sealing the open wound. Drissa moved on to the next blaster hole, giving the wound an even more vigorous cleaning. Perhaps the substance contained an analgesic.

"We had an interesting discussion upon the feasting fields," HaSSaam said in response to Nancy's raised eyebrow. His voice sounded stronger, and his big eyes glinted with mischief.

"More like a lecture." Drissa spared Nancy a glance before inspecting the joint where HaSSaam's wing connected to his shoulder ridge. "About the sanctity of life in the plant kingdom, and not blaming the victims for the sins of the ravishers. All while his people munched down more sunflowers and grasses than we ever burn through in a cycle!"

"There's a difference—" HaSSaam began, but Drissa cut him off.

"Yes, you told me, but between your poor grasp of galactic standard and the pounding headache preceding your 'gift' of translation, damned if I can tell the difference. Your people aren't enslaved by the nectar, mine are!"

Nancy looked from one to the other. HaSSaam radiated calm, though it carried a strained desperation. Drissa's mild disposition settled into hard angles and sharp barbs, fueled by her fundamentalist opposition to the aging Lobstra ruler. Clearly the Lokii disagreed with her idealism. The last thing she'd expect to find between such dissimilar races was a political standoff. But the priority for now was to keep HaSSaam alive.

"Explain it to them, HaSSaam." Reemer was plastered to the view port, watching their exchange.

"Not helping." Nancy glared at Reemer, but she needn't have bothered. Judging by the limp limbs and deep breathing, the Lokii had fallen asleep. It was likely the best thing for him. When the work at hand was done, they could debate at leisure—assuming they got clear of Urneck's crew.

* * *

The glob of translucent goo sagged under the constant strain of gravity, gathering its nerve for the long journey to the floor. Mica-like flecks within the gelatinous spittle reflected light as it teased. Nancy and Drissa stared at the globule, a thumb-sized smear halfway up on Reemer's side of the window between cells. The Squinch leaned expectantly toward the little projectile that she had worked her way up to daintily expelling as commentary on her disapproval of their current actions. Reemer nodded encouragement to the bit of goo, as if willing it into action. Even HaSSaam turned to watch from within the nest of blankets tucked around him.

"Really?" Nancy shook her head, trying to break the spell. Wait, did it move?

"Childish, I know," Reemer said. "But your abuse of that poor plant is just…infuriating. Yes, that's what it is, infuriating."

"I get that you're upset." Nancy tried to focus on the Squinch's pinched features, but her eyes kept wandering back to the clinging projectile. "But I've seen you hurl out volumes of noxious material, enough to choke a Slurg. Once, you even put a tree to sleep."

Reemer's eyes turned dreamy, the muscles of her face relaxing into a thoughtful grin. "That would be…" Nancy waited for her to fill in the blank with something like wonderful or awesome, but Reemer shuddered and scowled. "…improper."

Her head throbbed. They'd gone round and round with Reemer while HaSSaam slept. If anything, the Squinch grew more agitated. She insisted they release the Dolor Queen, conveniently ignoring the fact it would be impossible because they were all prisoners. The creature's thrashing resistance to Craig's electrostatic probe had grown frantic during the first two days, to the point of damaging the equipment, but Craig had made repairs and the Dolor finally settled down. Watching the extraction process would be unnerving for someone who didn't understand that the creature was simply a plant, especially if they hadn't seen what the Dolor were capable of. But Reemer had a front row seat to all the nastiness. Nancy rubbed her aching temples, hoping Dianne could scrounge up some good old-fashioned aspirin.

Low wailing—nearly inaudible—brought Nancy's head up. Craig probed as the automated brushes swept through the Dolor's vegetative hairdo. Dianne oversaw the controls. The twins and Urneck had left hours ago. The sound might have been an alarm, but nothing seemed out of place. Maybe it was a byproduct of her headache or simply vibration from unseen machinery. Her ears and jaw rattled as the tone sounded again.

Drissa and both humans paused to scan the room, so it wasn't her imagination. Reemer bounced up and down, and HaSSaam cocked his head like a curious puppy. The noise continued for a good twenty seconds before subsiding.

"Alarm?" Nancy asked.

"Maybe, but I could barely hear it. My antennae are still quivering," Drissa said.

"It's her!" Reemer cried. "Don't you see? She's in pain."

"For god's sake, Reemer, give it a rest!" Nancy turned to the Lokii. "Could your swarm be attacking again?"

HaSSaam rolled over so his thorax was cradled in the blankets and propped himself up on forelegs with those wickedly sharp tips brushing the floor. The motion cost him. She could tell by the painful hiss of air from the breathing tubes along his side and the fresh green ichor smearing the blankets. Those deep wounds saturated their bandages almost as quick as they could change them.

"We achieved our goal. They will not return. You should listen to your friend, Nancy Dickenson."

"Goal? Your people ran away as soon as things got tough. All you managed to do was get yourself shot and captured. Was that what you wanted?" Nancy asked, then clarified, "Not to get shot of course, but to be brought inside?"

"It also served as a diversion for your human friend." The echoed meaning in her head was not nearly as disturbing as it had been at their first encounter, and she'd had plenty of practice hearing the thoughts behind alien languages. There was definite nuance behind his words.

"You mean he's here?"

Jake was nearby! An unexpected fluttering warmth spread through her midsection as she let that sink in.

His silent language was accompanied by audible puffs of air, breathy hisses along the edge of his chitinous back. The sound reminded her of the orifices beneath Reemer's skirt, though thankfully without the flatulent overtones. The Squinch argued on with Drissa. Dianne would finish with the extractions today or tomorrow. Stopping right this instant wouldn't make any difference, and Nancy just couldn't dredge up the mental energy for more debate.

Nancy scooped up the medical kit, sat next to HaSSaam, and peeled off his sodden bandages. She reapplied sealant and clean dressings in silence, then washed the pale green blood from her hands. The antiseptic wipes worked well, except on those stubborn red patches she occasionally found along the edge of a nail or between her fingers. Just when she thought she'd gotten them all, another would present itself. She scrubbed harder.

Something brushed her temple, fluttering, butterfly kisses on the side of her head that tangled in her hair. She swatted with the cleaning rag only to find HaSSaam's angular face very close to her own. His fine antenna bent forward at ninety degrees and gently probed and tickled, an insect examining the edge of a doorway. She bit down on an exclamation as one cruelly serrated foreleg rose. She couldn't help shivering as the delicate fingers reached up to cradle her chin. Those orange-tipped teeth along his forearm, the entomological equivalent of a spiked medieval vambrace, could easily slice through things like beetle shells, roots, and, say, jugular veins. Nancy went very still.

"You must let this go." HaSSaam's voice was gentle.

Mom had sounded like that, sad and disappointed in Nancy's decision to join a space mission—a choice that in her mother's eyes shattered any prospects of a normal life for her daughter. A year was a long time to be away. At least her father had offered words of encouragement, his warm hand in hers as Mom finally came around and wrapped Nancy in a teary embrace. Dad smiled, but his eyes held the full measure of the coming separation. That one year would likely grow to two or three as more missions and opportunities presented themselves.

She'd watched the sadness in his eyes through her viewport as the shuttle engines had whined to life. The image filled her world. Then his gray eyes turned slate blue, the quiet sorrow replaced by bright, brittle fear. Pupils cast right and left as vines wrapped around Harry and pulled her closest friend into a dark, lonely grave. She studied her hands, the blood coating them, bright as the day they all died.

"It's back." Nancy moaned and tore open a new cleansing pack.

Those long alien fingers pressed firmly down on her hands, stilling them. She blinked in confusion as HaSSaam gently caressed her knuckles. In a moment of clarity, she saw that the only red across the backs of her hands was raw skin, where her fingernails scratched and the chemical scrub abraded. The real stains lurked below the surface, blood-red afterimages burnt into her mind.

HaSSaam's feathery touch withdrew at some point, leaving her cold and alone. She turned her palms up and looked numbly at the cracked skin, rubbed raw on so many occasions. She'd never get them clean.

Nancy blinked the room into focus. Despite dozing off, exhaustion still pulled at her. The Dolor's restraints and medical console were gone, the collection process complete. She tried to dredge up hate and contempt for the mass of vegetation slumped at the back of its enclosure. Its once-fearsome spiral arms twitched weakly and groomed through the crown of the opposing trunk, as if caressing and reassuring its other half—an absurd notion. None of it mattered. The hatred had fled, replaced by weary apathy and a throbbing head.

Drissa made a muffled exclamation. Arms snaked around Nancy from behind, breaking through her malaise. She looked down, expecting to again find those wicked Lokii front legs. But arms, real human arms with dirty hands and camouflaged sleeves rolled up to expose muscular forearms encircled her.

"You're okay," Jake murmured in her right ear.

He tried to draw her into a hug, but she pulled away.

"Don't touch me."

Nancy longed for human contact, but her body buzzed with agitation as if ants crawled across every inch of her skin. The warmth of those arms, the tenderness, was unbearable. She didn't deserve it; better to curl up and sleep.

But the arms were insistent. Iron gentleness encircled her, denied her efforts to stand. She shivered, lurched forward again, and then fell back into Jake. Hot tears spilled down her cheeks and gathered in the corners of her mouth. She tasted salt and shame and let his warmth enfold her.

29. A Bumpy Ride

"**D**O SOMETHING." Reemer was ready to gnaw off her antenna if it would stop the screams.

The Lokii were still an enigma. HaSSaam had been working with Nancy, trying to get the woman to see what was going on, to hear what Reemer herself heard all too clearly. The Lokii gift had spread like wildfire, and she assumed they were all affected equally. But the Squinch—or maybe just she—had proven more receptive to having their perception altered. The Lobstra and humans remained blissfully unaware of the screams of pain and anguish that Reemer couldn't block out. It was enough to drive a girl crazy.

"I do what I can." HaSSaam's patience was infuriating.

He sounded tired, which made sense. The Lokii had sat with Nancy for hours, keeping the woman from her incessant cleansing. The two surely communed in that silent way of the insect folk, and HaSSaam had only backed off due to Jake's surprise appearance. But Nancy had stayed locked in a trance, oblivious to the arrival of the other human and ignoring the hushed conversation between the others. Jake finally decided enough was enough and physically wrestled her out of whatever reverie had hold. At first, the waves of aguish rolling off Nancy after she collapsed into Jake's arms were physically painful. They had since eased into mere discomfort, but Reemer's strange human friend still hurt.

"Well, do it faster!"

Mother would be proud. Reemer had never realized the power females wielded. Aside from coaching and primping, Mother introduced her to several young male Squinch at the mating beach. That was an eye-opening experience indeed. They jumped at her beck and call, fetched her treats, and pretty much tripped over each other trying to win her approval—a taste of godhood! Sure, the sacred rituals probably had them swimming in their own hormones, but Mom assured her that getting the same devotion from anyone, anywhere, and at any time simply took practice.

Reemer occasionally missed the sliming fun and practical jokes, but these new abilities proved so much more practical. She slanted an imperious eye down at HaSSaam and the placid Lokii leader wilted as he let out a mental sigh. Yes, she was getting quite good!

* * *

"No!" Nancy cried.

The axe fell again, chipping at the wood of a forearm she'd thrust forward to stop her unseen attacker. A dark nimbus crowded close and cloying. Lights glowed just beyond her vision, though she saw only the gleaming steel of the axe as it hissed forward again. A fleshy chunk flew off, and her hand dropped away, lost to the mists climbing her legs.

Nancy couldn't see her feet and knew that they too had been taken. Things scuttled around in the mists, ignoring her pleas for help. They refused to even look her in the eyes. Indignation rose, and she suddenly towered above them. Her body was pitted and scored, her legs lost to the scourge below; she was greater, yet incomplete; safe, but threatened; omniscient, yet ignorant. So many conflicting feelings.

"Listen to me!" The darkness swallowed her words, her thoughts, and spun them back as echoing laughter, flat and humorless.

The ground lurched. Nancy stumbled, trying to get her feet beneath her, then realized her mistake and started to fall sideways. She scrambled, clomping about on wooden legs that refused to obey. It was a long way down. The ground rushed up toward her. She glimpsed the scurrying things as they scattered. Many were covered in smooth leaves with odd branches sticking out at waist and back. She fell upon them like an avenging, dying god, a burning comet from the heavens. Even as they ran for their lives, they refused to look upon her, to see her, to know her.

Had the floor tilted? Nancy could have sworn that a moment ago it had done just that. Now, all seemed perfectly level, though the deck did vibrate against her cheek. Her heart still pounded from the memory of the axe, and the pitiful wailing of some distant, dying piece of machinery didn't help. She sat up and blinked away the mist from the terrifying dream. She sat on the deck next to her cot under dim red lighting that simulated nighttime. HaSSaam rested in his nest of blankets near the viewport to Reemer's cell.

"Give me your hand," Jake said gently from the foot of her bed.

Nancy blinked at his hand before reaching out and letting him pull her to her feet.

"Oh god, my head." She massaged her forehead, feeling the swell of a lump, but the pain was an ice pick through her temple.

"Unexpected lift-off." Jake nodded across to Drissa and then Reemer, both were just picking themselves up off the deck. "Would have been nice if they had at least sounded the underway bells. The inertial dampeners do a decent job, but nothing's perfect."

"Where are we going?" Nancy realized she still gripped Jake's hand, hurriedly released it, and then smiled an apology. She massaged her temples with both hands and tried not to look like a total looney-bin. God, her head hurt, but an ugly thought slipped past the pain. "You're trapped!"

Jake shrugged and gave a boyish grin. The gesture was charming and probably meant to be reassuring, but he wasn't taking the situation seriously, which made her feel old. She winced as another terrible squeal pierced her already buzzing head. Did they forget to oil the damned engines? The sound came from deep in the craft, a sort of hollow and forlorn scream of equipment—t-rex meets Godzilla with a hint of cat's tail caught in a rocker. The sound blossomed to an all-encompassing screech. Nancy turned in a circle, then adjusted that thought. No, not everywhere, it came from straight across the room, from…there!

In the cell opposite her own, the quivering hulk of vegetation curled in a corner. The Dolor had also been thrown off its feet—or rather roots. The wispy appendages atop its crown, those organs that had released half of the diploid cells they harvested, swayed as the massive green head rocked with the rise and fall of the horrible sound. The spiral tentacles stroked the main trunk in time to the rhythm.

"Your eyes!" Reemer exclaimed. "You hear her."

Not the plant too. The Dolor queen made sounds that were not sounds, a rendering of simple thoughts, inarticulate wailings of despair and loss. But below the surface flitted images with thorny edges that resisted interpretation.

Nancy glared at HaSSaam. He rested painfully on his side, his praying mantis arms tucked contritely before him in seemingly placid meditation. "This is your doing." She didn't need to hear anything from this monster. It could wail and gnash all it liked, but she did…not…want…to…hear…it.

"Peace." The Lokii's mild word conveyed a world of meaning.

A wave of calm engulfed Nancy, which would have made her blood boil if it wasn't so damned peaceful! She wanted to complain, to lambaste the big insect monk for interfering, but it just wasn't going to happen. She turned back to Jake and tried to muster annoyance.

"Where are they taking us?" She asked—too damned calmly.

As Jake opened his mouth to reply, the main door whooshed open to admit Urneck and his two goons.

"Don't strain yourself, pretty-boy," Urneck said. "I'll answer the lady. And welcome aboard. Oh, don't look so glum, you had to know we'd be monitoring things down here." The twins took up station to either side of the entrance. As the man approached, Nancy smelled garlic. Urneck held his pistol casually and waived it at the plant. "We're putting the creature back where it belongs. Then we'll have to figure out where all of you belong."

"Really?" Nancy tried to think around the wailing in her head. At best, the man would strand them here on Fred. Assuming they could get a little help from the Lobstra until the navy rescue ship arrived, that wouldn't be so bad. But she doubted they could hope for the best-case scenario. Would his crew go along with murder? Nancy wished the damned Dolor would shut up for one minute. "Frankly, I'm shocked. A big bad renegade like yourself following the rules? It's so un-Grint-like."

Urneck's puzzled expression gave way to his signature sneer. "And you, Doc, with your fancy degree and navy appointment, just don't get it. The thing belongs on the plateau, so that's where we'll dump it."

Jake edged along the wall toward the partition into Reemer's cell. She didn't know how long he'd been aboard before coming to see her. If he had a plan, she needed to stall for time.

"Magnanimous of you, reseeding the hunting grounds so the next guy can get a piece of the action. I would think that drives down the value of your own harvest. Supply and demand and all—"

"No!" The faint mental command might have come from the Lokii. HaSSaam's head drooped, and it seemed to be all he could do to prop his upper body up on his forelegs. The color had washed from his shell, leaving it pale-green, and a hint of red made his eyes look bloodshot.

"You spoiled little—" Urneck's face flushed, but he bit off his statement, looked from Nancy to the Dolor, and shook his head as if to clear it. "Damned if you ain't right. I'm no conservationist. I…" His words faltered again as his eyes turned glassy, lids drooping. He raised his left hand and mouthed words into the blocky black device on his wrist, sounding half asleep. "QUEN, how far to the drop zone?"

"Five minutes, Mon Capitan." The familiar mechanical voice from the little comm unit sounded tinny.

Something powerful ruffled the edge of Nancy's perception as if she were outside a wind tunnel and only able to feel the turbulent edges. But what she did sense felt much like the wave of calm HaSSaam projected. The Lokii focused on Urneck, and the room grew quiet. Even the Dolor's lamenting ceased, as if the plant held its breath, waiting. Urneck's smile was forced, his movements wooden. He turned and walked stiffly toward the doorway. "Ray-Jay, box up the plant. Delivery in five."

Ray moved to comply, but Jay looked from Urneck to the open cell. "You okay, boss?"

"Did I ask you to play twenty questions?" Urneck snapped, and just like that was himself again.

In one smooth motion, Urneck spun back, raised his pistol, and fired. The bolt of energy sizzled as it struck HaSSaam where front legs connected to his long narrow chest. Air hissed from the alien, and he dropped into his nest of blankets, acrid smoke curling up from beneath him. The mental pressure winked out.

"Plan B," Urneck said to Jay, as he strode past the stunned man and swept through the sliding doors.

"HaSSaam!" Reemer's cry moved Nancy into action.

She rushed over to the crumpled alien. His antennae twitched weakly, and his thorax heaved with shallow breaths. One forearm had been cleanly severed from his body and lay in a tight vee off to the side. Green ichor seeped from the charred hole in his chest. She gagged at the sweet odor of burnt flesh. It wasn't the kind of wound you could patch.

Nancy held his remaining forearm and eased the Lokii leader onto his side. His eyes were misty red now, as if something within had ruptured. This was her fault. She'd goaded Urneck, trying to buy time, not realizing HaSSaam was…what? Manipulating him? She looked at the gaping hole, and her stomach churned. More blood on her hands.

"Peace, Nancy Dickenson." HaSSaam's mental voice was thready but insistent. "Do not blame yourself. We knew holding Urneck Grint to the pact would prove difficult."

So, the Lokii's mental manipulations kept the winning hunters in line. That was the force requiring the plant to be released.

"It is the best protection we can offer this planet's High One, the Lobstra's Szooda and your Dolor Queen."

He just read my mind.

"At times, your thoughts are clear." There was melancholy in his mental voice, true regret. "The deception is necessary. I grow careless as my journey ends and beg your discretion. If the extent of our abilities was widely known, it would cause undue complications. I have not the time to cite our reasons. We do what is necessary, while searching for a better way to help this planet. Direct intercession is rare. Most leaders respect the rules of the contest. But when the humans rejected their captain, more focused action was needed. So I came, but have failed."

The deck lurched as if punctuating HaSSaam's admission, and Nancy had to shift quickly to keep him semi-upright.

"Damn it! They've changed course. We're headed off planet. I hope this works," Jake called from the center of the bay, then spoke to the control panel. "QUEN, are you there? Daddy's home. I repeat, Daddy's home!"

"Hi, sweetie." The AI's voice was bright smiles. "Your files are still processing through quarantine, but it's sooooo good to hear your voice. How have you been? Is my man Veechy around?"

"There's little time," HaSSaam urged, pulling Nancy's attention back. "I give you what I have and ask that you return me to the swarm."

Something flowed from HaSSaam to Nancy. It wasn't an imperative or demand, as his attempt to calm her had been. This was a gentle power opening her mind for a few seconds of perfect attentiveness. Nancy wasn't religious, but divine radiance aptly described the experience.

Too soon, the moment passed, those rich colors that had drawn her deep into his fathomless eyes drained away leaving empty white orbs, and HaSSaam was gone. Nancy cradled his boney neck and rocked, clutching his body tight against the ache in her chest. Drops splashed onto the side of his delicate beak-of-a mouth. She hastily brushed the tears away and lowered him gently to her lap, the motion smearing her arms with green blood and ashy brown flecks. But she knew it was temporary, just dirt that would wash away.

"Listen to me, QUEN," Jake pleaded with the workstation. "You know my voice. Can't you—"

"Sorry, Jake." QUEN cut him off, and Jake swore under his breath. "Your files will finish processing and be loaded in thirty-three minutes."

"For the love of god, QUEN, don't make me do this." Jake slumped over the controls as though he'd cursed himself empty. Her newfound calm let Nancy smile at the absurdity of the handsome young man arguing with a computer. Jake shook his head and carefully articulated his next words. "QUEN, drop…the…ball, I repeat, drop…the…ball. Authentication, sierra niner three alpha alpha one."

The gentle acceleration that had kept them pressed to the deck a bit harder than simple artificial gravity suddenly vanished. For a terrifying instant, Nancy was falling.

"Everyone find a seat and brace yourself," Jake yelled. "It's going to get bumpy."

Bumpy did not begin to describe the ride.

30. Mind and Soul

"WHAT THE hell was that?" Reemer roared.

The angry words belied a gleam in the Squinch's eyes that had not been there in a long time. If Nancy didn't know better, she'd say Reemer enjoyed the jarring descent and crash landing despite the alarms, sparking wall panels, and crisp scent of ozone and burnt rubber.

Reemer pressed up against the clear partition, panting like a freight train. Green secretions flowed from the mouths beneath her skirt—an impressive volume of goo. Nancy braced for an old-school expulsion, but with visible effort Reemer reined in her mounting enthusiasm.

"Err...what I mean is, was all that strictly necessary, Jake?"

Nancy gave full points in decorum as Reemer peeled herself off the panel, although any attempt at dignity was undermined by slurping and sucking as she reabsorbed the mucus. Still, Reemer managed to draw herself into that regal pose so reminiscent of their brief encounter with Belinda.

"Yeah, sorry about that." Jake gave a nervous smile. "I had to use an old override code. QUEN pretty much dropped the shuttle like a rock. I figured if Grint's folks weren't quick to take manual control, the crash avoidance sensors would kick on the autonav. Looks like it worked!"

"If that was crash avoidance, I'd hate to see what you call a real crash." Drissa scuttled around the buckled floor plates in the open bay.

The Lobstra had the presence of mind to return to her own cell, which had adjustable webbing to fit her unique shape. Even so, she dragged two of her smaller legs, which seemed to have broken. The species' pain tolerance was astounding.

"Where are we?" Nancy asked.

"Can't tell from here." Jake glanced at the console. "I only had a voice link to QUEN. The rest of these controls are for the detention bay. We better get moving and plan for the worst. Could be a water landing, and if the shuttle doesn't catch fire we might sink and find ourselves…well…sunk."

Sweet man, not terribly articulate, but sweet. And now that she thought about it, the air was getting more than a little smoky. Weren't the shuttle fire suppression systems supposed to take care of things like that? Nancy looked down at the dead Lokii. He'd asked for her to "return him."

Nancy gathered up the edges of the blanket that curled out from under the body, making a sort of cocoon. She twisted the ends together and experimentally pulled. Unlike navy-issue blankets that remained remarkably thick and scratchy in spite of the space and weight restrictions inherent in interstellar travel, the material she held was gauzy thin, relying on reflected heat to do its job. That fact made it relatively easy to grasp and thankfully the material was quite strong, because HaSSaam was heavy. She managed to drag him a couple of feet, but it was a real chore and she found herself sweating. The sharp tang of burning insulation filled the room, and it was definitely getting warmer.

"Whatcha doing?"

Nancy jumped as something heavy and wet slithered over her right forearm. Reemer craned to look at her bundle.

"Don't do that! You nearly gave me a heart attack. How did you…" Nancy trailed off as she traced the glistening path leading from the Squinch back through the adjacent cell door that had twisted out of its frame. "Never mind. He asked me to take him back."

But she could barely drag the corpse to the cell entrance, let alone through the entire shuttle, up ladders, and out. And if they were sitting in a lagoon somewhere, then what? If she fashioned a harness, maybe Drissa could give her a hand dragging the body. The Lobstra currently helped Jake gather odds and ends from around the room. Bits of wire, the medical kit, and what looked like a toothbrush all got jammed into Jake's straining pack. The boy was such a packrat.

"Just take back the important bits." Reemer nudged one of the stiff little antenna in homage to the fallen alien.

Or maybe a cart, something with wheels would take the weight better. Hadn't the Lokii heard of the square-cube law? It was supposed to keep things from growing to arbitrary sizes, supposed to prohibit the existence of giants and mega-creatures. HaSSaam wasn't exactly Godzilla, but he was still a damned big bug, and proving hard to move.

"What important bits?"

"You know, the mind and soul, the head and heart." Reemer nodded at the corpse and burped out a wet sigh when Nancy blinked in confusion. "Cut off his flipping head and wings. That's what the bugs revere."

"Cut off his head!" Nancy choked as the Squinch nodded enthusiastically.

"And the wings. The soul flies, the mind…meditates, I guess. I've seen their ritual for the dead. I'm sure it's what he wanted."

The next few minutes were an exercise in frustration. Nancy tried to use the blunt little scissors from the medipak on a wing. The boney exoskeleton was tough where it hinged into his back, and her heart just wasn't in it. Reemer tried to gnaw at the plating to no avail. The attempt seemed a nostalgic nod to her past life, because she stopped as soon as the crunching and messy saliva forced Nancy to turn away. The other two finished their preps and came over with heads bowed.

"Would you be so kind," Reemer asked Drissa, with such a polite inflection that Nancy began to suspect the Squinch was a touch schizophrenic, or would that be bipolar?

"For goodness sake." Drissa reached out with her narrow cutting claw and snipped through one wing, then the other.

Nancy swallowed hard when Drissa slid her claw under HaSSaam's chin. When his boney neck sat firmly in the vee at the base of her claw, the claw snapped closed. With a pop and crunch the head came free, and the contents of Nancy's stomach rolled explosively up her throat.

It took a minute to gather her wits and clean up. Jake looked queasy as he passed her a wet blanket. She looped her travel pouch and the angular, soccer-ball-sized bundle the Lobstra handed her over one shoulder and tried not to think about its contents. Drissa lashed the severed wings together and crimped them onto Nancy's shoulder strap.

Though lifeless, the gossamer wings were beautiful. She'd never noticed the subtle iridescent spirals. Greens and yellows loosely wound around a darker reddish center of each to make a stylized set of eyes. The feather-light touch of the wings was somehow comforting. They cascaded down her back and brushed against her calves as she headed to the door with the others. She tucked her chin down into her collar to cover her mouth and nose.

"Everyone ready?" Jake stepped to the entrance, flipped opened an access panel, and grasped the lever within. "I'll manually override the fire boundaries, which is good and bad. Keep your faces covered to filter the smoke and stay to the side until we know what we're dealing with. If there's a backdraft, expect a gout of flame to roar past when the door opens. After it dies out, keep low and follow me. Use the wet blankets to protect yourselves from direct flames. We won't have far to go, but there is one ladder to climb. Drissa, help Reemer with that, will you?" The Lobstra bobbed in agreement. "Watch for weak spots and live wires. There could be flooding. If we hit water inside the ship, drop the blankets and use the floats we gave you. With luck the crew will be too busy getting things under control to worry about us."

Nancy gripped tight to her sodden half blanket and the string of four plastic bags that had been inflated into little pillows. The IV bags would serve as a life vest if the ship had come down in water.

"Here we go. Just keep your heads and stay together." Jake pulled the lever and Nancy braced herself as the doors began to move. "Let's see what we're dealing with, smoke, fire, water, or…" Jake stuttered to a halt and blinked in surprise "Sunshine?"

Sure enough, boulders and sparse tufts of grass baked in the midday sun just outside the big doorway. The doors themselves grating to a stop halfway open. Fresh air blew in through the opening, sweeping the smoke away and bringing with it a noticeably drier heat. It must have been near a hundred degrees out there.

"Wait here," Jake said before slipping outside.

He scrambled over rocks as his shadow moved out of sight. At the sound of muffled voices, she took a step toward the open doorway, straining to hear.

"Um, Nancy." Reemer's wet antenna tugged on her pant leg.

"Shh, not now."

"Holy crap!" Jake's exclamation dropped into muttered curses punctuated by more skittering stones.

"But you need to…"

"Give me a minute," Nancy hissed at the slug in her best schoolmarm voice.

Jake's footsteps grew louder, ringing as if he walked across broken terracotta pots. He slid down a short slope from the left and strode back in, blinking at the transition from bright sun to the relatively dark interior of the bay.

"You're not going to believe this. "Jake dusted his hands off and laughed, but his smile fled when he looked up. "Ah…we sort of forgot about that."

Nancy followed his gaze. The hulking Dolor queen towered over Reemer, who looked distinctly pale. Drissa hovered just out of reach as if uncertain what to do. Nancy's first instinct was to move back toward Jake, but her friends were too close. Jake's pistol wouldn't drop the plant. Even if he got off a fatal shot, Reemer and Drissa might be poisoned by its flailing arms.

Two of those spiral arms were already looped around the slug, one stroking between the eyestalks and the other patting her back. Reemer cringed yet leaned into the contact as if both nauseous and attentive.

"Reemer." Whispering felt silly. "Come toward the door."

The Squinch just sat there, head cocked to the left like a confused dog. Had the venom already started its work? Flatulent gurgles erupted from her skirt, a delicate giggle more melodious than the old Reemer's guffaws—but laughter nonetheless.

"Sorry." The Squinch blinked and focused on Nancy for the first time. "Rebecca was just telling me the funniest story." She patted the spiral that sat between her eyestalks with one sensory antenna.

"The poison!" Nancy surged forward, hand outstretched, but touching the tentacle that had laid Craig out didn't even faze Reemer. "Wait, who's Rebecca?"

"Why big, green, and scary here." Reemer gave the tentacle another pat.

The plant's other arms shot over its head, writhing and wriggling while the fleshy headpiece on the adjacent trunk swished back and forth. Pressure reminiscent of the powerful wailing built in Nancy's head, but without the undercurrent of mourning. If anything, it had an electrifying almost infectious quality, and the corners of her mouth quirked up. Incredibly, the Dolor was…laughing.

"You heard her." Reemer jabbed an antenna at her. "I saw that smirk."

"Please, just get away from it."

"Her," Reemer corrected.

"It, her, the creature from the black and blue lagoon, whatever!" Fear gnawed at Nancy's belly. "She's dangerous!"

"We have to go," Jake interjected. "The detention room was a modular expansion that QUEN sent down for the extraction process. Autonav managed a soft landing, but it got shorn off in the crash. The shuttle's mostly in one piece just on the other side of a rocky ridge maybe a quarter mile east. They'll be coming for us soon. Even if he doesn't need that thing, Grint will want my head now. Let the plant fend for itself. We have to get moving."

The Dolor swayed in agitation. The mirth drained from its wave of mental pressure, replaced by more lamenting wails. Was everyone around her bipolar? But this time there were rudimentary thoughts too, a language in the way primitive pictographs would compare to modern literary works, with the hint of words, grunts, and gestures in place of more complex syntax. Yet, her sense of loss overwhelmed Nancy with fleeting impressions of Dolor pain watchers and urchins, the shuttle intruders, and unfamiliar sub-species.

"Her children!" Reemer's wail matched the intensity of the Dolor's.

"Yeah, I get it," Nancy said. "We've met plenty of her kind, been attacked by most of them. Been there, done that. You seem to 'speak' better plant than the rest of us. Just shut her up so we can all get out of here."

Reemer extracted herself from the grasping arms and stalked up to Nancy, an impressive feat given the alien had no legs. She rose up on her tail, stretching until their eyes were level.

"You don't get to ignore her, Dr. Dickenson, not this time." Nancy backpedaled at the Squinch's intensity, but Reemer flowed forward, giving her no quarter. She slapped the gruesome bundle hanging at Nancy's hip with an antenna, then poked at the gossamer wings rising behind her head. "He gave his life for this, for us. You will not disrespect that gift. You will listen, or by god, Nancy, I'll see that you never work in this town again."

That last statement must have been a translation glitch, but Reemer's intent was perfectly clear. Nancy had never seen her—or him for that matter—so serious. "But my crew—"

"Just"—Reemer closed her eyes, and the rest of the sentence escaped in a breathy sigh—"listen. Use the gift he left."

Listen? That's what she'd been doing, to the screeching, to the wailing, to the catalogue of sub-species. And what the hell was the Lokii's gift? A severed head? Wings that could never again take flight? She looked into Reemer's eyes, now soft and pleading. Such passion for an alien slug. No, that wasn't fair. Reemer was as much a person as any of them. And then it dawned on her; the gift was understanding.

Of course, the translation ability had come from HaSSaam. Nancy was pretty certain she'd been patient zero, the carrier for that plague of understanding. By now damned near everyone on the planet probably had the ability to talk to one another, but it was more than just a language or simple translation. Reading body language, emotions, and intent helped her truly understand the creatures—damn it, the people—she'd met.

Nancy scanned their little group: Jake, a cute guy who she never would have given a second thought; Drissa, a giant lobster with a heart of gold and deep political views; Reemer, her friend and a surprisingly complex mollusk; and a giant, dual-stalked, deadly poisonous, Frankenstein of a cactus that just might also turn out to be a person in the broader sense of the word.

Just after HaSSaam's death, anguish radiating from the Dolor had crashed in on her. Had the Lokii pushed her abilities just that much further during his final moments? Nancy bowed her head and listened. With her ears, yes, but she also strove to open her mind, her heart, to lay aside the prejudices and preconceptions and forget about the blood, and pain, and fear. She didn't dare breathe.

It hurt. She almost shut down again, easier to listen to the wailing than that underlying song of grief and loss. And it was a song. Nancy found herself immersed in a seething tide of impressions, images, and true words this time. Yet, all of it was knitted together into a vibrant tapestry resembling contemporary music. The lament of loss laid in a melancholy blues, a tinkling of notes in a minor chord structure. Alien words drifted in a gentle melody of remembrance. Names?

"Mankin, Orion, Graya, Whavier…" The voice was feminine, matronly, and angry.

The litany of names flowed on at an ever-increasing tempo, overlaid now with tight strong chords of need and a driving determination to communicate and act.

"I must recover our…future."

The last word came across as a complex web of concepts including temporal shifts, growth, and realizing potential, but Nancy couldn't quite put the pieces together.

"Your future?" She opened her eyes and stared up at the strange creature that was suddenly not nearly as frightening. "I don't understand."

"Future!" Reemer exclaimed. "As in next generation. She wants to save her kids."

The undertone of children was there in the music, but survival mechanisms for the plant kingdom were pretty standard. Seeds and seedlings moved by a variety of means carried to new areas where overcrowding would not be an issue. They'd encountered Dolor specimens from the coast all the way to the upper elevations. The various sub-species seemed to be doing just fine if you discounted their tendency to attack.

Affirmation flowed from Rebecca—yes, the plant actually had a name for itself—along with words that became clearer by the moment. "We will not…survive? Yes, survive, another lost generation. I grow too old."

"Are you talking about the haploid cells, the nectar?" Nancy asked.

Stronger agreement. Nancy found herself nodding, and waves of gratitude rolled off Rebecca.

"That means taking on Grint." Reemer's mantle swelled.

"Wait, take on Grint?" Drissa asked. She and Jake looked confused. Neither of them seemed to follow the conversation, or at least not Rebecca's half of it.

Nancy summarized as best she could what the Dolor had broadcast.

"You can't seriously want to help that thing?" Drissa jabbed her battle claw at Rebecca. "The whole point has been to get rid of it. Now it parrots a few words and you want to fight for it? To bring more of its kind back? It's not a thinking creature. It's using some tricky survival technique. You're being manipulated, Nancy."

"Move now, talk later." Jake pushed them all toward the door.

None of them were sad to leave the holding area, but the Dolor—Rebecca—did not want to go through the partially open doorway. Her mental song flashed back to being zapped by the twins while in the transport crate. She feared the metal would come alive and the door would snap shut on her. Nancy waited outside with a bristling Drissa while Reemer helped Jake coax the plant creature through the opening.

Drissa was wrong about the Dolor being a mere plant. Rebecca didn't simply mimic intelligence. HaSSaam's gift made it clear there was logical thought behind that vegetative brow. Nancy and Reemer both saw it, perhaps due to their close proximity to the Lokii when he died and passed on more of his capabilities.

The Lobstra was clearly upset at Nancy's change of heart. A minute-long discussion with the Dolor hadn't totally allayed her reservations about the creature, but had served to humanize Rebecca. That alone made it easier to accept the plant as another in the diverse stream of individuals she'd met during her time on Fred. But the plant had a long way to go in gaining Nancy's trust, let alone respect.

But there was still the trail of corpses the plants—if not Rebecca herself—left in their wake. That thought twisted her gut into a conflicted knot, but Nancy had promised to retrieve the nectar if for no other reason than to keep it out of Urneck's clutches. Regardless, they needed to head back to the shuttle. Jake's link to QUEN had been severed when the holding bay tore free. So getting back to the ship was the only way to reestablish communications. He and the AI had a plan in mind.

The group stuck to the shadow cast by the detached holding bay. The module was wedged against a rocky ridge, like a battered and forgotten hockey puck. A cascade of slate sheets littered the ground and made it difficult to move quietly. They skirted a twisted array of docking clamps and umbilical cords that once connected them to the ship.

Nancy felt exposed under the bright sun, and every skittering stone made her jump. The shuttle sat at the end of the gully, a fresh gouge in the ground made by the unplanned landing. The ship sat at the other end and canted at perhaps fifteen degrees. That didn't seem too bad, but Jake assured them moving around inside would be a challenge.

"The shuttle has two hull breeches that Grint's people will need to patch to be space worthy," Jake said as they crept along the gully toward the main craft. "The nectar will either be in the med bay, with Dianne, or in Urneck's secured storage area near the bridge. We'll have to sneak past the teams doing exterior repairs, then split up to search those spots."

She could hug him. Jake's unquestioning support made the slippery footing of her moral shift more solid. Dissent still radiated from Drissa, but the Lobstra no longer argued, which Nancy took as a sign she was coming around.

"I find." Rebecca projected an image of recovering what was hers.

Jake looked up just before Nancy relayed the thought aloud. Rebecca could sense the material they'd taken from her if she got close.

"That would help." Jake scratched his chin and eyed the Dolor.

Nancy pushed an image of the cramped interior at the shambling plant. "No offense, but you'll barely fit inside, let alone be able to move through the passageways."

"That's not fair," Reemer countered. "She got to the holding bay just fine."

"Yeah, in a box. Not walking on her own, dealing with ladders. It just isn't practical."

"Please, stop bickering!" Drissa turned to Rebecca. "How close does it need to get?"

31. Hidden Agenda

T HEY SAT in the shade, just out of sight, waiting for the repair team to finish grinding down the edges and patching a two-foot tear in the shuttle's hull. Nancy agreed with Jake—they couldn't skirt Pete and the twin he worked with without being spotted.

"Eventually, they're going to have to seal off the docking area where the holding bay ripped loose." Jake rearranged the small collection of stones representing the shuttle and people. "That's around the far side. We'll be able to get to the rear gangway unseen, assuming they haven't set up proximity sensors. My access code will get us inside, but I'll need to find a control node quickly to check on QUEN and have her erase the door logs. Otherwise someone's bound to notice our digital trail."

"Where's the nearest node in relation to the bridge and medical?" Nancy asked

Jake added three new pebbles to form a triangle around the big rock. Of course they had to be on opposite sides of the ship.

"You do realize that if Dianne has begun processing, we might not be able to recover everything in good shape?" Nancy looked to the Dolor. Saying the next generation might already be dead sounded too final, plus the haploid cells were not fully-formed living organisms.

"I...do." The fronds of Rebecca's dominant head drooped.

"I just wanted to be sure, but we'll do our best."

It was entirely too easy to feel empathy for this creature. The plant would do anything to protect her young, and they could be in serious trouble if Rebecca had learned mind control from the Lokii. The two races must have been working together for decades, if not centuries. What were HaSSaam's people getting in return for helping the Dolor survive the insane hunting cycles? Worry crept in, concern that they were indeed being manipulated as Drissa had warned. But Rebecca's sorrow felt genuine, the concern for her children palpable. They were doing the right thing.

Drissa scurried up the slope to watch the shuttle repairs. After a few moments, she whispered down to the group, "They're leaving."

Getting inside the shuttle proved uneventful. They crept along the depression without being spotted, and Jake's access codes worked perfectly. The entrance was a kind of service port, and the small group crouched in a space twenty feet wide and bristling with equipment. As before, the Dolor hesitated.

"Get inside and out of sight," Drissa snapped, her patience clearly exhausted.

"Mean, angry...scary." Rebecca's leafy crown drooped in misery.

Nancy looked for some sign that Drissa heard the reply, but the Lobstra simply glared and waved an impatient claw, oblivious to any mind speak.

Seeing the planet Fred's massive apex creature cowed by the medical technician came as a surprise, but Nancy had to admit the Lobstra could be stern. Compromise didn't seem to take up a great portion of the race's psychological makeup. But she'd always found Captain Luftew to be reasonable in the end. Perhaps Drissa was coming around too, but her frantic insistence made the Dolor nervous instead of encouraging her to come inside.

"It's all right. We just need you to get out of sight." Reemer's voice rolled out in soothing waves, a good cop to Drissa's bad.

With a mental sigh, Rebecca shambled inside, gave Drissa a wide berth, and hunkered down in the corner. Survival suits, exoskeletal rigs, and excavating equipment hung along the bulkheads like suits of armor. The room bristled with instruments, and Jake gleefully worked at a console set next to an extra wide doorway leading to the interior. Nancy stopped her examination of a handheld drilling rig and walked over.

"Hello, beautiful," Jake crooned.

"Uh, hi," she stammered. There was that warm glow again. Nancy liked the way his voice dropped, making the letter o sound sultry.

"Hello yourself, Jakeypoo," that ridiculously sexy voice lilted from the console, raising the impossible image of a scantily clad, top-heavy blonde. "You have access to all of me now, honey. Think you can handle it?"

Nancy's ears were on fire, but fortunately Jake hadn't noticed her blunder. In fact, he turned to say something to the room and jumped at finding her so close.

"I'm back into QUEN." He gave them a thumbs up.

"Oh now, wouldn't that be interesting," the computer purred.

"Um, okay." Jake's smile froze, then slipped away as his ears went scarlet. "QUEN, I need you to suppress the door and boundary logs for a while. I don't want Urneck knowing where we're heading. Let him focus on the shuttle repairs. Oh, and I need you to open the armory and get a message off to the captain. He's waiting for the navy back with Endeavor."

"Affirmative on the door logs, lover, but no-can-do on the rest of that."

Jake refused to make eye contact as he consulted the digital map that blossomed on his screen, but paused at the AI's words. "Why not?"

"Well." QUEN let out a dainty huff—ridiculous, computers didn't breathe. "The G-man figured out that I was the one who cut power to the shuttle. He's quarantined the majority of my functions. I'm locked out of critical systems entirely. Without his say-so, I can't even maneuver the ship to keep my solar arrays charging. It's quite infuriating."

"Sorry. That's my fault." Jake looked truly chagrined, but then brightened. "Just critical systems? We can work around those."

They pulled supplies together from among the equipment. Nancy got herself a new cutting tool. It was bulkier than her old one and as long as a drumstick, but having the device made her feel whole again. Jake did his usual pack-rat thing, stuffing several small devices, rope, and kitchen sinks it into his bulging pack. Even Drissa managed to find a spare med kit and a few odds and ends that might prove useful. While the other three finished scavenging, Reemer spoke with Rebecca in quiet tones. Nancy made her way to the far corner and skidded to a halt on the slanting deck just before bowling Reemer over.

"Becky's staying here," Reemer said without preamble. "She says her young are that way."

Reemer pointed her feelers uphill toward what would be the far corner of the shuttle. So it was Becky now? The Squinch seemed even more protective of the Dolor than before. Jake came over with a flexible display of the shuttle layout. He'd marked two areas and rotated the device to orient the map. The direction Reemer indicated led to a blue area near the rear of the craft.

"That'll be Dianne's lab," Jake said. "We might not need to split up after all."

Jake took the lead. Nancy expected to run into trouble at every turn, but QUEN and Jake insisted that anyone not working on repairs would be on the bridge reestablishing navigation control. With all of her extra legs, the Lobstra had the best traction on inclines and took to scouting ahead to make sure the coast was clear. Their uphill climb along slanted decks was arduous, but not particularly dangerous. For the ladders, Reemer ended up clinging to Drissa's back.

A few scorched areas stood testament to recently smothered fires. Air scrubbers cleared the visible smoke but couldn't negate the odor of ozone and burnt plastic. Rebecca never could have made it through the debris and equipment that broke free during the violent landing and now littered the passageways. Nancy herself was sweaty and miserable as they drew to a halt outside medical.

"Nancy?" Dianne jumped up from a swivel seat bolted behind her desk, but froze halfway to the door.

Jake hadn't drawn his pistol, but his right hand hovered over the grip at his hip. Dianne blanched, but forced a measured smile. Bruising rose around a nasty lump on her forehead, a souvenir of the crash landing. Thanks to the equipment being neatly tucked into lockers and securely strapped to the bulkheads, the medical bay looked in better shape than the main corridors.

"We need the nectar," Nancy said. "Remember the analysis. It contains the haploid cells of the next Dolor generation. It's been stolen away for too many cycles. If this batch isn't returned, there won't be another cycle. The forests will die."

There was so much more to it: the burgeoning realization that the Dolor queen was more than just a plant, the symbiotic relationship with the Lokii, and the efforts to minimize the damage of the hunts. But blurting that out would sound crazy, too much like a desperate ploy to take advantage of Dianne's good nature.

The young woman wasn't cut from the same cloth as Urneck's goons. Not all of the human crew was poisoned by their selfish leader. One on one, Pete hadn't been so bad either and had taken risks to help them. Sure, the guy's deck was short a couple of cards, but he seemed decent once you got him away from Grint's influence. Craig and even Jay had likewise come across as rational and normal when they weren't being bossed around and threatened by Urneck.

By downplaying the idea that the Dolor was intelligent, Nancy could appeal to Dianne rationally, let her know the risk to the planet's ecosystem and remind her the navy was on its way, maybe even—

"You stole Becky's babies!" Reemer jabbed an accusing feeler at the woman.

Oh brother! Nancy liked Reemer better when she was less…caring.

"Who the hell's Becky?" Dianne whipped around to focus on the Squinch.

"The mother of Fred's next generation, the Dolor queen. You tortured them out of her."

"Oh, please, it's just a plant," Dianne scoffed, her face hardening as she turned back to Jake. "You know the size of our bonus. You could have killed us crashing the shuttle, and for what? This lunatic slug's idea that a plant will miss its babies?" The woman took a deep breath before continuing. "Nancy, if you're right, I am truly sorry, but the money is unimaginable. You know I have…things to take care of, responsibilities and bills to pay off. My parents won't have to worry about anything for the rest of their lives. I need this for my family."

Dianne took two quick steps toward her console, catching Nancy off guard. But Jake quickly intercepted the woman.

"Just give us the nectar." Jake voice was a low growl. "This is too important. I didn't want to hurt anyone. We've talked; you've seen it. There's something wrong with Urneck and his cronies. The rest of us will never see that bonus."

Something shifted behind the woman's eyes. Recognition? Agreement? But it flashed into fear as Drissa shot forward.

"There's no time for this. I can make her talk." The Lobstra moved like lightning, her battle claw clamping onto Dianne's shoulder.

"No!" Nancy grabbed the edge of her shell and tried to pull the Lobstra away.

Drissa could easily break Dianne's arm and collar bone without even trying. One slip could crush the woman's windpipe. Good lord, Drissa didn't budge. It was like pulling on a statue.

"Please, Dianne. How would you like it if your child was taken from you?" Nancy asked.

It was a low blow, and Nancy knew it. The woman had spoken of her pregnancy in confidence. All she wanted was to complete the mission and make a life for her unborn child, despite the crazy circumstances of its conception. Nancy wasn't sure who the father was, but hoped Dianne herself knew.

"How could you?" Dianne gaped at Nancy, eyes full of accusation, then slumped forward with a pointed look to the equipment rack in the far corner.

Drissa let go and strode to the corner. Dianne's knees buckled, and Nancy reached out to stabilize the woman, willing her to understand. The Lobstra poked at the equipment for a few moments. With a hiss, the round steel door Nancy had thought was for sterilizing surgical instruments opened. Cold vapor flowed out like liquid clouds to reveal the tray of nectar collection canisters.

"Got it!" Drissa removed the tray, double checked its contents, and stuffed the canisters into her oversized shoulder pack. "Let's get out of here."

"What about her?" Reemer asked. "We can't let her rat us out."

"Come with us." Nancy still had her arms around the woman.

"I can't." Dianne looked about in confusion, all her fire gone. "Jay's here."

"I understand, but think it over while we walk. I need you to stay with us until we're clear. Not as a hostage," Nancy quickly added when the woman's eyes went round. "Just to ensure you don't call the bridge and report us. Twenty minutes and we'll be out of your hair. But if you change your mind, you can stay with us until the navy arrives."

Nancy kept close to Dianne on the way out. The going was marginally easier downhill. As they picked their way through the debris, she asked if there was anything on the shuttle Dianne would need if she decided to leave. But the woman was in a daze, and rather than add to her confusion, Nancy eventually fell silent.

"Don't worry, little ones. We're taking you to mamma," Reemer cooed at the bag hanging at Drissa's side.

"Knock it off," the Lobstra growled with a halfhearted swipe at the Squinch.

At least, Nancy hoped it was halfhearted. Reemer squished nearly flat to the floor as the big claw swooshed over her head. The Lobstra still seemed to be holding a grudge against being outvoted, but things were going smoothly. They just needed to stay focused.

"Keep your eyes open, Reemer," Nancy said. "Let's get clear of the shuttle before getting all sappy."

"Well, I wouldn't call it sappy. Talking to gestating eggs has been shown to make the young ones more intelligent." Reemer drew herself up to her full height, sounding as prim and proper as a schoolmarm, but the illusion dropped away as she bent to pat the satchel with both antennae. "Isn't that right, little ones?"

This time Drissa's claw connected and snapped Reemer's head away with cruel force.

"Drissa!"

Even Jake and Dianne gasped at the sound of the hard claw smacking soft flesh. Drissa shrugged a half-apology and stomped on in silence. At least Reemer didn't seem any the worse for wear. She simply picked herself up, shook her head, and moved on with an indignant "well, I never!"

Instead of the normal swooshing sound, the doors to the equipment area let out a strange wailing tone as they parted to admit the group. The stringent noise brought everyone's head up in alarm. Rebecca still crouched in the far corner, but something was wrong. There were new burn marks on her hide, and a red elastic band pinned her tentacles up at a severe angle. The exterior door had been closed, and two men stepped from the shadows on either side of the plant—the twins. They held the familiar cattle prods and stern expressions.

Nancy backpedaled and spun toward the entrance, which was blocked by two more figures.

"Welcome back, Dr. Dickenson." Urneck Grint oozed through the door holding a nasty looking gun, as did the blonde on his right. Nancy couldn't recall the woman's name. "Jake, toss the gun to Angie."

"Bastard," Jake muttered as he handed over his pistol and the woman tucked it into her web belt.

"Come now," Urneck said. "You're the one who dropped us all out of the sky. You and that sad excuse for a computer. Damn nuisance having an AI aboard. I was seething about that, trying to get the ship repaired and a search organized, when you conveniently decide to bring my cargo back."

"She is not cargo," Reemer literally spat from next to Rebecca.

Urneck dodged the projectile that whizzed by his head. Ray jabbed Reemer with the prod, there was a crack of electric, and the slug fell onto her side in convulsions.

"Look, you have what you want," Jake said. "Just take the nectar and leave."

"No thanks to you. Captain's pet, always so eager to spy and spread your trackers around." Urneck grinned unpleasantly, managing to hold the gun steady as he flipped a small metallic disk into the air with his left hand and deftly caught it by the wisp of an antenna protruding from one end. "It took a while to figure out why a medevac transponder would be pinging from within the shuttle. Angie figured a field kit had broken loose and triggered one. But another popped up amidships and still another in medical near the nectar. Well, that's when I knew something was up. Oh, don't look at poor Dianne." That last was directed at Nancy, who had indeed turned to glare at the woman.

Thinking back, the girl couldn't have had a chance to activate any such device. And Urneck claimed two others had been set off within the ship. The image of Drissa rummaging in the med packs for supplies leapt to mind. The Lobstra had drifted away from the group several times under the pretext of scouting side passages as they picked their way through the shuttle.

"Drissa?" Nancy left the question—the accusation— unformed. The Lobstra moved to the exterior doorway and clutched her satchel with feathery upper legs.

"Dissent among the rabble?" Urneck asked with a satisfied smirk. "How fitting that one of your own misfits betrayed you. Although, I don't know what I did to instill such loyalty in one of the crustaceans. Still, I wouldn't want to look a gift horse in the mouth, as it were. Pony up, darling. I'll take that nectar back."

Drissa slapped the door controls on the bulkhead behind her, but nothing happened.

"I control the lock. Even your friendly AI can't get that open without my say so. Hand over the nectar." Urneck dropped the transponder and held out his hand.

Drissa stopped thrashing against the door. "I need your promise not to sell to any Lobstra."

That brought Urneck up short. Nancy could almost see the wheels turning behind his eyes as he tried to figure out if Drissa had a way of destroying the nectar if he tried to take it by force. A sly smile spread across the cretin's face. His conclusion was clear to Nancy, but likely lost on the Lobstra: promises were cheap.

"Not a problem. There are plenty of other buyers. Although I can't imagine why you'd want your own people cut out."

Drissa sagged in relief and cautiously removed the tray of canisters from her pack, oblivious to the man's insincerity. "And you'll let us all go."

"Not exactly a born negotiator, are you?" Urneck snatched the tray as he spoke. "You can't expect to modify an agreement after it's made. Boy, if they're all like you, I better make damned sure I do have lobsters at the bidding table. It's just business, you understand."

Drissa clearly didn't understand, at first. In the moments his words took to sink in, Urneck turned, crossed to the controls Jake used earlier, and punched something into the console. "This area should make a suitable holding cell for the creature. The brig is good for the rest, but with a guard this time."

As Urneck finished his entry, a horn blared out a warning, and a yellow light above the exterior door strobed in time to the undulating pitch.

"Self-destruct activated, in ten…nine…"

32. Where was That Hiding?

"WHAT THE HELL?" Jay squawked, speaking for the first time.

"Five…four…"

"No such thing." Urneck jumped back, then growled and leaned over the controls again as he frantically checked the readings.

"Three…two…"

"The stupid computer's screwing with us again." But Urneck's eyes were feverish as he looked from the flashing light to the panel.

"One…goodbye."

The amber light flicked off and a metallic clang sounded as clamp locks settled into place at the four corners of the outer door. The gentle snick of the locks closing and sudden silence were so anticlimactic that Nancy giggled.

"You go, QUEN," Jake muttered just loud enough for her to hear.

Urneck paused with his fingers over one last switch. When nothing further happened, he nodded, flipped the switch, and glared at the equipment as if daring QUEN to try something else.

With a distant click, the lights in the interior passageway changed from amber to cool blue, standard illumination for takeoff maneuvers.

"You've helped accelerate my timeline, doctor." Urneck waved an impatient hand at the twins. "One of you go with Angie to secure this lot in the brig."

"Not Dianne!" Jay gripped the cattle prod with white knuckles and stepped forward before catching himself. "I mean, she's not one of them, boss."

"Yes, Dianne too," Urneck snapped, then seemed to recognize the folly of angering the big man. "Just until I'm certain where her loyalties lie." He turned to go, then added an afterthought. "And keep Pete off the watch rotation this time."

The click of distant relays set the passage lights flickering from blue, to red, to green, and finally settling on a sort of vibrant magenta as a status report came through the console in a clipped mechanical tenor. "Airborne pathogens detected. Use extreme caution. Do you desire remediation?"

"What now?" Urneck glared at the console. "Yes, clean it up! No, wait—"

"No backsies," QUEN purred. The machine had impressive vocal control. Nancy could easily imagine a forefinger wagging back and forth in negation. "Commencing cleanup as instructed."

At that point, things became somewhat confusing.

Several small hatches along the base of the interior wall slid open, and three pint-sized robots trundled forth. Each was perhaps a foot and a half tall with a segmented oval top balanced on a spherical base. As they rolled across the smooth decking, long strands of brightly colored material slid from dozens of pores spaced around both top and bottom. The strands were made of a flat flexible cloth and whipped about like colorful hair caught in hurricane force winds.

The whip-crack of strands slapping the floor and stanchions holding the room's various equipment grew deafening. Dust and bits of detritus flew from the contact, then each unit discharged a dozen white hockey pucks. Or at least, that's what they looked like. The stream of smaller machines spilled down a ramp that extended from the lower section of each robot. The newcomers immediately began hoovering up the debris dislodged by their larger cousins.

"Cleaning bots," Jake said with a nod.

Urneck and the twins dodged the little units as they scurried about the room. It was an interesting distraction, but not enough to change their situation. Plus, the little robots kept heading to the grimier corners of the room. They needed to occupy Urneck and Angie long enough to wrestle those guns away.

"Don't get any ideas." Urneck held his pistol steady on Nancy as he called over his shoulder to the panel. "QUEN, abort cleaning. Abort."

But the robots merrily cleaned on.

"Reemer, oh master of grime and slime, we could use your help," Nancy said, keeping a wary eye on Urneck's gun.

"Oh, mother would not approve of that." The slug sighed.

Urneck swung the pistol toward Reemer, but snapped it back when Nancy spoke through a tight smile. "This is no time to be a dutiful daughter. I'm certain she would understand."

Reemer wrung her feelers together and moaned as she rocked back and forth. Her hide turned green around the gills. Nancy hated to cause her friend such distress, but they needed her help, they needed the old Reemer.

"What's with the slug? He's getting even uglier." Urneck sneered while keeping the nasty looking barrel trained on Nancy's stomach. "Little guy looks like he's going to hurl."

The ignorant buffoon didn't understand the forces he toyed with. Dark green patches rose along what passed for Reemer's jawline. Nancy had seen enough to never underestimate the unassuming mollusk. Reemer opened his mouth as if to speak. Green ribbons snaked beneath the translucent yellow hide, some moving toward Reemer's head, others disappearing at the edge of her skirt where a distinctly unpleasant sound arose—the sound of a cat preparing to spit up the mother of all furballs.

"Poor little fella's gonna be sick." Urneck said with a condescending pout.

"No. I'm…a…girl!" Reemer's gurgling and hocking peaked, paused in a pregnant moment of silent expectation during which no one so much as breathed. "Forgive me, Mother."

Urneck stood eight feet from the Squinch and undoubtedly expected the sick alien to dribble and drool vomit down her front. The man was totally unprepared for the gout of phlegm that geysered forth at firehose velocity. Reemer reared up as she hurled, raised her skirt, and gave the bastard a full broadside of noxious jelly from multiple orifices. Some of the alien's mouths were still available because Nancy heard laughter as Reemer sung her defiance, "Who's mama's little girl now? Fly, fly!"

Reemer's aim was excellent. The putrid stream of mucus, oils, and less-easily classified materials knocked their assailant back. Urneck choked and gagged, threatening to add his own output to the mess. Nancy blinked back tears and tried not to inhale through her nose. A few trailing spurts followed the geyser, a final insult that landed squarely on Urneck's shoes and across Angie's trim white jacket. The herd of little cleaning robots went wild.

All three robots made a beeline for Urneck, redoubling their frantic thrashing. The slapping tendrils must have stung, like being whipped with dozens of wet towels in a locker-room nightmare. Urneck went down under the sea of flailing appendages, and his gun danced dangerously as he tried to fend off the onslaught.

The robots ignored Angie and her gun to focus on the disastrous mess that was her leader. Luckily, the woman was not as stoic and doubled over with hands on knees to vomit. Nancy fished out her new cutting tool and slammed the laser blade down on the back of Angie's gun hand. The girl yelped, spraying globs of puke as she dropped the weapon. Nancy kicked it away.

Urneck was on his knees, still scrapping with the frenzied robots. Jake rushed over but couldn't get a hold of the man's pistol as he flailed and ranted.

"Enough!" Urneck pushed to his feet with a roar.

There was the hiss of actuating pistons, and the lead robot's head extended on top of a long metal neck. It went eye to eye with the jerk and continued to pummel Urneck's face and chest with its cleaning rags. Urneck roared again, grabbed the thing by the throat and snapped its neck. The head lolled off to the side, ridiculously far out from its still thrashing body. Then he aimed the blaster down and blew a hole dead center of the body. The machine went still.

Even dimwitted mechanicals could tell when they had gone too far. Nancy swore the remaining robots audibly gulped, then sucked in their cleaning wands amid a chorus of zips and pops. The pair trundled over to their fallen companion and swept the broken robot off to the wall cubbies while emitting sad little bleeps and whirs.

But the swarm of hockey pucks ignored the violence and continued to merrily suck up bits of goo that had been flash-dried into puffs of dust and brittle bits. Urneck stomped on one, crunching it flat like a big beetle, but ignored the rest and smashed Jake in the chest with his open palm. The younger man grunted and fell back, well out of reach of the gun.

From projectile vomiting to Urneck being back in control had taken all of two minutes. Ray took that time to ram his prod against Rebecca's trunk where it sizzled, sparked, and pinned the giant plant in her corner. Jay stood in the middle of the room, looking dazed by the sudden cessation of activity. Angie's gun had come to rest halfway to Drissa. Why hadn't Nancy picked it up instead of punting the thing away?

The handle of a sample rake jutted from a collection bag hanging near the robot ports. It was closer than the gun, and she wouldn't have to stoop to bring it to bear. As she tensed to make a grab for the improvised weapon a strange gurgling drew her attention back to Reemer. The little alien writhed and twisted into a ball. Fluid green ribbons again moved beneath her yellow hide. Urneck saw it too and jumped back in alarm.

"Watch the slug," he called out. "Get one of those sacks over it before it spews again."

Jay darted to the wall and grabbed a heavy cloth sack similar to the one she'd been about to go for. The twin held the bag like a shield and stepped between her and Reemer. There was a wet ripping sound and gasp from the slug. Urneck panicked, jabbed his blaster forward, and opened fire. For all his alleged weapons expertise, he shot wildly, heedless of the fact one of his men stood between him and the Squinch.

"No!" Drissa dove in front of Reemer, trying to shield her.

The Lobstra was fast, but the Dolor a breath quicker. The plant ignored the sparking prod and lunged forward, slamming Ray against the exterior bulkhead as she launched into the air. Rebecca twisted in mid-leap to avoid colliding with Drissa, her spiral tentacles snapping their binding and dragging her to the side.

Jay spun out of the way as a blast caught his left triceps. Urneck's next shot blackened the bulkhead above Reemer, then plant and Lobstra crashed to the deck, blocking his line of fire. Rebecca landed closest and took the next two shots on her secondary trunk. Gaping holes appeared just below the base of the arms, and all but two fell limp.

Nancy grabbed the rake. The grip was soft and pliable, but the tool itself had a fair amount of heft. She pivoted away from the wall and slammed the business end down on Urneck's wrist with a satisfying crunch. His curses cut off abruptly as another full arc brought the rake down on the man's thick skull. She was off balance, so the blow wasn't hard, but he dropped with a grunt.

It would have been too much to hope for his gun to tumble free. Instead, he fell directly on top of it like a football player scooping up a fumble. Angie's gun was nowhere in sight. Hadn't it been over by the door? The sound of wet fabric tearing had her looking past Drissa and the injured Dolor.

Reemer uncurled and ripped her stomach open with both antennae. Green blotches danced across her sides, neck, and head, warring with the golden hues. With one last mighty tear, a mucus-covered mass nearly as long as Nancy's arm dropped out of the Squinch. Reemer scooped up the oozing object with both antennae and waved it high in the air. Goo flew in all directions as she brandished what resolved into a dripping rifle with a damned big barrel.

"We're leaving…now!" Reemer's sonorous voice rang with authority, a gritty and primal tone replacing the regal intonation Belinda encouraged. Was Reemer smiling?

The slug spun toward the exit and brought the stubby rifle up using his sensory antennae like little arms to tuck the weapon alongside his face and take aim. Ray was just pushing to his feet with the cattle prod and found himself staring down the barrel. He dove to the side as Reemer fired. A blue bolt of energy splashed and sizzled against the door frame.

The Squinch looked down at the gun, adjusted its power setting with her right antenna, and fired again. The blast bolt was brighter and left a magenta afterimage as it struck the door's controls. The keypad exploded in a shower of sparks. The doors parted, but screeched to a stop halfway open with sunlight streaming through the four-foot gap.

"Everybody out." Reemer laughed and surged toward the exit.

The green edges of her skirt rippled wildly, looking for traction and at the same time spitting globs of gunk backward like a car accelerating out of mud. Nancy gave up on finding the other gun and leapt aside to avoid the noxious spray as it caught Urneck full in the face. He cursed and tried to push up, but collapsed when his broken wrist refused to support him.

Nancy gave the man a wide berth and urged Dianne to her feet. The woman hunched over Jay, frantically tying a rag around the hole in his arm. The pungent smell of burnt flesh told her the wound had self-cauterized—painful but not life-threatening. He still clutched the sack in his good hand and gazed up at Dianne as she clucked and worried at his wound.

"Come with us. Both of you have bigger things in your future than this," Nancy said.

Jay finally noticed her, looked to Dianne, and nodded. They helped him to his feet, and all three stumbled toward daylight. Nancy pushed the pair onward, but risked a glance back. The Dolor listed badly as she tried to follow, the weight of her limp arms pulling her off balance. She'd landed hard on her side and scrabbled at the deck with leafy feet, trying to right herself. Jake tried to help Rebecca, while Ray went to Urneck and Angie sat in the corner near the broken robot, clutching her burnt hand and retching.

Jake couldn't manage Rebecca's bulk, but Ray had Urneck back on his feet and pressed the gun into his uninjured hand. Nancy was too far away to do more than shout a warning. Drissa's eyestalks slid toward Urneck as he checked the gun, then swiveled to where Jake still struggled under the limp tentacles.

"Unbelievable," the Lobstra muttered.

Drissa lowered her head so she was parallel to the deck and shot forward, her spindly white legs finding purchase as they pumped furiously. In an instant, she was alongside the Dolor and locked her battle claw around the main torso between the vegetative crown and nectar-producing spikes. Two of her hind legs whipped out to encircle the lower trunk, and Drissa scurried toward the exit dragging Rebecca along sideways. It was easy to forget how big the Lobstra were. Drissa was nearly as long as the Dolor queen, longer if you included her antennae, which currently swept the path ahead for obstacles. Nancy backed through the doorway to give them room. Jake sprinted though just behind her.

The green and red mass hit the doorway hard and were so intertwined it was difficult to tell where Dolor ended and Lobstra began. Drissa heaved mightily to force them both through the too-narrow opening. Shell and wood scraped along metal as Drissa grunted and strained. The muffled discharge of a blaster sounded from inside. A final mighty heave forced the doors open a few extra inches and the two spilled through leaving chunks of leafy matter and shell chips along opposite sides of the exit.

"QUEN, close the hatch," Jake yelled into the handheld comms brick he'd managed to grab.

"I can't!" QUEN wailed. "He's locked me out. I'm sorry, Jake."

Nancy stumbled over the hillock that lined the trench, making room for the larger members of their party. Drissa and Rebecca followed just as Urneck and Ray stepped from the shuttle. The raised edge of the furrow left by the crash offered minimal protection. They wouldn't make it across the thirty yards of open ground to reach the rocky cliff rising on their left, and to the right there was literally nothing. The shuttle had landed on a flat ledge

covered in sparse grass and large blackened swaths. This was one
of the spots where Lobstra had burnt the acid grass away. They
were perched halfway up to the plateau itself. Landing the shuttle
on this narrow strip had to have been dicey. Her stomach
clenched. They were trapped.

Nancy did what she could to help Drissa pull Rebecca the final
few feet to level ground. With a coordinated heave, they got the
Dolor upright, though she had to lean hard against the lip of the
crater. Drissa collapsed against the dirt and rock wall. Reemer
oozed between them with gun at the ready to stand sentinel as the
humans strode from their ship.

Urneck didn't appear to be in any hurry. He'd plastered his fake
grin back on, but stopped every few steps to grimace and spit
something from the corner of his mouth. Jake joined the others at
the bottom of the trench, still quietly arguing with QUEN. Urneck
cradled his right arm against his stomach, managing to hold the
gun comfortably in his left hand. Ray carried Angie's pistol, which
made them officially outgunned.

"How good of a shot are you?" Nancy asked Reemer.

The Squinch's eyes rolled to look at her over the stock of his
short rifle. "Not very. I can hit things point blank, but I haven't
had any time to practice."

Reemer looked miserable. Her general coloration had darkened
significantly, and she was coated with globs of dirt and debris from
the climb. At least the gash in her stomach had closed up,
hopefully before getting dirt in the wound—if it was a wound.

"Where did you even get that gun?" Nancy asked. "I mean, it
can't be a natural part of the Squinch anatomy."

"Meinish made it special." Reemer grinned. "What a guy."

Nancy would have laughed at the wistful tone if their situation
wasn't so dire. Reemer clearly missed the old curmudgeon. She
considered using the weapon herself, but the controls appeared ill-

suited for human hands. The men working their way toward them looked even less friendly than usual.

"So now it ends…again," Urneck said.

He and Ray stopped twenty feet out to eye Reemer from a safe distance, apparently more worried about noxious projectiles than the Squinch's gun. Understandable—two guns were better than one. Nancy looked around one last time, hoping for inspiration. Rocks and grasses peeked along the cliffs behind them and atop the earthen ridge. No help there. Urneck had a strange look on his stupid face, as if working through how best to disarm the Squinch without losing control again. Or maybe he was preparing to launch into some nauseating recap of how he'd bested them.

"It's him!" Ray jabbed an accusing finger at Reemer. "The dude what wrecked us last time."

Urneck jerked around to gape at the other man, then squinted at Reemer and cursed. "Damned right it is. Those beady little eyes, that stupid 'who me' look."

"Hey!" Reemer complained. "You were the ones stupid enough to leave the engine room unlocked."

"Painted himself yellow so we wouldn't recognize him." Urneck leveled his gun at Reemer's head.

The Squinch's gun shook. Nancy looked at her friend's darkened hide, but the change in color was not simply from clinging dirt. Beneath the debris, Reemer had indeed turned back to her original pea-green coloration. There was absolutely no gold left anywhere. The swirling green pigments had risen while she dredged up those noxious ejections and become even more pervasive while retrieving the gun from its disgusting hiding spot. Nancy thought back to Reemer's wild cries as she let fly with her noxious brew—or he let fly. Perhaps the change had been necessary for what had to be done or was simply a physiological response from engaging in thoroughly disgusting behavior. Either way, incredibly, Reemer had turned male again.

"Drop it." Urneck looked down the barrel of Reemer's trembling weapon, then pointed his gun at Nancy's chest. "Now!"

33. The Silent Speak

"I T'S OKAY. You tried." Nancy tore her gaze away from Urneck's blaster and gave Reemer an understanding smile.

His eyestalks wilted, and those dark orbs crinkled into soulful almonds. With a sad nod, he lowered his gun and let it clatter to the ground.

"Now get back." Urneck waved Reemer away from the weapon.

The Squinch inched backward until he pressed against her leg. Nancy reached down to pat his head. The slick skin was cool and reassuring. A pleasant warmth fought against the chill of dread clutching her heart as she looked at the others. Reemer pressed against her thigh, trying to be brave.

Jake crouched on the balls of his feet, hands clenched and adorably ready to leap to her defense. Drissa leaned against the earth wall, her antennae drooping. Carrying the Dolor had taken a lot out of the Lobstra, and Nancy silently praised her friend for choosing life over political views. Rebecca towered over them all, a thinking, feeling marvel of the plant kingdom.

A flash of shame brought clarity. She'd focused so much hate and blame on Fred's inhabitants, been so willing to fight back, that she'd lost sight of the wonder of evolution. There'd been enough death; more wouldn't make things right—but understanding and friendship just might.

So much of the problem had been lack of communication. She looked to the sack hanging from her belt and the gossamer wing tips rising over her shoulder, and gave silent thanks to HaSSaam. The enigmatic insect brought sorely needed understanding to Fred. She'd only spoken to him a few times, but in retrospect considered the Lokii a friend.

They were all her friends, maybe even Dianne and Jay, who sat a bit apart from the aliens as the woman worried over Jay's wounded arm. They weren't so bad. Jake had told her that too, and the little she'd seen supported the idea. She grinned at the thought of dowdy, reclusive Nancy Dickenson making friends lightyears away from home—more than she'd made in a lifetime back on Earth. And now a few greedy people were going to take it all away, not just her circle of friends, but the entire Dolor species.

Nancy sighed and scratched Reemer one last time between his eyestalks. With her other hand, she palmed her little cutter. It wasn't much, but perhaps an opportunity would present itself.

"What now, you sad excuse for a human being?" The greedy bastard could rot for all she cared.

"Now, we do things properly," Urneck said coolly. "Ray, have Pete bring down the transport crate for our leafy friend and restraining harnesses for these others. We're done playing nice."

Ray looked to his brother, seemed about to say something, then turned away and spoke into his wrist communicator. "Repair team, we need you to fetch a few things."

"NO!" The unspoken word thundered in her head.

All heads turned to the source. Rebecca pushed away from the wall and stood tall. Her spiral arms still dangled, but her head was held high. She glared at Urneck despite having no eyes.

"What the?" The spacer shook his head as if to clear it.

Even Ray cut off his hushed conversation and looked about. They had both clearly "heard" something. Nancy patted the bundle at her waist. Maybe HaSSaam was still looking out for them.

"No more pain, no more hurt, no more…take." Images of loss and agony accompanied Rebecca's words, not just her own, but all their pain. Nancy saw her own face flash a panicked look during the crash, Jake's surprise as he was driven back by Urneck, Jay's shock at being shot, Reemer painfully extracting his rifle from its unholy hiding place, and finally Drissa going rigid in agony as she carried Rebecca from the shuttle and blaster shots tore through her back. Nancy looked to the Lobstra in alarm. Drissa still watched the proceedings, but sagged to the point that her head touched her tail.

"What are you doing?" Urneck stabbed his gun at Nancy and raised his free had to his temple, but dropped the broken wrist with a curse. "Stop it!"

"You're talking to the wrong person." Nancy waved at Rebecca. "Take it up with the locals."

Urneck's eyes went comically round as the jackass realized the giant tree he'd been abusing might actually be talking. He flicked his gun toward Rebecca. Movement on the ground caught Nancy's eye, but there was nothing there except the flickering shadow cast by Urneck and his gun arm—an arm that continued to waiver between herself and the Dolor.

Judging by his shadow, you'd have thought Urneck was tall and lean. His dark silhouette stretched away from the long shadows cast by the ridge. Even the lumps of rock along that ridge now cast elongated silhouettes across the rocky ground. The shadows stretched as the sun raced toward the distant horizon. They had better conclude this little standoff, or they'd soon be standing in the dark. Nancy cast another nervous glance at Drissa.

"You?" Urneck finally found his voice. The question was directed at the Dolor, although he kept looking over to Nancy as if trying to spot some feat of ventriloquism.

"I and mine. These...people." Rebecca swept her leafy crown to encompass the immediate group. "These friends. You will no hurt. Your greed"—she dipped her head forward, managing to indicate the tray of nectar slung across Urneck's shoulder—"You will no take...the future."

"Neat trick, but I already have the nectar." Urneck backed toward the shuttle as he spoke. "This is enough. You can all stay here and rot, for all I care."

He might not have understood all of Rebecca's words, but the man was clearly rattled. The Lokii gift spread at different rates, affecting some individuals more completely than others. Nancy didn't even know if the rest of her party understood the plant. Certainly Reemer would. Everyone looked to Rebecca and Urneck, apparently following at least some of the exchange.

Urneck patted the nectar with his gun and backed up another step. His foot caught, and he nearly went over backward. The shadow of his gun arm flailed, the erratic movement making her flinch. They'd be lucky if he didn't shoot one of them by accident. Half of his shadow disappeared into the shade cast by the ridge. The long shadows of the rocks crowding the crest had inexplicably sprouted protrusions, stubby upraised arms.

"We will not let you take them!" Rebecca's mental voice was hard-edged steel.

"Your little group isn't exactly in a position to demand anything." Urneck laughed, a nervous, forced sound, but he gained confidence as he spoke and a sneer colored his words. "Stupid plant, you negotiate worse than the lobsters."

He kept the gun trained fully on Rebecca now, ignoring Nancy and the others. The big plant made no move to advance, but the man's eyes were glued to her. Nancy clutched the laser cutter and Jake tensed. Getting control of that gun was top priority. Then they'd have Ray to contend with.

Urneck kicked blindly and tried to back around the rock he'd struck. More figures stretched above the hilltop shadow, many more. Nancy wrenched her eyes upward, past the shuttle to the newly turned dirt forming the trench. Tall green forms lined the ridge, a stubby arm protruding from either side of each—pain watchers.

"I don't think it's us you have to worry about," Nancy said.

Urneck followed her gaze. Ray did too and then slowly lowered his gun. Urneck did the opposite. He sighted on the closest watcher and fired. The creature was fifty feet away, but blue fire erupted near the base of the cactus and it collapsed. Urneck shot twice more at figures down the line, then turned his gun on Rebecca. Neither the Dolor queen nor the watchers moved. Urneck tried to retreat, but stumbled and fell backward. His gun discharged skyward. The foot-long thing he'd tripped over whipped into a u-shape, encircling his calf, and Urneck shrieked.

The green spiky head jabbed wicked thorns into his leg, the tapered brown body of the pain urchin refusing to be dislodged by Urneck's frantic kicks. Other dusty shapes crawled from among the rocks and converged on the screaming man. Soon his torso was covered by two other urchins and a fourth reared up, trying to snag his flailing gun hand. Ray backed away from the grisly affair, his gun gone and shaking hands held palms out. Nancy motioned him toward her.

"Rebecca, don't!" Nancy willed the Dolor to spare the man.

She'd much rather see Urneck behind bars, but the Dolor queen ignored her plea. Urneck attempted one last roar that trailed off into a moan as his lungs gave out, and it was over.

The effect of even one urchin's sting was devastating. Their powerful toxin spread quickly, disrupting neurological signals, paralyzing organs, and destroying cells. The human immune system didn't have a prayer of keeping the stuff at bay for more than a few minutes, seconds given the massive dose that had just been delivered. The urchins clung to the body for another minute, then slid off the dead man and flowed away on undulating needles.

"Not gonna need this anymore." Reemer hurried over to the corpse and tugged at the pouch of nectar until he'd worked it off the man's shoulder.

The Squinch's auxiliary antennae were more versatile than Nancy ever expected. Reemer carried his prize over and offered the containers to Rebecca. A skittering of rocks drew Nancy's attention to where Drissa sank the rest of the way to the ground. She cursed herself for a fool and dashed over. Drissa's legs and antennae hung loose and a pale blue tint crept into her shell. The broken legs from the crash didn't account for her shallow breathing; such things were more an inconvenience to the resilient species. A quick examination revealed a pair of fist sized holes on the back of her carapace. Blaster burns edged the wounds, where energy had punched through and melted the chitin. The shots tore through tissue, cartilage, and into Drissa's internal organs.

"Bastard shot me in the back," Drissa whispered, then giggled. "Joke's on him. No Lobstra would do such a cowardly thing." Her words slid into a painful bubbling cough.

"Oh, Drissa." Nancy held her friend's cutting claw and awkwardly slid down to lay an arm across her spiny shoulder. She wanted to say it would be all right, that they would patch her up good as new. But it would be a lie. That Drissa had managed to make it out of the ship at all was a miracle, especially while dragging Rebecca.

"Talk to Breena." Drissa paused to gather more strength before continuing. "About the virus."

"No need for that. Rebecca has the nectar, so your matriarch will have to do without."

"No. The virus"—her antennae quivered with the effort of speaking—"has already been released. I am sorry…my friend."

Bubbles and Drissa's final breath gurgled out from between the Lobstra's mandibles, and she was gone.

Nancy rocked the Lobstra in her arms, the heavy reassuring weight of her claw suddenly cold and empty. The world blurred into lights and shadows reflecting through her tears. She rocked on, swallowing the ache. She hadn't even gotten to say goodbye.

"You're my friend too," Nancy finally whispered. "We'll work it out. I promise."

Epilogue

"I THANK YOU." Waves of sorrow and gratitude accompanied Rebecca's thoughts as Nancy held Drissa.

Jake helped her lay the Lobstra back in a more relaxed pose. Nancy cradled one big claw in her lap as she rocked, absently arranging the limp smaller claws neatly across her friend's white underbelly. Drissa had gone from fearsome alien, to friend, to traitor and back in a few short weeks. Nancy could relate. Emotion, scientific curiosity, and reasoning didn't always make for the best bedfellows—nor the most stable decision making. She and Drissa had each acted on the available information, and each followed their heart. The Lobstra's yearning for political change had been a palpable force. Without the nectar her society would be forced to evolve—at least in the near term.

The hum of hoversled engines intruded on her silent vigil, and Nancy blinked up at Jake and Reemer who were in huddled conversation nearby. Three Lobstra vehicles settled to the ground and Captain Luftew and Joda shambled down the ramp that extended from the command sled.

"Where is everyone?" Nancy asked as the newcomers approached.

"Back inside," Jake said. "Dianne is patching Jay up. We'll keep Ray under ship arrest until we're well clear of here. Repairs to the shuttle are just about finished and QUEN is back online."

"Rebecca?" Now that she asked, Nancy realized the urchins and watchers were also absent.

"Took the nectar and ran." Reemer pointed off to a dark crevice in the side of the cliff. "She's got some way to reabsorb the stuff, but I think it's better if we keep that to ourselves."

"Dr. Dickenson." Captain Luftew crossed the last few yards and bent to examine Drissa, but his antenna wilted. "Too much loss."

She could only nod as Joda called back for help to move their fallen friend. Breena and two others brought a hoverboard from the medical sled. The med tech gently took Drissa's claw from Nancy, then all three grasped the edge of the dead Lobstra's shell and lifted her onto the board before drawing a silver sheet over the corpse.

"She saved us from him." Nancy pointed to the big weapons officer who lay curled on the ground. "He shot her in the back."

"No honor." Joda cast a disgusted look at Urneck's body, but his whiskers curved up in the same wry grin Drissa had used that said the joke was on the dead man.

"And the nectar?" the captain swiveled an inquisitive eyestalk her way.

"Gone," Reemer interjected. "Burned up in the crash. Spectacular fire in there. The whole med bay is gutted."

The captain had asked out of curiosity. Other races—like her own, unfortunately—dealt in espionage and backstabbing, but the Lobstra were proud and straightforward. She was not worried about them trying to steal the nectar back.

"That is...unfortunate." Virtues aside, the Lobstra leader raised a suspicious antenna at Reemer, but didn't press the matter. "We suspected the game had reached its conclusion. Plants across the plateau are already settling back down. Even the acid grass didn't react as we approached your crash site. We'll have a few more days to collect compounds before all goes quiet."

"And I see you're wearing battle trophies." Joda's statement had Nancy looking around until she realized HaSSaam's wings still rose behind her.

"Never!" Nancy's outrage melted away. Death didn't have the same stigma for the Lobstra, and the big security chief clearly meant no harm. "HaSSaam's people sent him in to help. Urneck objected. I promised to take him back."

"A worthy mission." Joda bobbed in understanding. "I'm sure the captain could spare a sled and one rather beat up pilot to help you find the Lokii."

"Herman's okay?" Relief flooded her, accompanied by a twinge of shame as she stood over Drissa with HaSSaam weighing heavy on her belt. "But I need a moment to talk to Breena before we go. It's about the vaccine," Nancy whispered as she pulled the small Lobstra off behind a boulder.

"Not to worry." Breena cast a sad look back as the techs floated Drissa's body away. "The first stage is complete. I found a virus that took well to manipulation. Propagation is by contact only, so it'll be slow. I released six infected urchins to get things started while we work up something hardy enough for airborne transmission. I know it's what she wanted."

"The thing is"— Nancy chose her words carefully—"we had it all wrong."

They argued in hushed whispers while more Lobstra vehicles settled into the clearing and a sleek sled rolled out under the expert guidance of a heavily bandaged Herman. Between Nancy's explanation of recent events and Reemer's not-so-helpful wailing about Becky just wanting to raise a family, the bewildered Lobstra promised not to launch any further viruses until Nancy came back. Luckily Breena had trackers on the urchins she had infected, so there was a chance they could recover and destroy the relatively slow-moving creatures before leaving Fred.

Interestingly, the previous communications silence among the various races involved in the hunt had lifted. All parties accepted that the cycle was over and took to frantically collecting the most valuable specimens they could get their collective hands, claws, and coils on before the jungles reverted to benign—and unprofitable—tranquility. Judging by the radio chatter Herman picked up as they headed north, trade among the competing groups broke out in earnest too. They skimmed past the beach adjacent to the Squinch mating grounds, where ships and piles of trinkets testified to the various races that were already deep in negotiation with Belinda and the Mayor.

Finding the Lokii proved easy because the main force had not moved far from the sunflower fields. At the end of their short visit, Nancy climbed onto the hoversled ahead of Reemer. They both turned to wave farewell to the Hassaams as Herman fired up their small craft. HaSSaam was home with his brothers now, and Nancy had borne witness to a somber and beautiful ceremony where the entire swarm shared in nibbling at HaSSaam's gossamer wings until they were fully reintegrated with his people.

The reverence and celebration of the silent masses helped her keep an open mind, but thankfully her friend's severed head was left intact as each insect paid homage. Eventually, HaSSaam's final remains were interred with others sealed in the hull of the massive pod that served as the Lokii ship—a poetic gesture allowing those who had gone before to guide future generations.

"I think they control a lot more of the hunting cycle than we ever realized," Reemer said as they pulled away. "Now that I'm more attuned to it, there's a game-over vibe coming from the Lokii."

"I sense it too. It's more than the jungle settling down. HaSSaam's people are declaring the end of the cycle, broadcasting it."

"Dr. Dickenson, this is Captain Gekko, do you read me?" The call sounded through the sled's communication panel.

"Sounds like it's for you. Twist this to talk." Herman waved at the dash and showed her how to work the controls. "Damned rolling language is too hard to follow over the radio."

In person, the Lokii gift let them all converse freely, but the capability faltered when the speaker was remote. In addition to the words getting harder to pick out, any semblance of underlying meaning disappeared completely. Most of the cross-species conversations over the air were in galactic or trade standard, resorting again to a common denominator language that put everyone at an equal disadvantage.

"Nancy here, Captain. It's good to hear your voice."

"Likewise, young lady. It took a while to raise Jake and get your frequency, but I knew you'd want to know the navy has arrived. SS Bernard and an escort frigate parked in orbit this morning. Their landing team is combing over the Endeavor and eager to speak to you."

"Are you still at our mission site?" Nancy asked.

"Yes. Jake gave me the quick and dirty on your mishaps. Losing the nectar is a real kick in the teeth, but I'd rather see it burnt up than have Urneck profit. My shuttle's already inbound. I'm transmitting our position if you'd care to join us."

"Okay to head over to these coordinates?" At Herman's nod she keyed the mic. "We're on our way."

They made it before nightfall, but Jake beat them by a solid hour. The bit of clear jungle they'd meticulously selected for the first stop on their ill-fated research mission was getting crowded. Between the two fleet transports, streams of naval personnel in crisp blue uniforms, and Captain Gekko's massive shuttle, Herman had to wedge the little sled into the underbrush. Despite the chaos, the clearing felt peaceful without hordes of killer plants roving about. Even the juvenile needler trees standing off on their own had fallen back into their five-year slumber.

Jake and his captain met them and introduced Commander Yi and Senior Chief Lowe who were in charge of the mission site. Despite being fully prepared to encounter Squinch, the pair was clearly surprised to meet Herman. Translators leapt into action since this new crew hadn't yet caught the Lokii gifts.

"Other survivors?" Nancy asked on the heels of introductions.

"Not yet." CDR Yi gave a curt head shake that carried more meaning than her terse reply—they didn't expect to find anyone else. "We'd like your account of what happened. It might help."

Nancy told what she could of the confusing attack that seemed like it happened ages ago. Chief Lowe took copious notes about the alien races and would have pulled more information from Nancy if the commander hadn't kept them focused on the whereabouts of Endeavor's crew. Unaware of how well Nancy read subtext, they were kind enough to try to keep her hope alive.

At the end of what would likely be many such sessions, Nancy walked them over to the needler that got Harry. They brought two crewmembers with body armor, but the tree made no move to perforate anyone. Nancy turned away, unable to watch them dig.

"I see he listed you as his shipboard emergency contact." CDR Yi took pity on her and walked Nancy back to the others as she scrolled through her datapad.

"Yeah, and Harry was mine." She said, happy for the distraction. "Neither of us had many friends onboard."

"The forensic crew is done going through the ship. We've been inventorying personal belongings before stowing everything for lift off. You're welcome to visit his quarters to ensure we haven't missed anything his family might want returned."

"Thanks. I'll take a look."

* * *

"So this was your partner before me?" Reemer asked as he nudged a photo of Harry and his dad pretending to inspect Endeavor's hull before launch.

"Do not slime that!" Nancy jerked the acrylic picture frame away and sat it on the boxes piled in the center of the room.

Harry had always been funny about collecting things like that. Most people would just keep their photos and holograms on their computer. Her friend had those too, but he also surrounded himself with physical knickknacks. It seemed reasonable to assume his parents would want any photos. She wasn't so certain about the other archaic items.

"Fascinating." Herman couldn't take his eyestalks off the Newton's cradle he'd pulled from the boxes.

The steel balls of the old Earth toy clacked back and forth, swinging on the end of their pendulum strings. The Lobstra was not immune to the hypnotic rhythm. Herman's eyestalks tracked the outermost balls as the kinetic energy transferred through the stationary ones in the center to alternately kick each end ball out along its tether—left, right, left...

"Can we focus here?" Nancy asked.

She'd segregated the piles into the clear memorabilia like the framed picture and journals, the superfluous junk like the toys, and an I-don't-know pile. Everything would be going back with the navy crew assigned to pilot the ship, but she wanted to make certain important items got to Harry's family as quickly as possible. He'd spoken enough about his father, that she was confident Gregory Coppola and his wife were still alive and kicking back on Earth. Good old dad's mission to Fred was his last before retiring to work solely with the Astronomical Bureau.

"Let's watch this." Reemer pulled a vidcube out of the first pile.

"Honestly, it's like having a two-year-old." Nancy took the cube labeled "home videos" away from the slug and wiped the goo off.

Scrubbing at the face activated the small device and a two-dimensional picture projected from one end to splash across the wall. She fumbled for the off switch, then reconsidered. There'd never been time to say goodbye to her friend. She wanted to remember more than his terrified eyes desperately searching for a way out. The curly hair on the washed-out figure playing across the bulkhead was Harry's through and through.

"Evening lighting," she told the room and slid a box toward the wall so she could set down the projector and properly size the picture.

Herman abandoned his steel balls and stretched out on the floor next to Nancy. Reemer wedged himself between.

"That's my friend Harry as a kid," Nancy said as the lights dimmed and the scene leapt into focus. "So young, I'm guessing he's around sixteen. This looks like a birthday party."

Harry sat cross-legged on the floor surrounded by boxes that he tore into with gusto. He wore blue pajamas decorated with stars and planets, as if the celebration had been held early in the morning. Someone just off screen reached over to take each new gift as it was unveiled. The arm and hand were small, so maybe a younger sibling.

The room was modern and sleek, with white floor and walls. The bit of austere furniture was all straight lines and synthetic leather. Sunlight glinted off a transparent panel to the left, and the camera panned over as the last gift got passed off. A boy a few years younger sat the plastic spacecraft he'd just grabbed with the others at his feet. He had Harry's long face and narrow nose, but his dark hair was cropped close. The clear wall was a head scratcher.

"Why's the little one in a cage?" Even Reemer noticed that the younger sibling had been reaching through a portal in the wall that divided the room.

As the camera zoomed out, the enclosed area resolved into a starkly furnished living compartment. The boy closed the portal he'd gathered the toys through and ran an ultraviolet cleansing rod up and down his arms, before turning to sanitize his gifts with a big toothy grin. His pajamas were more like hospital scrubs, although someone had printed "B-day Boy" across the smock.

"Why don't we have sound?" Reemer complained. For an alien slug who grew up underwater with no tech, he certainly was demanding.

"Just shut up and watch the show. That must be Harry's younger brother on his birthday. And he isn't in a cage. That's an isolation unit. He's sick or has a compromised immune system. The controlled environment keeps pollens and microorganisms from attacking his weakened system."

Of all the vehicles, books, and electronics Harry passed in, the boy latched onto a tiny potted plant with a spoonful of dirt and two shiny leaves that looked to have been cleaned within an inch of its life—a variegated Philodendron. The boy's face lit up, and he hugged the plant tight.

The scene shifted. Harry wore jeans and a tee-shirt and attacked a new pile of gifts. This time there were less toys and more boxes that Nancy thought were games. But after they were passed inside the chamber, the boy held them up to show off a hydroponic kit and botanical starter set. The Philodendron draped down behind the plastic sofa, apparently having thrived on a year of artificial lighting.

The years flew by as both boys grew, Harry outside with his stylish clothes and his brother in isolation wearing scrubs, but among an ever-increasing array of potted plants. By the time Harry showed up in his navy blues, little brother's room was a riot of color. The Phil covered the entire back wall and sent happy streamers along the couch to cascade down each end table to the floor.

"It's a shame that human cannot go outside, but he certainly likes his plants," Herman said.

"They keep him company." Nancy had met patients in intensive care before and knew how difficult the hours alone could be. "I bet he wanted a pet, but that wouldn't be safe if his system was severely compromised and unable to fight off disease. The plants would have been sterile enough to keep around and don't need to go out for walks. The oxygen they produce might have been just the ticket for his condition."

Then one year, there was a pile of cards instead of gifts. The door to the enclosure with its manicured jungle stood open and two men sat on the floor outside. Nancy was glad to see little brother out and about, but revised that thought when she realized CDR Coppola helped young Harry sort through the envelopes, opening each and jotting down notes on a tablet. Their solemn faces told what happened.

Several more random scenes showed the room change, the sparse, sterile furniture replaced by more decorative pieces. The jungle in its glass walls stood as a monument, but was slowly dismantled until just the Phil was left, trimmed into a terse cascade. Little brother was gone.

"Well, I didn't like that ending at all." Pale yellow blossomed along Reemer's flank as he grabbed the photograph with both antennae and shook it. "You shouldn't have let him leave! It isn't right to abandon your family."

"I don't think they had a choice," Nancy said gently. "His brother was sick, but they made the time he had special." She tried to take the picture frame, but Reemer yanked it back. The photo slipped halfway out of the frame, and another dropped to the deck.

Nancy scooped up the photo before the slug got his— bordering on her by the looks of the yellow still spreading across the Squinch—goo all over it. There had been a second photograph behind the picture of Harry and his dad. The two boys from those early movies looked out from among a sea of plants, with smiles so very similar. She turned the picture over and found an inscription. The first line was in beautiful flowing cursive, the second added with precise blocky print.

Harry & Fred lost in the jungle.

Now you have a whole planet to explore, little brother.

* * *

"I guess this is it," Nancy said to her little group of misfits, her friends.

Herman towered over Meinish and Reemer, while Jake cast a wary eye at the storm rolling in. She'd hoped Breena would be here, but the young Lobstra seemed to be avoiding her despite having rounded up the infected urchins without undue notice.

It would have been good to say goodbye to Rebecca too. The Dolor queen hadn't known just how close Nancy and the Lobstra had come to eradicating her kind here on Fred. That may have been for the best. A cold knot pulled tight in her stomach at the thought of how badly she'd wanted revenge. The cold spread to her hip and moisture seeped across her right leg. She sighed, knowing that wasn't a message from her conscience.

"A little close there, Reemer." She tried to pry the Squinch off.

"Don't leave! Nobody else understands me." Pustules along the Squinch's back ruptured, sending a wave of green-yellow slime down her pants.

The uniform was a write-off, so she gave her moaning friend a comforting hug. "I'm just going to help Jake and Captain Gekko finish synthesizing medicine from what they've gathered here and get it to a legal market."

Nancy's decision had come as a shock to the naval personnel sent to rescue her. Of course, they still had the Endeavor and the few remains they'd recovered to take back. As a civilian consultant it wasn't like she had a commission to resign or anything. After several messages to Fleet, Commander Yi conducted one final debriefing, had her sign a pile of paperwork, and cancelled her contract.

"Take me with you. I'll be the best space slug you know. Give me any job. I don't mind—really."

"I'll tell you what. Captain Gekko wants to come back this way after his debts are squared away. We'll stop back within the year and have a good long visit. That way we can catch up with Rebecca too without having to worry about the navy and all these other folks. In the meantime, you can get some more lessons from your mom. I know you were loving some of the perks."

"And what about me, Nancy?" Herman kicked at the dirt, his eyestalks downcast.

Nancy ducked down until she caught the Lobstra's eyes and gave him an awkward, spiny hug. "I'll miss you terribly. Who's going to drive me around at supersonic speed and swoop in to save the day the next time giant Slurg are closing in?" She looked to Jake who gave her a nod. "Maybe we can work things out so we can all meet up again. The navy seems awfully interested in your hover technology, something about it being low-reactive compared to ours. Maybe that will yield an opportunity."

"Well, missy, ya know there's always a chance with our Lady." Meinish patted Herman on the back, the sound of a horse galloping over a wooden bridge. "We'll get the lad trained up to be a right proper searcher. I bet if anyone can find you again, it'll be this lad. And you"—he jabbed a claw at Reemer, but his face went all soft and round—"don't get too prissy and ladylike. I'll need a right proper Reemer welcome when we return. Ya got that?"

"Loud and—" the words caught in Reemer's throat, and if Nancy didn't know better she'd say he was crying. But what started as wet little sobs grew into an all too familiar rumbling gurgle, followed by a fist-sized ball of mucus that splashed against the old searcher's chest plates and spattered them all with bits of goo. "Clear!"

"That's the spirit!" Meinish beamed every bit as broadly as Reemer—two peas in a pod.

"On that note"— Nancy pulled Jake toward the shuttle as she waved goodbye to her friends. "Let's go see what's out there and find some clean clothes."

∼

About the author

Jim Stein's hunger for stories transporting the reader to extraordinary realms began under one meager bulb, a towel stuffed beneath his door to avoid parental censure. He huddled with Tolkien, Asimov, and all the greats and unknowns plucked from the drugstore shelves to spin tales of the imagination. After writing short stories in school, two degrees in computer science, and several decades as a Naval officer, Jim has returned to his first passion. He writes speculative fiction advocating the underdog and embracing protagonists with strong moral fiber, often overlaid with supernatural elements and a few dark twists. Jim lives in northwestern Pennsylvania with his wife, Claudia, and his muse, Marley the Great Dane.

Thank you for spending time with Nancy and Reemer. I'd be eternally grateful if you'd share your opinion of *Planet Fred* or any other books on my Amazon author page at

https://amazon.com/author/steinjim.

Just click on the book you want to review, click on reviews, and select "write a review." It need not be long, only takes a minute, and is so very helpful to new authors. – Jim

41933264R00231